Praise for *The Love*

"Contemporary romance's unico... deeply brainy and delightfully escap... has wild commercial appeal, but the quieter secret is that there is a specific audience, made up of all of the Olives in the world, who have deeply, ardently waited for this exact book."

> —*New York Times* bestselling author Christina Lauren

"Funny, sexy, and smart. Ali Hazelwood did a terrific job with *The Love Hypothesis.*"

> —*New York Times* bestselling author Mariana Zapata

"This tackles one of my favorite tropes—Grumpy meets Sunshine—in a fun and utterly endearing way. . . . I loved the nods toward fandom and romance novels, and I couldn't put it down. Highly recommended!"

> —*New York Times* bestselling author Jessica Clare

"A beautifully written romantic comedy with a heroine you will instantly fall in love with, *The Love Hypothesis* is destined to earn a place on your keeper shelf."

> —Elizabeth Everett, author of *A Lady's Formula for Love*

the *Love* Hypothesis

ALI HAZELWOOD

JOVE
NEW YORK

A JOVE BOOK
Published by Berkley
An imprint of Penguin Random House LLC
penguinrandomhouse.com

Copyright © 2021 by Ali Hazelwood
Excerpt from *Love on the Brain* copyright © 2021 by Ali Hazelwood
Bonus Chapter copyright © 2022 by Ali Hazelwood
Penguin Random House supports copyright. Copyright fuels creativity,
encourages diverse voices, promotes free speech, and creates a vibrant culture.
Thank you for buying an authorized edition of this book and for complying
with copyright laws by not reproducing, scanning, or distributing any part of it
in any form without permission. You are supporting writers and allowing
Penguin Random House to continue to publish books for every reader.

A JOVE BOOK, BERKLEY, and the BERKLEY & B colophon are registered
trademarks of Penguin Random House LLC.

Library of Congress Cataloging-in-Publication Data

Names: Hazelwood, Ali, author.
Title: The love hypothesis / Ali Hazelwood.
Description: First edition. | New York: Jove, 2021.
Identifiers: LCCN 2020057346 (print) | LCCN 2020057347 (ebook) |
ISBN 9780593336823 (trade paperback) | ISBN 9780593336830 (ebook)
Subjects: GSAFD: Love stories.
Classification: LCC PS3608.A98845 L68 2021 (print) |
LCC PS3608.A98845 (ebook) | DDC 813/.6—dc23
LC record available at https://lccn.loc.gov/2020057346
LC ebook record available at https://lccn.loc.gov/2020057347

First Edition: September 2021

Printed in the United States of America
30th Printing

Book design by Tiffany Estreicher

To my women in STEM: Kate, Caitie, Hatun, and Mar.
Per aspera ad aspera.

hy·poth·e·sis (noun)

A supposition or proposed explanation made on the basis of limited evidence, as a starting point for further investigation.

Example: "Based on the available information and the data hitherto collected, my hypothesis is that the farther away I stay from love, the better off I will be."

Prologue

~~~~~~

Frankly, Olive was a bit on the fence about this whole grad school thing.

Not because she didn't like science. (She did. She *loved* science. Science was her *thing*.) And not because of the truckload of obvious red flags. She was well aware that committing to years of unappreciated, underpaid eighty-hour workweeks might *not* be good for her mental health. That nights spent toiling away in front of a Bunsen burner to uncover a trivial slice of knowledge might *not* be the key to happiness. That devoting her mind and body to academic pursuits with only infrequent breaks to steal unattended bagels might *not* be a wise choice.

She was well aware, and yet none of it worried her. Or maybe it did, a tiny bit, but she could deal. It was something else that held her back from surrendering herself to the most notorious and soul-sucking circle of hell (i.e., a Ph.D. program). Held her back, that is, until she was invited to interview for a spot in Stanford's biology department, and came across The Guy.

The Guy whose name she never really got.

The Guy she met after stumbling blindly into the first bath-room she could find.

The Guy who asked her, "Out of curiosity, is there a specific reason you're crying in my restroom?"

Olive squeaked. She tried to open her eyes through the tears and only barely managed to. Her entire field of view was blurry. All she could see was a watery outline—someone tall, dark haired, dressed in black, and . . . yeah. That was it.

"I . . . is this the ladies' restroom?" she stammered.

A pause. Silence. And then: "Nope." His voice was deep. So deep. Really deep. *Dreamy* deep.

"Are you sure?"

"Yes."

"Really?"

"Fairly, since this is my lab's bathroom."

Well. He had her there. "I'm so sorry. Do you need to . . ." She gestured toward the stall, or where she thought the stalls were. Her eyes stung, even closed, and she had to scrunch them shut to dull the burn. She tried to dry her cheeks with her sleeve, but the material of her wrap dress was cheap and flimsy, not half as absorbent as real cotton. Ah, the joys of being impoverished.

"I just need to pour this reagent down the drain," he said, but she didn't hear him move. Maybe because she was blocking the sink. Or maybe because he thought Olive was a weirdo and was contemplating siccing the campus police on her. That would put a brutally quick end to her Ph.D. dreams, wouldn't it? "We don't use this as a restroom, just to dispose of waste and wash equipment."

"Oh, sorry. I thought . . ." Poorly. She'd thought poorly, as was her habit and curse.

"Are you okay?" He must be really tall. His voice sounded like it came from ten feet above her.

"Sure. Why do you ask?"

"Because you are crying. In my bathroom."

"Oh, I'm not crying. Well, I sort of am, but it's just tears, you know?"

"I do not."

She sighed, slumping against the tiled wall. "It's my contacts. They expired some time ago, and they were never that great to begin with. They messed up my eyes. I've taken them off, but . . ." She shrugged. Hopefully in his direction. "It takes a while, before they get better."

"You put in expired contacts?" He sounded personally offended.

"Just a little expired."

"What's 'a little'?"

"I don't know. A few years?"

"*What?*" His consonants were sharp and precise. Crisp. Pleasant.

"Only just a couple, I think."

"Just a couple of *years*?"

"It's okay. Expiration dates are for the weak."

A sharp sound—some kind of snort. "Expiration dates are so I don't find you weeping in the corner of my bathroom."

Unless this dude was Mr. Stanford himself, he really needed to stop calling this *his* bathroom.

"It's fine." She waved a hand. She'd have rolled her eyes, if they hadn't been on fire. "The burning usually lasts only a few minutes."

"You mean you've done this before?"

She frowned. "Done what?"

"Put in expired contacts."

"Of course. Contacts are not cheap."

"Neither are *eyes*."

Humph. Good point. "Hey, have we met? Maybe last night, at the recruitment dinner with prospective Ph.D. students?"

"No."

"You weren't there?"

"Not really my scene."

"But the free food?"

"Not worth the small talk."

Maybe he was on a diet, because what kind of Ph.D. student said that? And Olive was *sure* that he was a Ph.D. student—the haughty, condescending tone was a dead giveaway. All Ph.D. students were like that: thinking they were better than everyone else just because they had the dubious privilege of slaughtering fruit flies in the name of science for ninety cents an hour. In the grim, dark hellscape of academia, graduate students were the lowliest of creatures and therefore had to convince themselves that they were the best. Olive was no clinical psychologist, but it seemed like a pretty textbook defense mechanism.

"Are you interviewing for a spot in the program?" he asked.

"Yup. For next year's biology cohort." God, her eyes were burning. "What about you?" she asked, pressing her palms into them.

"Me?"

"How long have you been here?"

"Here?" A pause. "Six years. Give or take."

"Oh. Are you graduating soon, then?"

"I . . ."

She picked up on his hesitation and instantly felt guilty. "Wait, you don't have to tell me. First rule of grad school—don't ask about other grads' dissertation timeline."

A beat. And then another. "Right."

"Sorry." She wished she could see him. Social interactions were hard enough to begin with; the last thing she needed was fewer cues to go by. "I didn't mean to channel your parents at Thanksgiving."

He laughed softly. "You could never."

"Oh." She smiled. "Annoying parents?"

"And even worse Thanksgivings."

"That's what you Americans get for leaving the Commonwealth." She held out her hand in what she hoped was his general direction. "I'm Olive, by the way. Like the tree." She was starting to wonder whether she'd just introduced herself to the drain disposal when she heard him step closer. The hand that closed around hers was dry, and warm, and so large it could have enveloped her whole fist. Everything about him must be huge. Height, fingers, voice.

It was not entirely unpleasant.

"You're not American?" he asked.

"Canadian. Listen, if you happen to talk with anyone who's on the admissions committee, would you mind not mentioning my contacts mishap? It might make me seem like a less-than-stellar applicant."

"You think so?" he deadpanned.

She would have glared at him if she could. Though maybe she was doing a decent job of it anyway, because he laughed—just a huff, but Olive could tell. And she kind of liked it.

He let go of her, and she realized that she'd been gripping his hand. Oops.

"Are you planning to enroll?" he asked.

She shrugged. "I might not get an offer." But she and the professor she'd interviewed with, Dr. Aslan, had really hit it off. Olive had stuttered and mumbled much less than usual. Plus, her GRE scores and GPA were almost perfect. Not having a life came in handy, sometimes.

"Are you planning to enroll if you get an offer, then?"

She'd be stupid not to. This was Stanford, after all—one of the best biology programs. Or at least, that was what Olive had been telling herself to cover the petrifying truth.

Which was that, frankly, she was a bit on the fence about this whole grad school thing.

"I . . . maybe. I must say, the line between excellent career choice and critical life screwup is getting a bit blurry."

"Seems like you're leaning toward screwup." He sounded like he was smiling.

"No. Well . . . I just . . ."

"You just?"

She bit her lip. "What if I'm not good enough?" she blurted out, and why, God, *why* was she baring the deepest fears of her secret little heart to this random bathroom guy? And what was the point, anyway? Every time she aired out her doubts to friends and acquaintances, they all automatically offered the same trite, meaningless encouragements. *You'll be fine. You can do it. I believe in you.* This guy was surely going to do the same.

Coming up.

Any moment now.

Any second—

"Why do you want to do it?"

Uh? "Do . . . what?"

"Get a Ph.D. What's your reason?"

Olive cleared her throat. "I've always had an inquisitive mind, and graduate school is the ideal environment to foster that. It'll give me important transferable skills—"

He snorted.

She frowned. "What?"

"Not the line you found in an interview prep book. Why do *you* want a Ph.D.?"

"It's true," she insisted, a bit weakly. "I want to sharpen my research abilities—"

"Is it because you don't know what else to do?"

"No."

"Because you didn't get an industry position?"

"No—I didn't even apply for industry."

"Ah." He moved, a large, blurry figure stepping next to her to pour something down the sink. Olive could smell a whiff of eugenol, and laundry detergent, and clean, male skin. An oddly nice combination.

"I need more freedom than industry can offer."

"You won't have much freedom in academia." His voice was closer, like he hadn't stepped back yet. "You'll have to fund your work through ludicrously competitive research grants. You'd make better money in a nine-to-five job that actually allows you to entertain the concept of weekends."

Olive scowled. "Are you trying to get me to decline my offer? Is this some kind of anti–expired-contacts-wearers campaign?"

"Nah."

She could hear his smile.

"I'll go ahead and trust that it was just a misstep."

"I wear them *all the time*, and they almost never—"

"In a long line of missteps, clearly." He sighed. "Here's the deal: I have no idea if you're good enough, but that's not what you should be asking yourself. Academia's a lot of bucks for very little bang. What matters is whether your *reason* to be in academia is good enough. So, why the Ph.D., Olive?"

She thought about it, and thought, and thought even more. And then she spoke carefully. "I have a question. A specific research question. Something that I want to find out." There. Done. This was the answer. "Something I'm afraid no one else will discover if I don't."

"A question?"

She felt the air shift and realized that he was now leaning against the sink.

"Yes." Her mouth felt dry. "Something that's important to

me. And—I don't trust anyone else to do it. Because they haven't
so far. Because . . ." *Because something bad happened. Because
I want to do my part so that it won't happen again.*

Heavy thoughts to have in the presence of a stranger, in the
darkness of her closed eyelids. So she cracked them open; her
vision was still blurry, but the burning was mostly gone. The
Guy was looking at her. Fuzzy around the edges, perhaps, but so
very *there*, waiting patiently for her to continue.

"It's important to me," she repeated. "The research that I
want to do." Olive was twenty-three and alone in the world. She
didn't want weekends, or a decent salary. She wanted to go back
in time. She wanted to be less lonely. But since that was impossible, she'd settle for fixing what she could.

He nodded but said nothing as he straightened and took a
few steps toward the door. Clearly leaving.

"Is mine a good enough reason to go to grad school?" she
called after him, hating how eager for approval she sounded. It was
possible that she was in the midst of some sort of existential crisis.

He paused and looked back at her. "It's the best one."

He was smiling, she thought. Or something like it.

"Good luck on your interview, Olive."

"Thanks."

He was almost out the door already.

"Maybe I'll see you next year," she babbled, flushing a little.
"If I get in. And if you haven't graduated."

"Maybe," she heard him say.

With that, The Guy was gone. And Olive never got his name.
But a few weeks later, when the Stanford biology department
extended her an offer, she accepted it. Without hesitating.

Chapter One

~~~~~~

♥ **HYPOTHESIS:** *When given a choice between A (a slightly inconveniencing situation) and B (a colossal shitshow with devastating consequences), I will inevitably end up selecting B.*

Two years, eleven months later

In Olive's defense, the man didn't seem to mind the kiss too much.

It did take him a moment to adjust—perfectly understandable, given the sudden circumstances. It was an awkward, uncomfortable, somewhat painful minute, in which Olive was simultaneously smashing her lips against his and pushing herself as high as her toes would extend to keep her mouth at the same level as his face. Did he *have* to be so tall? The kiss must have looked like some clumsy headbutt, and she grew anxious that she was not going to be able to pull the whole thing off. Her friend Anh, whom Olive had spotted coming her way a few seconds ago, was going to take one look at this and know at once that Olive and Kiss Dude couldn't possibly be two people in the middle of a date.

Then that agonizingly slow moment went by, and the kiss became . . . different. The man inhaled sharply and inclined his head a tiny bit, making Olive feel less like a squirrel monkey climbing a baobab tree, and his hands—which were large and pleasantly warm in the AC of the hallway—closed around her waist. They slid up a few inches, coming to wrap around Olive's rib cage and holding her to himself. Not too close, and not too far.

Just so.

It was more of a prolonged peck than anything, but it was quite nice, and for the life span of a few seconds Olive forgot a large number of things, including the fact that she was pressed against a random, unknown dude. That she'd barely had the time to whisper "Can I please kiss you?" before locking lips with him. That what had originally driven her to put on this entire show was the hope of fooling Anh, her best friend in the whole world.

But a good kiss will do that: make a girl forget herself for a while. Olive found herself melting into a broad, solid chest that showed absolutely no give. Her hands traveled from a defined jaw into surprisingly thick and soft hair, and then—then she heard herself sigh, as if already out of breath, and that's when it hit her like a brick on the head, the realization that— No. No.

Nope, nope, *no*.

She should not be enjoying this. Random dude, and all that.

Olive gasped and pushed herself away from him, frantically looking for Anh. In the 11:00 p.m. bluish glow of the biology labs' hallway, her friend was nowhere to be seen. Weird. Olive was sure she had spotted her a few seconds earlier.

Kiss Dude, on the other hand, was standing right in front of her, lips parted, chest rising and a weird light flickering in his eyes, which was exactly when it dawned on her, the enormity of what she had just done. Of *who* she had just—

Fuck her life.

Fuck. Her. Life.

Because Dr. Adam Carlsen was a known ass.

This fact was not remarkable in and of itself, as in academia every position above the graduate student level (Olive's level, sadly) required some degree of assness in order to be held for any length of time, with tenured faculty at the very peak of the ass pyramid. Dr. Carlsen, though—he was exceptional. At least if the rumors were anything to go by.

He was the reason Olive's roommate, Malcolm, had to completely scrap two research projects and would likely end up graduating a year late; the one who had made Jeremy throw up from anxiety before his qualifying exams; the sole culprit for half the students in the department being forced to postpone their thesis defenses. Joe, who used to be in Olive's cohort and would take her to watch out-of-focus European movies with microscopic subtitles every Thursday night, had been a research assistant in Carlsen's lab, but he'd decided to drop out six months into it for "reasons." It was probably for the best, since most of Carlsen's remaining graduate assistants had perennially shaky hands and often looked like they hadn't slept in a year.

Dr. Carlsen might have been a young academic rock star and biology's wunderkind, but he was also mean and hypercritical, and it was obvious in the way he spoke, in the way he carried himself, that he thought himself the only person doing decent science within the Stanford biology department. Within the entire world, probably. He was a notoriously moody, obnoxious, terrifying dick.

And Olive had just kissed him.

She wasn't sure how long the silence lasted—only that he was the one to break it. He stood in front of Olive, ridiculously intimidating with dark eyes and even darker hair, staring down from who knows how many inches above six feet—he must have been over half a foot taller than she was. He scowled, an expression that she recognized from seeing him attend the departmental seminar, a look that usually preceded him raising his hand to point out some perceived fatal flaw in the speaker's work.

Adam Carlsen. Destroyer of research careers, Olive had once overheard her adviser say.

It's okay. It's fine. Totally fine. She was just going to pretend nothing had happened, nod at him politely, and tiptoe her way out of here. *Yes, solid plan.*

"Did you . . . Did you just kiss me?" He sounded puzzled, and maybe a little out of breath. His lips were full and plump and . . . God. Kissed. There was simply no way Olive could get away with denying what she had just done.

Still, it was worth a try.

"Nope."

Surprisingly, it seemed to work.

"Ah. Okay, then." Carlsen nodded and turned around, looking vaguely disoriented. He took a couple of steps down the hallway, reached the water fountain—maybe where he'd been headed in the first place.

Olive was starting to believe that she might actually be off the hook when he halted and turned back with a skeptical expression.

"Are you sure?"

Dammit.

"I—" She buried her face in her hands. "It's not the way it looks."

"Okay. I . . . Okay," he repeated slowly. His voice was deep and low and sounded a lot like he was on his way to getting mad. Like maybe he was already mad. "What's going on here?"

There was simply no way to explain this. Any normal person would have found Olive's situation odd, but Adam Carlsen, who obviously considered empathy a bug and not a feature of humanity, could never understand. She let her hands fall to her sides and took a deep breath.

"I . . . listen, I don't mean to be rude, but this is really none of your business."

He stared at her for a moment, and then he nodded. "Yes. Of course." He must be getting back into his usual groove, because his tone had lost some of its surprise and was back to normal—dry. Laconic. "I'll just go back to my office and begin to work on my Title IX complaint."

Olive exhaled in relief. "Yeah. That would be great, since— Wait. Your what?"

He cocked his head. "Title IX is a federal law that protects against sexual misconduct within academic settings—"

"I know what Title IX is."

"I see. So you willfully chose to disregard it."

"I— What? No. No, I didn't!"

He shrugged. "I must be mistaken, then. Someone else must have assaulted me."

"Assault—I didn't 'assault' you."

"You did kiss me."

"But not *really*."

"Without first securing my consent."

"I *asked* if I could kiss you!"

"And then did so without waiting for my response."

"What? You said yes."

"Excuse me?"

She frowned. "I asked if I could kiss you, and you said yes."

"Incorrect. You asked if you could kiss me and I snorted."

"I'm *pretty sure* I heard you said yes."

He lifted one eyebrow, and for a minute Olive let herself day-dream of drowning someone. Dr. Carlsen. Herself. Both sounded like great options.

"Listen, I'm really sorry. It was a weird situation. Can we just forget that this happened?"

He studied her for a long moment, his angular face serious and something else, something that she couldn't quite decipher because she was too busy noticing all over again how damn towering and broad he was. Just massive. Olive had always been slight, just this side of too slender, but girls who are five eight rarely felt diminutive. At least until they found themselves standing next to Adam Carlsen. She'd known that he was tall, of course, from seeing him around the department or walking across campus, from sharing the elevator with him, but they'd never interacted. Never been this close.

Except for a second ago, Olive. When you almost put your tongue in his—

"Is there something wrong?" He sounded almost concerned.

"What? No. No, there isn't."

"Because," he continued calmly, "kissing a stranger at midnight in a science lab might be a sign that there is."

"There isn't."

Carlsen nodded, thoughtful. "Very well. Expect mail in the next few days, then." He began to walk past her, and she turned to yell after him.

"You didn't even ask my name!"

"I'm sure anyone could figure it out, since you must have swiped your badge to get in the labs area after hours. Have a good night."

"Wait!" She leaned forward and stopped him with a hand on his wrist. He paused immediately, even though it was obvious that it would take him no effort to free himself, and stared pointedly at the spot where her fingers had wrapped around his skin—right below a wristwatch that probably cost half her yearly graduate salary. Or all of it.

She let go of him at once and took one step back. "Sorry, I didn't mean to—"

"The kiss. Explain."

Olive bit into her lower lip. She had truly screwed herself over. She had to tell him, now. "Anh Pham." She looked around to make sure Anh was really gone. "The girl who was passing by. She's a graduate student in the biology department."

Carlsen gave no indication of knowing who Anh was.

"Anh has . . ." Olive pushed a strand of brown hair behind her ear. This was where the story became embarrassing. Complicated, and a little juvenile sounding. "I was seeing this guy in the department. Jeremy Langley, he has red hair and works with Dr. . . . Anyway, we went out just a couple of times, and then I brought him to Anh's birthday party, and they just sort of hit it off and—"

Olive shut her eyes. Which was probably a bad idea, because now she could see it painted on her lids, how her best friend and her date had bantered in that bowling alley, as if they'd known each other their whole lives; the never-exhausted topics of conversation, the laughter, and then, at the end of the night, Jeremy following Anh's every move with his gaze. It had been painfully clear who he was interested in. Olive waved a hand and tried for a smile.

"Long story short, after Jeremy and I ended things he asked Anh out. She said no because of . . . girl code and all that, but I can tell that she *really* likes him. She's afraid to hurt my feelings, and no matter how many times I told her it was fine she wouldn't believe me."

Not to mention that the other day I overheard her confess to our friend Malcolm that she thought Jeremy was awesome, but she could never betray me by going out with him, and she sounded so dejected. Disappointed and insecure, not at all like the spunky, larger-than-life Anh I am used to.

"So I just lied and told her that I was already dating someone else. Because she's one of my closest friends and I'd never seen her like a guy this much and I want her to have the good things she deserves and I'm positive that she would do the same for me and—" Olive realized that she was rambling and that Carlsen couldn't have cared less. She stopped and swallowed, even though her mouth felt dry. "Tonight. I told her I'd be on a date *tonight*."

"Ah." His expression was unreadable.

"But I'm not. So I decided to come in to work on an experiment, but Anh showed up, too. She wasn't supposed to be here. But she was. Coming this way. And I panicked—well." Olive wiped a hand down her face. "I didn't really think."

Carlsen didn't say anything, but it was there in his eyes that he was thinking, *Obviously*.

"I just needed her to believe that I was on a date."

He nodded. "So you kissed the first person you saw in the hallway. Perfectly logical."

Olive winced. "When you put it like that, perhaps it wasn't my best moment."

"Perhaps."

"But it wasn't my worst, either! I'm pretty sure Anh saw us. Now she'll think that I was on a date with you and she'll hopefully feel free to go out with Jeremy and—" She shook her head. "Listen. I'm so, so sorry about the kiss."

"Are you?"

"Please, don't report me. I really thought I heard you say yes. I promise I didn't mean to . . ."

Suddenly, the enormity of what she had just done fully dawned on her. She had just kissed a random guy, a guy who happened to be the most notoriously unpleasant faculty member in the biology department. She'd misunderstood a *snort* for consent, she'd basically attacked him in the hallway, and now he was staring at her in that odd, pensive way, so large and focused and close to her, and . . .

Shit.

Maybe it was the late night. Maybe it was that her last coffee had been sixteen hours ago. Maybe it was Adam Carlsen looking down at her, like *that*. All of a sudden, this entire situation was just too much.

"Actually, you're absolutely right. And I am so sorry. If you felt in any way harassed by me, you really should report me, because it's only fair. It was a horrible thing to do, though I really didn't want to . . . Not that my intentions matter; it's more like your perception of . . ."

Crap, crap, crap.

"I'm going to leave now, okay? Thank you, and . . . I am so, so, *so* sorry." Olive spun around on her heels and ran away down the hallway.

"Olive," she heard him call after her. "Olive, wait—"

She didn't stop. She sprinted down the stairs to the first floor and then out the building and across the pathways of the sparsely lit Stanford campus, running past a girl walking her dog and a group of students laughing in front of the library. She continued until she was standing in front of her apartment's door, stopping only to unlock it, making a beeline for her room in the hope of avoiding her roommate and whoever he might have brought home tonight.

It wasn't until she slumped on her bed, staring at the glow-in-the-dark stars glued to her ceiling, that she realized she had neglected to check on her lab mice. She had also left her laptop on her bench and her sweatshirt somewhere in the lab, and she had completely forgotten to stop at the store and buy the coffee she'd promised Malcolm she'd get for tomorrow morning.

Shit. What a disaster of a day.

It never occurred to Olive that Dr. Adam Carlsen—known ass—had called her by her name.

Chapter Two

♥ **HYPOTHESIS:** *Any rumor regarding my love life will spread with a speed that is directly proportional to my desire to keep said rumor a secret.*

Olive Smith was a rising third-year Ph.D. student in one of the best biology departments in the country, one that housed more than one hundred grads and what often felt like several million majoring undergrads. She had no idea what the exact number of faculty was, but judging from the mailboxes in the copy room she'd say that a safe guess was: too many. Therefore, she reasoned that if she'd never had the misfortune of interacting with Adam Carlsen in the two years before The Night (it had been only a handful of days since the kissing incident, but Olive already knew that she'd think of last Friday as The Night for the rest of her life), it was entirely possible that she might be able to finish grad school without crossing paths with him ever again. In fact, she was fairly sure that not only did Adam Carlsen have no idea who she was, but he also had no desire to learn—and had probably already forgotten all about what happened.

Unless, of course, she was catastrophically wrong and he did end up filing a Title IX lawsuit. In which case she supposed that she *would* see him again, when she pleaded guilty in federal court.

Olive figured that she could waste her time fretting about legal fees, or she could focus on what were more pressing issues. Like the approximately five hundred slides she had to prepare for the neurobiology class that she was slated to TA in the fall semester, which was starting in less than two weeks. Or the note Malcolm had left this morning, telling her he'd seen a cockroach scurry under the credenza even though their apartment was already full of traps. Or the most crucial one: the fact that her research project had reached a critical point and she desperately needed to find a bigger, significantly richer lab to carry out her experiment. Otherwise, what could very well become a groundbreaking, clinically relevant study might end up languishing on a handful of petri dishes stacked in the crisper drawer of her fridge.

Olive opened her laptop with half a mind to google "Organs one can live without" and "How much cash for them" but got sidetracked by the twenty new emails she'd received while busy with her lab animals. They were almost exclusively from predatory journals, Nigerian prince wannabes, and one glitter company whose newsletter she'd signed up for six years ago to get a free tube of lipstick. Olive quickly marked them as read, eager to go back to her experiments, and then noticed that one message was actually a reply to something she had sent. A reply from . . . Holy crap. *Holy crap.*

She clicked on it so hard she almost sprained her pointer finger.

Today, 3:15 p.m.
FROM: Tom-Benton@harvard.edu
TO: Olive-Smith@stanford.edu
SUBJECT: Re: Pancreatic Cancer Screening Project

Olive,
Your project sounds good. I'll be visiting Stanford in about
two weeks. Why don't we chat then?

Cheers,
TB

Tom Benton, Ph.D.
Associate Professor
Department of Biological Sciences, Harvard University

Her heart skipped a beat. Then it started galloping. Then it
slowed down to a crawl. And then she felt her blood pulsate in
her eyelids, which couldn't be healthy, but— *Yes.* Yes! She had a
taker. Almost. Probably? Maybe. Definitely maybe. Tom Benton
had said "good." He had said that it sounded "good." It had to
be a "good" sign, right?

She frowned, scrolling down to reread the email she'd sent
him several weeks earlier.

July 7, 8:19 a.m.
FROM: Olive-Smith@stanford.edu
TO: Tom-Benton@harvard.edu
SUBJECT: Pancreatic Cancer Screening Project

Dr. Benton,
My name is Olive Smith, and I am a Ph.D. student in the

biology department of Stanford University. My research focuses on pancreatic cancer, in particular on finding noninvasive, affordable detection tools that could lead to early treatment and increase survival rates. I have been working on blood biomarkers, with promising results. (You can read about my preliminary work in the peer-reviewed paper I have attached. I have also submitted more recent, unpublished findings to this year's Society for Biological Discovery conference; acceptance is pending but see the attached abstract.) The next step would be to carry out additional studies to determine the feasibility of my test kit.

Unfortunately my current lab (Dr. Aysegul Aslan's, who is retiring in two years) does not have the funding or the equipment to allow me to proceed. She is encouraging me to find a larger cancer research lab where I could spend the next academic year to collect the data I need. Then I would return to Stanford to analyze and write up the data. I am a huge fan of the work you have published on pancreatic cancer, and I was wondering whether there might be a possibility to carry out my work in your lab at Harvard.

I am happy to talk more in detail about my project if you are interested.

Sincerely,
Olive

Olive Smith
Ph.D. Candidate
Biology Department, Stanford University

If Tom Benton, cancer researcher extraordinaire, came to Stanford and gave Olive ten minutes of his time, she could convince him to help her out with her research predicament!

Well . . . maybe.

Olive was much better at actually *doing* research than at selling its importance to others. Science communication and public speaking of any sort were definitely her big weaknesses. But she had a chance to show Benton how promising her results were. She could list the clinical benefits of her work, and she could explain how little she required to turn her project into a huge success. All she needed was a quiet bench in a corner of his lab, a couple hundred of his lab mice, and unlimited access to his twenty-million-dollar electron microscope. Benton wouldn't even notice her.

Olive headed for the break room, mentally writing an impassioned speech on how she was willing to use his facilities only at night and limit her oxygen consumption to less than five breaths per minute. She poured herself a cup of stale coffee and turned around to find someone scowling right behind her.

She startled so hard that she almost burned herself.

"Jesus!" She clutched her chest, took a deep breath, and held tighter onto her Scooby-Doo mug. "Anh. You scared the shit out of me."

"Olive."

It was a bad sign. Anh never called her Olive—never, unless she was reprimanding her for biting her nails to the quick or for having vitamin gummies for dinner.

"Hey! How was your—"

"The other night."

Dammit. "—weekend?"

"Dr. Carlsen."

Dammit, dammit, dammit. "What about him?"

"I saw the two of you together."

"Oh. Really?" Olive's surprise sounded painfully playacted, even to her own ears. Maybe she should have signed up for drama club in high school instead of playing every single sport available.

"Yes. Here, in the department."

"Oh. Cool. Um, I didn't see you, or I'd have said hi."

Anh frowned. "Ol. I saw you. I saw you with Carlsen. You know that I saw you, and I know that you know that I saw you, because you've been avoiding me."

"I have not."

Anh gave her one of her formidable no-bullshit looks. It was probably the one she used as president of the student senate, as head of the Stanford Women in Science Association, as director of outreach for the Organization of BIPOC Scientists. There was no fight Anh couldn't win. She was fearsome and indomitable, and Olive loved this about her—but not right now.

"You haven't answered any of my messages for the past two days. We usually text every hour."

They did. Multiple times. Olive switched the mug to her left hand, for no reason other than to buy some time. "I've been . . . busy?"

"Busy?" Anh's eyebrow shot up. "Busy kissing Carlsen?"

"Oh. Oh, *that*. That was just . . ."

Anh nodded, as if to encourage her to finish the sentence. When it became obvious that Olive couldn't, Anh continued for her.

"That was—no offense, Ol—but that was the most bizarre kiss I have ever seen."

Calm. Stay calm. She doesn't know. She cannot know. "I doubt that," Olive retorted weakly. "Take that upside-down Spider-Man kiss. That was way more bizarre than—"

"Ol, you said you were on a date that night. You're not dating *Carlsen*, are you?" She twisted her face in a grimace.

It would have been so easy to confess the truth. Since starting grad school Anh and Olive had done heaps of moronic things, together and separately; the time Olive panicked and kissed none other than Adam Carlsen could become one of them, one they laughed about during their weekly beer-and-s'mores nights.

Or not. There was a chance that if Olive admitted to lying now, Anh might never trust her again. Or that she'd never go out with Jeremy. And as much as the idea of her best friend dating her ex had Olive wanting to puke just a bit, the thought of said best friend being anything but happy had her wanting to puke a lot more.

The situation was depressingly simple: Olive was alone in the world. She had been for a long time, ever since high school. She had trained herself not to make a big deal out of it—she was sure many people were alone in the world and found themselves having to write down made-up names and phone numbers on their emergency contact forms. During college and her master's, focusing on science and research had been her way of coping, and she had been perfectly ready to spend the rest of her life holed up in a lab with little more than a beaker and a handful of pipettes as her faithful companions—until . . . Anh.

In a way, it had been love at first sight. First day of grad school. Biology cohort orientation. Olive entered the conference room, looked around, and sat in the first free seat she could find, petrified. She was the only woman in the room, virtually alone in a sea of white men who were already talking about boats, and whatever sportsball was on TV the night before, and the best routes to drive places. *I have made a terrible mistake*, she thought. *The Guy in the bathroom was wrong. I should never have come here. I am never going to fit in.*

And then a girl with curly dark hair and a pretty, round face plopped in the chair next to hers and muttered, "So much for the STEM programs' commitment to inclusivity, am I right?" That was the moment everything changed.

They could have just been allies. As the only two non-cis-white-male students in their year, they could have found solace together when some bitching was needed and ignored each other otherwise. Olive had lots of friends like that—all of them, actually, circumstantial acquaintances whom she thought of fondly but not very often. Anh, though, had been different from the start. Maybe because they'd soon found out that they loved spending their Saturday nights eating junk food and falling asleep to rom-coms. Maybe it was the way she'd insisted on dragging Olive to every single "women in STEM" support group on campus and had wowed everyone with her bull's-eye comments. Maybe it was that she'd opened up to Olive and explained how hard it had been for her to get where she was today. The way her older brothers had made fun of her and called her a nerd for loving math so much growing up—at an age when being a nerd was not quite considered cool. That time a physics professor asked her if she was in the wrong class on the first day of the semester. The fact that despite her grades and research experience, even her academic adviser had seemed skeptical when she'd decided to pursue STEM higher education.

Olive, whose path to grad school had been rough but not nearly as rough, was befuddled. Then enraged. And then in absolute awe when she understood the self-doubt that Anh had been able to harness into sheer fierceness.

And for some unimaginable reason, Anh seemed to like Olive just as much. When Olive's stipend hadn't quite stretched to the end of the month, Anh had shared her instant ramen. When Olive's computer had crashed without backups, Anh had stayed up all night to help her rewrite her crystallography paper. When Olive had nowhere to go over the holidays, Anh would bring her friend home to Michigan and let her large family ply Olive with delicious food while rapid Vietnamese flowed around her. When Olive had felt too stupid for the program and had considered dropping out, Anh had talked her out of it.

The day Olive met Anh's rolling eyes, a life-changing friendship was born. Slowly, they'd begun to include Malcolm and become a bit of a trio, but Anh . . . Anh was *her person*. Family. Olive hadn't even thought that was possible for someone like her.

Anh rarely asked anything for herself, and even though they'd been friends for more than two years, Olive had never seen her show interest in dating anyone—until Jeremy. Pretending that she'd been on a date with Carlsen was the least Olive could do to ensure her friend's happiness.

So she bucked up, smiled, and tried to keep her tone reasonably even while asking, "What do you mean?"

"I mean that we talk every minute of every day, and you never mentioned Carlsen before. My closest friend is supposedly seeing the superstar professor of the department, and somehow I've never heard of it? You *know* his reputation, right? Is it some kind of joke? Do you have a brain tumor? Do *I* have a brain tumor?"

This was what happened whenever Olive lied: she ended up having to tell even more lies to cover her first, and she was horrible at it, which meant that each lie got worse and less convincing than the previous. There was no way she could fool Anh. There was no way she could fool *anybody*. Anh was going to get mad, then Jeremy was going to get mad, then Malcolm, too, and then Olive was going to find herself utterly alone. The heartbreak was going to make her flunk out of grad school. She was going to lose her visa and her only source of income and move back to Canada, where it snowed all the time and people ate moose heart and—

"Hey."

The voice, deep and even, came from somewhere behind Olive, but she didn't need to turn to know that it was Carlsen's. Just like she didn't need to turn to know that the large, warm weight suddenly steadying her, a firm but barely there pressure applied to the center of her lower back, was Carlsen's hand. About two inches above her ass.

Holy crap.

Olive twisted her neck and looked up. And up. And up. And a bit more up. She was not a short woman, but he was just *big*. "Oh. Um, hey."

"Is everything okay?" He said it looking into her eyes, in a low, intimate tone. Like they were alone. Like Anh was not there. He said it in a way that should have made Olive uncomfortable but didn't. For some inexplicable reason his presence in the room soothed her, even though until a second ago she had been freaking out. Perhaps two different types of unease neutralized each other? It sounded like a fascinating research topic. Worth pursuing. Maybe Olive should abandon biology and switch to psychology. Maybe she should excuse herself and go run a literature search. Maybe she should expire on the spot to avoid facing this crapfest of a situation she'd put herself in.

"Yes. Yes. Everything is *great*. Anh and I were just . . . chatting. About our weekends."

Carlsen looked at Anh, as though realizing for the first time that she was in the room. He acknowledged her existence with one of those brief nods dudes used to greet others. His hand slid lower on Olive's spine just as Anh's eyes widened.

"Nice to meet you, Anh. I've heard a lot about you," Carlsen said, and he was good at this, Olive had to admit. Because she was sure that from Anh's angle it looked like he was groping her, but in fact he was . . . not. Olive could barely feel his hand on her.

Just a little, maybe. The warmth, and the slight pressure, and—

"Nice to meet you, too." Anh looked thunderstruck. Like she might pass out. "Um, I was just about to leave. Ol, I'm going to text you when . . . yeah."

She was out of the room before Olive could answer. Which was good, because Olive didn't need to come up with more lies. But also slightly less good, because now it was just her and Carlsen. Standing way too close. Olive would have paid good money to say that she was the one to put some distance between them, but the embarrassing truth was that it was Carlsen who stepped away first. Enough to give her the space she needed, and then some.

"Is everything okay?" he asked again. His tone was still soft. Not something she would have expected from him.

"Yes. Yes, I just . . ." Olive waved her hand. "Thank you."

"You're welcome."

"Did you hear what she said? About Friday and . . ."

"I did. That's why I . . ." He looked at her, and then at his hand—the one that had been warming her back a few seconds ago—and Olive immediately understood.

"Thank you," she repeated. Because Adam Carlsen might have been a known ass, but Olive was feeling pretty damn grateful right at the moment. "Also, uh, I couldn't help noticing that no agents from the Federal Bureau of Investigation have knocked on my door to arrest me in the past seventy-two hours."

The corner of his mouth twitched. Minimally. "Is that so?"

Olive nodded. "Which makes me think that maybe you haven't filed that complaint. Even though it would have been totally within your rights. So, thank you. For that. And . . . and for stepping in, right now. You saved me a lot of trouble."

Carlsen stared at her for a long moment, looking suddenly like he did during seminar, when people mixed up theory and hypothesis or admitted to using listwise deletion instead of imputation. "You shouldn't need someone to step in."

Olive stiffened. Right. *Known ass.* "Well, it's not as if I asked you to do anything. I was going to handle it by myse—"

"And you shouldn't have to lie about your relationship status," he continued. "Especially not so that your friend and your boyfriend can get together guilt-free. That's not how friendship works, last I checked."

Oh. So he'd actually been listening when Olive vomited her life story at him. "It's not like that." He lifted an eyebrow, and Olive raised a hand in defense. "Jeremy wasn't really my boyfriend. And Anh didn't ask me for anything. I'm not some sort of victim, I just . . . want my friend to be happy."

"By lying to her," he added drily.

"Well, yeah, but . . . She thinks we're dating, you and I," Olive blurted out. God, the implications were too ridiculous to bear.

"Wasn't that the point?"

"Yeah." She nodded and then remembered the coffee in her hand and took a sip from her mug. It was still warm. The conversation with Anh couldn't have lasted more than five minutes. "Yeah. I guess it was. By the way—I'm Olive Smith. In case you're still interested in filing that complaint. I'm a Ph.D. student in Dr. Aslan's lab—"

"I know who you are."

"Oh." Maybe he had looked her up, then. Olive tried to imagine him combing through the Current Ph.D. Students' section on the department website. Olive's picture had been taken by the program secretary on her third day of grad school, well before she had become fully aware of what she was in for. She had made an effort to look good: tamed her wavy brown hair, put on mascara to pop the green of her eyes, even attempted to hide her freckles with some borrowed foundation. It had been before she'd realized how ruthless, how cutthroat academia could be. Before the sense of inadequacy, before the constant fear that even if she was good at research, she might never be able to truly make it as an academic. She had been smiling. A real, actual smile.

"Okay."

"I'm Adam. Carlsen. I'm faculty in—"

She burst out laughing in his face. And then regretted it immediately as she noticed his confused expression, as though he'd seriously thought Olive might not know who he was. As though he was unaware of being one of the most prominent scholars in the field. The modesty was not at all like Adam Carlsen. Olive cleared her throat.

"Right. Um, I know who you are, too, Dr. Carlsen."

"You should probably call me Adam."

"Oh. Oh, no." That would be way too . . . No. The department was not like that. Grads didn't call faculty by their first names. "I could never—"

"If Anh happens to be around."

"Oh. Yeah." It made sense. "Thank you. I hadn't thought of that." Or of anything else, really. Clearly, her brain had stopped working three days ago, when she'd decided that kissing him to save her own ass was a good idea. "If that's o-okay with you. I'm going to go home, because this whole thing was kind of stressful and . . ." *I was going to run an experiment, but I really need to sit on the couch and watch* American Ninja Warrior *for forty-five minutes while eating Cool Ranch Doritos, which taste surprisingly better than you'd give them credit for.*

He nodded. "I'll walk you to your car."

"I'm not *that* distraught."

"In case Anh's still around."

"Oh." It was, Olive had to admit, a kind offer. Surprisingly so. Especially because it came from Adam "I'm Too Good for This Department" Carlsen. Olive knew that he was a dick, so she couldn't quite understand why today he . . . didn't seem to be one. Maybe she should just blame her own appalling behavior, which would make anyone look good by comparison. "Thanks. But no need."

She could tell that he didn't want to insist but couldn't help himself. "I'd feel better if you let me walk you to your car."

"I don't have a car." *I'm a grad student living in Stanford, California. I make less than thirty thousand dollars a year. My rent takes up two-thirds of my salary. I've been wearing the same pair of contacts since May, and I go to every seminar that provides refreshments to save on meals,* she didn't bother adding. She had no idea how old Carlsen was, but it couldn't have been that long ago that he was a grad student.

"Do you take the bus?"

"I bike. And my bike is right at the entrance of the building."

He opened his mouth, and then closed it. And then opened it again.

You kissed that mouth, Olive. And it was a good kiss.

"There are no bike lanes around here."

She shrugged. "I like to live dangerously." *Cheaply,* she meant. "And I have a helmet." She turned to set her mug on the first surface she could find. She'd retrieve it later. Or not, if someone stole it. Who cared? She'd gotten it from a postdoc who'd left academia to become a DJ, anyway. For the second time in less than a week, Carlsen had saved her ass. For the second time, she couldn't stand being with him a minute longer.

"I'll see you around, okay?"

His chest rose as he inhaled deeply. "Yeah. Okay."

Olive got out of the room as fast as she could.

~~~~~~

"IS IT A prank? It must be a prank. Am I on national TV? Where are the hidden cameras? How do I look?"

"It's not a prank. There are no cameras." Olive adjusted the strap of her backpack on her shoulder and stepped to the side to avoid being run over by an undergrad on an electric scooter. "But now that you mention it—you look great. Especially for seven thirty in the morning."

Anh didn't blush, but it was a close thing. "Last night I did one of those face masks that you and Malcolm got me for my birthday. The one that looks like a panda? And I got a new sunscreen that's supposed to give you a bit of a glow. And I put on mascara," she added hastily under her breath.

Olive could ask her why she'd gone the extra mile to look nice on a run-of-the-mill Tuesday morning, but she already knew the answer: Jeremy's and Anh's labs were on the same floor, and while the biology department was large, chance encounters were very much a possibility.

She hid a smile. As weird as the idea of a best friend dating an ex might sound, she was glad that Anh was starting to allow herself to consider Jeremy romantically. Mostly, it was nice to know that the indignity Olive had put herself through with Carlsen on The Night was paying off. That, together with Tom Benton's very promising email about her research project, had Olive thinking that things might be finally looking up.

"Okay." Anh chewed on her lower lip, deep in concentration. "So it's not a prank. Which means that there must be another explanation. Let me find it."

"There is no explanation to be found. We just—"

"Oh my God, are you trying to get citizenship? Are they deporting you back to Canada because we've been sharing Malcolm's Netflix password? Tell them we didn't know it was a federal crime. No, wait, don't tell them anything until we get you a lawyer. And, Ol, I will marry you. I'll get you a green card and you won't have to—"

"Anh." Olive squeezed her friend's hand tighter to get her to shut up for a second. "I promise you, I'm not getting deported. I just went on a single date with Carlsen."

Anh scrunched her face and dragged Olive to a bench on the side of the path, forcing her to sit down. Olive complied, telling herself that were their positions inverted, had she caught Anh kissing Adam Carlsen, she'd probably have the same reaction. Hell, she'd probably be busy booking a full-blown psychiatric evaluation for Anh.

"Listen," Anh started, "do you remember last spring, when I held your hair back while you projectile vomited the five pounds of spoiled shrimp cocktail you ate at Dr. Park's retirement party?"

"Oh, yes. I do." Olive cocked her head, pensive. "You ate more than me and never got sick."

"Because I'm made of sterner stuff, but never mind that. The point is: I am here for you, and always will be, no matter what. No matter how many pounds of spoiled shrimp cocktail you projectile vomit, you can trust me. We're a team, you and I. And Malcolm, when he's not busy screwing his way through the Stanford population. So if Carlsen is secretly an extraterrestrial life-form planning a takeover of Earth that will ultimately result in humanity being enslaved by evil overlords who look like cicadas, and the only way to stop him is dating him, you can tell me and I'll inform NASA—"

"For God's sake"—Olive had to laugh—"it was just a date!"

Anh looked pained. "I just don't understand."

Because it doesn't make sense. "I know, but there is nothing to understand. It's just . . . We went on a date."

"But . . . why? Ol, you're beautiful and smart and funny and have excellent taste in knee socks, why would you go out with Adam Carlsen?"

Olive scratched her nose. "Because he is . . ." It cost her, to say the word. Oh, it cost her. But she had to. "Nice."

"Nice?" Anh's eyebrows shot up so high they almost merged with her hairline.

She does look extra cute today, Olive reflected, pleased.

"Adam 'Ass' Carlsen?"

"Well, yeah. He is . . ." Olive looked around, as if help could come from the oak trees, or the undergrads rushing to their summer classes. When it didn't seem forthcoming, she just finished, lamely, "He is a *nice* asshole, I guess."

Anh's expression went straight up disbelieving. "Okay, so you went from dating someone as cool as Jeremy to going out with Adam Carlsen."

Perfect. This was exactly the opening Olive had wanted. "I did. And happily, because I never cared that much about Jeremy." Finally some truth in this conversation. "It wasn't that hard to move on, honestly. Which is why— Please, Anh, put that boy out of his misery. He deserves it, and above all, *you* deserve it. I bet he's on campus today. You should ask him to accompany you to that horror movie festival so I don't have to come with you and sleep with the lights on for the next six months."

This time Anh blushed outright. She looked down at her hands, picked at her fingernails, and *then* she began to fiddle with the hem of her shorts before saying, "I don't know. Maybe. I mean, if you really think that—"

The sound of an alarm went off from Anh's pocket, and she

straightened to pull out her phone. "Crap, I've got a Diversity in STEM mentoring meeting and then I have to run two assays." She stood, picking up her backpack. "Want to get together for lunch?"

"Can't. Have a TA meeting." Olive smiled. "Maybe Jeremy's free, though."

Anh rolled her eyes, but the corners of her mouth were curving up. It made Olive more than a little happy. So happy that she didn't even flip her off when Anh turned around from the path and asked, "Is he blackmailing you?"

"Huh?"

"Carlsen. Is he blackmailing you? Did he find out that you're an aberration and pee in the shower?"

"First of all, it's time efficient." Olive glared. "Second, I find it oddly flattering that you'd think Carlsen would go to these ridiculous lengths to get me to date him."

"Anyone would, Ol. Because you're awesome." Anh grimaced before adding, "Except when you're peeing in the shower."

~~~~~~~

JEREMY WAS ACTING weird. Which didn't mean much, since Jeremy had always been a bit awkward, and having recently split from Olive to date her best friend was not going to make him any less so—but today he seemed even weirder than usual. He came into the campus coffee shop, a few hours after Olive's conversation with Anh, and proceeded to stare at her for two good minutes. Then three. Then five. It was more attention than he'd ever paid to Olive—yes, including their dates.

When it got borderline ridiculous, she lifted her eyes from her laptop and waved at him. Jeremy flushed, grabbed his latte from the counter, and found a table for himself. Olive went back to rereading her two-line email for the seventieth time.

Today, 10:12 a.m.
FROM: Olive-Smith@stanford.edu
TO: Tom-Benton@harvard.edu
SUBJECT: Re: Pancreatic Cancer Screening Project

Dr. Benton,
Thank you for your response. Chatting in person would be
fantastic. What day will you be at Stanford? Let me know
when it's most convenient for you to meet.

Sincerely,
Olive

Not twenty minutes later, a fourth-year who worked with
Dr. Holden Rodrigues over in pharmacology came in and took
a seat next to Jeremy. They immediately started whispering to
each other and pointing at Olive. Any other day she would have
been concerned and a little upset, but Dr. Benton had already
answered her email, which took priority over . . . anything else,
really.

Today, 10:26 a.m.
FROM: Tom-Benton@harvard.edu
TO: Olive-Smith@stanford.edu
SUBJECT: Re: Pancreatic Cancer Screening Project

Olive,
I'm on sabbatical from Harvard this semester, so I'll be
staying for several days. A Stanford collaborator and I were
just awarded a large grant, and we'll be meeting to talk
about setup, etc. Okay if we play it by ear once I'm there?

Cheers,

TB

Sent from my iPhone

Yes! She had several days to convince him to take on her project, which was much better than the ten minutes she'd originally anticipated. Olive fist-pumped—which led to Jeremy and his friend staring at her even more weirdly. What was up with them, anyway? Did she have toothpaste on her face or something? Who cared? She was going to meet Tom Benton and convince him to take her on. *Pancreatic cancer, I'm coming for you.*

She was in an excellent mood until two hours later, when she entered the biology TA meeting and a sudden silence dropped in the room. About fifteen pairs of eyes fixed on her—not a reaction she was accustomed to receiving.

"Uh—hi?"

A couple of people said hi back. Most averted their gazes. Olive told herself that she was just imagining things. *Must be low blood sugar. Or high. One of the two.*

"Hey, Olive." A seventh-year who had never before acknowledged her existence moved his backpack and freed the seat next to his. "How are you?"

"Good." She sat down gingerly, trying to keep the suspicion from her tone. "Um, you?"

"Great."

There was something about his smile. Something salacious and fake. Olive was considering asking about it when the head TA managed to get the projector to work and called everyone's attention to the meeting.

After that, things became even weirder. Dr. Aslan stopped by the lab just to ask Olive if there was anything she'd like to talk about; Chase, a grad in her lab, let her use the PCR machine first, even though he usually hoarded it like a third grader with his last piece of Halloween candy; the lab manager *winked* at Olive as he handed her a stack of blank paper for the printer. And then she met Malcolm in the all-gender restroom, completely by chance, and suddenly everything made sense.

"You sneaky monster," he hissed. His black eyes were almost comically narrow. "I've been texting you all day."

"Oh." Olive patted the back pocket of her jeans, and then the front one, trying to remember the last time she had seen her phone. "I think I might have left my phone at home."

"I cannot believe it."

"Believe what?"

"I cannot believe *you*."

"I don't know what you're talking about."

"I thought we were friends."

"We are."

"Good friends."

"We are. You and Anh are my best friends. What—"

"Clearly not, if I had to hear it from Stella, who heard it from Jess, who heard it from Jeremy, who heard it from Anh—"

"Hear what?"

"—who heard it from I don't even know who. And I thought we were friends."

Something icy crawled its way up Olive's back. Could it be . . . No. No, it couldn't be. "Hear what?"

"I'm done. I'm letting the cockroaches eat you. And I'm changing my Netflix password."

Oh no. "Malcolm. Hear what?"

"That you are dating *Adam Carlsen*."

OLIVE HAD NEVER been in Carlsen's lab, but she knew where to find it. It was the biggest, most functional research space in the whole department, coveted by all and a never-ending source of resentment toward Carlsen. She had to swipe her badge once and then once more to access it (she rolled her eyes both times). The second door opened directly onto the lab space, and maybe it was because he was as tall as Mount Everest and his shoulders were just as large, but Carlsen was the very first thing she noticed. He was peering at a Southern blot next to Alex, a grad who was one year ahead of Olive, but he turned toward the entrance the moment she came in.

Olive smiled weakly at him—mainly out of relief at having found him.

It was going to be all right. She was going to explain to him what Malcolm had told her, and without a doubt he was going to find the situation categorically unacceptable and fix it for the both of them, because Olive could *not* spend her next three years surrounded by people who thought that she was dating Adam freaking Carlsen.

The problem was, Carlsen wasn't the only one to notice Olive. There were over a dozen benches in the lab, and at least ten people working at them. Most of them—*all of them*—were staring at Olive. Probably because most of them—*all of them*—had heard that Olive was dating their boss.

Fuck her life.

"Can I talk to you for a minute, Dr. Carlsen?" Rationally, Olive knew that the lab was not furnished in a way that made echoing possible. Still, she felt as though her words bounced off the walls and repeated about four times.

Carlsen nodded, nonplussed, and handed the Southern blot

to Alex before heading in her direction. He appeared either unaware or uncaring that approximately two-thirds of his lab members were gaping at him. The remaining ones seemed to be on the verge of a hemorrhagic stroke.

He led Olive to a meeting room just outside the main lab space, and she followed him silently, trying not to dwell on the fact that a lab full of people who thought that she and Carlsen were dating had just seen them enter a private room. Alone.

This was the worst. The absolute worst.

"Everyone knows," she blurted out as soon as the door closed behind her.

He studied her for a moment, looking puzzled. "Are you okay?"

"Everyone knows. About us."

He cocked his head, crossing his arms over his chest. It had been barely a day since they'd last talked, but apparently long enough for Olive to have forgotten his . . . his presence. Or whatever it was that made her feel like she was small and delicate whenever he was around. "Us?"

"Us."

He seemed confused, so Olive elaborated.

"Us, dating—not that we're dating, but Anh clearly thought so, and she told . . ." She realized that the words were tumbling out and forced herself to slow down. "Jeremy. And he told everyone, and now everyone knows. Or they think they know, even though there's absolutely *nothing* to know. As you and I know."

He took it in for a moment and then nodded slowly. "And when you say everyone . . . ?"

"I mean *everyone*." She pointed in the direction of his lab. "Those people? They know. The other grads? They know. Cherie, the department secretary? She totally knows. Gossip in this department is the worst. And they all think that I am dating a *professor*."

"I see," he said, seeming strangely unbothered by this clusterfuck. It should have calmed Olive down, but it only had the effect of driving her panic up a notch.

"I am sorry this happened. *So* sorry. This is all my fault." She wiped a hand down her face. "But I didn't think that . . . I understand why Anh would tell Jeremy—I mean, getting those two together was the whole point of this charade—but . . . Why would Jeremy tell anyone?"

Carlsen shrugged. "Why wouldn't he?"

She looked up. "What do you mean?"

"A grad student dating a faculty member seems like an interesting piece of information to share."

Olive shook her head. "It's not that interesting. Why would people be interested?"

He lifted one eyebrow. "Someone once told me that 'Gossip in this department is the wor—'"

"Okay, okay. Point taken." She took a deep breath and started pacing, trying to ignore the way Carlsen was studying her, how relaxed he looked, arms across his chest while leaning against the conference table. He was not supposed to be calm. He was supposed to be incensed. He was a known dick with a reputation for arrogance—the idea of people thinking that he was dating a nobody should be mortifying to him. The burden of freaking out should not be falling on Olive alone.

"This is— We need to do something, of course. We need to tell people that this is not true and that we made it all up. Except that they'll think that I'm crazy, and maybe that you are, too, so we have to come up with some other story. Yes, okay, we need to tell people we're not together anymore—"

"And what will Anh and what's-his-face do?"

Olive stopped pacing. "Uh?"

"Won't your friends feel bad about dating if they think we're not together? Or that you lied to them?"

She hadn't thought of that. "I— Maybe. Maybe, but—"

It *was* true that Anh had seemed happy. Maybe she had already invited Jeremy to accompany her to that movie festival—possibly right after telling him about Olive and Carlsen, damn her. But this was exactly what Olive had wanted.

"Are you going to tell her the truth?"

She let out a panicked sound. "I can't. Not *now*." God, why did Olive ever agree to date Jeremy? She wasn't even into him. Yes, the Irish accent and the ginger hair were cute, but not worth any of this. "Maybe we can tell people that I broke up with you?"

"That's very flattering," Dr. Carlsen deadpanned. She couldn't quite figure out if he was joking.

"Fine. We can say that you broke up with me."

"Because that sounds credible," he said drily, almost below his breath. She was not sure she'd heard him correctly and had no idea what he might mean, but she was starting to feel very upset. Fine, she had been the one to kiss him first—God, she'd *kissed* Adam Carlsen; this was her life; these were her choices—but his actions in the break room the day before surely hadn't helped matters. He could at least display some concern. There was no way he was okay with everyone believing that he was attracted to some random girl with one point five publications—yes, that paper she had revised and resubmitted three weeks ago counted as half.

"What if we tell people that it was a mutual breakup?"

He nodded. "Sounds good."

Olive perked up. "Really? Great, then! We'll—"

"We could ask Cherie to add it to the departmental newsletter."

"What?"

"Or do you think a public announcement before seminar would be better?"

"No. No, it's—"

"Maybe we should ask IT to put it on the Stanford home page. That way people would know—"

"Okay, okay, fine! I get it."

He looked at her evenly for a moment, and when he spoke, his tone was reasonable in a way she would never have expected of Adam "Ass" Carlsen. "If what bothers you is that people are talking about you dating a professor, the damage is done, I'm afraid. Telling everyone that we broke up is not going to undo the fact that they think we dated."

Olive's shoulders slumped. She hated that he was right. "Okay, then. If you have any ideas on how to fix this mess, by all means I am open to—"

"You could let them go on thinking it."

For a moment, she thought she hadn't heard him correctly. "W-What?"

"You can let people go on thinking that we're dating. It solves your problem with your friend and what's-his-face, and you don't have much to lose, since it sounds like from a . . . reputation standpoint"—he said the word "reputation" rolling his eyes a little, as if the concept of caring about what others thought were the dumbest thing since homeopathic antibiotics—"things cannot get any worse for you."

This was . . . Out of everything . . . In her life, Olive had never, she had *never* . . .

"What?" she asked again, feebly.

He shrugged. "Seems like a win-win to me."

It *so* did not, to Olive. It seemed like a lose-lose, and then lose again, and then lose some more, type of situation. It seemed insane.

"You mean . . . forever?" She thought her voice came out whiny, but it was possible that it was just an effect of the blood pounding in her head.

"That sounds excessive. Maybe until your friends are not dating anymore? Or until they're more settled? I don't know. Whatever works best, I guess." He was serious about this. He was not joking.

"Are you not . . ." Olive had no idea how to even ask it. "Married, or something?" He must have been in his early thirties. He had a fantastic job; he was tall with thick, wavy black hair, clearly smart, even attractive looking; he was *built*. Yeah, he was a moody dick, but some women wouldn't mind it. Some women might even like it.

He shrugged. "My wife and the twins won't mind."

Oh, shit.

Olive felt a wave of heat wash over her. She blushed crimson and then almost died of shame, because— God, she had forced a married man, a *father*, to kiss her. Now people thought that he was having an affair. His wife was probably crying into her pillow. His kids would grow up with horrible daddy issues and become serial killers.

"I . . . Oh my God, I didn't— I am *so* sorry—"

"Just kidding."

"I really had no idea that you—"

"Olive. I was joking. I'm not married. No kids."

A wave of relief crashed into her. Followed by just as much anger. "Dr. Carlsen, this is not something you should joke—"

"You really need to start calling me Adam. Since we've reportedly been dating for a while."

Olive exhaled slowly, pinching the bridge of her nose. "Why would you even— What would you even get out of this?"

"Out of what?"

"Pretending to date me. Why do you care? What's in it for you?"

Dr. Carlsen—Adam—opened his mouth, and for a moment Olive had the impression that he was going to say something important. But then he averted his gaze, and all that came out was "It would help you out." He hesitated for a moment. "And I have my own reasons."

She narrowed her eyes. "What reasons?"

"Reasons."

"If it's criminal, I'd rather not be involved."

He smiled a bit. "It's not."

"If you don't tell me, I have no choice but to assume that it entails kidnapping. Or arson. Or embezzlement."

He seemed preoccupied for a moment, fingertips drumming against a large biceps. It considerably strained his shirt. "If I tell you, it cannot leave this room."

"I think we can both agree that *nothing* that has happened in this room should ever leave it."

"Good point," he conceded. He paused. Sighed. Chewed on the inside of his cheek for a second. Sighed again.

"Okay," he finally said, sounding like a man who knew that he was going to regret speaking the second he opened his mouth. "I'm considered a flight risk."

"Flight risk?" God, he was a felon on parole. A jury of his peers had convicted him for crimes against grad students. He'd probably whacked someone on the head with a microscope for mislabeling peptide samples. "So it *is* something criminal."

"What? No. The department suspects that I'm making plans to leave Stanford and move to another institution. Normally it wouldn't bother me, but Stanford has decided to freeze my research funds."

"Oh." Not what she'd thought. Not at all. "Can they?"

"Yes. Well, up to one-third of them. The reasoning is that

they don't want to fund the research and further the career of someone who—they believe—is going to leave anyway."

"But if it's only one-third—"

"It's millions of dollars," he said levelly. "That I had earmarked for projects that I planned to finish within the next year. Here, at Stanford. Which means that I need those funds soon."

"Oh." Come to think of it, Olive had been hearing scuttlebutt about Carlsen being recruited by other universities since her first year. A few months earlier there had even been a rumor that he might go work for NASA. "Why do they think that? And why now?"

"A number of reasons. The most relevant is that a few weeks ago I was awarded a grant—a very large grant—with a scientist at another institution. That institution had tried to recruit me in the past, and Stanford sees the collaboration as an indication that I am planning to accept." He hesitated before continuing. "More generally, I have been made aware that the . . . optics are that I have not put down roots because I want to be able to flee Stanford at the drop of a hat."

"Roots?"

"Most of my grads will be done within the year. I have no extended family in the area. No wife, no children. I'm currently renting—I'd have to buy a house just to convince the department that I'm committed to staying," he said, clearly irritated. "If I was in a relationship . . . that would really help."

Okay. That made sense. But. "Have you considered getting a real girlfriend?"

His eyebrow lifted. "Have you considered getting a real date?"

"Touché."

Olive fell silent and studied him for a few moments, letting him study her in return. Funny how she used to be scared of him. Now he was the only person in the world who knew about her worst fuckup ever, and it was hard to feel intimidated—even harder, after discovering that he was the kind of person who'd be desperate enough to pretend to date someone to get his research funds back. Olive was sure that she would do the exact same for the opportunity to finish her study on pancreatic cancer, which made Adam seem oddly . . . relatable. And if he was relatable, then she could go ahead and fake-date him, right?

No. Yes. No. What? She was crazy for even considering this. She was certifiably mental. And yet she found herself saying, "It would be complicated."

"What would be?"

"To pretend that we're dating."

"Really? It would be complicated to make people think that we're dating?"

Oh, he was impossible. "Okay, I see your point. But it would be hard to do so convincingly for a prolonged period."

He shrugged. "We'll be fine, as long as we say hi to each other in the hallways and you don't call me Dr. Carlsen."

"I don't think people who are dating just . . . say hi to each other."

"What do people who are dating do?"

It beat Olive. She had gone on maybe five dates in her life, including the ones with Jeremy, and they had ranged from moderately boring to anxiety inducing to horrifying (mostly when a guy had monologued about his grandmother's hip replacement in frightening detail). She would have loved to have someone in her life, but she doubted it was in store for her. Maybe she was unlovable. Maybe spending so many years alone had warped her in some fundamental way and that was why she seemed to be unable to develop a true romantic connection, or even the type of attraction she often heard others talk about. In the end, it didn't really matter. Grad school and dating went poorly together, anyway, which was probably why Dr. Adam Carlsen, MacArthur Fellow and genius extraordinaire, was standing here at thirtysomething years old, asking Olive what people did on dates.

Academics, ladies and gentlemen.

"Um . . . things. Stuff." Olive racked her brain. "People go out and do activities together. Like apple picking, or those Paint and Sip things." *Which are idiotic*, Olive thought.

"Which are idiotic," Adam said, gesturing dismissively with those huge hands of his. "You could just go to Anh and tell her that we went out and painted a Monet. Sounds like she'd take care of letting everyone else know."

"Okay, first of all, it was Jeremy. Let's agree to blame Jeremy. And it's more than that," Olive insisted. "People who date, they—they talk. A lot. More than just greetings in the hallway. They know each other's favorite colors, and where they were born, and they . . . they hold hands. They *kiss*."

Adam pressed his lips together as if to suppress a smile. "We could never do *that*."

A fresh wave of mortification crashed into Olive. "I *am* sorry about the kiss. I really didn't think, and—"

He shook his head. "It's fine."

He did seem uncharacteristically indifferent to the situation, especially for a guy who was known to freak out when people got the atomic number of selenium wrong. No, he wasn't indifferent. He was *amused*.

Olive cocked her head. "Are you enjoying this?"

"'Enjoying' is probably not the right word, but you have to admit that it's quite entertaining."

She had no idea what he was talking about. There was nothing entertaining about the fact that she had randomly kissed a faculty member because he was the only person in the hallway and that, as a consequence of that spectacularly idiotic action, everyone thought she was dating someone she'd met exactly twice before today—

She burst into laughter and folded into herself before her train of thought was even over, overwhelmed by the sheer improbability of the situation. *This* was her life. *These* were the results of her actions. When she could finally breathe again, her abs hurt and she had to wipe her eyes. "This is the worst."

He was smiling, staring at her with a strange light in his eyes. And would you look at that: Adam Carlsen had dimples. Cute ones. "Yep."

"And it's all my fault."

"Pretty much. I kind of yanked Anh's chain yesterday, but yeah, I'd say that it's mostly your fault."

Fake dating. Adam Carlsen. Olive would have to be a lunatic. "Wouldn't it be a problem that you're faculty and I'm a graduate student?"

He tilted his head, going serious. "It wouldn't look great, but I don't think so, no. Since I have no authority whatsoever over you and am not involved in your supervision. But I can ask around."

It was an epically bad idea. The worst idea ever entertained in the epically bad history of bad ideas. Except that it really would solve this current problem of hers, as well as some of Adam's, in exchange for saying hi to him once a week and making an effort not to call him Dr. Carlsen. It seemed like a pretty good deal.

"Can I think about it?"

"Of course," he said calmly. Reassuringly.

She hadn't thought he'd be like this. After hearing all the

stories, and seeing him walk around with that perpetual frown of his, she really hadn't thought he'd be like this. Even if she didn't quite know what *this* even meant.

"And thank you, I guess. For offering. Adam." She added the last word like an afterthought. Trying it out on her lips. It felt weird, but not too weird.

After a long pause, he nodded. "No problem. Olive."

Chapter Three

~~~~~~

♥ **HYPOTHESIS:** *A private conversation with Adam Carlsen will become 150 percent more awkward after the word "sex" is uttered. By me.*

Three days later, Olive found herself standing in front of Adam's office.

She'd never been there before, but she had no problem finding it. The student scurrying out with misty eyes and a terrified expression was a dead giveaway, not to mention that Adam's door was the only one in the hallway completely devoid of pictures of kids, pets, or significant others. Not even a copy of his article that had made the cover of *Nature Methods*, which she knew about from looking him up on Google Scholar the previous day. Just dark brown wood and a metal plaque that read: *Adam J. Carlsen, Ph.D.*

Maybe the *J* stood for "Jackass."

Olive had felt a bit like a creep the night before, scrolling down his faculty web page and going through his list of ten million publications and research grants, staring at a picture of him clearly taken in the middle of a hiking trip and not by Stanford's official photographer. Still, she'd quickly quashed the feeling, telling herself that a thorough academic background check was only logical before embarking on a fake-dating relationship.

She took a deep breath before knocking and then another between Adam's "Come in" and the moment she finally managed to force herself to open the door. When she entered the office, he didn't immediately look up and continued typing on his iMac. "My office hours were over five minutes ago, so—"

"It's me."

His hands halted, hovering half an inch or so above the keyboard. Then he turned his chair toward her. "Olive."

There was something about the way he talked. Maybe it was an accent, maybe just a quality of his voice. Olive didn't quite know what, but it was there, in the way he said her name. Precise. Careful. Deep. Unlike anyone else. Familiar—impossibly so.

"What did you say to her?" she asked, trying not to care about how Adam Carlsen spoke. "The girl who ran out in tears?"

It took him a moment to remember that less than sixty seconds ago there had been someone else in the office—someone whom he clearly made cry. "I just gave her feedback on something she wrote."

Olive nodded, silently thanking all the gods that he was not her adviser and never would be, and studied her surroundings. He had a corner office, of course. Two windows that together must total seventy thousand square meters of glass, and so much light, just standing in the middle of the room would cure twenty people's seasonal depression. It made sense, what with all the grant money he brought in, what with the prestige, that he'd been given a nice space. Olive's office, on the other hand, had no windows and smelled funny, probably because she shared it with three other Ph.D. students, even though it was meant to accommodate two at the most.

"I was going to email you. I talked to the dean earlier today," Adam told her, and she looked back at him.

He was gesturing to the chair in front of his desk. Olive pulled it back and took a seat.

"About you."

"Oh." Olive's stomach dropped. She'd much rather the dean didn't know about her existence. Then again, she'd also rather not be in this room with Adam Carlsen, have the semester begin in a handful of days, have climate change be a thing. And yet.

"Well, about us," he amended. "And socialization regulations."

"What did she say?"

"There's nothing against you and me dating, since I'm not your adviser."

A mix of panic and relief flooded through Olive.

"However, there are some issues to consider. I won't be able to collaborate with you in any formal capacity. And I'm part of the program's awards committee, which means that I'll have to excuse myself if you are nominated for fellowships or similar opportunities."

She nodded. "Fair enough."

"And I absolutely cannot be part of your thesis committee."

Olive huffed out a laugh. "That won't be a problem. I wasn't going to ask you to be on my committee."

He narrowed his eyes. "Why not? You study pancreatic cancer, right?"

"Yep. Early detection."

"Then your work would benefit from the perspective of a computational modeler."

"Yeah, but there are other computational modelers in the department. And I'd like to eventually graduate, ideally without sobbing in a bathroom stall after each committee meeting."

He glared at her.

Olive shrugged. "No offense. I'm a simple girl, with simple needs."

To that, he lowered his gaze to his desk, but not before Olive could see the corner of his mouth twitch. When he looked up again, his expression was serious. "So, have you decided?"

She pressed her lips together as he watched her calmly. She took a deep breath before saying, "Yes. Yes, I . . . I want to do it. It's a good idea, actually."

For so many reasons. It would get Anh and Jeremy off her back, but also . . . also everyone else. It was as if since the rumor had begun to spread, people had been too intimidated by Olive to give her the usual shit. The other TAs had quit trying to switch her nice 2:00 p.m. sections with their horrifying 8:00 a.m. ones, her lab mates had stopped cutting in front of her in the line for the microscope, and two different faculty members Olive had been trying to get ahold of for weeks had finally deigned to answer her emails. It felt a little unfair to exploit this huge misunderstanding, but academia was a lawless land and Olive's life in it had been nothing but miserable for the past two years. She had learned to grab whatever she could get away with. And if some—okay, if most of the grads in the department looked at her suspiciously because she was dating Adam Carlsen, so be it. Her friends seemed to be largely fine with this, if a little bemused.

Except for Malcolm. He'd been shunning her like she had the pox for three solid days. But Malcolm was Malcolm—he'd come around.

"Very well, then." He was completely expressionless—almost *too* expressionless. Like it was no big deal and he didn't care either way; like if she'd said no, it wouldn't have changed anything for him.

"Though, I've been thinking about this a lot."

He waited patiently for her to continue.

"And I think that it would be best if we laid down some ground rules. Before starting."

"Ground rules?"

"Yes. You know. What we are allowed and not allowed to do. What we can expect from this arrangement. I think that's pretty standard protocol, before embarking on a fake-dating relationship."

He tilted his head. "Standard protocol?"

"Yup."

"How many times have you done this?"

"Zero. But I am familiar with the trope."

"The . . . what?" He blinked at her, confused.

Olive ignored him. "Okay." She inhaled deeply and lifted her index finger. "First of all, this should be a strictly on-campus arrangement. Not that I think you'd want to meet me off campus, but just in case you were planning to kill two birds with one stone, I'm not going to be your last-minute backup if you need to bring a date home for Christmas, or—"

"Hanukkah."

"What?"

"My family is more likely to celebrate Hanukkah than Christmas." He shrugged. "Though I'm unlikely to celebrate either."

"Oh." Olive pondered it for a moment. "I guess this is something your fake girlfriend should know."

The ghost of a smile appeared on his mouth, but he said nothing.

"Okay. Second rule. Actually, it could be interpreted as an extension of the first rule. But"—Olive bit into her lip, willing herself to bring it up—"no sex."

For several moments he simply didn't move. Not even a milli-meter. Then his lips parted, but no sound came out, and that's when Olive realized that she had just rendered Adam Carlsen speechless. Which would have been funny any other day, but the fact that he seemed dumbfounded by Olive not wanting to include sex in their fake-dating relationship made her stomach sink.

Had he assumed that they would? Was it something she'd said? Should she explain that she'd had very little sex in her life? That for years she'd wondered whether she was asexual and she had realized only recently that she *might* be able to experience sexual attraction, but only with people she trusted deeply? That if for some inexplicable reason Adam wanted to have sex with her, she wasn't going to be able to go through with it?

"Listen"—she made to stand from the chair, panic rising in her throat—"I'm sorry, but if one of the reasons you offered to fake-date is that you thought that we would—"

"*No.*" The word half exploded out of him. He looked genu-inely appalled. "I'm shocked that you'd even feel the need to bring it up."

"Oh." Olive's cheeks heated at the indignation in his voice. Right. Of course he didn't expect that. Or even want that, with her. Look at him—why would he? "I'm sorry, I didn't mean to assume—"

"No, it makes sense to be up-front. I was just surprised."

"I know." Olive nodded. Honestly, she was a little surprised, too. That she was sitting in Adam Carlsen's office, talking about sex—not the meiosis kind of sex, but potential sexual inter-course between the two of them. "Sorry. I didn't mean to make things weird."

"It's okay. This whole thing is weird." The silence between them stretched, and Olive noticed that he was blushing faintly.

Just a dusting of red, but he looked so . . . Olive couldn't stop staring.

"No sex," he confirmed with a nod.

She had to clear her throat and shake herself out of inspecting the shape and color of his cheekbones.

"No sex," she repeated. "Okay. Third. It's not really a rule, but here goes: I won't date anyone else. As in real dating. It would be messy and complicate everything and . . ." Olive hesitated. Should she tell him? Was it too much information? Did he need to know? Oh, well. Why not, at this point? It wasn't like she hadn't kissed the man, or brought up sex in his place of work. "I don't date, anyway. Jeremy was an exception. I've never . . . I've never dated seriously before, and it's probably for the best. Grad school is stressful enough, and I have my friends, and my project on pancreatic cancer, and honestly there's better things to use my time for." The last few words came out more defensively than she'd intended.

Adam just stared and said nothing.

"But you can date, of course," she added hastily. "Though I'd appreciate it if you could avoid telling people in the department, just so I don't look like an idiot and you don't look like you're cheating on me and rumors don't balloon out of control. It would benefit you, too, since you're trying to look like you're in a committed relationship—"

"I won't."

"Okay. Great. Thanks. I know lying by omission can be a pain, but—"

"I mean, I won't date someone else."

There was a certainty, a finality in his tone that took her by surprise. She could only nod, even though she wanted to protest that he couldn't possibly know, even though a million questions surfaced in her mind. Ninety-nine percent of them were inappropriate and not her business, so she shooed them away.

"Okay. Fourth. We obviously can't keep on doing this forever, so we should give ourselves a deadline."

His lips pressed together. "When would that be?"

"I'm not sure. A month or so would probably be enough to convince Anh that I'm firmly over Jeremy. But it might not be enough on *your* end, so . . . you tell me."

He mulled it, and then nodded once. "September twenty-ninth."

It was a little over a month from now. But also . . . "That's a weirdly specific date." Olive racked her head, trying to figure out why it could be meaningful. The only thing that came to mind was that she'd be in Boston that week for the annual biology conference.

"It's the day after the department's final budget review. If they don't release my funds by then, they won't release them at all."

"I see. Well, then, let's agree that on September twenty-ninth we part ways. I'll tell Anh that our breakup was amicable but that I'm a little sad about it because I still have a bit of a crush on you." She grinned at him. "Just so she won't suspect that I'm still hung up on Jeremy. Okay." She took a deep breath. "Fifth and last."

This was the tricky one. The one she was afraid he'd object to. She noticed that she was wringing her hands and placed them firmly in her lap.

"For this to work we should probably . . . do things together. Every once in a while."

"Things?"

"Things. Stuff."

"Stuff," he repeated dubiously.

"Yep. Stuff. What do you do for fun?" He was probably into something atrocious, like cow-tipping excursions or Japanese beetle fighting. Maybe he collected porcelain dolls. Maybe he was an avid geocacher. Maybe he frequented vaping conventions. Oh God.

"Fun?" he repeated, like he'd never heard the word before.

"Yeah. What do you do when you're not at work?"

The length of time that passed between Olive's question and his answer was alarming. "Sometimes I work at home, too. And I work out. And I sleep."

She had to actively stop herself from face-palming. "Um, great. Anything else?"

"What do *you* do for fun?" he asked, somewhat defensively.

"Plenty of things. I . . ." *Go to the movies.* Though she hadn't been since the last time Malcolm had dragged her. *Play board games.* But every single one of her friends was too busy lately, so not that, either. She'd participated in that volleyball tournament, but it had been over a year ago.

"Um. I work out?" She would have loved to wipe that smug expression off his face. So much. "Whatever. We should do something together on a regular basis. I don't know, maybe get coffee? Like, once a week? Just for ten minutes, at a place where people could easily see us. I know it sounds annoying and like a waste of time, but it'll be super short, and it would make the fake dating more credible, and—"

"Sure."

Oh.

She'd thought it would take more convincing. A lot more. Then again, this was in his interest, too. He needed his colleagues to believe in their relationship if he was to cajole them into releasing his funding.

"Okay. Um . . ." She forced herself to stop wondering why he was being so accommodating and tried to visualize her schedule. "How about Wednesday?"

Adam angled his chair to face his computer and pulled up a calendar app. It was so full of colorful boxes that Olive felt a surge of vicarious anxiety.

"It works before eleven a.m. And after six p.m."

"Ten?"

He turned back to her. "Ten's good."

"Okay." She waited for him to type it in, but he made no move to. "Aren't you going to add it to your calendar?"

"I'll remember," he told her evenly.

"Okay, then." She made an effort to smile, and it felt relatively sincere. Way more sincere than any smile she'd ever thought she'd be able to muster in Adam Carlsen's presence. "Great. Fake-dating Wednesday it is."

A line appeared between his eyebrows. "Why do you keep saying that?"

"Saying what?"

"'Fake dating.' Like it's a thing."

"Because it is. Don't you watch rom-coms?"

He stared at her with a puzzled expression, until she cleared her throat and looked down at her knees. "Right." God, they had nothing in common. They'd never find anything to talk about. Their ten-minute coffee breaks were going to be the most painful, awkward parts of her already painful, awkward weeks.

But Anh was going to have her beautiful love story, and Olive wouldn't have to wait for ages to use the electron microscope. That was all that mattered.

She stood and thrust her hand out to him, figuring that every fake-dating arrangement deserved at least a handshake. Adam studied it hesitantly for a couple of seconds. Then he stood and clasped her fingers. He stared at their joined hands before meeting her eyes, and Olive ordered herself not to notice the heat of his skin, or how broad he was, or . . . anything else about him. When he finally let go, she had to make a conscious effort not to inspect her palm.

Had he done something to her? It sure felt like it. Her flesh was tingling.

"When do you want to start?"

"How about next week?" It was Friday. Which meant that she had fewer than seven days to psychologically prepare for the experience of getting coffee with Adam Carlsen. She knew that she could do this—if she had worked her way up to a ninety-seventh percentile on the verbal portion of the GRE, she could do anything, or as good as—but it still seemed like a horrible idea.

"Sounds good."

It was happening. Oh God. "Let's meet at the Starbucks on campus. It's where most of the grads get coffee—someone's bound to spot us." She headed for the door, pausing to glance back at Adam. "I guess I'll see you for fake-dating Wednesday, then?"

He was still standing behind his desk, arms crossed on his chest. Looking at Olive. Looking entirely less irritated by this mess than she'd ever have expected. Looking . . . nice. "See you, Olive."

~~~~~~

"PASS THE SALT."

Olive would have, but Malcolm looked like he was already salty enough. So she leaned her hip against the kitchen counter and folded her arms across her chest. "Malcolm."

"And the pepper."

"Malcolm."

"And the oil."

"Malcolm . . ."

"Sunflower. Not that grape-seed crap."

"Listen. It's not what you think—"

"Fine. I'll get them myself."

To be fair, Malcolm had every right to be mad. And Olive did feel for him. He was one year ahead of her, and the scion of STEM royalty. The product of generations of biologists, geologists, botanists, physicists, and who knows what other -ists mixing their DNA and spawning little science machines. His father was a dean at some state school on the East Coast. His mother had a TED Talk on Purkinje cells with several million views on YouTube. Did Malcolm want to be in a Ph.D. program, headed for an academic career? Probably no. Did he have any other choice, considering the pressure his family had put on him since he was in diapers? Also no.

Not to say that Malcolm was unhappy. His plan was to get his Ph.D., find a nice cushy industry job, and make lots of money working nine-to-five—which technically qualified as "being a scientist," which in turn was not something his parents would be able to object to. At least, not too strenuously. In the meantime, all he wanted was to have a grad school experience that was as un-traumatizing as possible. Out of everyone in Olive's program, he was the one who best managed to have a life outside of grad school. He did things that were unimaginable to most grads, like cooking real food! Going for hikes! Meditating! Acting in a play! Dating like it was an Olympic sport! ("It *is* an Olympic sport, Olive. And I am training for gold.")

Which was why when Adam forced Malcolm to throw out tons of data and redo half his study, it made for a very, very miserable few months. In retrospect, that might have been when Malcolm started wishing a plague on the Carlsen house (he had been rehearsing for *Romeo and Juliet* at the time).

"Malcolm, can we please talk about this?"

"We're talking."

"No, you are cooking and I am just standing here, trying to get you to acknowledge that you are mad because Adam—"

Malcolm turned away from his casserole, wagging his finger in Olive's direction. "Do not say it."

"Do not say what?"

"You know what."

"Adam Carl—?"

"Do *not* say his name."

She threw her hands up. "This is crazy. It's fake, Malcolm."

He went back to chopping the asparagus. "Pass the salt."

"Are you even listening? It's not real."

"And the pepper, and the—"

"The relationship, it's fake. We're not really dating. We're pretending so people will *think* that we're dating."

Malcolm's hands stopped mid-chop. "What?"

"You heard me."

"Is it a . . . friends-with-benefits arrangement? Because—"

"No. It's the opposite. There are no benefits. Zero benefits. Zero sex. Zero friends, too."

He stared at her, narrow-eyed. "To be clear, oral and butt stuff totally counts as sex—"

"Malcolm."

He took a step closer, grabbing a dishrag to wipe his hands, nostrils flaring. "I'm scared to ask."

"I know it sounds ridiculous. He's helping me out by pretending we're together because I lied to Anh, and I need her to feel okay about dating Jeremy. It's all fake. Adam and I have talked exactly"—she decided on the spot to omit any information pertinent to The Night—"three times, and I know nothing about him. Except that he's willing to help me handle this situation, and I jumped at the chance."

Malcolm was making that face, the one he reserved for people who wore sandals paired with white socks. He could be a little scary, she had to admit.

"This is . . . wow." There was a vein pulsating on his forehead. "Ol, this is breathtakingly stupid."

"Maybe." Yes. Yes, it was. "But it is what it is. And you have to support me in my idiocy, because you and Anh are my best friends."

"Isn't Carlsen your best friend now?"

"Come on, Malcolm. He's an ass. But he's actually been pretty nice to me, and—"

"I'm not even—" He grimaced. "I'm not going to address this."

She sighed. "Okay. Don't address this. You don't have to. But can you just not hate me? Please? I know he's been a nightmare to half the grads in the program, you included. But he's helping me out. You and Anh are the only ones I care about knowing the truth. But I can't tell Anh—"

"—for obvious reasons."

"—for obvious reasons," she finished at the same time, and smiled. He just shook his head disapprovingly, but his expression had softened.

"Ol. You're amazing. And kind, way too kind. You should find someone better than Carlsen. Someone to date for real."

"Yeah, right." She rolled her eyes. "Because it went so well with Jeremy. Who, by the way, I only agreed to date following *your* advice! 'Give the boy a chance,' you said. 'What could possibly go wrong?' you said."

Malcolm glared, and she laughed.

"Listen, I'm clearly bad at real dating. Maybe fake dating will be different. Maybe I've found my niche."

He sighed. "Does it have to be Carlsen? There are better faculty members to fake-date."

"Like who?"

"I don't know. Dr. McCoy?"

"Didn't her wife just give birth to triplets?"

"Oh, yeah. What about Holden Rodrigues? He's hot. Cute smile, too. I would know—he always smiles at me."

Olive burst into laughter. "I could never fake-date Dr. Rodrigues, not with how assiduously you've been thirsting after him for the past two years."

"I have, haven't I? Did I ever tell you about the serious flirting that happened between us at the undergrad research fair? I'm pretty sure he winked at me multiple times from the other side of the room. Now, some say he just had something in his eye, but—"

"Me. *I* said that he probably had something in his eye. And you tell me about it every other day."

"Right." He sighed. "You know, Ol, I would have fake-dated you myself in a heartbeat, to spare you from goddamned Carlsen. I would have held hands with you, and given you my jacket when you were cold, and very publicly gifted you chocolate roses and teddy bears on Valentine's Day."

How refreshing, to talk with someone who'd watched a romcom. Or ten. "I know. But you also bring home a different person every week, and you love it, and I love that you love it. I don't want to cramp your style."

"Fair." Malcolm looked pleased—whether at the fact that he really did get around a fair bit or at Olive's thorough understanding of his dating habits, she wasn't sure.

"Can you please not hate me, then?"

He tossed the kitchen cloth onto the counter and stepped closer. "Ol. I could never hate you. You'll always be my kalamata." He pulled her into his chest, hugging her tight. At the beginning, when they'd just met, Olive had been constantly disoriented by how physical he was, probably because it had been years since she'd experienced such affectionate contact. Now, Malcolm's hugs were her happy place.

She laid her head on his shoulder and smiled into the cotton of his T-shirt. "Thanks."

Malcolm held her tighter.

"And I promise if I ever bring Adam home, I'll put a sock on my door— *Ouch!*"

"You evil creature."

"I was kidding! Wait, don't leave, I have something important to tell you."

He paused by the door, scowling. "I've reached my maximum daily intake of Carlsen-related conversation. Anything further will be lethal, so—"

"Tom Benton, the cancer researcher from Harvard, reached out to me! It's not decided yet, but he might be interested in having me in his lab next year."

"Oh my God." Malcolm walked back to her, delighted. "Ol, this is amazing! I thought none of the researchers you contacted had gotten back to you?"

"Not for the longest time. But now Benton has, and you know how famous and well-known he is. He probably has more research funds than I could ever dream of. It would be—"

"Fantastic. It would really be fantastic. Ol. I am so proud of you." Malcolm took her hands in his. His face-splitting grin slowly gentled. "And your mom would be so proud, too."

Olive looked away, blinking rapidly. She didn't want to cry, not tonight. "Nothing is set in stone. I'll have to persuade him. It will involve quite a bit of politicking and going through the whole 'pitch me your research' bit. Which as you know is not my forte. It might still not work out—"

"It *will* work out."

Right. Yes. She needed to be optimistic. She nodded, attempting a smile.

"But even if it didn't . . . she would still be proud."

Olive nodded again. When a single tear managed to slide down her cheek, she decided to let it be.

Forty-five minutes later, she and Malcolm sat on their minuscule couch, arms pressed together, watching reruns of *American Ninja Warrior* while they ate a very undersalted veggie casserole.

Chapter Four

~~~~~~

♥ **HYPOTHESIS:** *Adam Carlsen and I have absolutely nothing in common, and having coffee with him will be twice as painful as a root canal. Without anesthesia.*

Olive arrived to the first fake-dating Wednesday late and in the foulest of moods, after a morning spent growling at her cheap, knockoff reagents for not dissolving, then not precipitating, then not sonicating, then not being enough for her to run her entire assay.

She paused outside the coffee shop's door and took a deep breath. She needed a better lab if she wanted to produce decent science. Better equipment. Better reagents. Better bacteria cultures. Better *everything*. Next week, when Tom Benton arrived, she had to be on top of her game. She needed to prepare her spiel, not waste time on a coffee she didn't particularly want, with a person she most definitely didn't want to talk to, halfway through her experimental protocol.

Ugh.

When she stepped inside the café, Adam was already there, wearing a black Henley that looked like it was ideated, designed, and produced specifically with the upper half of his body in mind. Olive was momentarily bemused, not so much that his clothes fit him well, but that she'd noticed what someone was wearing to begin with. It was not like her. She'd been seeing Adam traipse around the biology building for the better part of two years, after all, not to mention that in the past couple of weeks they'd spoken an inordinate amount of times. They had even kissed, if one counted what had happened on The Night as a proper kiss. It was dizzying and a little unsettling, the realization that sank into her as they got in line to order their coffee.

Adam Carlsen was handsome.

Adam Carlsen, with his long nose and wavy hair, with his full lips and angular face that shouldn't have fit together but somehow did, was really, really, *really* handsome. Olive had no clue why it hadn't registered before, or why what made her realize it was him putting on a plain black shirt.

She willed herself to stare ahead at the drink menu instead of his chest. In the coffee shop, there were a total of three biology grad students, one pharmacology postdoc, and one undergraduate research assistant eyeing them. *Perfect.*

"So. How are you?" she asked, because it was the thing to do.

"Fine. You?"

"Fine."

It occurred to Olive that maybe she hadn't thought this through as thoroughly as she should have. Because being seen together might have been their goal, but standing next to each other in silence was not going to fool anyone into thinking that they were blissfully dating. And Adam was . . . well. He seemed unlikely to initiate any kind of conversation.

"So." Olive shifted her weight to the balls of her feet a couple of times. "What's your favorite color?"

He looked at her, confused. "What?"

"Your favorite color."

"My favorite color?"

"Yep."

There was a crease between his eyes. "I—don't know?"

"What do you mean you don't know?"

"They're colors. They're all the same."

"There must be one you like most."

"I don't think so."

"Red?"

"I don't know."

"Yellow? Vomit green?"

His eyes narrowed. "Why are you asking?"

Olive shrugged. "It feels like something I should know."

"Why?"

"Because. If someone tries to figure out whether we're really dating, it might be one of the first questions they ask. Top five, for sure."

He studied her for a few seconds. "Does that seem like a likely scenario to you?"

"About as likely as me fake-dating you."

He nodded, as if conceding her point. "Okay. Black, I guess."

She snorted. "Figures."

"What's wrong with black?" He frowned.

"It's not even a color. It's no colors, technically."

"It's better than vomit green."

"No, it isn't."

"Of course it is."

"Yeah, well. It suits your scion-of-darkness personality."

"What does that even—"

"Good morning." The barista smiled at them cheerfully. "What will you have today?"

Olive smiled back, gesturing at Adam to order first.

"Coffee." He darted a glance at her before adding, sheepishly, "Black."

She had to duck her head to hide her smile, but when she glanced at him again, the corner of his mouth was curved upward. Which, she reluctantly admitted to herself, was not a bad look for him. She ignored it and ordered the most fatty, sugary thing on the drink menu, asking for extra whipped cream. She was wondering if she should try to make up for it by buying an apple, too, or if she should just lean into it and top it off with a cookie, when Adam took a credit card out of his wallet and held it to the cashier.

"Oh, no. No, no, no. *No*." Olive put her hand in front of his and lowered her voice. "You can't pay for my stuff."

He blinked. "I can't?"

"That's not the kind of fake relationship we're having."

He looked surprised. "It isn't?"

"Nope." She shook her head. "I would never fake-date a dude who thinks that he has to pay for my coffee just because he's a dude."

He lifted an eyebrow. "I doubt a language exists in which the thing you just ordered could be referred to as 'coffee.'"

"Hey—"

"And it's not about me being a 'dude'"—the word came out a touch pained—"but about you still being a grad student. And your yearly income."

For a moment she hesitated, wondering if she should be offended. Was Adam being his well-known ass self? Was he patronizing her? Did he think she was poor? Then she remembered that she *was*, in fact, poor, and that he probably made five times as much as her. She shrugged, adding a chocolate chip cookie, a banana, and a pack of gum to her coffee. To his credit, Adam said nothing and paid the resulting $21.39 without batting an eye.

While they were waiting for their drinks, Olive's mind began drifting off to her project and to whether she could convince Dr. Aslan to buy her better reagents soon. She looked distractedly around the coffee shop, finding that even though the research assistant, the postdoc, and one of the students were gone, two grads (one of whom serendipitously happened to work in Anh's lab) were still sitting at a table by the door, glancing toward them every few minutes. Excellent.

She leaned her hip against the counter and looked up at Adam. Thank God this thing was only going to be ten minutes a week, or she'd develop a permanent crick in her neck.

"Where were you born?" she asked.

"Is this another one of your green card marriage interview questions?"

She giggled. He smiled in response, as if pleased to have made her laugh. Though it was certainly for some other reason.

"Netherlands. The Hague."

"Oh."

He leaned against the counter, too, directly in front of her. "Why 'oh'?"

"I don't know." Olive shrugged. "I think I expected . . . New York? Or maybe Kansas?"

He shook his head. "My mother used to be a US ambassador to the Netherlands."

"Wow." Weird, to imagine that Adam had a mother. A family. That before being tall and scary and infamous, he'd been a kid. Maybe he spoke Dutch. Maybe he had smoked herring for breakfast on the reg. Maybe his mother had wanted him to follow in her footsteps and become a diplomat, but his shiny personality had emerged and she'd given up on that dream. Olive found herself acutely eager to know more about his upbringing, which was . . . weird. Very weird.

"Here you go." Their drinks appeared on the counter. Olive told herself that the way the blond barista was obviously checking out Adam as he turned to retrieve a lid for his cup was none of her business. She also reminded herself that as curious as she was about his diplomat mother, how many languages he spoke, and whether he liked tulips, it was information that went well beyond their arrangement.

People had seen them together. They were going to go back to their labs and tell improbable tales of Dr. Adam Carlsen and the random, unremarkable student they'd spotted him with. Time for Olive to go back to her science.

She cleared her throat. "Well. This was fun."

He looked up from his cup, surprised. "Is fake-dating Wednesday over?"

"Yep. Great job, team, now hit the showers. You're free until next week." Olive stabbed her straw into her drink and took a sip, feeling the sugar explode in her mouth. Whatever she'd ordered, it was disgustingly good. She was probably developing diabetes as she spoke. "I'll see you—"

"Where were *you* born?" Adam asked before she could leave.

Oh. They were doing this, then. He was probably just trying to be polite, and Olive sighed inwardly, thinking longingly of her lab bench. "Toronto."

"Right. You're Canadian," he said, like he'd already known. "Yep."

"When did you move here?"

"Eight years ago. For college."

He nodded, as if storing up the information. "Why the US? Canada has excellent schools."

"I got a full ride." It was true. If not the whole truth.

He fidgeted with the cardboard cup holder. "Do you go back a lot?"

"Not really, no." Olive licked some whipped cream off her straw. She was puzzled when he immediately looked away from her.

"Do you plan to move back home once you graduate?"

She tensed. "Not if I can help it." She had lots of painful memories in Canada, and her only family, the people she wanted nearby, were Anh and Malcolm, both US citizens. Olive and Anh had even made a pact that if Olive was ever on the verge of losing her visa, Anh would marry her. In hindsight, this entire fake-dating business with Adam was going to be great practice for when Olive leveled up and started defrauding the Department of Homeland Security in earnest.

Adam nodded, taking a sip of his coffee. "Favorite color?"

Olive opened her mouth to tell him her favorite color, which was so much better than his, and . . . "Dammit."

He gave her a knowing look. "Difficult, isn't it?"

"There are so many good ones."

"Yup."

"I'm going to go with blue. Light blue. No, wait!"

"Mmm."

"Let's say white. Okay, white."

He clucked his tongue. "You know, I don't think I can accept that. White's not really a color. More like all colors put together—"

Olive pinched him on the fleshy part of his forearm.

"Ow," he said, clearly not in pain. With a sly smile, he waved goodbye and turned away, heading for the biology building.

"Hey, Adam?" she called after him.

He paused and looked back at her.

"Thanks for buying me three days' worth of food."

He hesitated and then nodded, once. That thing he was doing

with his mouth—he was *definitely* smiling down at her. A little begrudgingly, but still.

"My pleasure, Olive."

~~~~~~

Today, 2:40 p.m.
FROM: Tom-Benton@harvard.edu
TO: Olive-Smith@stanford.edu
SUBJECT: Re: Pancreatic Cancer Screening Project

Olive,
I'll be flying in on Tuesday afternoon. How about we meet on Wednesday around 3:00 p.m. in Aysegul Aslan's lab? My collaborator can point me in its direction.

TB
Sent from my iPhone

~~~~~~

OLIVE WAS LATE for her second fake-dating Wednesday, too, but for different reasons—all Tom Benton related.

First, she'd overslept after staying up late the previous night rehearsing how she was going to sell him her project. She'd repeated her spiel so many times that Malcolm had started finishing her sentences, and then, at 1:00 a.m., he'd hurled a nectarine at her and begged her to go practice in her room. Which she had, until 3:00 a.m.

Then, in the morning, she'd realized that her usual lab outfit (leggings, ratty 5K T-shirt, and very, very messy bun) would probably not communicate "valuable future colleague" to Dr. Benton, and spent an excessive amount of time looking for something appropriate. Dress for success and all that.

Finally, it occurred to her that she had no idea what Dr.

Benton—arguably the most important person in her life at the moment, and yes, she was aware of how sad that sounded but decided not to dwell on it—even *looked* like. She looked him up on her phone and found out that he was somewhere in his late thirties, blond with blue eyes, and had very straight, very white teeth. When she arrived at the campus Starbucks, Olive was whispering to his Harvard headshot, "Please, let me come work in your lab." Then she noticed Adam.

It was an uncharacteristically cloudy day. Still August, but it almost felt like late fall. Olive glanced at him, and she immediately knew that he was in the nastiest of moods. That rumor of him throwing a petri dish against a wall because his experiment hadn't worked out, or because the electron microscope needed repairs, or because something equally inconsequential had happened came to mind. She considered ducking under the table.

It's okay, she told herself. *This is worth it.* Things with Anh were back to normal. Better than normal: she and Jeremy were officially dating, and last weekend Anh had showed up to beers-and-s'mores night wearing leggings and an oversize MIT sweater she'd clearly borrowed from him. When Olive had eaten lunch with the two of them the other day, it hadn't even felt awkward. Plus, the first-, second-, and even third-year grads were too scared of Adam Carlsen's "girlfriend" to steal Olive's pipettes, which meant that she didn't have to stuff them in her backpack and take them home for the weekend anymore. And she was getting some grade A free food out of this. She could take Adam Carlsen—yes, even this pitch-black-mood Adam Carlsen. For ten minutes a week, at the very least.

"Hey." She smiled. He responded with a look that exuded moodiness and existential angst. Olive took a fortifying breath. "How are you?"

"Fine." His tone was clipped, his expression tenser than

usual. He was wearing a red plaid shirt and jeans, looking more like a wood-chopping lumberjack than a scholar pondering the mysteries of computational biology. She couldn't help noticing the muscles and wondered again if he had his clothes custom-made. His hair was still a bit long but shorter than the previous week. It seemed a little surreal that she and Adam Carlsen were at a point where she was able to keep track of both his moods and his haircuts.

"Ready to get coffee?" she chirped.

He nodded distractedly, barely looking at her. On a table in the back, a fifth-year was glancing at them while pretending to clean the monitor of his laptop.

"Sorry if I was late. I just—"

"It's fine."

"Did you have a good week?"

"Fine."

Okay. "Um . . . did you do anything fun last weekend?"

"I worked."

They got in line to order, and it was all Olive could do to stop herself from sighing. "Weather's been nice, right? Not too hot."

He grunted in response.

It was starting to be a bit much. There was a limit to what Olive would do for this fake-dating relationship—even for a free mango Frappuccino. She sighed. "Is it because of the haircut?"

That got his attention. Adam looked down at her, a vertical line deep between his eyebrows. "What?"

"The mood. Is it because of the haircut?"

"What mood?"

Olive gestured broadly toward him. "This. The bad mood you're in."

"I'm not in a bad mood."

She snorted—though that was probably not the right term for

what she just did. It was too loud and derisive, more like a laugh. A snaugh.

"What?" He frowned, unappreciative of her snaugh.

"Come on."

"What?"

"You *ooze* moodiness."

"I do not." He sounded indignant, which struck her as oddly endearing.

"You so do. I saw that face, and I immediately knew."

"You did not."

"I did. I do. But it's fine, you're allowed to be in a bad mood."

It was their turn, so she took a step forward and smiled at the cashier.

"Good morning. I'll have a pumpkin spice latte. And that cream cheese danish over there. Yep, that one, thank you. And"—she pointed at Adam with her thumb—"he'll have chamomile tea. No sugar," she added cheerfully. She immediately took a few steps to the side, hoping to avoid damage in case Adam decided to throw a petri dish at her. She was surprised when he calmly handed his credit card to the boy behind the counter. Really, he wasn't as bad as they made him out to be.

"I hate tea," he said. "And chamomile."

Olive beamed up at him. "That is unfortunate."

"You smart-ass."

He stared straight ahead, but she was almost certain that he was about to crack a smile. There was a lot to be said about him but not that he didn't have a sense of humor.

"So . . . not the haircut?"

"Mm? Ah, no. It was a weird length. Getting in my way while I was running."

Oh. So he was a runner. Like Olive. "Okay. Great. Because it doesn't look bad."

It looks good. As in, really good. You were probably one of the most handsome men I'd ever talked to last week, but now you look even better. Not that I care about these things. I don't care at all. I rarely notice guys, and I'm not sure why I'm noticing you, or your hair, or your clothes, or how tall and broad you are. I really don't get it. I never care. Usually. Ugh.

"I . . ." He seemed flustered for a second, his lips moving without making a sound as he looked for an appropriate response. Then, out of the blue, he said, "I talked with the department chair this morning. He's still refusing to release my research funds."

"Oh." She cocked her head. "I thought they weren't due to decide until the end of September."

"They aren't. This was an informal meeting, but the topic came up. He said that he's still monitoring the situation."

"I see." She waited for him to continue. When it became clear that he wouldn't, she asked, "Monitoring . . . how?"

"Unclear." He was clenching his jaw.

"I'm sorry." She felt for him. She really did. If there was something she could empathize with, it was scientific studies coming to an abrupt halt because of a lack of resources. "Does that mean that you can't continue your research?"

"I have other grants."

"So . . . the problem is that you cannot start new studies?"

"I can. I had to rearrange different pots, but I should be able to afford to start new lines of research, too."

Uh? "I see." She cleared her throat. "So . . . let me recap. It sounds like Stanford froze your funds based on rumors, which I agree is a crappy move. But it also sounds like for now you can afford to do what you were planning, so . . . it's not the end of the world?"

Adam gave her an affronted glare, suddenly looking even more cross.

Oh, boy. "Don't get me wrong, I understand the principle of the matter, and I'd be mad, too. But you have, how many other grants? Actually, don't answer that. I'm not sure I want to know."

He probably had fifteen. He also had tenure, and dozens of publications, and there were all those honors listed on his website. Not to mention that she'd read on his CV that he had one patent. Olive, on the other hand, had cheap knockoff reagents and old pipettes that regularly got stolen. She tried not to dwell on how much further ahead than her he was in his career, but it was unforgettable, how good he was at what he did. How *annoyingly* good.

"My point is, this is not an insurmountable problem. And we're actively working on it. We're in this together, showing people that you're going to stay here forever because of your amazing girlfriend."

Olive pointed to herself with a flourish, and his glare followed her hand. Clearly he was not a fan of rationalizing and working through his emotions.

"Or, you could stay mad, and we could go to your lab and throw test tubes full of toxic reagents at each other until the pain of third-degree burns overrides your shitty mood? Sounds like fun, no?"

He looked away and rolled his eyes, but she could see it in the curve of his cheeks that he was amused. Likely against his will. "You are such a smart-ass."

"Maybe, but I'm not the one who grunted when I asked how your week was."

"I did not grunt. And you ordered me chamomile tea."

She smiled. "You're welcome."

They were quiet for a few moments as she chewed through the first bite of her Danish. Once she'd swallowed she said, "I'm sorry about your funds."

He shook his head. "I'm sorry about the mood."

Oh. "It's okay. You're famous for that."

"I am?"

"Yep. It's kind of your thing."

"Is that so?"

"Mmm."

His mouth twitched. "Maybe I wanted to spare you."

Olive smiled, because it was actually a nice thing to say. And he was not a nice person, but he was very kind to her most of the time—if not always. He was almost smiling back, staring down at her in a way that she couldn't quite interpret but that made her think weird thoughts, until the barista deposited their drinks on the counter. He suddenly looked like he was about to retch.

"Adam? Are you okay?"

He stared at her cup and took a step back. "The *smell* of that thing."

Olive inhaled deeply. Heaven. "You hate pumpkin spice latte?"

He wrinkled his nose, moving even farther away. "Gross."

"How can you hate it? It's the best thing your country has produced in the past century."

"Please, stand back. The stench."

"Hey. If I have to choose between you and pumpkin spice latte, maybe we should rethink our arrangement."

He eyed her cup like it contained radioactive waste. "Maybe we should."

He held the door open for her as they exited the coffee shop, taking care not to come too close to her drink. Outside it was starting to drizzle. Students were hastily packing up their laptops and notebooks from the patio tables to head to class or move to the library. Olive had been in love with the rain since as far back as she could remember. She inhaled deeply and filled her lungs with petrichor, stopping with Adam under the canopy. He took a sip of his chamomile tea, and it made her smile.

"Hey," she said, "I have an idea. Are you going to the fall biosciences picnic?"

He nodded. "I have to. I'm on the biology department's social-and-networking committee."

She laughed out loud. "No way."

"Yep."

"Did you actually sign up for it?"

"It's service. I was forced to rotate into the position."

"Ah. That sounds . . . fun." She winced sympathetically, almost laughing again at his appalled expression. "Well, I'm going, too. Dr. Aslan makes us all go, says it promotes bonding among lab mates. Do you make your grads go?"

"No. I have other, more productive ways of making my grads miserable."

She chuckled. He *was* funny, in that weird, dark way of his. "I bet you do. Well, here's my idea: we should hang when we're there. In front of the department chair—since he's 'monitoring.' I'll bat my eyelashes at you; he'll see that we're basically one step away from marriage. Then he'll make a quick phone call and a truck will drive up and unload your research funds in cash right there in front of—"

"Hey, man!"

A blond man approached Adam. Olive fell silent as Adam turned to smile at him and exchanged a handshake—a *close bros* handshake. She blinked, wondering if she was seeing things, and took a sip of her latte.

"I thought you'd sleep in," Adam was saying.

"The time difference screwed me up. I figured I might as well come to campus and get to work. Something to eat, too. You have no food, man."

"There are apples in the kitchen."

"Right. No food."

Olive took a step back, ready to excuse herself, when the blond man turned his attention to her. He looked eerily familiar, even though she was certain she had never met him before.

"And who's this?" he asked curiously. His eyes were a very piercing blue.

"This is Olive," Adam said. There was a beat after her name, in which he should have probably specified *how* he knew Olive. He did not, and she really couldn't blame him for not wanting to feed their fake-dating crap to someone who was clearly a good friend. She just kept her smile in place and let Adam continue. "Olive, this is my collaborator—"

"Dude." The man pretended to bristle. "Introduce me as your friend."

Adam rolled his eyes, clearly amused. "Olive, this is my *friend* and collaborator. Dr. Tom Benton."

Chapter Five

💜 **HYPOTHESIS:** *The more I need my brain to be on top of its game, the higher the probability that it will freeze on me.*

"Wait a minute." Dr. Benton tilted his head. His smile was still in place, but his gaze became a little sharper, his focus on Olive less superficial. "Do you happen to be . . ."

Olive froze.

Her mind was never calm, or orderly—more like a garbled mess of thoughts, really. And yet, standing there in front of Tom Benton, the inside of her head went uncharacteristically quiet, and several considerations stacked themselves neatly into place.

The first was that she was comically luckless. The chances that the person she depended on to finish her beloved research project would be acquainted—no, *friends* with the person she depended on to ensure her beloved Anh's romantic happiness were laughably low. And yet. Then again, Olive's special brand of luck was no news, so she moved on to the next consideration.

She needed to admit who she was to Tom Benton. They were scheduled to meet at 3:00 p.m., and pretending not to recognize him now would mean the kiss of death to her plans to infiltrate herself into his lab. Academics had huge egos, after all.

Last consideration: if she phrased this right, she could probably avoid Dr. Benton hearing about the whole fake-dating mess. Adam hadn't mentioned it, which probably meant that he wasn't planning to. Olive just needed to follow his lead.

Yes. Excellent plan. She had this in the bag.

Olive smiled, held on to her pumpkin spice latte, and answered, "Yes, I'm Olive Smith, the—"

"Girlfriend I've heard so much about?"

Shit. Shit, shit, *shit.* She swallowed. "Um, actually I—"

"Heard from whom?" Adam asked, frowning.

Dr. Benton shrugged. "Everyone."

"Everyone," Adam repeated. He was scowling now. "In Boston?"

"Yeah."

"Why are people at Harvard talking about my girlfriend?"

"Because you're you."

"Because I'm *me*?" Adam looked perplexed.

"There have been tears. Some hair-pulling. A few broken hearts. Don't worry, they'll get over it."

Adam rolled his eyes, and Dr. Benton returned his attention to Olive. He smiled at her, offering his hand. "It's very nice to meet you. I had written off the whole girlfriend thing as rumors, but I'm glad you . . . exist. Sorry, I didn't catch your name—I'm terrible at names."

"I'm Olive." She shook his hand. He had a nice grip, not too tight and not too soft.

"Which department do you teach, Olive?"

Oh, crap. "Actually, I don't. Teach, that is."

"Oh, sorry. I didn't mean to assume." He smiled, apologetic and self-effacing. There was a smooth charm to him. He was young to be a professor, though not as young as Adam. And he was tall, though not as tall as Adam. And he was handsome, though . . . yeah. Not as handsome as Adam.

"What do you do, then? Are you a research fellow?"

"Um, I actually—"

"She's a student," Adam said.

Dr. Benton's eyes widened.

"A *graduate* student," Adam clarified. There was a hint of warning in his tone, like he really wanted Dr. Benton to drop the subject.

Dr. Benton, naturally, did not. "*Your* graduate student?"

Adam frowned. "No, of course she's not my—"

This was the perfect opening. "Actually, Dr. Benton, I work with Dr. Aslan." Maybe this meeting was still salvageable. "You probably don't recognize my name, but we've corresponded. We're supposed to meet today. I'm the student who's working on the pancreatic cancer biomarkers. The one who asked to come work in your lab for a year."

Dr. Benton's eyes widened even more, and he muttered something that sounded a lot like "*What the hell?*" Then his face stretched into a wide, openmouthed grin. "Adam, you *absolute ass*. You didn't even tell me."

"I didn't know," Adam muttered. His gaze was fixed on Olive.

"How could you not know that your girlfriend—"

"I didn't tell Adam, because I didn't know you two were friends," Olive interjected. And then she thought that maybe it wasn't quite believable. If Olive really were Adam's girlfriend, he'd have told her about his friends. Since, in a shocking plot twist, he did appear to have at least one.

"That is, I, um . . . never put two and two together, and didn't know that you were the Tom he always talked about." There, better. Kind of. "I'm sorry, Dr. Benton. I didn't mean to—"

"Tom," he said, grin still in place. His shock seemed to be settling into pleasant surprise. "Please, call me Tom." His eyes darted between Adam and Olive for a few seconds. Then he said, "Hey, are you free?" He pointed at the coffee shop. "Why don't we go inside and chat about your project now? No point in waiting until this afternoon."

She took a sip of her latte to temporize. Was she free? Technically, yes. She would have loved to run to the edge of campus and scream into the void until modern civilization collapsed, but that wasn't exactly a pressing matter. And she wanted to look as accommodating as possible to Dr. Benton—Tom. Beggars and choosers and all that.

"I'm free."

"Great. You, Adam?"

Olive froze. And so did Adam, for about a second, before pointing out, "I don't think I should be present, if you're about to interview her—"

"Oh, it's not an interview. Just an informal chat to see if Olive's and my research match. You'll want to know if your girlfriend is moving to Boston for a year, right? Come on." He motioned for them to follow him and then stepped inside the Starbucks.

Olive and Adam exchanged a silent look that somehow managed to speak volumes. It said, *What the hell do we do?* and *How the hell would I know?* and *This is going to be weird*, and *No, it's going to be plain bad*. Then Adam sighed, put on a resigned face, and headed inside. Olive followed him, regretting her life choices.

"Aslan's retiring, huh?" Tom asked after they'd found a secluded table in the back. Olive had no choice but to sit across from him—and on Adam's left. Like a good "girlfriend," she supposed. Her "boyfriend," in the meantime, was sullenly sipping his chamomile tea next to her. *I should snap a picture*, she reflected. *He'd make for an excellent viral meme.*

"In the next few years," Olive confirmed. She loved her adviser, who had always been supportive and encouraging. Since the very beginning she had given Olive the freedom to develop her own research program, which was almost unheard of for Ph.D. students. Having a hands-off mentor was great when it came to pursuing her interests, but . . .

"If Aslan's retiring soon, she's not applying for grants anymore—understandable, since she won't be around long enough to see the projects through—which means that your lab is not exactly flush with cash right now," Tom summarized perfectly. "Okay, tell me about your project. What's cool about it?"

"I . . . ," Olive began—she scrambled to collect her thoughts. "So, it's—" Another pause. Longer this time, and more painfully awkward. "Um . . ."

This, precisely, was her problem. Olive knew that she was an excellent scientist, that she had the discipline and the critical-thinking skills to produce good work in the lab. Unfortunately succeeding in academia also required the ability to pitch one's work, sell it to strangers, present it in public, and . . . *that* was not something she enjoyed or excelled at. It made her feel panicky and judged, as though pinned to a microscope slide, and her ability to produce syntactically coherent sentences invariably leaked out of her brain.

Like right now. Olive felt her cheeks heat and her tongue tie and—

"What kind of question is that?" Adam interjected.

When she glanced at him, he was scowling at Tom, who just shrugged.

"What's *cool* about your project?" Adam repeated back.

"Yeah. Cool. You know what I mean."

"I don't think I do, and maybe neither does Olive."

Tom huffed. "Fine, what would *you* ask?"

Adam turned to Olive. His knee brushed her leg, warm and oddly reassuring through her jeans. "What issues does your project target? Why do you think it's significant? What gaps in the literature does it fill? What techniques are you using? What challenges do you foresee?"

Tom huffed. "Right, sure. Consider all those long, boring questions asked, Olive."

She glanced at Adam, finding that he was studying her with a calm, encouraging expression. The way he'd formulated the questions helped her reorganize her thoughts, and realizing that she had answers for each one melted most of her panic. It probably hadn't been intentional on Adam's part, but he'd done her a solid.

Olive was reminded of that guy from the bathroom, from years ago. *I have no idea if you're good enough,* he'd told her. *What matters is whether your* reason *to be in academia is good enough.* He'd said that Olive's reason was the best one, and therefore, she could do this. She *needed* to do this.

"Okay," she started again after a deep breath, gathering what she'd rehearsed the previous night with Malcolm. "Here's the deal. Pancreatic cancer is very aggressive and deadly. It has very poor prognosis, with only one out of four people alive a year after diagnosis." Her voice, she thought, sounded less breathy and more self-assured. Good. "The problem is that it's so hard to detect, we are only able to diagnose it very late in the game. At that point, the cancer has already spread so widely, most treatments can't do much to counteract it. But if diagnosis were faster—"

"People could get treatment sooner and have a higher chance of survival," Tom said, nodding a bit impatiently. "Yep, I'm well aware. We already have some screening tools, though. Like imaging."

She wasn't surprised he brought it up, since imaging was what Tom's lab focused on. "Yes, but that's expensive, time-consuming, and often not useful because of the pancreas's position. But . . ." She took another deep breath. "I think I have found a set of biomarkers. Not from tissue biopsy—blood biomarkers. Noninvasive, easy to obtain. Cheap. In mice they can detect pancreatic cancer as early as stage one."

She paused. Tom and Adam were both staring at her. Tom was clearly interested, and Adam looked . . . a little weird, to be honest. Impressed, maybe? Nah, impossible.

"Okay. This sounds promising. What's the next step?"

"Collecting more data. Running more analyses with better equipment to prove that my set of biomarkers is worthy of a clinical trial. But for that I need a larger lab."

"I see." He nodded with a thoughtful expression and then leaned back in his chair. "Why pancreatic cancer?"

"It's one of the most lethal, and we know so little about how—"

"No," Tom interrupted. "Most third-year Ph.D. students are too busy infighting over the centrifuge to come up with their own line of research. There must be a reason you're so motivated. Did someone close to you have cancer?"

Olive swallowed before reluctantly answering, "Yes."

"Who?"

"Tom," Adam said, a trace of warning in his voice. His knee was still against her thigh. Still warm. And yet, Olive felt her blood turn cold. She really, really didn't want to say it. And yet she couldn't ignore the question. She needed Tom's help.

"My mother."

Okay. It was out there now. She'd said it, and she could go back to trying not to think about it—

"Did she die?"

A beat. Olive hesitated and then nodded silently, not looking at either of the men at the table. She knew Tom wasn't trying to be mean—people were curious, after all. But it wasn't something Olive wanted to discuss. She barely ever talked about it, even with Anh and Malcolm, and she had carefully avoided writing about her experience in her grad school applications, even when everyone had told her it would give her a leg up.

She just . . . She couldn't. She just couldn't.

"How old were you—"

"*Tom*," Adam interrupted, tone sharp. He set his tea down with more force than necessary. "Stop harassing my girlfriend." It was less of a warning and more of a threat.

"Right. Yes. I'm an insensitive ass." Tom smiled, apologetic.

Olive noticed that he was looking at her shoulder. When she followed his gaze, she realized that Adam had placed his arm on the back of her chair. He wasn't touching her, but there was something . . . protective about his position. He seemed to generate large amounts of heat, which was not at all unwelcome. It helped melt the yucky feeling the conversation with Tom had left behind.

"Then again, so is your boyfriend." Tom winked at her. "Okay, Olive. Tell you what." Tom leaned forward, elbows on the table. "I've read your paper. And the abstract you submitted to the SBD conference. Are you still planning to go?"

"If it's accepted."

"I'm sure it will be. It's excellent work. But it sounds like your project has progressed since you submitted that, and I need to know more about it. If I decide that you can work in my lab next year, I'll cover you completely—salary, supplies, equipment, whatever you need. But I need to know where you're at to make sure that you're worth investing in."

Olive felt her heart racing. This sounded promising. Very promising.

"Here's the deal. I'm going to give you two weeks to write up a report on everything you've been doing so far—protocols, findings, challenges. In two weeks, send me the report and I'll make a decision based on it. Does that sound feasible?"

She grinned, nodding enthusiastically. "Yes!" She could absolutely do that. She'd need to pull the intro from one of her papers, the methods from her lab protocols, the preliminary data from that grant she'd applied for and not won. And she'd have to rerun some of her analyses—just to make sure that the report was absolutely flawless for Tom. It would be lots of work in little time, but who needed sleep? Or bathroom breaks?

"Great. In the meantime I'll see you around and we can chat more. Adam and I will be joined at the hip for a couple of weeks, since we're working on that grant we just got. Are you coming to my talk tomorrow?"

Olive had no idea he was giving a talk, let alone when or where, but she said "Of course! Can't wait!" with the certainty of someone who had installed a countdown widget on her smartphone.

"And I'm staying with Adam, so I'll see you at his place."

Oh no. "Um . . ." She risked a glance at Adam, who was unreadable. "Sure. Though we usually meet at my place, so . . ."

"I see. You disapprove of his taxidermy collection, don't you?" Tom stood with a smirk. "Excuse me. I'll get some coffee and be right back."

The second he was gone, Olive instantly turned to Adam. Now that they were alone there were about ten million topics for them to debrief on, but the only thing she could think of was, "Do you really collect taxidermied animals?"

He gave her a scathing look and took his arm away from around her shoulders. She felt cold all of a sudden. Bereft.

"I'm sorry. I had no idea he was your friend, or that you two had a grant together. You do such different research, the possibility didn't even cross my mind."

"You did mention that you don't believe cancer researchers can benefit from collaborating with computational modelists."

"You—" She noticed the way his mouth was twitching and wondered when exactly they'd gotten on teasing terms. "How do you two know each other?"

"He was a postdoc in my lab, back when I was a Ph.D. student. We've kept in touch and collaborated through the years."

So he must be four or five years older than Adam.

"You went to Harvard, right?"

He nodded, and a terrifying thought occurred to her. "What if he feels obliged to take me on because I'm your fake girlfriend?"

"Tom won't. He once fired his cousin for breaking a flow cytometer. He's not exactly tenderhearted."

Takes one to know one, she thought. "Listen, I'm sorry this is forcing you to lie to your friend. If you want to tell him that this is fake . . ."

Adam shook his head. "If I did, I'd never live it down."

She let out a laugh. "Yeah, I can see that. And honestly it wouldn't reflect well on me, either."

"But, Olive, if you do end up deciding that you want to go to Harvard, I'll need you to keep it a secret until the end of September."

She gasped, realizing the implications of his words. "Of course. If people know that I'm leaving, the department chair will never believe that you're not leaving, too. I hadn't even thought of it. I promise I won't tell anyone! Well, except for Malcolm and Anh, but they're great at keeping secrets, they'd never—"

His eyebrow rose. Olive winced.

"I will *make* them keep this secret. I swear."

"I appreciate it."

She noticed that Tom was on his way back to the table and leaned closer to Adam to quickly whisper, "One more thing. The talk he mentioned, the one he's giving tomorrow?"

"The one you 'can't wait' for?"

Olive bit the inside of her cheek. "Yes. When and where is it going to be?"

Adam laughed silently just as Tom sat down again. "Don't worry. I'll email you the details."

Chapter Six

♥ **HYPOTHESIS:** *When compared with multiple types and models of furniture, Adam Carlsen's lap will be rated in the top fifth percentile for comfort, coziness, and enjoyment.*

The moment Olive opened the door of the auditorium she and Anh exchanged a wide-eyed look and said, in unison, "Holy shit."

In her two years at Stanford she had been to countless seminars, trainings, lectures, and classes in this lecture hall, and yet she'd never seen the room this full. Maybe Tom was giving out free beer?

"I think they made the talk mandatory for immunology and pharmacology," Anh said. "And I overheard at least five people in the hallway saying that Benton is 'a known science hottie.'" She stared critically at the podium, where Tom was chatting with Dr. Moss from immunology. "I guess he's cute. Though not nearly as cute as Jeremy."

Olive smiled. The air in the room was hot and humid, smelling like sweat and too many human beings. "You don't have to stay. This is probably a fire hazard and not even remotely relevant to your research—"

"It beats doing actual work." She grabbed Olive's wrist, pulling her through the throng of grads and postdocs crowding the entrance and down the stairs on the side. They were just as packed. "And if this guy is going to take you away from me and to Boston for an entire year, I want to make sure that he deserves you." She winked. "Consider my presence the equivalent of a father cleaning his rifle in front of his daughter's boyfriend before prom."

"Aww, Daddy."

There was nowhere to sit, of course, not even on the floor or on the steps. Olive spotted Adam in an aisle seat a few meters away. He was back to his usual black Henley and deep in conversation with Holden Rodrigues. When Adam's eyes met Olive's, she grinned and waved at him. For some yet unknown reason that likely had to do with the fact that they were sharing this huge, ridiculous, unlikely secret, Adam now felt like a friendly face. He didn't wave back, but his gaze seemed softer and warmer, and his mouth curved into that tilt that she'd learned to recognize as his version of a smile.

"I can't believe they didn't switch the talk to one of the bigger auditoriums. There is not nearly enough space for— Oh, *no*. No, no, no."

Olive followed Anh's gaze, and saw at least twenty new people arrive. The crowd immediately started pushing Olive toward the front of the room. Anh yelped when a first-year from neuroscience who weighed about four times as much as she did stepped on her toe. "This is ridiculous."

"I know. I can't believe more people are—"

Olive's hip bumped against something—someone. She turned to apologize, and—it was Adam. Or, Adam's shoulder. He was still chatting with Dr. Rodrigues, who wore a displeased expression and was muttering, "Why are we even here?"

"Because he's a friend," Adam said.

"Not *my* friend."

Adam sighed and turned to look at Olive.

"Hey—sorry." She gestured in the direction of the entrance. "A bunch of new people just came in and apparently the space in this room is finite. I think it's a law of physics, or something."

"It's okay."

"I'd take a step back, but . . ."

On the podium, Dr. Moss took the mic and began introducing Tom.

"Here," Adam told Olive, making to stand from his chair. "Take my seat."

"Oh." It was nice of him to offer. Not fake-dating-to-save-her-ass, spend-twenty-bucks-on-junk-food-for-her nice, but still very nice. Olive couldn't possibly accept. Plus, Adam was a professor, which meant that he was older and all that. Thirtysomething. He did look fit, but he probably had a bum knee and was only a few years short of osteoporosis. "Thank you, but—"

"Actually, that would be a terrible idea," Anh interjected. Her eyes were darting between Olive and Adam. "No offense, Dr. Carlsen, but you're three times larger than Olive. If you stand, the room's going to burst."

Adam stared at Anh like he had no idea whether he'd just been insulted.

"But," she continued, this time looking at Olive, "it'd be great if you could do me a solid and sit on your boyfriend's lap, Ol. Just so I don't have to stand on my toes?"

Olive blinked. And then she blinked again. And then she blinked some more. Near the podium, Dr. Moss was still introducing Tom—"Got his Ph.D. from Vanderbilt and then moved to a postdoctoral fellowship at Harvard University, where he pioneered several techniques in the field of imaging"—but her voice sounded as if it was coming from far, far away. Possibly because Olive couldn't stop thinking about what Anh had proposed, which was just . . .

"Anh, I don't think it's a good idea," Olive mumbled under her breath, avoiding glancing in Adam's direction.

Anh gave her a look. "Why? You're taking up space we don't have, and it's only logical that you use Carlsen as a chair. I would, but he's your boyfriend, not mine."

For a moment, Olive tried to imagine what Adam would do if Anh decided to sit on his lap, and figured that it would probably end up involving someone being murdered and someone doing the murdering—she wasn't sure who'd be doing what. The mental image was so ridiculous that she almost giggled out loud. Then she noticed the way Anh was looking at her expectantly. "Anh, I *can't*."

"Why?"

"*Because*. This is a scientific talk."

"Psh. Remember last year, when Jess and Alex made out for half of that CRISPR lecture?"

"I do—and it was *weird*."

"Nah, it wasn't. Also, Malcolm swears that during a seminar he saw that tall guy from immunology get a hand job from—"

"*Anh*."

"The point is, no one cares." Anh's expression softened into a plea. "And this girl's elbow is puncturing my right lung, and I have about thirty seconds of air left. Please, Olive."

Olive turned to face Adam. Who was, very unsurprisingly, looking up at her with that nonexpression of his, the one that Olive couldn't quite decipher. Except that his jaw was working, and she wondered if maybe this was it. The last straw. The moment he backed out of their arrangement. Because millions of dollars in research funds couldn't be worth having some girl he barely knew sit on his lap in the most crowded room in the history of crowded rooms.

Is this okay? she tried to ask him with her eyes. *Because maybe this is a little too much. Way more than saying hi to each other and having coffee together.*

He gave her a brief nod, and then—Olive, or at least Olive's body, was stepping toward Adam and gingerly sitting on his thigh, her knees tucked between his spread legs. It was happening. It had happened already. Olive was here.

Sitting.

On.

Adam.

This. Yep, *this.*

This was her life now.

She was going to murder Anh for this. Slowly. Maybe painfully, too. She was going to be jailed for bestfriendicide, and she was a-okay with it.

"I'm sorry," she whispered to Adam. He was so tall, her mouth was not quite level with his ear. She could smell him—the woodsiness of his shampoo, his body wash, and something else underneath, dark and good and clean. It all felt familiar, and after a few seconds Olive realized that it was because of the last time they had been this close. Because of The Night. Because of the kiss. "So, *so* sorry."

He didn't immediately answer. His jaw tensed, and he looked in the direction of the PowerPoint. Dr. Moss was gone, Tom was talking about cancer diagnostics, and Olive would have gobbled this up on a regular day, but right now she just needed *out.* Of the talk. Of the room. Of her own life.

Then Adam turned his face a little and told her, "It's okay."

He sounded a bit strained. Like nothing about this situation was, in fact, okay.

"I'm sorry. I had no idea she would suggest this, and I couldn't think of a way to—"

"Sssh." His arm slid around her waist, his hand coming to rest on her hip in a gesture that should have been unpleasant but just felt reassuring. His voice was low when he added, "It's fine." The words vibrated in her ear, rich and warm. "More material for my Title IX complaint."

Shit. "God, I'm so sorry—"

"Olive."

She lifted her eyes to catch his and was shocked to find him . . . not smiling, but something like it.

"I was kidding. You weigh nothing. I don't mind."

"I—"

"Ssh. Just focus on the talk. Tom might ask you questions about it."

This was just . . . Seriously, this whole business, it was completely, *utterly* . . .

Comfortable. Adam Carlsen's lap was one of the most comfortable places on earth, as it turned out. He was warm and solid in a pleasant, soothing way, and he didn't seem to mind too much having Olive half draped over him. After a short while she realized that the room was truly too full for anyone to be paying attention to them, except for a quick glance from Holden Rodrigues, who studied Adam for a long moment and then smiled warmly at Olive before focusing on the talk. She stopped pretending to be able to hold her spine upright for more than five minutes and just let herself lean into Adam's torso. He didn't say anything but angled himself a little, just to help her fit more comfortably.

Somewhere halfway through the talk she realized that she

had been sliding down Adam's thigh. Or, to be fair, Adam realized and lifted her up, straightening her in a firm, quick pull that made her feel like she really didn't weigh anything. Once she was stable again, he didn't move his arm from where it was snaked around her waist. The talk had been happening for thirty-five minutes going on a century, so no one could blame Olive if she sank into him a little bit more.

It was fine. It was more than fine, actually. It was nice.

"Don't fall asleep," he murmured. She felt his lips move against the tendrils of hair above her temple. It should have been Olive's cue to straighten, but she couldn't quite make herself.

"I'm not. Though you're so comfy."

His fingers tightened on her, maybe to wake her up, maybe to hold her closer. She was about to melt off the chair and start snoring.

"You look like you're about to take a nap."

"It's just that I've read all of Tom's articles. I already know what he's saying."

"Yeah, same. We cited all this stuff in our grant proposal." He sighed, and she felt his body move under hers. "This is dull."

"Maybe you should ask a question. To liven this up."

Adam turned slightly to her. "Me?"

She angled her head to speak in his ear. "I'm sure you can come up with something. Just raise your hand and make a mean observation with that tone of yours. Glare at him. It might devolve into an entertaining outbreak of fisticuffs."

His cheek curved. "You are such a smart-ass."

Olive looked back to the slides, smiling. "Has it been weird? Having to lie to Tom about us?"

Adam seemed to think about it. "No." He hesitated. "It looks like your friends are buying that we're together."

"I think so. I'm not exactly a convincing liar, and sometimes

I worry that Anh might get suspicious. But I walked in on her and Jeremy making out in the grad lounge the other day."

They fell quiet and listened to the last few minutes of the talk in silence. In front of them, Olive could see at least two professors taking a nap, and several surreptitiously working on their laptops. Next to Adam, Dr. Rodrigues had been playing Candy Crush on his phone for the past half an hour. Some people had left, and Anh had found a seat about ten minutes ago. So had several of the students who had been next to Olive, which meant that she could have technically stood up and left Adam alone. Technically. Technically, there was an open chair somewhere in the third-to-last row. Technically.

Instead she brought her lips to Adam's ear once more and whispered, "It's working out well for me, I have to say. This whole fake-dating thing." More than well. Better than she ever thought it would.

Adam blinked once and then nodded. Maybe his arm tensed a little around her. Maybe it didn't, and Olive's mind was playing tricks on her. It was starting to get late, after all. Her last coffee had been too long ago, and she wasn't fully awake, her thoughts fuzzy and relaxed.

"What about you?"

"Mmm?" Adam wasn't looking at her.

"Is it working for you?" It came out a little needy. Olive told herself that it was only because of how low she had to pitch her voice. "Or do you maybe want to fake–break up early?"

He didn't reply for a second. Then, just as Dr. Moss took the mic to thank Tom and ask the audience for questions, she heard him say, "No. I don't want to fake–break up."

He really did smell good. And he was funny in a weird, deadpan way, and yes, a known ass, but friendly enough to her that she could sort of ignore that about him. Plus, he was spending a small fortune on sugar for her. Truly, she had nothing to complain about.

Olive settled herself more comfortably and turned her attention back to the podium.

~~~~~~~~

AFTER THE TALK, Olive considered walking down to the podium to compliment Tom and ask him one or two questions she already knew the answers to. Sadly, there were dozens of people waiting to speak to him, and she decided that the ass-kissing wasn't worth standing in line. So she said goodbye to Adam, waited for Anh to wake up from her nap while contemplating getting revenge by drawing a dick on her face, and then slowly headed with her across campus back to the biology building.

"Is it going to be a lot of work, the report Benton asked for?"

"A fair amount. I need to run a few control studies to make my results stronger. Plus there's other stuff I should be working on—the TA'ing, and my poster presentation for the SBD conference in Boston." Olive bent her head back, felt the sun warm her skin, and smiled. "If I hole up in the lab every night this week and the next, I should be able to finish it on time."

"SBD is something to look forward to, at least."

Olive nodded. She usually wasn't a fan of academic conferences, given how prohibitively expensive registration, travel, and lodgings could be. But Malcolm and Anh were going to be at SBD, too, and Olive was excited to explore Boston with them. Plus, the intradepartmental drama that always happened at academic functions with open bars was sure to be A+ entertainment.

"I am organizing this outreach event for BIPOC women in STEM from all over the country—I'm going to get Ph.D. students like me to talk face-to-face with undergrads who are applying and reassure them that if they come to grad school they won't be alone."

"Anh, this is amazing. *You* are amazing."

"I know." Anh winked, sliding her arm through Olive's. "We can all share a hotel room. And get free gadgets from the exhibit booths, and get sloshed together. Remember at Human Genetics, when Malcolm got wasted and began hitting random passersby with his poster tube— What's going on there?"

Olive squinted against the sun. The parking lot of the biology building was uncharacteristically jammed with traffic. People were blowing their horns and getting out of their cars, trying to figure out the source of the holdup. She and Anh walked around a line of vehicles stuck in the lot, until they ran into a group of biology grads.

"Someone's battery died, and it's blocking the exit line." Greg, one of Olive's lab mates, was rolling his eyes and bouncing impatiently on his feet. He pointed at a red truck stuck sideways in the most inconvenient turn.

Olive recognized it as Cherie's, the department secretary.

"I defend my dissertation proposal tomorrow—I need to drive home to prepare. This is ridiculous. And why the fuck is Cherie just standing there, chatting leisurely with Carlsen? Do they want us to bring them tea and cucumber sandwiches?"

Olive looked around, searching for Adam's tall frame.

"Oh yeah, there's Carlsen," Anh said. Olive looked where she was pointing, just in time to see Cherie get back behind the wheel and Adam jogging around the truck.

"What is he—" was all Olive managed to say, before he came to a stop, put his hands on the back of the truck in neutral, and started . . .

Pushing.

His shoulders and biceps strained his Henley. The firm muscles of his upper back visibly shifted and tensed under the black fabric as he bent forward and rolled several tons of truck across . . . quite a bit of a distance and into the closest empty parking space.

Oh.

There was some applause and whistling from bystanders when the truck was out of the way, and a couple of faculty members from neuroscience clapped Adam on the shoulder as the line of cars started driving out of the lot.

"Fucking finally," Olive heard Greg say from behind her, and she stood there, blinking, a little shocked. Had she hallucinated it? Had Adam really just pushed a giant truck all by himself? Was he an alien from planet Krypton who moonlighted as a superhero?

"Ol, go give him a kiss."

Olive whirled around, abruptly reminded of Anh's existence. "What?" No. *No.* "I'm good. I just said goodbye to him a minute ago and—"

"Ol, why don't you want to go kiss your boyfriend?"

Ugh. "I . . . It's not that I don't want to. I just—"

"Dude, he just moved a truck. By himself. On uphill ground. He deserves a damn kiss." Anh shoved Olive and made a shooing motion.

Olive clenched her teeth and headed in Adam's direction, wishing she'd gone ahead and drawn twenty dicks all over Anh's face. Maybe she did suspect that Olive was faking her relationship with Adam. Or maybe she just got a kick out of pressuring her into PDA'ing, that ingrate. Either way, if this was what one got for masterminding an intricate fake-dating scheme that was supposed to benefit a friend's love life, then maybe—

Olive halted abruptly.

Adam's head was bent forward, black hair covering his forehead as he wiped the sweat from his eyes with the hem of his shirt. It left a broad strip of flesh visible on his torso, and—it was nothing indecent, really, nothing unusual, just some fit guy's midriff, but for some reason Olive couldn't help staring at Adam Carlsen's uncovered skin like it was a slab of Italian marble, and—

"Olive?" he said, and she immediately averted her eyes. Crap, he'd totally caught her staring. First she'd forced him to kiss her, and now she was ogling him like some perv in the biology parking lot and—

"Did you need anything?"

"No, I . . ." She felt her cheeks go crimson.

His skin, too, was flushed from the effort of pushing, and his eyes were bright and clear, and he seemed . . . well, at least he didn't seem unhappy to see her.

"Anh sent me to give you a kiss."

He froze halfway through wiping his hands on his shirt. And then he said "Ah" in his usual neutral, unreadable tone.

"Because you moved the truck. I—I know how ridiculous that sounds. I know. But I didn't want her to get suspicious, and there are faculty members here, too, so maybe they'll tell the department chair and it will be two birds with one stone and I can leave if you—"

"It's okay, Olive. Breathe."

Right. Yes. Good suggestion. Olive did breathe, and the act made her realize that she hadn't done that in a while, which in turn made her smile up at Adam—who did his mouth-twitch thing back at her. She was really starting to get used to him. To his expressions, his size, his distinctive way of being in the same space as her.

"Anh's staring at us," he said, looking over Olive's head.

Olive sighed and pinched the bridge of her nose. "I just bet she is," she mumbled.

Adam wiped sweat from his forehead with the back of his hand.

Olive squirmed. "So . . . Should we hug or something?"

"Oh." Adam looked at his hands and down at himself. "I don't think you want to do that. I'm pretty gross."

Before she could stop herself Olive studied him from head to toe, taking in his large body, his broad shoulders, the way his hair was curling around his ears. He didn't *look* gross. Not even to Olive, who was usually not a fan of dudes built like they spent a double-digit percentage of their time at the gym. He looked . . .

Not gross.

Still, maybe it was better if they didn't hug. Olive might end up doing something egregiously stupid. She should just say goodbye and leave—yes, that was the thing to do.

Except that something absolutely insane came out of her mouth.

"Should we just kiss, then?" she heard herself blurt out. And then she instantly wished a stray meteorite would hit the exact spot where she was standing, because—had she just asked Adam Carlsen for a kiss? Was that what she'd done? Was she a lunatic all of a sudden?

"I mean, not like a *kiss* kiss," she hastened to add. "But like the last time? You know."

He didn't seem to know. Which made sense, because their other kiss had definitely been a *kiss* kiss. Olive tried not to think about it too much, but it flashed in her mind every once in a while, mostly when she was doing something important that required her utmost concentration, like implanting electrodes inside a mouse's pancreas or trying to decide what to order at Subway. Occasionally it would pop up during a quiet moment, like when she was in bed and about to fall asleep, and she would feel a mixture of embarrassment and incredulity and something else. Something that she had no intention of examining too closely, not now and not ever.

"Are you sure?"

She nodded, even though she wasn't sure at all. "Is Anh still staring at us?"

His eyes flicked up. "Yes. She's not even pretending not to. I . . . why does she care so much? Are you famous?"

"No, Adam." She gestured at him. "*You* are."

"Am I?" He looked perplexed.

"Anyway, no need to kiss. You're right that it would probably be a bit weird."

"No. No, I didn't mean that . . ." There was a droplet of sweat running down his temple, and he wiped his face again, this time with the sleeve of his shirt. "We can kiss."

"Oh."

"If you think that . . . If your friend is watching."

"Yeah." Olive swallowed. "But we don't have to."

"I know."

"Unless you want to." Olive's palms felt damp and clammy, so she surreptitiously wiped them on her jeans. "And by 'want to' I mean, unless you think it's a good idea." It so was *not* a good idea. It was a horrible idea. Like *all* her ideas.

"Right." He looked past Olive and toward Anh, who was probably in the middle of doing an entire Instagram Story on them. "Okay, then."

"Okay."

He stepped a little closer, and really, he was not gross. How someone this sweaty, someone who'd just pushed a truck, still managed to smell good was a topic worthy of a Ph.D. dissertation, for sure. Earth's finest scientists should have been hard at work on this.

"Why don't I . . ." Olive inched slightly into him, and after letting her hand hover for a moment she rested it over Adam's shoulder. She pushed up on her toes, angling her head up toward him. It helped very little, as Olive was still not tall enough to reach his mouth, so she tried to get more leverage by putting her other hand on his arm, and immediately realized that she was basically hugging him. Which was the exact thing he had asked her not to do a second ago. *Crap.*

"Sorry, too close? I didn't mean to—"

She would have finished the sentence, if he hadn't closed the distance between them and just—kissed her. Just like that.

It was little more than a peck—just his lips pressing against hers, and his hand on her waist to steady her a little. It was a kiss, but barely, and it certainly didn't warrant the way her heart pounded in her chest, or the fact that there was something warm and liquid looping at the bottom of her belly. Not unpleasant, but confusing and a bit scary nonetheless, and it had Olive pull back after only a second. When she eased back on her heels, it seemed like for a fraction of a moment Adam followed her, try-ing to fill the gap between their mouths. Though by the time she'd blinked herself free of the haze of the kiss, he was standing tall in front of her, cheekbones dusted with red and chest moving up and down in shallow breaths. She must have dreamed up that last bit.

She needed to avert her eyes from him, now. And he needed to look elsewhere, too. Why were they staring at each other?

"Okay," she chirped. "That, um . . . worked."

Adam's jaw twitched, but he didn't reply.

"Well, then. I'm going to . . . um . . ." She gestured behind her shoulders with her thumb.

"Anh?"

"Yeah. Yeah, to Anh."

He swallowed heavily. "Okay. Yeah."

They had kissed. They had kissed—twice, now. *Twice*. Not that it mattered. No one cared. But. Twice. Plus, the lap. Earlier today. Again, not that it mattered.

"I'll see you around, right? Next week?"

He lifted his fingers to his lips, then let his arm drop to his side. "Yes. On Wednesday."

It was Thursday now. Which meant that they were going to see each other in six days. Which was fine. Olive was fine, no matter when or how often they met. "Yep. See you Wed— Hey, what about the picnic?"

"The— Oh." Adam rolled his eyes, looking a little more like himself. "Right. That fu—" He stopped short. "That picnic."

She grinned. "It's on Monday."

He sighed. "I know."

"You're still going?"

He gave her a look that clearly stated: *It's not like I have a choice, even though I'd rather have my nails extracted one by one. With pliers.*

Olive laughed. "Well. I'm going, too."

"At least there's that."

"Are you bringing Tom?"

"Probably. He actually *likes* people."

"Okay. I can network with him a bit, and you and I can show off how steady and committed we are to the department chair. You'll look like a wingless bird. No flight risk whatsoever."

"Perfect. I'll bring a counterfeit marriage license to casually drop at his feet."

Olive laughed, waved goodbye, and then jogged up to Anh. She rubbed the side of her hand against her lips, as if trying to scrub her mind clean of the fact that she had just kissed Adam— Dr. Adam Carlsen—for the second time in her life. Which, again, was fine. It had been barely a kiss. Not important.

"Well, then," Anh said, tucking her phone into her pocket. "You really just made out in front of the biology building with associate professor Adam MacArthur Carlsen."

Olive rolled her eyes and started up the stairs. "I'm pretty sure that's not his middle name. And we did not."

"But it was clear that you wanted to."

"Shut up. Why were you looking at us, anyway?"

"I wasn't. I happened to glance up when he was about to jump you, and I just couldn't look away."

Olive snorted, plugging her headphones into her phone's port. "Right. Of course."

"He's really into you. I can tell from the way he stares at—"

"I'm gonna listen to music very loudly now. To tune you out."

"—you."

It wasn't until much later, after Olive had been working on Tom's report for several hours, that she remembered what Adam had said when she'd told him she'd be at the picnic.

At least there's that.

Olive ducked her head and smiled at her toes.

Chapter Seven

~~~~~~

♥ **HYPOTHESIS:** *There will be a significant positive correlation between the amount of sunscreen poured in my hands and the intensity of my desire to murder Anh.*

Tom's report was about a third done and sitting tight at thirty-four pages single-spaced, Arial (11 point), no justification. It was 11:00 a.m., and Olive had been working in the lab since about five—analyzing peptide samples, writing down protocol notes, taking covert naps while the PCR machine ran—when Greg barged in, looking absolutely furious.

It was unusual, but not *too* unusual. Greg was a bit of a hot-head to begin with, and grad school came with a lot of angry outbursts in semipublic places, usually for reasons that, Olive was fully aware, would appear ridiculous to someone who'd never stepped foot in academia. *They're making me TA Intro to Bio for the fourth time in a row; the paper I need is behind a paywall; I had a meeting with my supervisor and accidentally called her "Mom."*

Greg and Olive shared an adviser, Dr. Aslan, and while they'd always gotten along fine, they had never been particularly close.

Olive had hoped, by picking a female adviser, to avoid some of the nastiness that was so often directed at women in STEM. Unfortunately she had still found herself in an all-male lab, which was . . . a less-than-ideal environment. That was why when Greg came in, slammed the door, and then threw a folder on his bench, Olive was not sure what to do. She watched him sit down and begin to sulk. Chase, another lab mate, followed him inside a moment later with an uneasy expression and started gingerly patting his back.

Olive looked longingly at her RNA samples. Then she stepped closer to Greg's bench and asked, "What's wrong?"

She had expected the answer to be *The production of my reagent has been discontinued*, or *My p-value is .06*, or *Grad school was a mistake, but now it's too late to back out of it because my self-worth is unbreakably tied to my academic performance, and what would even be left of me if I decided to drop out?*

Instead what she got was: "Your stupid boyfriend is what's wrong."

By now the fake dating had been going on for over two weeks: Olive didn't startle anymore when someone referred to Adam as her boyfriend. Still, Greg's words were so unexpected and full of venom that she couldn't help but answer, "Who?"

"Carlsen." He spat the name out like a curse.

"Oh."

"He's on Greg's dissertation committee," Chase explained in a significantly milder tone, not quite meeting Olive's eyes.

"Oh. Right." This could be bad. Very bad. "What happened?"

"He failed my proposal."

"Shit." Olive bit into her lower lip. "I'm sorry, Greg."

"This is going to set me back a lot. It'll take me months to revise it, all because Carlsen had to go and nitpick. I didn't even want him on my committee; Dr. Aslan forced me to add him because she's so obsessed with his stupid computational stuff."

Olive chewed on the inside of her cheek, trying to come up with something meaningful to say and failing miserably. "I'm really sorry."

"Olive, do you guys talk about this stuff?" Chase asked out of the blue, eyeing her suspiciously. "Did he tell you he wasn't going to pass Greg?"

"What? No. No, I . . ." *I talk to him for exactly fifteen minutes a week. And, okay, I've kissed him. Twice. And I sat on his lap. Once. But it's just that, and Adam—he speaks very little. I actually wish he spoke more, since I know nothing about him, and I'd like to know at least something.* "No, he doesn't. I think it would be against regulations if he did."

"God." Greg slammed his palm against the edge of the bench, making her jump. "He's such a dick. What a sadistic piece of shit."

Olive opened her mouth to—to do what, precisely? To defend Adam? He *was* a dick. She had seen him be a dick. In full action. Maybe not recently, and maybe not to her, but if she'd wanted to count on her fingers the number of acquaintances who'd ended up in tears because of him, well . . . She would need both her hands, and then her toes. Maybe borrow some of Chase's, too.

"Did he say why, at least? What you have to change?"

"Everything. He wants me to change my control condition and add another one, which is going to make the project ten times more time-consuming. And the way he said it, his air of superiority—he is *so* arrogant."

Well. It was no news, really. Olive scratched her temple, trying not to sigh. "It sucks. I'm sorry," she repeated once more, at a loss for anything better and genuinely feeling for Greg.

"Yeah, well." He stood and walked around his bench, coming to a stop in front of Olive. "You should be."

She froze. Surely she must have misheard. "Excuse me?"

"You're his girlfriend."

"I . . ." *Really am not.* But. Even if she had been. "Greg, I'm only *dating* him. I am not him. How would I have anything to do with—"

"You're fine with all of this. With him acting like that—like an asshole on a power trip. You don't give a shit about the way he treats everyone in the program, otherwise you wouldn't be able to stomach being with him."

At his tone, she took a step back.

Chase lifted his hands in a peacekeeping gesture, coming to stand between them. "Hey, now. Let's not—"

"I'm not the one who failed you, Greg."

"Maybe. But you don't care that half of the department lives in terror of your boyfriend, either."

Olive felt anger bubbling up. "That is not true. I am able to separate my professional relationships and my personal feelings for him—"

"Because you don't give a shit about anyone but yourself."

"That is unfair. What am I supposed to do?"

"Get him to stop failing people."

"Get him—" Olive sputtered. "Greg, how is this a rational response for you to have about Adam's failing you—"

"Ah. Adam, is it?"

She gritted her teeth. "Yes. Adam. What should I call my boyfriend to better please you? Professor Carlsen?"

"If you were a half-decent ally to any of the grads in the department, you would just dump your fucking boyfriend."

"How— Do you even realize how little sense you are . . ."

No reason to finish her sentence, since Greg was storming out of the lab and slamming the door behind him, clearly uninterested in anything Olive might have wanted to add. She ran a hand down her face, unsettled by what had just happened.

"He's not . . . he doesn't really mean it. Not about you, at least," Chase said while scratching his head. A nice reminder that he'd been standing there, in the room, for the entirety of this conversation. Front-row seat. It was going to take maybe fifteen minutes before everyone in the program knew about it. "Greg needs to graduate in the spring with his wife. So that they can find postdocs together. They don't want to live apart, you know."

She nodded—she hadn't known, but she could imagine. Some of her anger dissipated. "Yeah, well." *Being horrible to me isn't going to make his thesis work go any faster*, she didn't add.

Chase sighed. "It's not personal. But you have to understand that it's weird for us. Because Carlsen . . . Maybe he wasn't on any of your committees, but you must know the kind of guy he is, right?"

She was unsure how to respond.

"And now you guys are dating, and . . ." Chase shrugged with a nervous smile. "It shouldn't be a matter of taking sides, but sometimes it can feel like it, you know?"

Chase's words lingered for the rest of the day. Olive thought about them as she ran her mice through her experimental protocols, and then later while she tried to figure out what to do with those two outliers that made her findings tricky to interpret. She mulled it over while biking home, hot wind warming her cheeks and ruffling her hair, and while eating two slices of the saddest pizza ever. Malcolm had been on a health kick for weeks now (something about cultivating his gut microbiome) and refused to admit that cauliflower crust did not taste good.

Among her friends, Malcolm and Jeremy had had unpleasant

dealings with Adam in the past, but after the initial shock they didn't seem to hold Olive's relationship with him against her. She hadn't concerned herself too much with the feelings of other grads. She had always been a bit of a loner, and focusing on the opinion of people she barely interacted with seemed like a wasteful use of time and energy. Still, maybe there was a glimmer of truth in what Greg had said. Adam had been anything but a jerk to Olive, but did accepting his help while he acted horribly toward her fellow grads make her a bad person?

Olive lay on her unmade bed, looking up at the glow-in-the-dark stars. It had been more than two years since she'd borrowed Malcolm's stepladder and carefully stuck them on the ceiling; the glue was starting to give out, and the large comet in the corner by the window was going to fall off any day. Without letting herself think it through too much, she rolled out of bed and rummaged inside the pockets of her discarded jeans until she found her cell phone.

She hadn't used Adam's number since he'd given it to her a few days ago—"If anything comes up or you need to cancel, just give me a call. It's quicker than an email." When she tapped the blue icon under his name a white screen popped up, a blank slate with no history of previous messages. It gave Olive an odd rush of anxiety, so much so that she typed the text with one hand while biting the thumbnail on the other.

Olive: Did you just fail Greg?

Adam was *never* on his phone. Never. Whenever Olive had been in his company, she'd not seen him check it even once— even though with a lab as big as his he probably got about thirty new emails every minute. Truth was, she didn't even know that he owned a cell phone. Maybe he was a weird modern-day hippie and hated technology. Maybe he'd given her his office landline number, and that's why he'd told her to call him. Maybe he didn't know how to text, which meant that Olive was never going to get an answer from—

Her palm vibrated.

Adam: Olive?

It occurred to her that when Adam had given her his number, she'd neglected to give hers in return. Which meant that he had no way of knowing who was texting him now, and the fact that he'd guessed correctly revealed an almost preternatural intuition.

Damn him.

Olive: Yup. Me.

Olive: Did you fail Greg Cohen? I ran into him after his meeting. He was very upset.

At me. Because of you. Because of this stupid thing we're doing.

There was a pause of a minute or so, in which, Olive reflected, Adam might very well be cackling evilly at the idea of all the pain he'd caused Greg. Then he answered:

Adam: I can't discuss other grads' dissertation meetings with you.

Olive sighed, exchanging a loaded look with the stuffed fox Malcolm had gotten her for passing her qualifying examinations.

Olive: I'm not asking you to tell me anything. Greg already told me. Not to mention that I'm the one taking the heat for it, since I'm your girlfriend.

Olive: "Girlfriend."

Three dots appeared at the bottom of her screen. Then they disappeared, and then they appeared again, and then, finally, Olive's phone vibrated.

Adam: Committees don't fail students. They fail their proposals.

She snorted, half wishing he could hear her.

Olive: Yeah, well. Tell it to Greg.

Adam: I have. I explained the weaknesses in his study. He'll revise his proposal accordingly, and then I'll sign off on his dissertation.

Olive: So you admit that you are the one behind the decision to fail him.

Olive: Or, whatever. To fail his proposal.

Adam: Yes. In its current state, the proposal is not going to produce findings of scientific value.

Olive bit the inside of her cheek, staring at her phone and wondering if continuing this conversation was a terrible idea. If what she wanted to say was too much. Then she remembered the way Greg had treated her earlier, muttered, "Fuck it," and typed:

Olive: Don't you think that maybe you could have delivered that feedback in a nicer way?

Adam: Why?

Olive: Because if you had maybe he wouldn't be upset now?

Adam: I still don't see why.

Olive: Seriously?

Adam: It's not my job to manage your friend's emotions. He's in a Ph.D. program, not grade school. He'll be inundated by feedback he doesn't like for the rest of his life if he pursues academia. How he chooses to deal with it is his own business.

Olive: Still, maybe you could try not to look like you enjoy delaying his graduation.

Adam: This is irrational. The reason his proposal needs to be modified is that in its current state it's setting him up for failure. Me and the rest of the committee are giving him feedback that will allow him to produce useful knowledge. He is a scientist in training: he should value guidance, not be upset by it.

Olive gritted her teeth as she typed her responses.

Olive: You must know that you fail more people than anyone

else. And your criticism is needlessly harsh. As in, immediately-drop-out-of-grad-school-and-never-look-back harsh. You must know how grads perceive you.

Adam: I don't.

Olive: Antagonistic. And unapproachable.

And that was sugarcoating it. *You're a dick*, Olive meant. *Except that I know you can not be, and I can't figure out why you're so different with me. I'm absolutely nothing to you, so it doesn't make any sense that you'd have a personality transplant every time you're in my presence.*

The three dots at the bottom of the screen bounced for ten seconds, twenty, thirty. A whole minute. Olive reread her last text and wondered if this was it—if she'd finally gone too far. Maybe he was going to remind her that being insulted over text at 9:00 p.m. on a Friday night was not part of their fake-dating agreement.

Then a blue bubble appeared, filling up her entire screen.

Adam: I'm doing my job, Olive. Which is not to deliver feedback in a pleasant way or to make the department grads feel good about themselves. My job is to form rigorous researchers who won't publish useless or harmful crap that will set back our field. Academia is cluttered with terrible science and mediocre scientists. I couldn't care less about how your friends perceive me, as long as their work is up to standard. If they want to drop out when told that it's not, then so be it. Not everyone has what it takes to be a scientist, and those who don't should be weeded out.

She stared at her phone, hating how unfeeling and callous he sounded. The problem was—Olive understood exactly where Greg was coming from, because she'd been in similar situations. Perhaps not with Adam, but her overall experience in STEM academia had been punctuated by self-doubt, anxiety, and a sense of inferiority. She'd barely slept the two weeks before her qualifying exams, often wondered if her fear of public speaking was going to prevent her from having a career, and she was constantly terrified of being the stupidest person in the room. And yet, most of her time and energy was spent trying to be the best possible scientist, trying to carve a path for herself and amount to *something*. The idea of someone dismissing her work and her feelings this coldheartedly cut deep, which is why her response was so immature, it was almost fetal.

Olive: Well, fuck you, Adam.

She immediately regretted it, but for some reason she couldn't bring herself to send an apology. It wasn't until twenty minutes later that she realized that Adam wasn't going to reply. A warning popped up on the upper part of her screen, informing her that her battery was at 5 percent.

With a deep sigh, Olive stood up from her bed and looked around the room in search of her charger.

~~~~~~

"NOW GO RIGHT."

"Got it." Malcolm's finger flicked the turn signal lever. A clicking sound filled the small car. "Going right."

"No, don't listen to Jeremy. Turn left."

Jeremy leaned forward and swatted Anh's arm. "Malcolm, trust me. Anh has never been to the farm. It's on the right."

"Google Maps says left."

"Google Maps is wrong."

"What do I do?" Malcolm made a face in the rearview mirror. "Left? Right? Ol, what do I do?"

In the back seat, Olive looked up from the car window and shrugged. "Try right; if it's wrong, we'll just turn around." She shot Anh a quick, apologetic glance, but she and Jeremy were too busy mock-glaring at each other to notice.

Malcolm grimaced. "We'll be late. God, I hate these stupid picnics."

"We are, like"—Olive glanced at the car's clock—"one hour late, already. I think we can add ten minutes to that." *I just hope there's some food left.* Her stomach had been growling for the past two hours, and there was no way everyone in the car hadn't noticed.

After her argument with Adam three days ago, she'd been tempted to just skip the picnic. Hole herself up in the lab and continue with what she had been doing the whole weekend— ignore the fact that she had told him to fuck off, and with very little reason. She could use the time to work on Tom's report, which was proving to be trickier and more time-consuming than she'd initially thought—probably because Olive couldn't forget how much was at stake and kept rerunning analyses and agonizing over every single sentence. But she'd changed her mind last minute, telling herself that she'd promised Adam that they'd put on a show for the department chair. It would be unfair of her to back out after he'd done more than his share of the deal when it came to convincing Anh.

That was, of course, in the very unlikely case that he still wanted anything to do with Olive.

"Don't worry, Malcolm," Anh said. "We'll get there eventually. If anyone asks, let's just say that a mountain lion attacked us. God, why is it so hot? I brought sunblock, by the way. SPF thirty and fifty. No one is going anywhere before putting it on."

In the back seat Olive and Jeremy exchanged a resigned look, well acquainted with Anh's sunscreen obsession.

The picnic was in full swing when they finally arrived, as crowded as most academic events with free food. Olive made a beeline for the tables and waved at Dr. Aslan, who was sitting in the shade of a giant oak with other faculty members. Dr. Aslan waved back, no doubt pleased to note that her authority extended to commandeering her grads' free time on top of the eighty hours a week they already spent in the lab. Olive smiled weakly in a valiant attempt not to look resentful, grabbed a cluster of white grapes, and popped one into her mouth while letting her gaze wander around the fields.

Anh was right. This September was uncommonly hot. There were people everywhere, sitting on the lawn chairs, lying down in the grass, walking in and out of the barns—all enjoying the weather. A few were eating from plastic plates on folding tables close to the main house, and there were at least three games going on—a version of volleyball with the players standing in a circle, a soccer match, and something that involved a Frisbee and over a dozen half-dressed dudes.

"What are they even playing?" Olive asked Anh. She spotted Dr. Rodrigues tackle someone from immunology and looked back to the almost empty tables, cringing. Slim pickings was all that was left. Olive wanted a sandwich. A bag of chips. Anything.

"Ultimate Frisbee, I think? I don't know. Did you put on sunblock? You're wearing a tank top and shorts, so you really should."

Olive bit into another grape. "You Americans and your fake sports."

"I'm pretty sure there are Canadian tournaments of Ultimate Frisbee, too. You know what's not fake?"

"What?"

"Melanoma. Put on some sunscreen."

"I will, Mom." Olive smiled. "Can I eat first?"

"Eat what? There's nothing left. Oh, there's some corn bread over there."

"Oh, cool. Pass it over."

"Don't eat the corn bread, guys." Jeremy's head popped up between Olive and Anh. "Jess said that a pharmacology first-year sneezed all over it. Where did Malcolm go?"

"Parking— *Holy. Shit.*"

Olive looked up from her perusal of the table, alarmed by the urgency in Anh's tone. "What?"

"Just, *holy shit.*"

"Yeah, what—"

"*Holy shit.*"

"You mentioned that already."

"Because—*holy shit.*"

She glanced around, trying to figure out what was going on. "What is— Oh, there's Malcolm. Maybe he found something to eat?"

"Is that *Carlsen*?"

Olive was already walking toward Malcolm to find something edible and skip the whole sunscreen nonsense altogether, but when she heard Adam's name, she stopped dead in her tracks. Or maybe it wasn't Adam's name but the way Anh was saying it. "What? Where?"

Jeremy pointed at the Ultimate Frisbee crowd. "That's him, right? Shirtless?"

"*Holy shit,*" Anh repeated, her vocabulary suddenly pretty limited, given her twentysomething years of education. "Is that a six-pack?"

Jeremy blinked. "Might even be an eight-pack."

"Are those his real shoulders?" Anh asked. "Did he have shoulder-enhancement surgery?"

"That must be how he used the MacArthur grant," Jeremy said. "I don't think shoulders like that exist in nature."

"God, is that Carlsen's *chest*?" Malcolm leaned his chin over Olive's shoulder. "Was that thing under his shirt while he was ripping my dissertation proposal a new one? *Ol.* Why didn't you say that he was *shredded*?"

Olive just stood there, rooted to the ground, arms dangling uselessly at her sides. *Because I didn't know. Because I had no idea.* Or maybe she had, a bit, from seeing him push that truck the other day—though she'd been trying to suppress that particular mental image.

"Unbelievable." Anh pulled Olive's hand toward herself, overturning it to squirt a healthy dose of lotion on her palm. "Here, put this on your shoulders. And your legs. And your face, too—you're probably at high risk for all sorts of skin stuff, Freckles McFreckleface. Jer, you too."

Olive nodded numbly and began to massage the sunscreen into her arms and thighs. She breathed in the smell of coconut oil, trying hard not to think about Adam and about the fact that he really *did* look like that. Mostly failing, but hey.

"Are there actual studies?" Jeremy asked.

"Mmm?" Anh was pulling her hair up in a bun.

"On the link between freckles and skin cancer."

"I don't know."

"Feels like there would be."

"True. I wanna know now."

"Hold on. Is there Wi-Fi here?"

"Ol, do you have internet?"

Olive wiped her hands on a napkin that looked mostly unused. "I left my phone in Malcolm's car."

She turned her head away from Anh and Jeremy, who were now studying the screen of Jeremy's iPhone, until she had a good view of the Ultimate Frisbee group—fourteen men and zero women. It probably had to do with the general excess of testosterone in STEM programs. At least half the players were faculty or postdocs. Adam, of course, and Tom, and Dr. Rodrigues, and several others from pharmacology. All equally shirtless. Though, no. Not equal at all. There was really nothing equal about Adam.

Olive wasn't like this. She really was not. She could count the number of guys she'd been this viscerally attracted to on one hand. Actually—on one finger. And at the moment said guy was running toward her, because Tom Benton, bless his heart, had just thrown the Frisbee way too clumsily, and it was now in a patch of grass approximately ten feet from Olive. And Adam, shirtless Adam, just happened to be the one closest to where it landed.

"Oh, check out this paper." Jeremy sounded excited.

"Khalesi et al., 2013. It's a meta-analysis. 'Cutaneous markers of photo-damage and risk of basal cell carcinoma of the skin.' In *Cancer Epidemiology, Biomarkers & Prevention.*"

Jeremy fist-pumped. "Olive, are you listening to this?"

Nope. No, she was not. She was mostly trying to empty her brain, and her eyes, too. Of her fake boyfriend and the sudden warm ache in her stomach. She just wished she were elsewhere. That she were temporarily blind and deaf.

"Hear this: solar lentigines had weak but positive associations with basal cell carcinoma, with odds ratios around 1.5. Okay, I don't like this. Jeremy, hold the phone. I'm giving Olive more sunscreen. Here's SPF fifty; it's probably what you need."

Olive tore her eyes from Adam's chest, now alarmingly close, and turned around, stepping away from Anh. "Wait. I already put some on."

"Ol," Anh told her, with that sensible, motherly tone she used whenever Olive slipped and confessed that she mostly got her veggie servings from french fries, or that she washed her colors and whites in the same load. "You know the literature."

"I do not know the literature, and neither do you, you just know one line from one abstract and—"

Anh grabbed Olive's hand again and poured half a gallon of lotion in it. So much of it that Olive had to use her left palm to prevent it from spilling over—until she was just standing there like an idiot, her hands cupped like a beggar as she half drowned in goddamn sunscreen.

"Here you go." Anh smiled brightly. "Now you can protect yourself from basal cell carcinoma. Which, frankly, sounds awful."

"I . . ." Olive would have face-palmed, if she'd had the freedom to move her upper limbs. "I hate sunscreen. It's sticky and it makes me smell like a piña colada and—this is way too much."

"Just put on as much as your skin will absorb. Especially around the freckled areas. The rest, you can share with someone."

"Okay. Anh, then, you take some. You too, Jeremy. You're a ginger, for God's sake."

"A redhead with no freckles, though." He smiled proudly, like he'd created his genotype all on his own. "And I already put on a ton. Thanks, babe." He leaned down for a brief kiss to Anh's cheek, which almost devolved into a make-out session.

Olive tried not to sigh. "Guys, what do I do with this?"

"Just find someone else. Where did Malcolm go?"

Jeremy snorted. "Over there, with Jude."

"Jude?" Anh frowned.

"Yeah, that neuro fifth-year."

"The MD-Ph.D.? Are they dating or—"

"Guys." It took Olive all she had not to yell. "I have no mobility. Please, fix this sunscreen mess you created."

"God, Ol." Anh rolled her eyes. "You're so dramatic sometimes. Hang on—" She waved at someone behind Olive, and when she spoke, her voice was much louder. "Hey, Dr. Carlsen! Have you put on sunscreen yet?"

In the span of a microsecond Olive's entire brain burst into flames—and then crumbled into a pile of ashes. Just like that, one hundred billion neurons, one thousand billion glial cells, and who knew how many milliliters of cerebrospinal fluid, just ceased to exist. The rest of her body was not doing very well, either, since Olive could feel all her organs shut down in real time. From the very beginning of her acquaintance with Adam there had been about ten instances of Olive wishing to drop dead on the spot, for the earth to open and swallow her whole, for a cataclysm to hit and spare her from the embarrassment of their interactions. This time, though, it felt as though the end of the world might happen for real.

Don't turn around, what's left of her central nervous system told her. *Pretend you didn't hear Anh. Will this into nonexistence.* But it was impossible. There was this triangle of sorts, formed by Olive, and Anh in front of her, and Adam probably—surely—standing behind her; it wasn't as if Olive had a choice. Any choice. Especially when Adam, who couldn't possibly imagine the depraved direction of Anh's thoughts, who couldn't possibly see the bucketful of sunscreen that had taken residence in Olive's hands, said, "No."

Well. Shit.

Olive spun around, and there he was—sweaty, holding a Frisbee in his left hand, and so very, very shirtless. "Perfect, then!" Anh said, sounding so chipper. "Olive has way too much and was wondering what to do with it. She'll put some on you!"

No. No, no, *no*. "I can't," she hissed at Anh. "It would be *highly* inappropriate."

"Why?" Anh blinked at her innocently. "I put sunscreen on Jeremy all the time. Look"—she squirted lotion on her hand and haphazardly slapped it across Jeremy's face— "*I* am putting sunscreen on my boyfriend. Because I don't want him to get melanoma. Am I 'inappropriate'?"

Olive was going to murder her. Olive was going to make her lick every drop of this stupid sunscreen and watch her writhe in pain as she slowly died of oxybenzone poisoning.

Later, though. For now, Adam was looking at her, expression completely unreadable, and Olive would have apologized, she would have crawled under the table, she would have at least waved at him—but all she could do was stare and notice that even though the last time they'd talked she'd insulted him, he didn't really seem angry. Just thoughtful and a little confused as he looked between Olive's face and the small lake of white goop that now lived in her hands, probably trying to figure out if there was a way to get out of this latest shitshow—and then, finally, just giving up on it.

He nodded once, minutely, and turned around, the muscles in his back shifting as he threw Dr. Rodrigues the Frisbee and yelled, "I'm taking five!"

Which, Olive assumed, meant that they were actually doing this. Of course they damn were. Because this was her life, and these were her poor, moronic, harebrained choices.

"Hey," Adam said to her once they were closer. He was looking at her hands, at the way she had to hold them in front of her body like a supplicant. Behind her, Anh and Jeremy were no doubt ogling them.

"Hey." She was wearing flip-flops, and he had sneakers on, and—he was always tall, but right now he towered over her. It put her eyes right in front of his pecs, and . . . *No. Nope. Not doing that.*

"Can you turn around?"

He hesitated for a moment, but then he did, uncharacteristically obedient. Which ended up resolving none of Olive's problems, since his back was in no way less broad or impressive than his chest.

"Can you, um . . . duck a bit?"

Adam bent his head until his shoulders were . . . still abnormally high but somewhat easier to reach. As she lifted her right hand, some of the lotion dripped to the ground—*Where it belongs*, she thought savagely—and then she was doing it, this thing that she had never thought she would ever, ever do. Putting sunscreen on Adam Carlsen.

It wasn't her first time touching him. Therefore, she shouldn't have been surprised by how hard his muscles were, or that there was no give to his flesh. Olive remembered the way he'd pushed the truck, imagined that he could probably bench-press three times her weight, and then ordered herself to stop, because that was *not* an appropriate train of thought. Still, the issue remained that there was nothing between her hand and his skin. He was hot from the sun, his shoulders relaxed and immobile under her touch. Even in public, close as they were, it felt like something intimate was happening.

"So." Her mouth was dry. "This might be a good time to mention how sorry I am that we keep getting stuck in these situations."

"It's fine."

"I really am, though."

"It's not your fault." There was an edge in his voice.

"Are you okay?"

"Yep." He nodded, though the movement seemed taut. Which had Olive realizing that maybe he was not as relaxed as she'd initially thought.

"How much do you hate this, on a scale from one to 'correlation equals causation'?"

He surprised her by chuckling, though he still sounded strained. "I don't hate it. And it's not your fault."

"Because I know this is the worst possible thing, and—"

"It isn't. Olive." He turned a bit to look her in the eyes, a mix of amusement and that odd tension. "These things are going to keep on happening."

"Right."

His fingers brushed softly against her left palm as he stole a bit of her sunscreen for his front. Which, all in all, was for the best. She really didn't want to be massaging lotion into his chest in front of 70 percent of her Ph.D. program—not to mention her boss, since Dr. Aslan was probably watching them like a hawk. Or maybe she wasn't. Olive had no intention of turning around to check. She'd rather live in less-than-blissful ignorance. "Mostly because you hang out with some really nosy people."

She burst out laughing. "I know. Believe me, I'm *really* regretting befriending Anh right now. Kind of contemplating assassinating her, to tell the truth."

She moved to his shoulder blades. He had a lot of small moles and freckles, and she wondered exactly how inappropriate it would be if she played connect the dots on them with her fingers. She could just imagine the amazing pictures it would reveal.

"But hey, the long-term benefits of sunscreen have been proven by scientists. And you *are* pretty pale. Here, duck a bit more, so I can get your neck."

"Mmm."

She walked around him to get to the front part of his shoulders. He was so big, she was going to have to use all this stupid lotion. Might even need to ask Anh for more. "At least the department chair is getting a show. And you look like you're having fun."

He glanced pointedly at the way her hand was spreading sunscreen on his collarbone. Olive's cheeks burned. "No, I mean—not because I am . . . I meant, you look like you're having a good time playing Frisbee. Or whatever."

He made a face. "Beats chitchatting, for sure."

She laughed. "That makes sense. I bet that's why you're so fit. You played lots of sports growing up because it got you out of talking with people. It also explains why now that you're an adult your personality is so—" Olive stopped short.

Adam lifted one eyebrow. "Antagonistic and unapproachable?"

Crap. "I didn't say that."

"You just typed it."

"I-I'm sorry. I'm very sorry. I didn't mean to—" She pressed her lips together, flustered. Then she noticed that the corners of his eyes were crinkling. "Damn you."

She pinched him lightly on the underside of his arm. He yelped and smiled wider, which made her wonder what he would do if she retaliated by writing her name with sunscreen on his chest, just enough for him to only get a tan around it. She tried to imagine his face after taking off his T-shirt, finding the five letters printed on his flesh in the reflection of his bathroom mirror. The expression he'd make. Whether he'd touch them with his fingertips.

Crazy, she told herself. *This whole thing, it's driving you crazy. So he's handsome, and you find him attractive. Big deal. Who cares?*

She wiped her mostly lotion-free hands down the columns of his biceps and took a step back. "You're good to go, Dr. Antagonistic."

He smelled of fresh sweat, himself, and coconut. Olive wasn't going to get to talk with him again until Wednesday, and why the thought came with an odd pang in her chest, she had no clue.

"Thanks. And thank Anh, I guess."

"Mm. What do you think she'll have us do next time?"

He shrugged. "Hold hands?"

"Feed each other strawberries?"

"Good one."

"Maybe she'll up her game."

"Fake wedding?"

"Fake-buy a house together?"

"Fake-sign the mortgage paperwork?"

Olive laughed, and the way he looked at her, kind and curious and patient . . . she must be hallucinating it. Her head was not right. She should have brought a sun hat.

"Hey, Olive."

She tore her gaze from Adam's and noticed Tom approaching. He, too, was shirtless, and clearly fit, and had a large number of abs that were defined enough to be easily counted. And yet, for some reason, it did absolutely nothing for Olive.

"Hi, Tom." She smiled, even though she was a little irritated by the interruption. "Loved your talk the other day."

"It was good, wasn't it? Did Adam tell you about our change of plans?"

She tilted her head. "Change of plans?"

"We've been making great progress on the grant, so we're going to Boston next week to finish setting up stuff on the Harvard side."

"Oh, that's great." She turned to Adam. "How long will you be gone?"

"Just a few days." His tone was quiet. Olive felt relief that it wasn't going to be longer. For indiscernible reasons.

"Would you be able to send me your report by Saturday, Olive?" Tom asked. "Then I'll have the weekend to look it over, and we'll discuss it while I'm still here."

Her brain exploded in a flurry of panic and bright red-alert signs, but she managed to keep her smile in place. "Yeah, of course. I'll send it to you on Saturday." Oh God. Oh *God*. She was going to have to work around the clock. She wasn't going to get any sleep this week. She was going to have to bring her laptop to the toilet and write while she peed. "No problem at all," she added, leaning even harder into her lie.

"Perfect." Tom winked at her, or maybe just squinted in the sun. "You going back to play?" he asked Adam, and when Adam nodded, Tom spun around and headed back into the game.

Adam hesitated for just a second longer, then he nodded at Olive and left. She tried hard not to stare at his back as he rejoined his team, which seemed to be overjoyed to have him again. Clearly, sports were another thing Adam Carlsen excelled at—unfairly so.

She didn't even have to check to know that Anh and Jeremy and pretty much everyone else had been staring at them for the past five minutes. She fished a seltzer can out of the nearest cooler, reminding herself that this was exactly what they wanted from this arrangement, and then found a spot under an oak tree next to her friends—all this sunscreen fuss, and now they were sitting in the shade. Go figure.

She wasn't even that hungry anymore, a small miracle courtesy of having to apply sunscreen to her fake boyfriend very publicly.

"So, what's he like?" Anh asked. She was lying down with her head on Jeremy's lap. Above her, Malcolm was staring at the Frisbee players, probably swooning over how pretty Holden Rodrigues looked in the sun.

"Mm?"

"Carlsen. Oh, actually"—Anh smirked—"I meant to say *Adam*. You call him Adam, right? Or do you prefer Dr. Carlsen? If you guys role-play with schoolgirl uniforms and rulers, I totally want to hear about it."

"Anh."

"Yeah, how *is* Carlsen?" Jeremy asked. "I'm assuming he's different with you than with us. Or does he also tell *you* repeat-

edly that the font for the labels of your x- and y-axis is irritatingly small?"

Olive smiled into her knees, because she could totally imagine
Adam saying that. Could almost hear his voice in her head.
"No. Not yet, at least."

"What's he like, then?"

She opened her mouth to answer, thinking it would be easy.
Of course, it was everything but. "He's just . . . you know."

"We don't," Anh said. "There must be more to him than
meets the eye. He's so moody and negative and angry and—"

"He's not," Olive interrupted. And then regretted it a little, because it wasn't entirely true. "He *can* be. But he can *not* be, too."

"If you say so." Anh seemed unconvinced. "How did you
even start dating? You never told me."

"Oh." Olive looked away and let her gaze wander. Adam
must have just done something noteworthy, because he and Dr.
Rodrigues were exchanging a high five. She noticed Tom staring
at her from the field and waved at him with a smile. "Um, we
just talked. And then got coffee. And then . . ."

"How does that even happen?" Jeremy interrupted, clearly
skeptical. "How does one decide to say yes to a date with
Carlsen? Before seeing him half-naked, anyway."

*You kiss him. You kiss him, and then, next thing you know,
he's saving your ass and he's buying you scones and calling you
a smart-ass in a weirdly affectionate tone, and even when he's
being his moody asshole self, he doesn't seem to be that bad. Or
bad at all. And then you tell him to fuck off over the phone and
possibly ruin everything.*

"He just asked me out. And I said yes." Though it was obviously a lie. Someone with a *Lancet* publication and back muscles
that defined would never ask someone like Olive out.

"So you didn't meet on Tinder?"

"What? No."

"Because that's what people are saying."

"I'm not on Tinder."

"Is Carlsen?"

No. Maybe. Yes? Olive massaged her temples. "Who's saying that we met on Tinder?"

"Actually, rumor's that they met on Craigslist," Malcolm said distractedly, waving at someone. She followed his gaze and noticed that he was staring at Holden Rodrigues—who appeared to be smiling and waving back.

Olive frowned. Then she parsed what Malcolm had just said. "*Craigslist?*"

Malcolm shrugged. "Not saying that I believed it."

"Who are *people*? And why are they even talking about us?"

Anh reached up to pat Olive on the shoulder. "Don't worry, the gossip about you and Carlsen died down after Dr. Moss and Sloane had that very public argument about people disposing of blood samples in the ladies' restroom. Well, for the most part. Hey."

She sat up and wrapped an arm around Olive, pulling her in for an embrace. She smelled like coconut. Stupid, stupid sunscreen.

"Chill. I know some people have been weird about this, but Jeremy and Malcolm and I are just happy for you, Ol." Anh smiled at her reassuringly, and Olive felt herself relax. "Mostly that you're finally getting laid."

Chapter Eight

❤ **HYPOTHESIS:** *On a Likert scale ranging from one to ten, Jeremy's timing will be negative fifty, with a standard error of the mean of zero point two.*

Number thirty-seven—salt-and-vinegar potato chips—was sold out. It was frankly inexplicable: Olive had come in at 8:00 p.m., and there had been at least one bag left in the break room's vending machine. She distinctly remembered patting the back pocket of her jeans for quarters, and the feeling of triumph at finding exactly four. She recalled looking forward to that moment, approximately two hours later, by which time she estimated that she'd have completed exactly a third of her work and would thus be able to reward herself with the indisputable best among the snacks that the fourth floor had to offer. Except that the moment had come, and there were no chips left. Which was a problem, because Olive had already inserted her precious quarters inside the coin slot, and she was very hungry.

She selected number twenty-four (Twix)—which was okay, though not her favorite by a long shot—and listened to its dull, disappointing thud as it fell to the bottom shelf. Then she bent to pick it up, staring wistfully at the way the gold wrapper shined in her palm.

"I wish you were salt-and-vinegar chips," she whispered at it, a trace of resentment in her voice.

"Here."

"Aaah!" She startled and instantly turned around, hands in front of her body and ready to defend—possibly even to attack. But the only person in the break room was Adam, sitting on one of the small couches in the middle, looking at her with a bland, slightly amused expression.

She relaxed her pose and clutched her hands to her chest, willing her racing heartbeat to slow down. "When did you get here?!"

"Five minutes ago?" He regarded her calmly. "I was here when you came in."

"Why didn't you *say* something?"

He tilted his head. "I could ask the same."

She covered her mouth with her hand, trying to recover from the scare. "I didn't see you. Why are you sitting in the dark like a creep?"

"Light's broken. As usual." Adam lifted his drink—a bottle of Coke that hilariously read "Seraphina"—and Olive remembered Jess, one of his grads, complaining about how strict Adam was about bringing food and drinks into his lab. He grabbed something from the cushion and held it out to Olive. "Here. You can have the rest of the chips."

Olive narrowed her eyes. "You."

"Me?"

"You stole my chips."

His mouth curved. "Sorry. You can have what's left." He peeked into the bag. "I didn't have many, I don't think."

She hesitated and then made her way to the couch. She distrustfully accepted the small bag and took a seat next to him. "Thanks, I guess."

He nodded, taking a sip of his drink. She tried not to stare at his throat as he tipped his head back, averting her eyes to her knees.

"Should you be having caffeine at"—Olive glanced at the clock—"ten twenty-seven p.m.?" Come to think of it, he shouldn't be having caffeine at all, given his baseline shiny personality. And yet the two of them got coffee together every Wednesday. Olive was nothing but an enabler.

"I doubt I'll be sleeping much, anyway."

"Why?"

"I need to run a set of last-minute analyses for a grant due on Sunday night."

"Oh." She leaned back, finding a more comfortable position. "I thought you had minions for that."

"As it turns out, asking your grads to pull an all-nighter for you is frowned upon by HR."

"What a travesty."

"Truly. What about you?"

"Tom's report." She sighed. "I'm supposed to send it to him tomorrow and there's a section that I just don't . . ." She sighed again. "I'm rerunning a few analyses, just to make sure that everything is *perfect*, but the equipment I'm working with is not exactly . . . *ugh.*"

"Have you told Aysegul?"

Aysegul, he'd said. Naturally. Because Adam was a colleague of Dr. Aslan, not her grad, and it made sense that he'd think of her as Aysegul. It wasn't the first time he'd called her that; it wasn't even the first time Olive had noticed. It was just hard to reconcile, when they were sitting alone and talking quietly, that Adam was faculty and Olive was very much not. Worlds apart, really.

"I did, but there's no money to get anything better. She's a great mentor, but . . . last year her husband got sick and she decided to retire early, and sometimes it feels like she's stopped caring." Olive rubbed her temple. She could feel a headache coming up and had a long night ahead of her. "Are you going to tell her I told you that?"

"Of course."

She groaned. "Don't."

"Might also tell her about the kisses you've been extorting, and the fake-dating scheme you roped me into, and above all about the sunscreen—"

"Oh God." Olive hid her face in her knees, arms coming up to wrap around her head. "God. The sunscreen."

"Yeah." His voice sounded muffled from down here. "Yeah, that was . . ."

"Awkward?" she offered, sitting back straight with a grimace. Adam was looking elsewhere. She was probably imagining it, the way he was flushing.

He cleared his throat. "Among other things."

"Yep." It had been other things, too. A lot of things that she was not going to mention, because *her* other things were sure to not be *his* other things. His other things were probably "terrible" and "harrowing" and "invasive." While hers . . .

"Is the sunscreen going in the Title IX complaint?"

His mouth twitched. "Right on the first page. *Nonconsensual sunblock application.*"

"Oh, come on. I saved you from basal cell carcinoma."

"*Groped under SPF pretense.*"

She swatted him with her Twix, and he ducked a bit to avoid her, amused. "Hey, you want half of this? Since I fully plan to eat what's left of your chips."

"Nah."

"You sure?"

"Can't stand chocolate."

Olive stared at him, shaking her head in disbelief. "You would, wouldn't you? Hate everything that is delicious and lovely and comforting."

"Chocolate's disgusting."

"You just want to live in your dark, bitter world made of black coffee and plain bagels with plain cream cheese. And occasionally salt-and-vinegar chips."

"They are clearly your favorite chips—"

"Not the point."

"—and I am flattered that you've memorized my orders."

"It does help that they're always the same."

"At least I've never ordered something called a *unicorn Frappuccino*."

"That was so good. It tasted like the rainbow."

"Like sugar and food coloring?"

"My two favorite things in the universe. Thank you for buying it for me, by the way." It had made for a nice fake-dating Wednesday treat this week, even though Olive had been so busy with Tom's report that she hadn't been able to exchange more than a couple of words with Adam. Which, she had to admit, had been a little disappointing.

"Where's Tom by the way, while you and I slave our Friday night away?"

"Out. On a date, I think."

"On a date? Does his girlfriend live here?"

"Tom has lots of girlfriends. In lots of places."

"But are any of them fake?" She beamed at him, and could tell that he was tempted to smile back. "Would you like half a dollar, then? For the chips?"

"Keep it."

"Great. Because it's about a third of my monthly salary."

She actually managed to make him laugh, and—it didn't just transform his face, it changed the entire space they were inhabiting. Olive had to convince her lungs not to stop working, to keep taking in oxygen, and her eyes not to get lost in the little lines at the corners of his eyes, the dimples in the center of his cheeks. "Glad to hear that grad students' stipends have not increased since I was one."

"Did you use to live on instant ramen and bananas during your Ph.D., too?"

"I don't like bananas, but I remember having lots of apples."

"Apples are expensive, you fiscally irresponsible splurger." She tilted her head and wondered if it was okay to ask the one thing she'd been dying to know. She told herself that it was probably inappropriate—and then went for it anyway. "How old are you?"

"Thirty-four."

"Oh. Wow." She'd thought younger. Or older, maybe. She'd thought he existed in an ageless dimension. It was so weird to hear a number. To have a year of birth, almost a whole decade before hers. "I'm twenty-six." Olive wasn't sure why she offered up the information, since he hadn't asked. "It's odd to think that you used to be a student, too."

"Is it?"

"Yep. Were you like this as an undergrad, too?"

"Like this?"

"You know." She batted her eyes at him. "Antagonistic and unapproachable."

He glared, but she was starting to not take that too seriously. "I might have been worse, actually."

"I bet." There was a brief, comfortable silence as she sat back and began to tackle her bag of chips. It was all she'd ever wanted from a vending machine snack. "So does it get better?"

"What?"

"This." She gestured inchoately around herself. "Academia. Does it get better, after grad school? Once you have tenure?"

"No. God, no." He looked so horrified by the assumption, she had to laugh.

"Why do you stick around, then?"

"Unclear." There was a flash of something in his eyes that Olive couldn't quite interpret, but—nothing surprising about that. There was a lot about Adam Carlsen she didn't know. He was an ass, but with unexpected depths. "There's an element of sunk-cost fallacy, probably—hard to step away, when you've invested so much time and energy. But the science makes it worth it. When it works, anyway."

She hummed, considering his words, and remembered The Guy in the bathroom. He'd said that academia was a lot of bucks for little bang, and that one needed a good reason to stick around. Olive wondered where he was now. If he'd managed to graduate. If he knew that he'd helped someone make one of the hardest decisions of their life. If he had any idea that there was a girl, somewhere in the world, who thought about their random encounter surprisingly often. Doubtful.

"I know grad school is supposed to be miserable for everyone, but it's depressing to see tenured faculty here on a Friday night, instead of, I don't know, watching Netflix in bed, or getting dinner with their girlfriend—"

"I thought you were my girlfriend."

Olive smiled up at him. "Not quite." *But, since we're on the topic: why exactly don't you have one? Because it's getting harder and harder for me to figure that one out. Except that maybe you just don't want one. Maybe you just want to be on your own, like everything about your behavior suggests, and here I am, annoying the shit out of you. I should just pocket my*

chips and my candy and go back to my stupid protein samples,
but for some reason you are so comfortable to be around. And
I am drawn to you, even though I don't know why.

"Do you plan to stay in academia?" he asked. "After you
graduate."

"Yes. Maybe. No."

He smiled, and Olive laughed.

"Undecided."

"Right."

"It's just . . . there are things that I love about it. Being in the
lab, doing research. Coming up with study ideas, feeling that I'm
doing something meaningful. But if I go the academic route,
then I'll also need to do a lot of other things that I just . . ." She
shook her head.

"Other things?"

"Yeah. The PR stuff, mostly. Write grants and convince people to fund my research. Network, which is a special kind of
hell. Public speaking, or even one-on-one situations where I have
to impress people. That's the worst, actually. I hate it so much—
my head explodes and I freeze and everyone is looking at me
ready to judge me and my tongue paralyzes and I start wishing
that I was dead and then that *the world* was dead and—" She
noticed his smile and gave him a rueful look. "You get the gist."

"There are things you can do about that, if you want. It just
takes practice. Making sure your thoughts are organized. Stuff
like that."

"I know. And I try to do that—I did it before my meeting
with Tom. And I still stammered like an idiot when he asked me
a simple question." *And then you helped me, ordered my*
thoughts, and saved my ass, without even meaning to. "I don't
know. Maybe my brain is broken."

He shook his head. "You did great during that meeting with

Tom, especially considering that you were forced to have your fake boyfriend sit next to you." She didn't point out that his presence had actually made things better. "Tom certainly seemed impressed, which is no small feat. And if anyone screwed up, it was definitely him. I'm sorry he did that, by the way."

"Did what?"

"Force you to talk about your personal life."

"Oh." Olive looked away, toward the blue glow of the vending machine. "It's okay. It's been a while." She was surprised to hear herself continue. To feel herself *wanting* to continue. "Since high school, really."

"That's . . . young." There was something about his tone, maybe the evenness, maybe the lack of overt sympathy, that she found reassuring.

"I was fifteen. One day my mom and I were there, just . . . I don't even know. Kayaking. Thinking about getting a cat. Arguing over the way I'd pile stuff on top of the trash can when it was overflowing and I didn't want to take it out. And next thing I knew she had her diagnosis, and three weeks later she'd already—" She couldn't say it. Her lips, her vocal folds, her heart, they just wouldn't form the words. So she swallowed them. "The child welfare system couldn't figure out where to send me until I became of age."

"Your dad?"

She shook her head. "Never in the picture. He's an asshole, according to my mom." She laughed softly. "The never-takes-out-the-trash gene clearly came from his side of the family. And my grandparents had died when I was a kid, because apparently that's what people around me do." She tried to say it jokingly, she really tried. To not sound bitter. She thought she even succeeded. "I was just . . . alone."

"What did you do?"

"Foster home until sixteen, then I emancipated." She shrugged, hoping to brush off the memory. "If only they'd caught it earlier, even just by a few months—maybe she'd be here. Maybe surgery and chemo would have actually done something. And I . . . I was always good at science stuff, so I thought that the least I could do was . . ."

Adam dug into his pockets for a few moments and held out a crumpled paper napkin. Olive stared at it, confused, until she realized that her cheeks had somehow grown wet.

Oh.

"Adam, did you just offer me a used tissue?"

"I . . . maybe." He pressed his lips together. "I panicked."

She chuckled wetly, accepting his gross tissue and using it to blow her nose. They'd kissed twice, after all. Why not share a bit of snot? "I'm sorry. I'm usually not like this."

"Like what?"

"Weepy. I . . . I shouldn't talk about this."

"Why?"

"Because." It was hard to explain, the mix of pain and affection that always resurfaced when she talked about her mother. It was the reason she almost never did it, and the reason she hated cancer so much. Not only had it robbed her of the person she loved the most, but it had also turned the happiest memories of her life into something bittersweet. "It makes me weepy."

He smiled. "Olive, you can talk about it. And you should let yourself be weepy."

She had a sense that he really meant it. That she could have talked about her mom for however long she liked, and he would have listened intently to every second of it. She wasn't sure she was ready for it, though. So she shrugged, changing the topic. "Anyway, now here I am. Loving lab work and barely dealing with the rest—abstracts, conferences, networking. Teaching.

Rejected grants." Olive gestured in Adam's direction. "Failed dissertation proposals."

"Is your lab mate still giving you a hard time?"

Olive waved her hand dismissively. "I'm not his favorite person, but it's fine. He'll get over it." She bit into her lip. "I'm sorry about the other night. I was rude. You have every right to be mad."

Adam shook his head. "It's okay. I understand where you were coming from."

"I do get what you're saying. About not wanting to form a new generation of crappy millennial scientists."

"I don't believe I've ever used the expression 'crappy millennial scientists.'"

"But FYI, I still think that you don't need to be that harsh when you give feedback. We get the gist of what you're saying, even if you give criticism more nicely."

He looked at her for a long time. Then he nodded, once. "Noted."

"Are you going to be less harsh, then?"

"Unlikely."

She sighed. "You know, when I have no more friends and everyone hates me because of this fake-dating thing, I'll be super lonely and you are going to have to hang out with me every day. I'll annoy you all the time. Is it really worth being mean to every grad in the program?"

"Absolutely."

She sighed again, this time with a smile, and let the side of her head rest on his shoulder. It might have been a bit forward, but it felt natural—maybe because they seemed to have a knack for getting themselves in situations that required PDA of some sort, maybe because of everything they'd been talking about, maybe because of the hour of the night. Adam . . . well, he didn't act as if he minded. He was just there, quiet, relaxed, warm and solid through the cotton of his black shirt under her temple. It felt like a long time before he broke the silence.

"I'm not sorry for asking Greg to revise his proposal. But I am sorry that I created a situation that led him to take it out on you. That as long as this continues, it might happen again."

"Well, I am sorry about the texts I sent," she said again. "And you're fine. Even if you're antagonistic and unapproachable."

"Good to hear."

"I should go back to the lab." She sat up, one hand coming to massage the base of her neck. "My disastrous blotting is not going to fix itself."

Adam blinked, and there was a gleam in his eyes, as if he hadn't thought she'd leave so soon. As if he'd have liked for her to stay. "Why disastrous?"

She groaned. "It's just . . ." She reached for her phone and tapped on the home button, pulling up a picture of her last Western blot. "See?" She pointed at the target protein. "This—it shouldn't . . ."

He nodded, thoughtful. "You're sure the starting sample was good? And the gel?"

"Yep, not runny, or dried out."

"It looks like the antibody might be the problem."

She looked up at him. "You think so?"

"Yep. I'd check the dilution and the buffer. If not that, it might also be a wonky secondary antibody. Come by my lab if it still doesn't work; you can borrow ours. Same for other pieces of equipment or supplies. If there's anything you need, just ask my lab manager."

"Oh, wow. Thank you." She smiled. "Now I'm actually a bit sorry that I can't have you on my dissertation committee. Perhaps rumors of your cruelty have been greatly exaggerated."

His mouth twitched. "Maybe you just pull out the best in me?"

She grinned. "Then maybe I should stick around. Just, you know, to save the department from your terrible moods?"

He glanced at the picture of the failed Western blot in her hand. "Well, it doesn't look like you're going to graduate anytime soon."

She half laughed, half gasped. "Oh my God. Did you just—?"

"Objectively—"

"This is the rudest, meanest thing—" She was laughing. Holding her stomach as she waved her finger at him.

"—based on your blotting—"

"—that anyone could *ever* say to a Ph.D. student. Ever."

"I think I can find meaner things. If I really put myself to it."

"We're done." She wished she weren't smiling. Then maybe he'd take her seriously instead of just looking at her with that patient, amused expression. "Seriously. It was nice while it lasted." She made to stand and leave indignantly, but he grabbed the sleeve of her shirt and gently tugged at it until she was sitting down again, next to him on the narrow couch—maybe even a little closer than before. She continued glaring, but he regarded her blandly, clearly unperturbed.

"There's nothing bad about taking more than five years to graduate," he offered in a conciliatory tone.

Olive huffed. "You just want me to stay around forever. Until you have the biggest, fattest, strongest Title IX case to ever exist."

"That was my plan all along, in fact. The one and only reason I kissed you out of the blue."

"Oh, shut up." She ducked her chin into her chest, biting into her lip and hoping he wouldn't notice her grinning like the idiot she was. "Hey, can I ask you something?"

Adam looked at her expectantly, like he seemed to a lot lately, so she continued, her tone softer and quieter.

"Why are you really doing this?"

"Doing what?"

"The fake dating. I understand that you want to look like you're not a flight risk, but . . . Why aren't you *really* dating someone? I mean, you're not that bad."

"High praise."

"No, come on, what I meant was . . . Based on your fake-dating behavior, I'm sure that a lot of women . . . well, *some* women would love to real-date you." She bit into her lip again, playing with the hole that was opening up on the knee of her jeans. "We're friends. We weren't when we started, but we are now. You can tell me."

"Are we?"

She nodded. *Yes. Yes, we are. Come on.* "Well, you did just break one of the sacred tenets of academic friendships by mentioning my graduation timeline. But I'll forgive you if you tell me if this is really better for you than . . . you know, getting a *real* girlfriend."

"It is."

"Really?"

"Yes." He seemed honest. He was honest. Adam was not a liar; Olive would bet her life on it.

"Why, though? Do you enjoy the sunscreen-mediated fondling? And the opportunity to donate hundreds of your dollars to the campus Starbucks?"

He smiled faintly. And then he wasn't smiling anymore. Not looking at her, either, but somewhere in the direction of the crumpled plastic wrapper that she'd tossed on the table a few minutes go.

He swallowed. She could see his jaw work.

"Olive." He took a deep breath. "You should know that—"

"Oh my God!"

They both startled, Olive considerably more so than Adam, and turned toward the entrance. Jeremy stood there, one hand dramatically clutching his sternum. "You guys scared the shit out of me. What are you doing sitting in the dark?"

What are you *doing here?* Olive thought ungraciously. "Just chatting," she said. Though it didn't seem like a good descriptor of what was going on. And yet, she couldn't put her finger on why.

"You scared me," Jeremy repeated once more. "Are you working on your report, Ol?"

"Yeah." She stole a quick glance at Adam, who was motionless and expressionless next to her. "Just taking a quick break. I was about to go back, actually."

"Oh, cool. Me too." Jeremy smiled, pointing in the direction of his lab. "I need to go isolate a bunch of virgin fruit flies. Before they're not virgins anymore, you know?" He wiggled his eyebrows, and Olive had to force out a small, unconvincing laugh. She usually enjoyed his sense of humor. Usually. Now she just wished . . . She wasn't sure what she wished. "You coming with, Ol?"

No, I'm fine right here, actually. "Sure." Reluctantly, she stood. Adam did the same, gathering their wrappers and his empty bottle and sorting them in the recycling bins.

"Have a good night, Dr. Carlsen," Jeremy said from the entrance. Adam just nodded at him, a touch curtly. The set of his eyes was yet again impossible to decipher.

I guess that's it, then, she thought. Where the weight in her chest had come from, she had no clue. She was probably just tired. Had eaten too much, or not enough.

"See you, Adam. Right?" she murmured before he could head for the entrance and leave the room. Her voice was pitched low enough that Jeremy couldn't possibly have heard her. Maybe Adam hadn't, either. Except that he paused for a moment. And then, when he walked past her, she had the impression of knuckles brushing against the back of her hand.

"Good night, Olive."

Chapter Nine

~~~~~~

♥ **HYPOTHESIS:** *The more I mention an attachment in an email, the less likely I will be to actually include said attachment.*

SATURDAY, 6:34 p.m.
FROM: Olive-Smith@stanford.edu
TO: Tom-Benton@harvard.edu
SUBJECT: Re: Report on Pancreatic Cancer Study

Hi Tom,
Here is the report you asked for, with a detailed description of what I have done so far, as well as my thoughts on future directions and the resources I will need to expand. I'm excited to hear your thoughts on my work!

Sincerely,
Olive

SATURDAY, 6:35 p.m.
FROM: Olive-Smith@stanford.edu
TO: Tom-Benton@harvard.edu
SUBJECT: Re: Report on Pancreatic Cancer Study

Hi Tom,
Oops, forgot the attachment.

Sincerely,
Olive

Today, 3:20 p.m.
FROM: Tom-Benton@harvard.edu
TO: Olive-Smith@stanford.edu
SUBJECT: Re: Report on Pancreatic Cancer Study

Olive,
Done reading the report. Do you think you could come over to Adam's to chat about it? Maybe tomorrow morning (Tue) at nine? Adam and I will be leaving for Boston on Wed afternoon.

TB

Olive's heart beat faster—whether at the idea of being in Adam's home or at the thought of getting her answer from Tom, she wasn't sure. She immediately texted Adam.

Olive: Tom just invited me to your place to talk about the report I sent him. Would it be okay if I came over?

Adam: Of course. When?

Olive: Tomorrow at 9 a.m. Will you be home?

Adam: Probably. There are no bike lanes to my house. Do you need a ride? I can pick you up.

She thought about it for a few moments and decided that she liked the idea a little too much.

Olive: My roommate can drive me, but thanks for offering.

〰〰〰

MALCOLM DROPPED HER off in front of a beautiful Spanish colonial house with stucco walls and arched windows and refused to back out of the driveway until Olive agreed to slide a can of pepper spray in her backpack. She walked over the brick-tile path and up to the entrance, marveling at the green of the yard and at the cozy atmosphere of the porch. She was about to ring the doorbell when she heard her name.

Adam was behind her, bathed in sweat and clearly just back from his morning run. He was wearing sunglasses, shorts, and a Princeton Undergrad Mathletes T-shirt that stuck to his chest. Out of the ensemble, the only nonblack items were the AirPods in his ears, peeking through the damp waves of his hair. She felt her cheeks curve into a smile, trying to imagine what he was listening to. Probably Coil, or Kraftwerk. The Velvet Underground. A TED Talk on water-efficient landscaping. Whale noises.

She would have given a huge chunk of her salary in exchange for five minutes alone with his phone, just to mess with his playlist. Add Taylor Swift, Beyoncé, maybe some Ariana. Broaden his horizons. She couldn't see his eyes behind the dark lenses, but she didn't need to. His mouth had curved as soon as he'd noticed her, his smile slight but definitely there.

"You okay?" he asked.

Olive realized that she'd been staring. "Um, yeah. Sorry. You?"

He nodded. "Did you find the house all right?"

"Yes. I was just about to knock."

"No need." He passed her and opened the door for her, waiting until she'd stepped inside to close it after them. She caught a whiff of his scent—sweat and soap and something dark and good—and wondered anew at how familiar it had become to her. "Tom's probably this way."

Adam's place was light, spacious, and simply furnished. "No taxidermied animals?" she asked under her breath.

He was clearly about to flip her off when they found Tom in the kitchen, typing on his laptop. He looked up at her and grinned—which, she hoped, was a good sign.

"Thanks for coming, Olive. I wasn't sure I'd have time to go to campus before leaving. Sit down, please." Adam disappeared from the room, probably to go shower, and Olive felt her heart pick up. Tom had made his decision. Her destiny was going to be defined by the next few minutes.

"Can you clarify a couple of things for me?" he asked, turning his laptop toward her and pointing at one of the figures she'd sent. "To make sure I understand your protocols correctly."

When Adam came back twenty minutes later, hair damp and wearing one of his ten million black Henleys that were all a tiny bit different and yet still managed to fit him in the most irritatingly perfect way, she was just wrapping up an explanation of her RNA analyses. Tom was taking notes on his laptop.

"Whenever you guys are done, I can give you a ride back to campus, Olive," Adam offered. "I need to drive in, anyway."

"We're done," Tom said, still typing. "She's all yours."

Oh. Olive nodded and gingerly stood up. Tom hadn't given her an answer yet. He'd asked lots of interesting, smart questions about her project, but he hadn't told her whether he wanted to work with her next year. Did it mean that the answer was a no, but he'd rather not communicate it to Olive in her "boyfriend's" home? What if he'd never really thought that her work was worth funding? What if he'd just been faking it because

Adam was his friend? Adam had said that Tom wasn't like that, but what if he'd been wrong and now—

"You ready to go?" Adam asked. She grabbed her backpack, trying to collect herself. She was fine. This was fine. She could cry about this later.

"Sure." She rocked once on her heels, giving Tom one last look. Sadly, he seemed taken with his laptop. "Bye, Tom. It was nice to meet you. Have a safe trip home."

"Likewise," he said, not even glancing at her. "I had lots of interesting conversations."

"Yeah." It must have been the section on genome-based prognostics, she thought, following Adam out of the room. She'd suspected it was too weak, but she'd been stupid and she'd sent the report anyway. Stupid, stupid, *stupid*. She should have beefed it up. The most important thing now was to avoid crying until she was—

"And, Olive," Tom added.

She paused under the doorframe and looked back at him. "Yes?"

"I'll see you next year at Harvard, right?" His gaze finally slid up to meet hers. "I have the perfect bench set aside for you."

Her heart detonated. It absolutely exploded with joy in her chest, and Olive felt a violent wave of happiness, pride, and relief all wash over her. It could have easily knocked her to the floor, but by some miracle of biology she managed to stay upright and smile at Tom.

"I can't wait," she said, voice thick with happy tears. "Thank you so much."

He gave her a wink and one last smile, kind and encouraging. Olive barely managed to wait until she was outside to fist-pump, then jump around a few times, then fist-pump again.

"You all done?" Adam asked.

She turned around, remembering that she wasn't alone. His arms were folded on his chest, fingers drumming against his biceps. There was an indulgent expression in his eyes, and—she should have been embarrassed, but she just couldn't help it. Olive threw herself at him and hugged his torso as tight as she could. She closed her eyes when, after a few seconds of hesitation, he wrapped his arms around her.

"Congratulations," he whispered softly against her hair. Just like that Olive was on the verge of tears all over again.

Once they were in Adam's car—a Prius, to exactly no one's surprise—and driving to campus, she felt so happy she couldn't possibly be quiet.

"He'll take me. He said he'll take me."

"He'd be an idiot not to." Adam was smiling softly. "I knew he would."

"Had he told you?" Her eyes widened. "You knew, and you didn't even tell me—"

"He hadn't. We haven't discussed you."

"Oh?" She tilted her head, turning around in the car seat to better look at him. "Why?"

"Unspoken agreement. It might be a conflict of interest."

"Right." Sure. It made sense. Close friend and girlfriend. Fake girlfriend, actually.

"Can I ask you something?"

She nodded.

"There are lots of cancer labs in the US. Why did you choose Tom's?"

"Well, I sort of didn't. I emailed several people—two of whom are at UCSF, which is much closer than Boston. But Tom was the only one who answered." She leaned her head against the seat. It occurred to her for the first time that she was going to have to leave her life for an entire year. Her apartment with

Malcolm, her nights spent with Anh. Adam, even. She immediately pushed the thought away, not ready to entertain it. "Why do professors never answer students' emails, by the way?"

"Because we get approximately two hundred a day, and most of them are iterations of 'why do I have a C minus?'" He was quiet for a moment. "My advice for the future is to have your adviser reach out, instead of doing it yourself."

She nodded and stored away the information. "I'm glad Harvard worked out, though. It's going to be amazing. Tom is such a big name, and the amount of work I can do in his lab is limitless. I'll be running studies twenty-four seven, and if the results are what I think they'll be, I'll be able to publish in high-impact journals and probably get a clinical trial started in just a few years." She felt high on the prospect. "Hey, you and I now have a collaborator in common, on top of being excellent fake-dating partners!" A thought occurred to her. "What is your and Tom's big grant about, anyway?"

"Cell-based models."

"Off-lattice?"

He nodded.

"Wow. That's cool stuff."

"It's the most interesting project I'm working on, for sure. Got the grant at the right moment, too."

"What do you mean?"

He was silent for a beat while he switched lanes. "It's different from my other grants—mostly genetic stuff. Which is interesting, don't get me wrong, but after ten years researching the same exact thing, I was in a rut."

"You mean . . . bored?"

"To death. I briefly considered going into industry."

Olive gasped. Switching from academia to industry was considered the ultimate betrayal.

"Don't worry." Adam smiled. "Tom saved the day. When I told him I wasn't enjoying research anymore, we brainstormed some new directions, found something we were both enthusiastic about, and wrote the grant."

Olive felt a sudden surge of gratitude toward Tom. Not only was he going to rescue her project, but he was the reason Adam was still around. The reason she'd gotten the opportunity to know him. "It must be nice to be excited about work again."

"It is. Academia takes a lot from you and gives back very little. It's hard to stick around without a good reason to do so."

She nodded absentmindedly, thinking that the words sounded familiar. Not just the content, but the delivery, too. Not surprising, though: it was exactly what The Guy in the bathroom had told her all those years ago. *Academia's a lot of bucks for very little bang. What matters is whether your reason to be in academia is good enough.*

Suddenly, something clicked in her brain.

The deep voice. The blurry dark hair. The crisp, precise way of talking. Could The Guy in the bathroom and Adam be . . .

No. Impossible. The Guy was a student—though, had he explicitly said so? No. No, what he'd said was *This is my lab's bathroom* and that he'd been there for six years, and he hadn't answered when she'd asked about his dissertation timeline, and—

Impossible. Improbable. Inconceivable.

Just like everything else about Adam and Olive.

Oh God. What if they'd *really* met years ago? He probably didn't remember, anyway. Surely. Olive had been no one. Still was no one. She thought about asking him, but why? He had no idea that a five-minute conversation with him had been the exact push Olive needed. That she'd thought about him for years.

Olive remembered her last words to him—*Maybe I'll see you next year*—and oh, if only she'd known. She felt a surge of something warm and soft in the squishy part of herself that she guarded most carefully. She looked at Adam, and it swelled even larger, even stronger, even hotter.

You, she thought. *You. You are just the most—*

The worst—

The best—

Olive laughed, shaking her head.

"What?" he asked, puzzled.

"Nothing." She grinned at him. "Nothing. Hey, you know what? You and I should go get coffee. To celebrate."

"Celebrate what?"

"Everything! Your grant. My year at Harvard. How great our fake dating is going."

It was probably unfair of her to ask, since they were not due for fake-dating coffee until tomorrow. But the previous Wednesday had lasted just a few short minutes, and since Friday night, there had been about thirty times when Olive had to forcibly remove her phone from her hands to avoid texting him things he couldn't possibly care about. He didn't need to know that he was right and the problem with her Western blot had been the antibody. There was no way he'd have answered her if on Saturday at 10:00 p.m., when she'd been dying to know if he was in his office, she had sent that *Hey, what are you up to?* message that she'd written and deleted twice. And she was glad she'd ended up chickening out of forwarding him that *Onion* article on sun-safety tips.

It was probably unfair of her to ask, and yet today was a momentous day, and she found herself wanting to celebrate. With him.

He bit the inside of his cheek, looking pensive. "Would it be actual coffee, or chamomile tea?"

"Depends. Will you go all moody on me?"

"I will if you get pumpkin stuff."

She rolled her eyes. "You have no taste." Her phone pinged with a reminder. "Oh, we should go to Fluchella, too. Before coffee."

A vertical line appeared between his brows. "I'm afraid to ask what that is."

"Fluchella," Olive repeated, though it was clearly not helpful, judging from how the line bisecting his forehead deepened. "Mass flu vaccination for faculty, staff, and students. At no charge."

Adam made a face. "It's called Fluchella?"

"Yep, like the festival. Coachella?"

Adam was clearly not familiar.

"Don't you get university emails about this stuff? There've been at least five."

"I have a great spam filter."

Olive frowned. "Does it block Stanford emails, too? Because it shouldn't. It might end up filtering out important messages from admin and students and—"

Adam arched one eyebrow.

"Oh. Right."

Don't laugh. Don't laugh. He doesn't need to know how much he makes you laugh.

"Well, we should go get our flu shots."

"I'm good."

"You got one already?"

"No."

"I'm pretty sure it's mandatory for everyone."

The set of Adam's shoulders clearly broadcasted that he was, in fact, *not* everyone. "I never get sick."

"I doubt it."

"You shouldn't."

"Hey, the flu is more serious than you might think."

"It's not that bad."

"It is, especially for people like you."

"Like me?"

"You know . . . people of a certain age."

His mouth twitched as he turned into the campus parking lot. "You smart-ass."

"Come on." She leaned forward, poking his biceps with her index finger. They had touched so much at this point. In public, and alone, and a mixture of the two. It didn't feel weird. It felt good and natural, like when Olive was with Anh, or Malcolm. "Let's go together."

He didn't budge, parallel parking in a spot that would have taken Olive about two hours of maneuvering to fit into. "I don't have time."

"You just agreed to go get coffee. You must have some time."

He finished parking in less than a minute and pressed his lips together. Not answering her.

"Why don't you want to get the shot?" She studied him suspiciously. "Are you some kind of anti-vaxxer?"

Oh, if looks could kill.

"Okay." She furrowed her brow. "Then why?"

"It's not worth the hassle." Was he fidgeting a little? Was he biting the inside of his lip?

"It literally takes ten minutes." She reached for him, tugging at the sleeve of his shirt. "You get there, they scan your university badge. They give you the shot." She felt his muscles tense under her fingertips as she said the last word. "Easy peasy, and the best part is, you don't get the flu for a whole year. Totally— *Oh*." Olive covered her mouth with her hand.

"What?"

"Oh my God."

"What?"

"Are you— Oh, Adam."

"What?"

"Are you afraid of needles?"

He went still. Completely immobile. He wasn't breathing anymore. "I'm not *afraid* of needles."

"It's okay," she said, making her tone as reassuring as possible.

"I know, since I'm not—"

"This is a safe space for you and your fear of needles."

"There is no fear of—"

"I get it, needles *are* scary."

"It's not—"

"You are allowed to be scared."

"I am *not*," he told her, a little too forcefully, and then turned away, clearing his throat and scratching the side of his neck.

Olive pressed her lips together, and then said, "Well, *I* used to be scared."

He looked at her, curious, so she continued.

"As a child. My . . ." She had to clear her throat. "My mother would have to hold me in a bear hug every time I needed a shot, or I'd thrash around too much. And she had to bribe me with ice cream, but the problem was that I wanted it *immediately* after my shot." She laughed. "So she'd buy an ice cream sandwich before the doctor's appointment, and by the time I was ready to eat, it'd be all melted in her purse and make a huge mess and . . ."

Dammit. She was weepy, again. In front of Adam, *again.*

"She sounds lovely," Adam said.

"She was."

"And to be clear, I'm not afraid of needles," he repeated. This time, his tone was warm and kind. "They just feel . . . disgusting."

She sniffled and looked up at him. The temptation to hug him was almost irresistible. But she'd already done that today, so she made do with patting him on the arm. "Aww."

He pinned her with a withering look. "Don't *aww* me."

Adorable. He was adorable. "No, really, they *are* gross. Stuff pokes at you, and then you bleed. The feeling of it—yikes."

She got out of the car and waited for him to do the same. When he joined her, she smiled at him reassuringly.

"I get it."

"You do?" He didn't seem convinced.

"Yep. They're horrible."

He was still a little distrustful. "They are."

"And scary." She wrapped her hand around his elbow and began to pull him in the direction of the Fluchella tent. "Still, you need to get over it. For science. I'm taking you to get a flu shot."

"I—"

"This is nonnegotiable. I'll hold your hand, during."

"I don't need you to hold my hand. Since I'm not going." Except that he *was* going. He could have planted his feet and stood his ground, and he would have turned into an immovable object; Olive would have had no way of dragging him anywhere. And yet.

She let her hand slide down to his wrist and looked up at him. "You *so* are."

"Please." He looked pained. "Don't make me."

He was *so* adorable. "It's for your own good. And for the good of the elderly people who might come in any proximity to you. Even more elderly than you, that is."

He sighed, defeated. "Olive."

"Come on. Maybe we're lucky and the chair will spot us. And I'll buy you an ice cream sandwich afterward."

"Will I be paying for this ice cream sandwich?" He sounded resigned now.

"Likely. Actually, scratch that, you probably don't like ice cream anyway, because you don't enjoy anything that's good in life." She kept on walking, pensively chewing on her lower lip. "Maybe the cafeteria has some raw broccoli?"

"I don't deserve this verbal abuse on top of the flu shot."

She beamed. "You're such a trooper. Even though the big bad needle is out to get you."

"You are a smart-ass." And yet, he didn't resist when she continued to pull him behind her.

It was ten on an early-September morning, the sun already shining too bright and too hot through the cotton of Olive's shirt, the sweetgum leaves still a deep green and showing no sign of turning. It felt different from the past few years, this summer that didn't seem to want to end, that was stretched full and ripe past the beginning of the semester. Undergrads must have been either dozing off in their midmorning classes or still asleep in bed, because for once that harried air of chaos that always coated the Stanford campus was missing. And Olive—Olive had a lab for next year. Everything she'd worked toward since fifteen, it was finally going to happen.

Life didn't get much better than this.

She smiled, smelling the flower beds and humming a tune under her breath as she and Adam walked quietly, side by side. As they made their way across the quad, her fingers slid down from his wrist and closed around his palm.

Chapter Ten

♥ **HYPOTHESIS:** *If I fall in love, things will invariably end poorly.*

The knockout mouse had been hanging from a wire for a length of time that should have been impossible, considering how it had been genetically modified. Olive frowned at it and pressed her lips together. It was missing crucial DNA. All the hanging-from-a-wire proteins had been erased. There was no way it could hold on for this long. It was the whole point of knocking out its stupid genes—

Her phone lit up, and the corner of her eye darted to its screen. She was able to read the name of the sender (Adam) but not the content of the message. It was 8:42 on Wednesday, which immediately had her worried that he might want to cancel their fake date. Maybe he thought that because he'd let Olive pick out an ice cream sandwich for him yesterday after Fluchella (which she may or may not have ended up eating herself) they didn't need to meet today. Maybe she shouldn't have forced him to sit on a bench with her and recount the marathons they had run, and possibly she had come off as annoying when she'd stolen his phone, downloaded her favorite running app, and then friended herself on it. He had seemed to be enjoying himself, but maybe he hadn't been.

Olive glanced at her gloved hands, and then back at her mouse, who was still holding on to the wire.

"Dude, stop trying so hard." She kneeled until she was at eye level with the cage. The mouse kicked around with its little legs, its tail flopping back and forth. "You're supposed to be bad at this. And I'm supposed to write a dissertation about how bad you are. And then you get a chunk of cheese, and I get a real job that pays real money and the joy of saying 'I'm not that kind of doctor' when someone is having a stroke on my airplane."

The mouse squeaked and let go of the wire, flopping on the floor of the testing cage with a thud.

"That'll do it." She quickly got rid of her gloves and unlocked her phone with her thumb.

Adam: My arm hurts.

She initially thought that he was giving her a reason why they couldn't meet up. Then she remembered waking up and rubbing her own achy arm.

Olive: From the flu shot?

Adam: It's really painful.

She giggled. She truly had not thought she was the type to, but here she was, covering her mouth with her hand and . . . yes, giggling like a fool in the middle of the lab. Her mouse was staring up at her, its tiny red eyes a mix of judgment and surprise. Olive hastily turned away and looked back at her phone.

Olive: Oh, Adam. I'm so sorry.

Olive: Should I come over and kiss it better?

Adam: You never said it would hurt so bad.

Olive: As someone once told me, it's not my job to work on your emotion regulation skills.

Adam's answer was one single emoji (a yellow hand with a raised middle finger), and Olive's cheeks pulled with how hard she was grinning. She was about to reply with a kiss emoji when a voice interrupted her.

"Gross."

She looked up from her phone. Anh stood in the lab's entrance, sticking out her tongue.

"Hey. What are you doing here?"

"Borrowing gloves. *And* being grossed out."

Olive frowned. "Why?"

"We're out of the small size." Anh stepped inside, rolling her eyes. "Honestly, they never buy enough because I'm the only woman in the lab, but it's not like I don't go through gloves as fast as—"

"No, why are you grossed out?"

Anh made a face and plucked two purple gloves from Olive's stash. "Because of how in love you are with Carlsen. Is it okay if I take a few pairs?"

"What are you—" Olive blinked at her, still clutching her phone. Was Anh going crazy? "I'm not *in love* with him."

"Uh-huh, sure." Anh finished stuffing her pockets with gloves and then looked up, finally noticing Olive's distressed expression. Her eyes widened. "Hey, I was kidding! You're not gross. I probably look the same when I'm texting Jeremy. And it's actually very sweet, how gone you are for him—"

"But I'm *not*. Gone." Olive was starting to panic. "I don't— It's just—"

Anh pressed her lips together, as if biting back a smile. "Okay. If you say so."

"No, I'm serious. We're just—"

"Dude, it's okay." Anh's tone was reassuring and a little emotional. "It's just, you're so amazing. And special. And honestly, my favorite person in the whole world. But sometimes I get worried that no one but Malcolm and me will ever get to experience how incredible you are. Well, until now. Now I'm not worried anymore, because I've seen you and Adam together, at the picnic. And in the parking lot. And . . . every other time, really. You're *both* crazy in love, and over the moon about it. It's cute! Except that first night," she added, pensive. "I maintain *that* was pretty awkward."

Olive stiffened. "Anh, it's not like that. We're just . . . dating. Casually. Hanging out. Getting to know each other. We're not . . ."

"Okay, sure. If you say so." Anh shrugged, clearly not believing a word of what Olive was saying. "Hey, I gotta go back to my bacterial culture. I'll come bug you when I'm on break, okay?"

Olive nodded slowly, watching her friend's back as she headed for the door. Olive's heart skipped a beat when Anh paused and turned around, her expression suddenly serious.

"Ol. I just want you to know that . . . I was very worried about you getting hurt from my dating Jeremy. But now I'm not anymore. Because I know what you really look like when you . . . Well." Anh gave her a sheepish grin. "I won't say it, if you don't want me to."

She left with a wave of her hand, and Olive stood frozen, watching the doorframe long past the moment Anh had disappeared. Then she lowered her gaze to the floor, slumped on the stool behind her, and thought one single thing:

Shit.

~~~~~~

IT WASN'T THE end of the world. These things happened. Even the best of people developed crushes—Anh had said love, oh

God, she had said *love*—on the person they were fake-dating. It didn't mean anything.

Except that: Fuck. Fuck, fuck, *fuck*.

Olive locked the door of her office behind her and plopped herself into a chair, hoping today wouldn't be the one time in the semester that her office mates decided to show up before 10:00 a.m.

It was all her fault. Her stupid doing. She had known, she *had known*, that she'd begun to find Adam attractive. She had known almost from the very beginning, and then she'd started talking with him, she'd started getting to know him even though it was never part of the plan, and—damn him to hell for being so different from what she'd expected. For making her want to be with him more and more. Damn him. It had been there, staring at Olive for the past few days, and she hadn't noticed. Because she was an idiot.

She stood abruptly and dug into her pocket for her phone, pulling up Malcolm's contact.

Olive: We have to meet.

Bless Malcolm, because it took him fewer than five seconds to answer.

Malcolm: Lunch? I'm about to dig into the neuromuscular junction of a juvenile rat.

Olive: I need to talk to you NOW.

Olive: Please.

Malcolm: Starbucks. In 10.

~~~~~~

"I TOLD YOU SO."

Olive didn't bother lifting her forehead from the table. "You didn't."

"Well, maybe I didn't say, 'Hey, don't do this fake-dating shit because you're going to fall for Carlsen,' but I did say that the whole idea was idiotic and a car wreck waiting to happen—which I believe encompasses the current situation."

Malcolm was sitting across from her, by the window of the crowded coffee shop. Around them students chatted, laughed, ordered drinks—rudely unaware of the sudden maelstrom in Olive's life. She pushed up from the cold surface of the table and pressed her palms into her eyes, not quite ready to open them yet. She might never be ready again. "How could this happen? I am not like this. This is not me. How could I—and Adam Carlsen, of everyone. *Who is into Adam Carlsen?*"

Malcolm snorted. "Everyone, Ol. He's a tall, broody, sullen hunk with a genius IQ. Everyone likes tall, broody, sullen hunks with genius IQs."

"I don't!"

"Clearly you do."

She squeezed her eyes shut and whimpered. "He's really not that sullen."

"Oh, he is. Just, you don't notice, because you're halfway gone for him."

"I am not—" She smacked her forehead. Repeatedly. "Shit."

He leaned forward and grabbed her hand, his skin dark and warm against hers. "Hey," he told her, voice pitched to a comforting tone. "Settle down. We'll figure it out." He even tacked on a smile. Olive loved him so much in that moment, even with all the I told you sos. "First of all, how bad is it?"

"I don't know. Is there a scale?"

"Well, there is liking, and there is *liking.*"

She shook her head, feeling utterly lost. "I just like him. I want to spend time with him."

"Okay, that doesn't mean anything. You also want to spend time with me."

She grimaced, feeling herself blush scarlet. "Not quite like that."

Malcolm was quiet for a beat. "I see." He knew how big of a deal this was for Olive. They'd talked about it multiple times—how rare it was for her to experience attraction, especially sexual attraction. If there was something wrong with her. If her past had stunted her in some way.

"God." She just wanted to retreat inside her hoodie like a turtle until it all went away. Go run a race. Start writing her dissertation proposal. Anything but deal with this. "It was there, and I didn't figure it out. I just thought he was smart and attractive and that he had a nice smile and that we could be friends and—" She rubbed her palms into her eye sockets, wishing she could go back and erase her life choices. The entire past month. "Do you hate me?"

"Me?" Malcolm sounded surprised.

"Yes."

"No. Why would I hate you?"

"Because he's been horrible to you, made you throw out a ton of data. It's just—with me he's not—"

"I know. Well," he amended, waving his hand, "I don't *know* know. But I can believe he's different with you than when he was in my damn graduate advisory committee."

"You hate him."

"Yeah—*I* hate him. Or . . . I dislike him. But you don't have to dislike him because I do. Though I do reserve the right to comment on your abysmal taste in men. Every other day or so. But, Ol, I saw you guys at the picnic. He definitely wasn't interacting with you like he does with me. Plus, you know," he added begrudgingly, "he's not *not* hot. I can see why you'd hit that."

"This is not what you said when I first told you about the fake dating."

"No, but I'm trying to be supportive here. You weren't in love with him at the time."

She groaned. "Can we please not use that word? Ever again? It seems a little premature."

"Sure." Malcolm brushed nonexistent dust off his button-down. "Way to bring a rom-com to life, by the way. So, how are you going to break the news?"

She massaged her temple. "What do you mean?"

"Well, you have a thing for him, and you two are friendly. I'm assuming you're planning to inform him of your . . . feelings? Can I use the word 'feelings'?"

"No."

"Whatever." He rolled his eyes. "You're going to tell him, right?"

"Of course not." She snorted out a laugh. "You can't tell the person you're fake-dating that you"—her brain scanned itself for the correct word, didn't find it, and then stumbled on—"*like* them. It's just not done. Adam will think I orchestrated this. That I was after him all along."

"That's ridiculous. You didn't even know him at the time."

"Maybe I did, though. Do you remember the guy I told you about, who helped me decide about grad school? The one I met in the bathroom over my interview weekend?"

Malcolm nodded.

"He might have been Adam. I think."

"You *think*? You mean you didn't ask him?"

"Of course not."

"Why 'of course'?"

"Because maybe it *wasn't* him. And if he was, he clearly doesn't remember, or he'd have mentioned it weeks ago."

He hadn't been the one wearing expired contacts, after all.

Malcolm rolled his eyes. "Listen, Olive," he said earnestly, "I need you to consider something: What if Adam likes you, too? What if he wants something more?"

She laughed. "There is no way."

"Why not?"

"Because."

"Because what?"

"Because he's him. He's Adam Carlsen, and I . . ." She trailed off. No need to continue. *And I'm me. I am nothing special.*

Malcolm was quiet for a long moment. "You have no idea, do you?" His tone was sad. "You're great. You're beautiful, and loving. You're independent, and a genius scientist, and selfless, and loyal—hell, Ol, look at this ridiculous mess you created just so your friend could date the guy she likes without feeling guilty. There's no way Carlsen hasn't noticed."

"No." She was resolute. "Don't get me wrong, I do think he likes me, but he thinks of me as a friend. And if I tell him and he doesn't want to . . ."

"To what? Doesn't want to fake-date you anymore? It's not like you have much to lose."

Maybe not. Maybe all the talking, and those looks Adam gave her, and him shaking his head when she ordered extra whipped cream; the way he let himself be teased out of his moods; the texts; how he seemed to be so at ease with her, so noticeably different from the Adam Carlsen she used to be half-scared of—maybe all of that was not much. But she and Adam were friends now, and they could remain friends even past September twenty-ninth. Olive's heart sank at the thought of giving up the possibility of it. "I do, though."

Malcolm sighed, once again enveloping her hand with his. "You have it bad, then."

She pressed her lips together, blinking rapidly to push back the tears. "Maybe I do. I don't know—I've never had it before. I've never wanted to have it."

He smiled reassuringly, even though Olive felt anything but reassured. "Listen, I know it's scary. But this is not necessarily a bad thing."

One single tear was making its way down Olive's cheek. She hastened to clean it with her sleeve. "It's the worst."

"You've finally found someone you're into. And okay, it's Carlsen, but this could still turn out to be great."

"It couldn't. It can't."

"Ol, I know where you're coming from. I get it." Malcolm's hand tightened on hers. "I know it's scary, being vulnerable, but you can *allow* yourself to care. You can want to be with people as more than just friends or casual acquaintances."

"But I can't."

"I don't see why not."

"Because all the people I've cared about are *gone*," she snapped.

Somewhere in the coffee shop, the barista called for a caramel macchiato. Olive immediately regretted her harsh words.

"I'm sorry. It's just . . . it's the way it works. My mom. My grandparents. My father—one way or another, everyone is gone. If I let myself care, Adam will go, too." There. She'd put it into words, said it out loud, and it sounded all the truer because of it.

Malcolm exhaled. "Oh, Ol." He was one of the few people to whom Olive had opened up about her fears—the constant feeling of not belonging, the never-ending suspicions that since so much of her life had been spent alone, then it would end the same way. That she'd never be worthy of someone caring for her. His knowing expression, a combination of sorrow and understanding and pity, was unbearable to watch. She looked elsewhere—at the laughing students, at the coffee cup lids stacked next to the counter, at the stickers on a girl's MacBook—and slid her hand away from under his palm.

"You should go." She attempted a smile, but it felt wobbly. "Finish your surgeries."

He didn't break eye contact. "*I* care. *Anh* cares—Anh would have chosen you over Jeremy. And you care, too. We all care about one another, and I'm still here. I'm not going anywhere."

"It's different."

"How?"

Olive didn't bother answering and used her sleeve to dry her cheek. Adam was different, and what Olive wanted from him was different, but she couldn't—didn't want to articulate it. Not now. "I won't tell him."

"Ol."

"No," she said, firm. With her tears gone, she felt marginally better. Maybe she was not who she had thought, but she could fake it. She could pretend, even to herself. "I'm not going to tell him. It's a horrible idea."

"Ol."

"How would that conversation even work? How would I phrase it? What are the right words?"

"Actually you should probably—"

"Do I tell him that I'm into him? That I think about him all the time? That I have a huge crush on him? That—"

"*Olive.*"

In the end, what tipped her off was not Malcolm's words, or his panicky expression, or the fact that he was clearly looking at a spot somewhere above her shoulders. In the end, Anh chose that exact moment to text her, which drew Olive's eyes to the numbers on the screen.

10:00 a.m.

It was ten. On a Wednesday morning. And Olive was currently sitting in the campus Starbucks, the very same Starbucks where she had spent her Wednesday mornings for the past few weeks. She whirled around and—

She wasn't even surprised to find Adam. Standing behind her. Close enough that unless both his eardrums had ruptured since the last time they'd talked, he must have heard every single word that came out of Olive's mouth.

She wished she could expire on the spot. She wished she could crawl outside her body and this café, melt in a pool of sweat, and seep between the tiles on the floor, just vanish into thin air. But all these things were currently beyond her skill set, so she fixed a weak smile on her face and looked up at Adam.

Chapter Eleven

❤ **HYPOTHESIS:** *Whenever I lie, things will get worse by a factor of 743.*

"Did you . . . did you hear that?" she blurted out.

Malcolm hurried to clear the table of his stuff, muttering tightly, "I was just about to go."

Olive barely noticed, busy watching Adam slide the chair back to sit across from her.

Shit.

"Yes," he said, bland and even, and Olive felt like she was about to disintegrate into a million tiny pieces, here, in this exact spot. She wanted him to take it back. Wanted him to say "No, heard what?" She wanted to go back to earlier this morning and rewind it all, this horrible mess of a day. Not look at the texts on her phone, not let Anh walk in on her mooning over her fake boyfriend, not pour her heart out to Malcolm in the worst possible place.

Adam couldn't know. He simply couldn't. He'd think that

Olive had kissed him on purpose, that she'd masterminded this whole fiasco, that she'd manipulated him into this situation. He'd feel compelled to break up with her well before he could reap any benefits from their arrangement. And he would hate her.

The prospect was terrifying, so she said the one thing she could think of.

"It wasn't about you."

The lie rolled off her tongue like a mudslide: unpremeditated, quick, and bound to leave a huge mess behind.

"I know." He nodded, and . . . he didn't even look surprised. It was as though it had never occurred to him that Olive might have been interested in him. It made her want to cry—a frequent state on this stupid morning—but instead of doing that, she just vomited out another lie.

"I just . . . I have a thing. For a guy."

He nodded again, this time slowly. His eyes darkened, and the corner of his jaw twitched, just for a moment. She blinked, and his expression was blank again. "Yeah. I gathered that."

"This guy, he's . . ." She swallowed. What was he? *Quick, Olive,* quick. An immunologist? Icelandic? A giraffe? What was he?

"You don't have to explain if you don't want." Adam's voice seemed slightly offbeat, but also comforting. Tired. Olive realized that she was wringing her hands, and instead of stopping she simply hid them under the table.

"I . . . It's just that . . ."

"It's okay." He offered her a reassuring smile, and Olive—she couldn't possibly look at him. Not a second longer. She averted her eyes, desperately wishing she had something to say. Something to fix this. Right outside the café's window, a group of undergrads were huddling together in front of a laptop, laughing at something playing on the screen. A gust of wind scattered a stack of notes, and a boy scrambled to retrieve them. In the distance, Dr. Rodrigues was walking in the direction of Starbucks.

"This . . . our arrangement." Adam's voice pulled her back inside. To the lies and the table between them; to the gentle, soft way he was talking to her. Kind, he'd been so kind.

Adam. I used to think the worst of you, and now . . .

"It's supposed to help both of us. If it stops doing so . . ."

"No." Olive shook her head. "No. I . . ." She forced her face into a smile. "It's complicated."

"I see."

She opened her mouth to say that no, he couldn't possibly see. He couldn't possibly see anything, because Olive had just made all of this up. This clusterfuck of a situation. "I don't—" She wet her lips. "There is no need to stop our arrangement early, because I can't tell him that I like him. Because I—"

"Dude." A hand clapped on Adam's shoulder. "Since when are you not in your offi— Oh. I see." Dr. Rodrigues's gaze slid from Adam to Olive and settled on her. For a second, he just stood by the table and took her in, surprised to find her there. Then his mouth widened into a slow grin. "Hey, Olive."

During Olive's first year of grad school, Dr. Rodrigues had been on her preassigned graduate advisory committee—an admittedly odd choice, given his relative lack of relevance to her research. And yet, Olive had mostly pleasant memories of her interactions with him. When she'd stammered her way through her committee meetings, he'd always been the first to smile at her, and once he'd even complimented her Star Wars T-shirt—and then proceeded to hum the Darth Vader theme under his breath every time Dr. Moss would start one of her rants against Olive's methods.

"Hey, Dr. Rodrigues." She was positive that her smile was not nearly as convincing as it should have been. "How are you?"

He waved a hand. "Pssh. Please, call me Holden. You're not my student anymore." He patted Adam on the back with relish. "And you have the very dubious pleasure of dating my oldest, most socially impaired friend."

It was all Olive could do not to let her jaw drop. They were friends? Charming, devil-may-care Holden Rodrigues and surly, taciturn Adam Carlsen were *old* friends? Was this something she was supposed to know? Adam's girlfriend would have known, right?

Dr. Rodrigues—Holden? God, Holden. She was never going to get used to the fact that professors were real people and had first names—turned to Adam, who appeared untroubled by having been decreed socially impaired.

He asked, "You're leaving for Boston tonight, right?" and his speech pattern changed a little—pitched lower and faster, more casual. Comfortable. They really were old friends.

"Yeah. Can you still give Tom and me a ride to the airport?"

"Depends."

"On what?"

"Is Tom going to be gagged and tied up in the trunk?"

Adam sighed. "Holden."

"I'll allow him in the back seat, but if he doesn't keep his mouth shut, I'll ditch him on the highway."

"Fine. I'll let him know."

Holden seemed satisfied. "Anyway, I didn't mean to interrupt." He patted Adam's shoulder once more, but he was looking at Olive.

"It's okay."

"Really? Well, then." His smile broadened and he pulled up a chair from a nearby table. Adam closed his eyes, resigned.

"So, what are we talking about?"

Why, I was just in the middle of lying my ass off, thank you for asking. "Ah . . . nothing much. How do you two . . ." She looked between them, clearing her throat. "Sorry, I forgot how you and Adam know each other."

A thud—Holden kicking Adam under the table. "You little shit. You didn't tell her about our decades-deep history?"

"Just trying to forget."

"You wish." Holden turned to grin at her. "We grew up together."

She frowned at Adam. "I thought you grew up in Europe?"

Holden waved his hand. "He grew up all over the place. And so did I, since our parents worked together. Diplomats—the worst kind of people. But then our families settled in DC." He leaned forward. "Guess who went to high school, college, *and* grad school together."

Olive's eyes widened, and Holden noticed, at least judging by how he kicked Adam again.

"You really haven't told her shit. I see you're still going for brooding and mysterious." He rolled his eyes fondly and looked at her again. "Did Adam tell you that he almost didn't graduate high school? He got suspended for punching a guy who insisted that the Large Hadron Collider would destroy the planet."

"Interesting how you're not mentioning that you got suspended alongside me for doing the exact same thing."

Holden ignored him. "My parents were out of the country on some kind of assignment and briefly forgot that I existed, so we spent the week at my place playing *Final Fantasy*—it was glorious. What about when Adam applied to law school? He must have told you about that."

"I never *technically* applied to law school."

"Lies. All lies. Did he at least tell you that he was my prom date? It was *phenomenal*."

Olive looked at Adam, expecting him to deny that, too. But

Adam just half smiled, met Holden's eyes, and said, "It was quite phenomenal."

"Picture this, Olive. Early two thousands. Preppy, ridiculously expensive all-male DC school. Two gay students in grade twelve. Well, two of us that were out, anyway. Richie Muller and I date for the entirety of senior year—and then he dumps me three days before prom for some guy he'd been having a thing with for *months*."

"He was a prick," Adam muttered.

"I have three choices. Not go to the dance and mope at home. Go alone and mope at school. *Or*, have my best friend—who was planning on staying home and moping over gamma-aminobutyric acids—come as my date. Guess which?"

Olive gasped. "How did you convince him?"

"That's the thing, I didn't. When I told him about what Richie did, he *offered*!"

"Don't get used to it," Adam mumbled.

"Can you believe it, Olive?"

That Adam would pretend to be in a relationship with someone to get them out of a miserable situation? "Nope."

"We held hands. We slow-danced. We made Richie spit out his punch and regret every single one of his wretched choices. Then we went home and played even more *Final Fantasy*. It was the shit."

"It was surprisingly fun," Adam conceded, almost reluctantly.

Olive looked at him, and a realization dawned on her: Holden was Adam's Anh. His person. It was obvious that Adam and Tom were very close, too, but the relationship Adam had with Holden was something else, and . . . and Olive had no idea what to do with this piece of information.

Maybe she should tell Malcolm. He'd either have a field day or go completely berserk.

"Well," Holden said, standing up. "This was fantastic. I'll go get coffee, but we should hang out soon, the three of us. I can't remember the last time I had the pleasure of embarrassing Adam in front of a girlfriend. For now, though, he's all yours." He followed the word "yours" with a smirk that had Olive blushing.

Adam rolled his eyes when Holden left for the coffee counter. Fascinated, Olive followed him with her gaze for several moments. "Um, that was . . . ?"

"Holden for you." Adam seemed barely annoyed.

She nodded, still a little dazed. "I can't believe I'm not your first."

"My first?"

"Your first fake date."

"Right. I guess prom qualifies." He seemed to mull it over. "Holden has had some . . . bad luck with relationships. *Undeserved* bad luck."

It warmed her chest, the protective concern in his tone. Made her wonder if he was even aware of it.

"Did he and Tom ever . . . ?"

He shook his head. "Holden would be outraged if he knew you asked."

"Why doesn't he want to drive Tom to the airport, then?"

Adam shrugged. "Holden has always had a very deep, very irrational dislike of Tom, ever since grad school."

"Oh. Why?"

"Not sure. Not sure Holden knows, either. Tom says he's jealous. I think it's just a personality thing."

Olive fell silent, absorbing the information. "You didn't tell Holden about us, either. That it's not real."

"No."

"Why?"

Adam looked away. "I don't know." His jaw tensed. "I think

I just didn't . . ." His voice trailed off, and he shook his head before giving her a smile, small and a little forced. "He speaks very highly of you, you know?"

"Holden? Of me?"

"Of your work. And your research."

"Oh." She had no idea what to say to that. *When did you talk about me? And why?* "Oh," she repeated uselessly.

She wasn't sure why now, in this very moment, but the possible ramifications of their arrangement on Adam's life hit her in full for the first time. They had agreed to fake-date because they both had something to gain from it, but it occurred to her that Adam also had significantly more to lose. Out of all the people she loved, Olive was only lying to one, Anh, and that was absolutely unavoidable. She could not care less about other students' opinions. Adam, though . . . he was lying on a daily basis to his colleagues and his friends. His grads interacted with him every day believing that he was dating one of their peers. Did they think him lecherous? Had his relationship with Olive changed their perception of him? And what about other faculty members in the department, or in adjacent programs? Just because dating a grad student was allowed, it didn't mean that it wasn't frowned upon. And what if Adam met—or had *already* met—someone he actually liked? When they'd struck their deal, he'd said he wasn't going to date, but that had been weeks ago. Olive herself had been convinced that she'd never be interested in dating anyone at the time—and didn't that make her want to laugh now, in a remarkably unfunny way? Not to mention that she alone was benefitting from their arrangement. Anh and Jeremy had bought her lie, but Adam's research funds were still frozen.

And yet, he was still helping her despite all of this. And Olive was repaying his kindness by getting ideas and developing feelings that were sure to make him feel uncomfortable.

"Do you want to get coffee?"

Olive looked up from her hands. "No." She cleared her throat against the burning sensation lodged behind her sternum. The idea of coffee made her nauseous. "I think I need to go back to the lab."

She bent down to retrieve her backpack, meaning to stand and leave immediately, but halfway through, a thought swept over her, and she found herself staring at him. He was sitting across from her with a concerned expression, a slight frown creasing his brow.

She attempted a smile. "We are friends, right?"

His frown deepened. "Friends?"

"Yes. You and I."

He studied for a long moment. Something new passed through his face, stark and a little sad. Too fleeting to interpret. "Yes, Olive."

She nodded, unsure as to whether she should be feeling relieved. This was not how she'd thought today would go, and there was a strange pressure behind her eyelids, which had her sliding her arms through the straps of her backpack that much quicker. She waved him goodbye with a tremulous smile, and she'd have already been out of this damn Starbucks, if he hadn't said with that voice of his: "Olive."

She paused right in front of his chair and looked down at him. It was so odd, to be the taller one for once.

"This might be inappropriate, but . . ." His jaw shifted, and he closed his eyes for a second. As if to collect his thoughts. "Olive. You are really . . . You are extraordinary, and I cannot imagine that if you told Jeremy how you feel he wouldn't . . ." He trailed off and then nodded. A punctuation of sorts, as his words and the way he'd said them brought her that much closer to tears.

He thought it was Jeremy. Adam thought Olive had been in love with Jeremy when they'd begun their arrangement—he thought she was *still* in love with him. Because she'd just told a half-assed lie that she was too afraid to take back and—

It was going to happen. She was going to cry, and what she wanted most in the world was to not do it in front of Adam.

"I'll see you next week, okay?" She didn't wait for his response and walked briskly toward the exit, her shoulder bumping into someone she should have apologized to. Once she was outside, she took a deep breath and marched to the biology building, trying to empty her mind, forcing herself to think about the section she was slated to TA later today, the fellowship application she'd promised Dr. Aslan she'd send by tomorrow, the fact that Anh's sister would be in town next weekend and had made plans to cook Vietnamese food for everyone.

A chilly wind weaved through the leaves of the campus trees, pushing Olive's sweater against her body. She hugged herself and didn't look back to the café. Fall had finally begun.

Chapter Twelve

❤ **HYPOTHESIS:** *If I am bad at doing activity A, my chances of being asked to engage in activity A will rise exponentially.*

Campus felt strangely empty with Adam gone, even on days in which she likely wouldn't have met him anyway. It didn't make much sense: Stanford was most definitely not empty, but teeming with loud, annoying undergrads on their way to and from class. Olive's life, too, was full: her mice were old enough for the behavioral assays to be run, she'd finally gotten revisions for a paper she'd submitted months earlier, and she had to start making concrete plans for her move to Boston next year; the class she was TA'ing had a test coming up, and undergrads magically began to pop by during office hours, looking panicky and asking questions that were invariably answered in the first three lines of the syllabus.

Malcolm spent a couple of days trying to convince Olive to tell Adam the truth, and then became—thankfully—too discouraged by her stubbornness and too busy trying to meditate away his own dating drama to insist. He did bake several batches of butterscotch cookies, though, patently lying that he was "not rewarding your self-destructive behaviors, Olive, but just perfecting my recipe." Olive ate them all, and hugged him from behind while he sprinkled sea salt on top of the last batch.

On Saturday, Anh came over for beer and s'mores, and she and Olive daydreamed about leaving academia and finding industry jobs that paid a proper salary and acknowledged the existence of free time.

"We could, like, sleep in on Sunday mornings. Instead of having to check on our mice at six a.m."

"Yeah." Anh sighed wistfully. *Pride and Prejudice and Zombies* was running in the background, but neither of them was paying attention. "We could buy real ketchup instead of stealing packets from Burger King. And order that wireless vacuum cleaner I saw on TV."

Olive giggled drunkenly and turned to her side, making the bed squeak. "Seriously? A vacuum cleaner?"

"A wireless one. It's *the shit*, Ol."

"That is . . ."

"What?"

"Just . . ." Olive giggled some more. "It's the most random thing."

"Shut up." Anh smiled but didn't open her eyes. "I have severe dust allergies. You know what, though?"

"Are you going to hit me with a Trivial Pursuit vacuum cleaner fact?"

The corners of Anh's eyes crinkled. "Nah," she said, "I don't have any. Wait—I think that maybe the first female corporate CEO worked for a vacuum cleaner company."

"No way. That is *actually* cool."

"But maybe I'm making it up." Anh shrugged. "Anyway, what I meant to say is . . . I think I still want it?"

"The vacuum cleaner?" Olive yawned without bothering to cover her mouth.

"No. An academic job. And everything that comes with it. The lab, the grad students, the outrageous teaching load, the race for the NIH grants, the disproportionately low salary. The whole shebang. Jeremy says that Malcolm has it right. That industry jobs are where it's at. But I think I want to stay and become a professor. It'll be miserable, for sure, but it's the only way to create a good environment for women like us, Ol. Give some competition to all these entitled white men." She grinned, beautiful and fierce. "Jeremy can go into industry and make a ton of blood money that I'll invest in wireless vacuum cleaners."

Olive drunkenly studied the drunken determination on Anh's drunken face, thinking that there was something reassuring in knowing that her closest friend was starting to figure out what she wanted her life to be like. Who she wanted to live it with. It did send a pang deep in Olive's stomach, in that spot that seemed to feel Adam's absence most acutely, but she pushed it down, trying not to think about it too hard. Instead she reached for her friend's hand, squeezed it once, and inhaled the sweet scent of apple from her hair.

"You'll be so good at it, Anh. I can't wait to see you change the world."

~~~~~~

ALL IN ALL, Olive's life continued as it always had—except that for the first time, there was something else she'd rather be doing. Someone else she'd rather be with.

So, this is liking someone, she mused. Feeling like the biology building was not worth going to because if Adam was out of town, even the most remote chance of running into him had been taken away from her; constantly spinning around after catching a glimpse of jet-black hair, or when hearing a deep voice that sounded as rich as Adam's but really wasn't; thinking of him because her friend Jess mentioned planning a trip to the Netherlands, or when on *Jeopardy!* the correct answer to "Aichmophobia" turned out to be "What is fear of needles?"; feeling stuck in an odd limbo, waiting, just waiting, waiting . . . for nothing. Adam was going to come back in a few days, and Olive's lie that she was in love with someone else was still going to be there. September twenty-ninth would arrive all too soon, and anyway, the assumption that Adam could ever see Olive in any romantic light was preposterous. All considered, she was lucky he liked her enough to want to be her friend.

On Sunday, her phone pinged while she was running at the gym. When Adam's name popped up at the top of the screen, she immediately jumped to read it. Except that there wasn't much to read: just the image of a huge drink in a plastic cup, topped with what looked like a muffin. The bottom of the image proudly stated "Pumpkin Pie Frappuccino," and below that, Adam's text:

Adam: Think I can smuggle this on the plane?

She didn't need to be told that she was grinning at her phone like an idiot.

Olive: Well, TSA is notoriously incompetent.

Olive: Though maybe not that incompetent?

Adam: Too bad.

Adam: Wish you were here, then.

Olive's smile stayed in place for a long time. And then, when she remembered the mess she was in, it faded into a heavy sigh.

～～～～～

SHE WAS CARRYING a tray of tissue samples to the electron microscope lab when someone patted her on the shoulder, startling her. Olive nearly tripped and destroyed several thousand dollars' worth of federal grant funding. When she turned, Dr. Rodrigues was staring at her with his usual boyish grin—like they were best buddies about to go for a beer and a jolly good time, instead of a Ph.D. student and a former member of her advisory committee who'd never quite gotten around to reading any of the paperwork she'd turned in.

"Dr. Rodrigues."

His brow wrinkled. "I thought we'd settled on Holden?"

Had they? "Right. Holden."

He smiled, pleased. "Boyfriend's out of town, huh?"

"Oh. Um . . . Yes."

"You going in there?" He pointed at the microscope lab with his chin, and Olive nodded. "Here, let me get it." He swiped his badge to unlock the door and held it open for her.

"Thank you." She settled her samples on a bench and smiled gratefully, sliding her hands into her back pockets. "I was going to get a cart, but I couldn't find one."

"There's only one left on this floor. I think someone's bringing them home and reselling them."

He grinned, and—Malcolm was right. Had been right for the past two years: there really was something easygoing and effortlessly attractive about Holden. Not that Olive seemed to be interested in anything but tall, broody, sullen hunks with genius IQs.

"Can't blame 'em. I'd have done the same in my grad school days. So, how's life?"

"Um, fine. You?"

Holden ignored her question and casually leaned against the wall. "How bad is it?"

"Bad?"

"Adam being gone. Hell, even I miss that little shit." He chuckled. "How are you holding up?"

"Oh." She took her hands out of her pockets, crossed her arms in front of her chest, and then changed her mind and dropped them woodenly by her sides. *Yep. Perfect. Acting natural.* "Fine. Good. Busy."

Holden looked genuinely relieved. "Great. Have you guys been talking on the phone?"

No. Of course not. Talking on the phone is the hardest, most stressful thing in the world, and I can't do it with the nice lady who schedules my dental cleanings, let alone with Adam Carlsen. "Ah, mostly texting, you know?"

"Yeah, I do know. However buttoned-up and sulky Adam is with you, please know that he's making an effort and he's a million times worse with everyone else. Me included." He sighed and shook his head, but there was a fondness behind it. An easy affection that Olive couldn't miss. *My oldest friend,* he'd said about Adam, and clearly he hadn't been lying. "He's actually gotten a lot better, since you guys started dating."

Olive felt on the verge of a full-body cringe. Unsure of what to say, she settled for a simple, painful, awkward: "Really?"

Holden nodded. "Yep. I'm so glad he finally scrounged up the courage to ask you out. He'd been going on and on about this 'amazing girl' for years, but he was concerned about being in the same department, and you know how he is . . ." He shrugged and waved his hand. "I'm glad he finally managed to pull his head out of his ass."

Olive's brain stuttered. Her neurons went sluggish and cold, and it took her several seconds to process that Adam had been wanting to ask her out for years. She couldn't wrap her head around it, because . . . it was not possible. It didn't make sense. Adam didn't even remember Olive existed before she'd Title-IXed him in the hallway a few weeks ago. The more she thought about it, the more she grew convinced that if he'd had any recollection of their bathroom meeting, he would have said as much. Adam was famously direct, after all.

Holden must have been referring to someone else. And Adam must have feelings for that someone. Someone he worked with, someone who was in their department. Someone who was "amazing."

Olive's mind, half frozen until a few seconds ago, began to spiral with the knowledge. Setting aside the fact that this conversation was an utter invasion of Adam's privacy, Olive couldn't stop herself from considering the implications of their arrangement for him. If the person Holden was talking about was one of Adam's colleagues, there was no chance that she hadn't heard about Adam and Olive dating. It was possible that she'd seen the two of them get coffee together on a Wednesday, or Olive sitting on Adam's lap during Tom's talk, or—God, Olive slathering him with sunblock at that godforsaken picnic. Which couldn't be good for his prospects. Unless Adam didn't mind, because he was sure beyond any doubt that his feelings were unrequited—and oh, wouldn't that be funny? About as funny as a Greek tragedy.

"Anyway." Holden pushed away from the wall, his hand coming up to scratch his nape. "I think we should go on a double date one of these days. I've been taking a break from dating— too much heartache—but maybe it's time to dip my toes in again. Hopefully I'll snatch myself a boyfriend soon."

The weight in Olive's stomach sank even lower. "That would be lovely." She attempted a smile.

"Right?" He grinned. "Adam would hate it with the intensity of a thousand suns."

He really would.

"But I could tell you so many juicy stories about him, approximately aged ten to twenty-five." Holden was delighted at the prospect. "He'd be mortified."

"Are they about taxidermy?"

"Taxidermy?"

"Nothing. Just something Tom had said about . . ." She waved her hand. "Nothing."

Holden's gaze turned sharp. "Adam said you might be going to work with Tom next year. Is that true?"

"Oh . . . yeah. That's the plan."

He nodded, pensive. Then seemed to come to some sort of decision and added, "Watch your back while you're around him, okay?"

"My back?" What? Why? Did this have anything to do with what Adam had mentioned—Holden not liking Tom? "What do you mean?"

"Adam's back, too. *Especially* Adam's back." Holden's expression remained intense for a moment, and then lightened up. "Anyway. Tom only met Adam in grad school. But I was there in his teenage years—that's when the good stories are from."

"Oh. You probably shouldn't tell me. Since . . ." *Since he's faking a relationship with me and surely doesn't want me in his business. Also, he's probably in love with someone else.*

"Oh, of course. I'll wait until he's present. I want to see his face when I tell you everything about his newsboy-cap phase."

She blinked. "His . . . ?"

He nodded solemnly and stepped out, closing the door behind him and leaving her alone in the chilly, semidark lab. Olive had to take several deep breaths before she could focus on her work.

~~~~~~

WHEN SHE RECEIVED the email, she initially thought it must be an error. Maybe she'd misread—she hadn't been sleeping well, and as it turned out, having an unwanted, unreciprocated crush came with all sorts of scatter-headedness—though after a second look, then a third and a fourth, she realized that wasn't the case. So maybe the mistake was on the SBD conference's side. Because there was no way—absolutely *no way*—that they'd really meant to inform her that the abstract she'd submitted had been selected to be part of a panel.

A panel with faculty.

It was just not possible. Graduate students were rarely selected for oral presentations. Most of the time they just made posters with their findings. Talks were for scholars whose careers were already advanced—except that when Olive logged into the conference website and downloaded the program, her name was there. And out of all the speakers' names, hers was the only one not followed by any letters. No MD. No Ph.D. No MD-Ph.D.

Crap.

She ran out of the lab clutching her laptop to her chest. Greg gave her a dirty look when she almost crashed into him in the hallway, but she ignored him and stormed inside Dr. Aslan's office out of breath, her knees suddenly made of jelly.

"Can we talk?" She closed the door without waiting for an answer.

Her adviser looked up from behind her desk with an alarmed expression. "Olive, what is—"

"I don't want to give a talk. I can't give a talk." She shook her head, trying to sound reasonable but only managing panic-stricken and frantic. "I *can't*."

Dr. Aslan cocked her head and steepled her hands. The veneer of calm her adviser projected was usually comforting, but now it made Olive want to flip the nearest piece of furniture.

Calm down. Deep breaths. Use your mindfulness and all that stuff Malcolm's always yapping his mouth about. "Dr. Aslan, my SBD abstract was accepted as a talk. Not as a poster, a *talk*. Out loud. On a panel. Standing. In front of *people*." Olive's voice had made its way to a shriek. And yet, for reasons beyond understanding, Dr. Aslan's face split into a grin.

"This is wonderful news!"

Olive blinked. And then blinked again. "It's . . . not?"

"Nonsense." Dr. Aslan stood and walked around her desk,

running her hand up and down Olive's arm in what she clearly intended as a congratulatory gesture. "This is fantastic. A talk will give you much more visibility than a poster. You might be able to network for a postdoctoral position. I am so, *so* happy for you."

Olive's jaw dropped. "But . . ."

"But?"

"I cannot give a talk. I can't *talk*."

"You're talking right now, Olive."

"Not in front of people."

"I am people."

"You're not *many* people. Dr. Aslan, I can't talk in front of a lot of people. Not about science."

"Why?"

"Because." *Because my throat will dry up and my brain will shut down and I will be so bad that someone from the audience will take out a crossbow and shoot me in the kneecap.* "I'm not ready. To speak. In public."

"Of course you are. You're a good public speaker."

"I'm not. I stammer. I blush. I meander. A lot. Especially in front of large crowds, and—"

"Olive," Dr. Aslan interrupted her with a stern tone. "What do I always tell you?"

"Um . . . 'Don't misplace the multichannel pipette'?"

"The other thing."

She sighed. "'Carry yourself with the confidence of a mediocre white man.'"

"More than that, if possible. Since there is absolutely nothing mediocre about you."

Olive closed her eyes and took enough deep breaths to pull back from the verge of a panic attack. When she opened them, her adviser was smiling encouragingly.

"Dr. Aslan." Olive grimaced. "I *really* don't think I can do this."

"I know you don't." There was some sadness in her expression. "But you can. And we'll work together until you feel up to the task." This time, she put both her hands on Olive's shoulders. Olive was still hugging her laptop to her chest, like she would a life buoy in the open sea, but the touch was oddly comforting. "Don't worry. We have a couple of weeks to get you ready."

You say that. You say "we," but I'll be the one to speak in front of hundreds of people, and when someone asks a three-minute-long question meant to get me to admit that deep down my work is poorly structured and useless, I'll be the one to crap her pants. "Right." Olive had to force her head into an up-and-down motion and take a deep breath. She exhaled slowly. "Okay."

"Why don't you put together a draft? You could practice during the next lab meeting." Another reassuring smile, and Olive was nodding again, not feeling reassured in the least. "And if you have any questions, I'm always here. Oh, I am so disappointed that I won't get to see your talk. You must promise to record it for me. It will be just as if I was there."

Except that you won't be there, and I'll be alone, she thought bitterly while closing the door of Dr. Aslan's office behind her. She slumped against the wall and squeezed her eyes shut, trying to quiet the agitated mess of thoughts fluttering inside her head. And then she opened them again when she heard her name in Malcolm's voice. He was standing in front of her with Anh, studying her with a half-amused, half-worried expression. They were holding Starbucks cups. The smell of caramel and peppermint wafted over, making her stomach churn.

"Hey."

Anh took a sip of her drink. "Why are you taking a standing nap next to your adviser's office?"

"I . . ." Olive pushed away from the wall and walked a few steps away from Dr. Aslan's door, rubbing her nose with the back of her hand. "My abstract got accepted. The SBD one."

"Congrats!" Anh smiled. "But that was pretty much a given, right?"

"It was accepted as a *talk*."

For a few seconds, two pairs of eyes just stared at her in silence. Olive thought that Malcolm might be wincing, but when she turned to check, there was just a vague smile pasted on his face. "That's . . . awesome?"

"Yeah." Anh's eyes darted to Malcolm and back to Olive. "That's, um, great."

"It's a disaster of epic proportions."

Anh and Malcolm exchanged a worried glance. They knew very well how Olive felt about public speaking.

"What is Dr. Aslan saying about it?"

"The usual." She rubbed her eyes. "That it will be fine. That we'll work on it together."

"I think she's right," Anh said. "I'll help you practice. We'll make sure you know it by heart. And it *will* be fine."

"Yeah." *Or it won't.* "Also, the conference is in less than two weeks. We should book the hotel—or are we doing Airbnb?"

Something odd happened the moment she asked the question. Not with Anh—she was still peacefully sipping on her coffee—but Malcolm's cup froze halfway to his mouth, and he bit his lip while studying the sleeve of his sweater.

"About that . . . ," he began.

Olive frowned. "What?"

"Well." Malcolm shuffled his feet a little, and maybe it was accidental, the way he seemed to be drifting away from Olive—but she didn't think so. "We already have."

"You already booked something?"

Anh nodded cheerfully. "Yes." She didn't appear to notice that Malcolm was about to have a stroke. "The conference hotel."

"Oh. Okay. Let me know what I owe you then, since—"

"The thing is . . ." Malcolm seemed to move even farther away.

"What thing?"

"Well." He fidgeted with the cardboard holder of his cup, and his eyes darted to Anh, who seemed blissfully oblivious to his discomfort. "Jeremy's hotel room is paid for because of that fellowship he's on, and he asked Anh to stay with him. And then Jess, Cole, and Hikaru offered for me to stay with them."

"What?" Olive glanced at Anh. "Seriously?"

"It will save all of us a lot of money. And it will be my first trip with Jeremy," Anh interjected distractedly. She was typing something on her phone. "Oh my God, guys, I think I found it! A location for the Boston event for BIPOC women in STEM! I think I've got it!"

"That's great," Olive said weakly. "But I thought . . . I thought we'd room together."

Anh glanced up, looking contrite. "Yeah, I know. That's what I told Jeremy, but he pointed out that you . . . you know." Olive tilted her head, confused, and Anh continued, "I mean, why would you want to spend money on a room when you could stay with Carlsen?"

Oh. "Because." Because. Because, because, *because.* "I . . ."

"I'll miss you, but it's not as if we'll be in the rooms for anything other than sleeping."

"Right. . . ." She pressed her lips together, and added, "Sure."

Anh's grin made her want to groan. "Awesome. We'll get meals together and hang out for poster sessions. And at night, of course."

"Of course." It was all Olive could do not to sound bitter. "I look forward to it," she added with as good a smile as she could muster.

"Okay. Great. I gotta go—the Women in Science outreach committee is meeting in five. But let's get together this weekend to plan fun activities for Boston. Jeremy said something about a ghost tour!"

Olive waited until Anh was out of earshot before turning to face Malcolm. He was already raising his hands defensively.

"First of all, Anh came up with this plan while I was monitoring that twenty-four-hour experiment—worst day of my life, I *cannot* graduate soon enough. And after that—what was I supposed to do? Inform her that you're not going to stay with Carlsen because you're fake-dating? Oh, but wait—now that you've got a huge crush on him maybe it's sort of real—"

"Okay, I get it." Her stomach was starting to ache. "You still could have told me."

"I was going to. And then I dumped Neuro Jude and he went crazy and egged my car. And after that my dad called me to say hi and asked me about how my projects are going, which devolved into him grilling me on why I'm not using a C. *elegans* model, and, Ol, you know how incredibly nosy and micromanaging he can be, which led to us having an argument and my mom got involved and—" He stopped and took a deep breath. "Well, you were there. You heard the screams. Bottom line is, it totally slipped my mind, and I'm so sorry."

"It's fine." She scratched her temple. "I'm going to have to find someplace to stay."

"I'll help you," Malcolm told her eagerly. "We can look online tonight."

"Thanks, but don't worry about it. I'll manage." Or not. Probably. Likely. Since the conference was in less than two weeks, and everything was likely already booked up. What was left was undoubtedly so out of her price range, she'd have to sell a kidney to be able to afford it. Which could be an option—she did have two.

"You're not mad, right?"

"I . . ." *Yes. No. Maybe a little.* "No. It's not your fault." She hugged Malcolm back when he leaned into her, reassuring him with a few awkward pats on the shoulder. As much as she'd have liked to blame him for this, she only had to look at herself. The crux of her problems—most of them, at least—was her moronic, harebrained decision to lie to Anh in the first place. To begin this fake-dating sham. Now she was giving a *talk* at this stupid conference, probably after sleeping at a bus station and eating moss for breakfast, and despite all of this she couldn't stop thinking about Adam. Just perfect.

Laptop under her arm, Olive headed back to the lab, the prospect of getting her slides in order for her talk simultaneously daunting and depressing. There was something leaden and unpleasant weighing on her stomach, and on impulse she made a detour to the restroom and entered the stall farthest from the door, leaning against the wall until the back of her head hit the cold tile surface.

When the weight in her belly began to feel too heavy, her knees gave out on her and her back slid down until she sat on the floor. Olive stayed like that for a long time, trying to pretend that this wasn't her life.

Chapter Thirteen

❤ **HYPOTHESIS:** *Approximately two out of three fake-dating situations will eventually involve room-sharing; 50 percent of room-sharing situations will be further complicated by the presence of only one bed.*

There was an Airbnb twenty-five minutes from the conference center, but it was an inflatable mattress on the floor of a storage room, charging 180 bucks per night, and even if she could have afforded it, one of the reviews reported that the host had a penchant for role-playing Viking with the guests, so . . . No, thank you. She found a more affordable one forty-five minutes away by subway, but when she went to reserve the room, she discovered that someone had beaten her to it by mere seconds, and she was tempted to hurl her laptop across the coffee shop. She was trying to decide between a seedy motel and a cheap couch in the suburbs when a shadow cast over her. She looked up with a frown, expecting an undergrad wanting to use the outlet she'd been hoarding, and instead found . . .

"Oh."

Adam was standing in front of her, the late-afternoon sunlight haloing his hair and shoulders, fingers closed around an iPad as he looked down at her with a somber expression. It had been less than a week since she'd last seen him—six days to be precise, which was just a handful of hours and minutes. Nothing, considering that she'd barely known him a month. And yet it was as if the space she was in, the whole campus, the entire city was transformed by knowing that he was back.

Possibilities. That's what Adam's presence felt like. Of what, she was not certain.

"You're . . ." Her mouth was dry. An event of great scientific interest, considering that she'd taken a sip from her water bottle maybe ten seconds ago. "You're back."

"I am."

She hadn't forgotten his voice. Or his height. Or the way his stupid clothes fit him. She couldn't have—she had two medial temporal lobes, fully functioning and tucked nicely inside her skull, which meant that she was perfectly able to encode and store memories. She hadn't forgotten anything, and she wasn't sure why right now it felt as if she had. "I thought . . . I didn't—" *Yes, Olive. Wonderful. Very eloquent.* "I didn't know that you were back."

His face was a little closed off, but he nodded. "I flew in last night."

"Oh." She should have probably prepared something to say, but she hadn't expected to see him until Wednesday. If she had, maybe she wouldn't have been wearing her oldest leggings and most tattered T-shirt, and her hair wouldn't have been a mess. Not that she was under any illusion that Adam would have noticed her if she'd been wearing a swimsuit or a gala dress. But still. "Do you want to sit?" She leaned forward to gather her phone and notebook, making room on the other side of the small table. It was only when he hesitated before taking a seat that it occurred to her that maybe he had no intention of staying, that now he might feel forced to do so. He folded himself into the chair gracefully, like a big cat.

Great job, Olive. Who doesn't love a needy person who hounds them for attention?

"You don't have to. I know you're busy. MacArthur grants to win and grads to brutalize and broccoli to eat." He'd probably rather be anywhere else. She bit her thumbnail, feeling guilty, starting to panic, and—

And then he smiled. And suddenly there were grooves around his mouth and dimples in his cheeks and his face was completely altered by them. The air at the table thinned. Olive couldn't quite breathe.

"You know, there's a middle ground between living off brownies and exclusively eating broccoli."

She grinned, for no reason other than—Adam was *here*, with *her*. And he was *smiling*. "That's a lie."

He shook his head, mouth still curved. "How are you?"

Better now. "Good. How was Boston?"

"Good."

"I'm glad you're back. I'm pretty sure the biology dropout rates have seen a steep reduction. We can't have that."

He gave her a patient, put-upon look. "You look tired, smart-ass."

"Oh. Yeah, I . . ." She rubbed her cheek with her hand, ordering herself not to feel self-conscious about her looks, just like she'd always made a point not to. It would be an equally stupid idea to wonder what the woman Holden mentioned the other day looked like. Probably stunning. Probably feminine, with curves; someone who actually needed to wear a bra, someone who was not half covered in freckles, who had mastered the art of applying liquid eyeliner without making a mess of herself.

"I'm fine. It's been a week, though." She massaged her temple.

He cocked his head. "What happened?"

"Nothing . . . My friends are stupid, and I hate them." She felt instantly guilty and made a face. "Actually, I don't hate them. I do hate that I love them, though."

"Is this the sunscreen friend? Anh?"

"The one and only. And my roommate, too, who really should know better."

"What did they do?"

"They . . ." Olive pressed into both eyes with her fingers. "It's a long story. They found alternative accommodations for SBD. Which means that now I have to find a place on my own."

"Why did they do that?"

"Because . . ." She briefly closed her eyes and sighed. "Because they assumed that I'd want to stay with you. Since you're my . . . you know. 'Boyfriend.'"

He went still for a couple of seconds. And then: "I see."

"Yep. A pretty bold assumption, but . . ." She spread her arms and shrugged.

He bit the inside of his cheek, looking pensive. "I'm sorry you won't get to room with them."

She waved her hand. "Oh, that's not it. That would have been fun, but it's just that now I need to find something else nearby, and there are no affordable options." Her eyes fell on the screen of her laptop. "I'm thinking of booking this motel that's an hour away and—"

"Won't they know?"

She looked up from the grainy, shady-looking picture of the place. "Mm?"

"Won't Anh know that you're not staying with me?"

Oh. "Where are you staying?"

"The conference hotel."

Of course. "Well." She scratched her nose. "I wouldn't tell her. I don't think she'll pay too much attention."

"But she'll notice if you're staying one hour away."

"I . . ." Yes. They would notice, and ask questions, and Olive would have to come up with a bunch of excuses and even more half-truths to deal with it. Add a few blocks to this Jenga tower of lies she'd been building for weeks. "I'll figure it out."

He nodded slowly. "I'm sorry."

"Oh, it's not your fault."

"One could argue that it is, in fact, my fault."

"Not at all."

"I would offer to pay for your hotel room, but I doubt there's anything left in a ten-mile radius."

"Oh, no." She shook her head emphatically. "And I wouldn't accept it. It's not a cup of coffee. And a scone. And a cookie. And a pumpkin Frappuccino." She batted her eyes at him and leaned forward, trying to change the topic. "Which, by the way, is new on the menu. You could totally buy it for me, and that would make my day."

"Sure." He looked slightly nauseous.

"Awesome." She grinned. "I think it's cheaper today, some kind of Tuesday sale, so—"

"But you could room with me."

The way he put it forward, calm and sensible, almost made it sound like it was no big deal. And Olive almost fell for it, until her ears and brain seemed to finally connect with each other and she was able to process the meaning of what he'd just said.

That she.

Could room.

With him.

Olive knew full well what sharing quarters with someone

entailed, even for a very short period. Sleeping in the same room meant seeing embarrassing pajamas, taking turns to use the bathroom, hearing the swish of someone trying to find a comfortable position under the sheets loud and clear in the dark. Sleeping in the same room meant— No. Nope. It was a terrible idea. And Olive was starting to think that maybe she had maxed those out for a while. So she cleared her throat.

"I could not, actually."

He nodded calmly. But then, then he asked equally calmly, "Why?" and she wanted to bang her head against the table.

"I couldn't."

"The room is a double, of course," he offered, as if that piece of information could have possibly changed her mind.

"It's not a good idea."

"Why?"

"Because people will think that we . . ." She noticed Adam's look and immediately hushed. "Okay, *fine*. They already think that. But."

"But?"

"Adam." She rubbed her forehead with her fingers. "There will be only one bed."

He frowned. "No, as I said it's a double—"

"It's not. It won't be. There will be only one bed, for sure."

He gave her a puzzled look. "I got the booking confirmation the other day. I can forward it to you if you want; it says that—"

"It doesn't matter what it says. It's *always* one bed."

He stared at her, perplexed, and she sighed and leaned helplessly against the back of her chair. He'd clearly never seen a rom-com or read a romance novel in his life. "Nothing. Ignore me."

"My symposium is part of a satellite workshop the day before the conference starts, and then I'll be speaking on the first day of the actual conference. I have the room for the entire conference, but I'll probably need to leave for some meetings after night two, so you'd be by yourself from night three. We'd only overlap for one night."

She listened to the logical, methodical way he listed sensible reasons why she should just accept his offer and felt a wave of panic sweep over her. "It seems like a bad idea."

"That's fine. I just don't understand why."

"Because." *Because I don't want to. Because I have it bad. Because I'd probably have it even worse, after that. Because it's going to be the week of September twenty-ninth, and I've been trying hard not to think about it.*

"Are you afraid that I'll try to kiss you without your consent? To sit on your lap, or fondle you under the pretext of applying sunscreen? Because I would never—"

Olive chucked her phone at him. He caught it in his left hand, studied its glitter amino-acid case with a pleased expression, and then carefully set it next to her laptop.

"I hate you," She told him, sullen. She might have been pouting. And smiling at the same time.

His mouth twitched. "I know."

"Am I ever going to live that stuff down?"

"Unlikely. And if you do, I'm sure something else will come up."

She huffed, crossing her arms over her chest, and they exchanged a small smile.

"I can ask Holden or Tom if I can stay with them, and leave you my room," he suggested. "But they know that I already have one, so I'd have to come up with excuses—"

"No, I'm not going to kick you out of your room." She ran a hand through her hair and exhaled. "You'd hate it."

He tilted his head. "What?"

"Rooming with me."

"I would?"

"Yeah. You seem like a person who . . ." *You seem like you like to keep others at arm's length, uncompromising and ever so hard to know. You seem like you care very little about what people think of you. You seem like you know what you're doing. You seem equally horrible and awesome, and just the thought that there's someone you'd like to open up to, someone who's not me, makes me feel like I can't sit at this table any longer.* "Like you'd want your own space."

He held her gaze. "Olive. I think I'll be fine."

"But if you end up *not* being fine, then you'd be stuck with me."

"It's one night." His jaw clenched and relaxed, and he added, "We are friends, no?"

Her own words, thrown back at her. *I don't want to be your friend*, she was tempted to say. Thing was, she also didn't want to *not* be his friend. What she wanted was completely outside of her ability to obtain, and she needed to forget it. Scrap it from her brain.

"Yes. We are."

"Then, as a friend, don't force me to worry about you using public transportation late at night in a city you're not familiar with. Biking on roads without bike lanes is bad enough," he muttered, and she immediately felt a weight sink into her stomach. He was trying to be a good friend. He cared for her, and instead of being satisfied with what she currently had, she had to ruin it all and—and want more.

She took a deep breath. "Are you sure? That it wouldn't bother you?"

He nodded, silent.

"Okay, then. Okay." She forced herself to smile. "Do you snore?"

He huffed out a laugh. "I don't know."

"Oh, come on. How can you not know?"

He shrugged. "I just don't."

"Well, that probably means you don't. Otherwise, someone would have told you."

"Someone?"

"A roommate." It occurred to her that Adam was thirty-four and likely hadn't had a roommate in about a decade. "Or a girl-friend."

He smiled faintly and lowered his gaze. "I guess my 'girlfriend' will tell me after SBD, then." He said it in a quiet, unassuming tone, clearly trying to make a joke, but Olive's cheeks warmed, and she couldn't quite bear to look at him anymore. Instead she picked at a thread on the sleeve of her cardigan, and searched for something to say.

"My stupid abstract." She cleared her throat. "It was accepted as a talk."

He met her eyes. "Faculty panel?"

"Yeah."

"You're not happy?"

"No." She winced.

"Is it the public-speaking thing?"

He'd remembered. Of course he had. "Yeah. It will be awful."

Adam stared at her and said nothing. Not that it would be fine, not that the talk would go smoothly, not that she was over-reacting and underselling a fantastic opportunity. His calm acceptance of her anxiety had the exact opposite effect of Dr. Aslan's enthusiasm: it relaxed her.

"When I was in my third year of grad school," he said quietly, "my adviser sent me to give a faculty symposium in his stead. He told me only two days before, without any slides or a script. Just the title of the talk."

"Wow." Olive tried to imagine what that would have felt like, being expected to perform something so daunting with so little forewarning. At the same time, part of her marveled at Adam self-disclosing something without being asked a direct question. "Why did he do that?"

"Who knows?" He tilted his head back, staring at a spot above her head. His tone held a trace of bitterness. "Because he had an emergency. Because he thought it'd be a formative experience. Because he could."

Olive just bet that he could. She didn't know Adam's former adviser, but academia was very much an old boys' club, where those who held the power liked to take advantage of those who didn't without repercussions.

"Was it? A formative experience?"

He shrugged again. "As much as anything that keeps you awake in a panic for forty-eight hours straight can be."

Olive smiled. "And how did you do?"

"I did . . ." He pressed his lips together. "Not well enough." He was silent for a long moment, his gaze locked somewhere outside the café's window. "Then again, nothing was ever good enough."

It seemed impossible that someone might look at Adam's scientific accomplishments and find them lacking. That he could ever be anything less than the best at what he did. Was that why he was so severe in his judgment of others? Because he'd been taught to set the same impossible standards for himself?

"Do you still keep in touch with him? Your adviser, I mean."

"He's retired now. Tom has taken over what used to be his lab."

It was such an uncharacteristically opaque, carefully worded answer. Olive couldn't help being curious. "Did you like him?"

"It's complicated." He rubbed a hand over his jaw, looking pensive and far away. "No. No, I didn't like him. I still don't. He was . . ." It took him so long to continue, she almost convinced herself that he wouldn't. But he did, staring at the late-afternoon sunlight disappearing behind the oak trees. "Brutal. My adviser was brutal."

She chuckled, and Adam's eyes darted back to her face, narrow with confusion.

"Sorry." She was still laughing a little. "It's just funny, to hear you complain about your old mentor. Because . . ."

"Because?"

"Because he sounds exactly like you."

"I'm not like him," he retorted, more sharply than Olive had come to expect from him. It made her snort.

"Adam, I'm pretty sure that if we were to ask anyone to describe you with one word, 'brutal' would come up one or ten times."

She saw him stiffen before she was even done speaking, the line of his shoulders suddenly tense and rigid, his jaw tight and with a slight twitch to it. Her first instinct was to apologize, but she was not sure for what. There was nothing new to what she'd just told him—they'd discussed his blunt, uncompromising mentoring style before, and he'd always taken it in stride. Owned it, even. And yet his fists were clenched on the table, and his eyes were darker than usual.

"I . . . Adam, did I—" she stammered, but he interrupted her before she could continue.

"Everyone has issues with their advisers," he said, and there was a finality to his tone that warned her not to finish her sentence. Not to ask *What happened? Where did you just go?*

So she swallowed and nodded. "Dr. Aslan is . . ." She hesitated. His knuckles were not quite as white anymore, and the tension in his muscles was slowly dissolving. It was possible that she'd imagined it. Yes, she must have. "She's great. But sometimes I feel like she doesn't really understand that I need more . . ."

Guidance. Support. Some practical advice, instead of blind encouragement. "I'm not even sure what I need, myself. I think that might be part of the problem—I'm not very good at communicating it."

He nodded and appeared to choose his words carefully. "It's hard, mentoring. No one teaches you how to do it. We're trained to become scientists, but as professors, we're also in charge of making sure that students learn to produce rigorous science. I hold my grads accountable, and I set high standards for them. They're scared of me, and that's fine. The stakes are high, and if being scared means that they're taking their training seriously, then I'm okay with it."

She tilted her head. "What do you mean?"

"My job is to make sure that my adult graduate students don't become mediocre scientists. That means I'm the one who's tasked with demanding that they rerun their experiments or adjust their hypotheses. It comes with the territory."

Olive had never been a people pleaser, but Adam's attitude toward others' perception of him was so cavalier, it was almost fascinating. "Do you really not care?" she asked, curious. "That your grads might dislike you as a person?"

"Nah. I don't like them very much, either." She thought of Jess and Alex and the other half a dozen grads and postdocs mentored by Adam whom she didn't know very well. The thought of him finding them as annoying as they found him despotic made her chuckle. "To be fair, I don't like people in general."

"Right." *Don't ask, Olive. Do not ask.* "Do you like me?"

A millisecond of hesitation as he pressed his lips together. "Nope. You're a smart-ass with abysmal taste in beverages." He traced the corner of his iPad, a small smile playing on his lips. "Send me your slides."

"My slides?"

"For your talk. I'll take a look at them."

Olive tried not to gape at him. "Oh—you . . . I'm not your grad. You don't have to."

"I know."

"You really don't have to—"

"I want to," he said, voice pitched low and even as he looked into her eyes, and Olive had to avert her gaze because something felt too tight in her chest.

"Okay." She finally managed to snap out the loose thread on her sleeve. "How likely is it that your feedback will cause me to cry under the shower?"

"That depends on the quality of your slides."

She smiled. "Don't feel like you have to hold back."

"Believe me, I don't."

"Good. Great." She sighed, but it was reassuring, knowing that he was going to be checking her work. "Will you come to my talk?" she heard herself ask, and was as surprised by the request as Adam seemed to be.

"I . . . Do you want me to?"

No. No, it's going to be horrible, and humiliating, and probably a disaster, and you're going to see me at my worst and weakest. It's probably best if you lock yourself into the bathroom for the entire duration of the panel. Just so you don't accidentally wander in and see me making a fool of myself.

And yet. Just the idea of having him there, sitting in the audience, made the prospect seem like less of an ordeal. He was not her adviser, and he wasn't going to be able to do much if she got inundated by a barrage of impossible questions, or if the projector stopped working halfway through the talk. But maybe that wasn't what she needed from him.

It hit her then what was so special about Adam. That no matter his reputation, or how rocky their first meeting, since the very beginning, Olive had felt that he was on her side. Over and over, and in ways that she could never have anticipated, he had made her feel unjudged. Less alone.

She exhaled slowly. The realization should have been rattling, but it had an oddly calming effect. "Yes," she told him, thinking that this might very well turn out to be all right. She might never have what she wanted from Adam, but for now at least, he was in her life. That was going to have to be enough.

"I will, then."

She leaned forward. "Will you ask a long-winded, leading question that will cause me to ramble incoherently and lose the respect of my peers, thus forever undermining my place in the field of biology?"

"Possibly." He was smiling. "Should I buy you that disgusting"— Adam gestured toward the register—"pumpkin sludge now?"

She grinned. "Oh, yes. I mean, if you want to."

"I'd rather buy you anything else."

"Too bad." Olive jumped to her feet and headed for the counter, tugging at his sleeve and forcing him to stand with her. Adam followed meekly, mumbling something about black coffee that Olive chose to ignore.

Enough, she repeated to herself. *What you have now, it will have to be enough.*

Chapter Fourteen

♥ HYPOTHESIS: *This conference will be the worst thing to ever happen to my professional career, general well-being, and sense of sanity.*

There were two beds in the hotel room.

Two double beds to be precise, and as she stared at them, Olive felt her shoulders sag with relief and had to resist the urge to fist-pump. *Take that, you stupid rom-coms.* She may have fallen for the dude she'd begun to fake-date like some born-yesterday fool, but at least she wouldn't be sharing a bed with him any time soon. Given her disastrous past couple of weeks, she'd really, really needed the win.

There were a number of little clues that Adam had slept on the bed closest to the entrance—a book on the bedside table in a language that looked like German, a thumb drive and the same iPad she'd seen him carry around on several occasions, an iPhone charger dangling from the power outlet. A suitcase tucked by the foot of the bed, black and expensive-looking. Unlike Olive's, it probably hadn't been fished out of the Walmart bargain bin.

"I guess this is mine, then," she murmured, sitting on the bed closest to the window and bouncing a few times to test the firmness of the mattress. It was a nice room. Not ridiculously fancy, but Olive was suddenly grateful for the way Adam had snorted and looked at her like she was crazy when she'd offered to pay for half of it. At least the place was wide enough that they weren't going to have to brush up against each other every time they moved around. Staying in here with him wouldn't feel like a singularly sadistic version of seven minutes in heaven.

Not that they'd be together much. She was going to give her talk in a couple of hours—*ugh*—then go to the department's social and hang out with her friends until . . . well, as long as she feasibly could. Odds were that Adam already had tons of meetings scheduled, and maybe they wouldn't even see each other. Olive would be asleep when he came back tonight, and tomorrow morning one of them would pretend not to wake up while the other got ready. It was going to be fine. Harmless. At the very least, not make things worse than they currently were.

Olive's usual conference outfit was black jeans and her least-frayed cardigan, but a few days ago Anh had mentioned that the ensemble might be too casual for a talk. After sighing for hours Olive had decided to bring the black wrap dress she'd bought on sale before interviewing for grad school and black pumps borrowed from Anh's sister. It had seemed like a good idea at the time, but as soon as she slipped into the bathroom to put on the dress, she realized that it must have shrunk the last time she washed it. It didn't quite hit her knees anymore, not by a couple of inches. She groaned and snapped a picture for Anh and Malcolm, who texted her, respectively, **Still conference appropriate** and a fire emoji. Olive prayed that Anh was right as she combed the waves in her hair and fought against dried-out mascara—her fault for buying makeup at the dollar store, clearly.

She had just got out of the bathroom, rehearsing her talk under her breath, when the door opened and someone—Adam, of course it was *Adam*—entered the room. He was holding his key card and typing something in his phone, but stopped as soon as he looked up and noticed Olive. His mouth opened, and—

That was it. It just stayed open.

"Hey." Olive forced her face into a smile. Her heart was doing something weird in her chest. Beating a little too quickly. She should probably have it checked as soon as she got back home. One could never be too careful about cardiovascular health. "Hi."

He snapped his mouth closed and cleared his throat. "You're . . ." He swallowed and shifted on his feet. "Here."

"Yep." She nodded, still smiling. "Just arrived. My flight landed on time, surprisingly."

Adam seemed a little slow. Maybe jet-lagged from his own flight, or perhaps last night he'd been out late with his famous scientist friends, or with the mysterious woman Holden had talked about. He just stared at Olive, silent for several moments, and when he spoke, it was only to say, "You look . . ."

She glanced down at her dress and heels, wondering if her eye makeup was already smudged. She'd put it on three whole minutes ago, so it was more than likely. "Professional?"

"That's not what I . . ." Adam closed his eyes and shook his head, as if collecting himself. "But, yes. You do. How are you?"

"Good. Fine. I mean, I wish I were dead. But aside from that."

He laughed silently and moved closer. "You'll be okay." She had thought sweaters were a good look for him, but only because she'd never seen him wear a blazer. *He had a secret weapon all along*, she thought, trying not to stare too hard. *And now he's unleashing it. Damn him.*

"Agreed." She pushed her hair back and smiled. "After I die."

"You're fine. You have a script. You memorized it. Your slides are good."

"I think they were better before you made me change the PowerPoint background."

"It was acid green."

"I know. It made me happy."

"It made *me* nauseous."

"Mm. Anyway, thanks again for helping me figure it out." *And for answering the 139 questions I asked. Thank you for taking less than ten minutes to reply to my emails, every time, even when it was 5:30 a.m. and you misspelled "consensus," which is unusual of you and makes me suspect that maybe you were still half asleep.* "And for letting me crash with you."

"No problem."

She scratched the side of her nose. "I figured you were using that bed, so I put my stuff here, but if you . . ." She gestured confusedly at the room.

"No, that's where I slept last night."

"Okay." She was *not* counting how many inches there were between the two beds. Definitely not. "So how's the conference so far?"

"Same old. I was mostly at Harvard for a few meetings with Tom. I only got back for lunch."

Olive's stomach rumbled loudly at the mention of food.

"You okay?"

"Yeah. I think I forgot to eat today."

His eyebrows arched. "I didn't think you capable."

"Hey!" She glared at him. "The sustained levels of despair I've been engaging in for the past week require a staggering number of calories, in case you— What are you doing?"

Adam was leaning over his suitcase, rummaging for something that he held out to Olive.

"What is it?"

"Calories. To fuel your despair habits."

"Oh." She accepted it and then studied the protein bar in her hands, trying not to burst out crying. It was just food. Probably a snack he'd brought for the plane ride and ended up not eating. He didn't need to despair, after all. He was Dr. Adam Carlsen. "Thanks. Are you . . ." The wrapping of the bar crinkled as she shifted it from one hand to another. "Are you still coming to my talk?"

"Of course. When is it exactly?"

"Today at four, room 278. Session three-b. The good news is that it partially overlaps with the keynote address, which means that hopefully only a handful of people will show up . . ."

His spine stiffened noticeably. Olive hesitated.

"Unless you were planning to go to the keynote address?"

Adam wet his lips. "I . . ."

Her eyes chose that precise moment to fall to the conference badge dangling from his neck.

> Adam Carlsen, Ph.D.
> Stanford University
> Keynote Speaker

Her jaw dropped.

"Oh my God." She looked up at him, wide-eyed, and . . . Oh *God*. At least he had the grace to look sheepish. "How did you *not* tell me that you are the keynote speaker?"

Adam scratched his jaw, oozing discomfort. "I didn't think of it."

"Oh my God," she repeated.

To be fair, it was on her. The name of the keynote speaker was likely printed in font size 300 in the program, and all the promotional material, not to mention the conference app and the emails. Olive must have had her head very much up her butt to fail to notice.

"Adam." She made to rub her eyes with her fingers, and then thought better of it. Damn makeup. "I can't be fake-dating SBD's keynote speaker."

"Well, there are technically three keynote speakers, and the other two are married women in their fifties who live in Europe and Japan, so—"

Olive crossed her arms on her chest and gave him a flat look until he quieted. She couldn't help laughing. "How did this not come up?"

"It's not a big deal." He shrugged. "I doubt I was their first choice."

"Right." Sure. Because a person existed who'd refuse to be keynote speaker at SBD. She tilted her head. "Did you think I was an idiot, when I started complaining about my ten-minute talk that will be attended by fourteen and a half people?"

"Not at all. Your reaction was understandable." He thought about it for a moment. "I do sometimes think you're an idiot, mostly when I see you put ketchup and cream cheese on bagels."

"It's a great mix."

He looked pained. "When are you presenting in your panel? Maybe I can still make it."

"No. I'm exactly halfway through." She waved a hand, hoping to seem unconcerned. "It's fine, really." And it was. "I'm going to have to record myself with my iPhone, anyway." She rolled her eyes. "For Dr. Aslan. She couldn't come to the conference, but she said she wants to listen to my first talk. I can send it to you, if you're a fan of stammering and secondhand embarrassment."

"I'd like that."

Olive flushed and changed the topic. "Is that why you have a room for the entire length of the conference even though you're not staying? Because you're a big shot?"

He frowned. "I'm not."

"Can I call you 'big shot' from now on?"

He sighed, walking to the bedside table and pocketing the USB she'd noticed earlier. "I have to take my slides downstairs, smart-ass."

"Okay." He could leave. It was fine. Totally fine. Olive didn't let her smile falter. "I guess I'll maybe see you after my talk, then?"

"Of course."

"And after yours. Good luck. And congrats. It's such a huge honor."

Adam didn't seem to be thinking about that, though. He lingered by the door, his hand on the knob as he looked back at Olive. Their eyes held for a few moments before he told her, "Don't be nervous, okay?"

She pressed her lips together and nodded. "I'll just do what Dr. Aslan always says."

"And what's that?"

"Carry myself with the confidence of a mediocre white man."

He grinned, and—there they were. The heart-stopping dimples. "It will be fine, Olive." His smile softened. "And if not, at least it will be over."

It wasn't until a few minutes later, when she was sitting on her bed staring at the Boston skyline and chewing on her lunch, that Olive realized that the protein bar Adam had given her was covered in chocolate.

~~~~~

SHE CHECKED WHETHER she had the correct room for the third time—nothing like talking about pancreatic cancer to a crowd that expected a presentation on the Golgi apparatus to make an impression—and then felt a hand close around her shoulder. She spun around, noticed who it belonged to, and immediately grinned.

"Tom!"

He was wearing a charcoal suit. His blond hair was combed back, making him look older than he had in California, but also professional. He was a friendly face in a sea of unfamiliar ones, and his presence took the edge off her intense desire to puke in her own shoe.

"Hey, Olive." He held the door open for her. "I thought I might see you here."

"Oh?"

"From the conference program." He looked at her oddly. "You didn't notice we're on the same panel?"

Oh, *crap*. "Uh—I . . . I didn't even read who else was on the panel." *Because I was too busy panicking.*

"No worries. It's mostly boring people." He winked, and his hand slid to her back, guiding her toward the podium. "Except for you and me, of course."

Her talk didn't go poorly.

It didn't go perfectly, either. She stumbled on the word "channelrhodopsin" twice, and by some weird trick of the projector her staining looked more like a black blob than a slice. "It looks different on my computer," Olive told the audience with a strained smile. "Just trust me on this one."

People chuckled, and she relaxed marginally, grateful that she'd spent hours upon hours memorizing everything she was supposed to say. The room was not as full as she'd feared, and there were a handful of people—likely working on similar projects at other institutions—who took notes and listened raptly to her every word. It should have been overwhelming and anxiety inducing, but about halfway through she realized that it made her oddly giddy, knowing that someone else was passionate about the same research questions that had taken up most of the past two years of her life.

In the second row, Malcolm faked a fascinated expression, while Anh, Jeremy, and a bunch of other grads from Stanford nodded enthusiastically whenever Olive happened to look in their direction. Tom alternated between staring intensely at her and checking his phone with a bored expression—fair, since he'd already read her report. The session was running late, and the moderator ended up giving her time for only one question—an easy one. At the end, two of the other panelists—well-known cancer researchers whom Olive had to restrain herself not to fangirl over—shook her hand and asked her several questions about her work. She was simultaneously flustered and overjoyed.

"You were so amazing," Anh told her when it was over, pushing up to hug her. "Also, you look hot and professional, and while you were talking, I had a vision of your future in academia."

Olive wrapped her arms around Anh. "What vision?"

"You were a high-powered researcher, surrounded by students who hung on your every word. And you were answering a multiparagraph email with an uncapitalized no."

"Nice. Was I happy?"

"Of course not." Anh snorted. "It's academia."

"Ladies, the department social starts in half an hour." Malcolm leaned in to kiss Olive on the cheek and squeeze her waist. When she was wearing heels, he was just a tiny bit shorter than her. She definitely wanted a picture of the two of them side by side. "We should go celebrate the single time Olive managed to pronounce 'channelrhodopsin' right with some free booze."

"You dick."

He pulled her in for a tight hug and whispered in her ear,

"You did amazing, Kalamata." And then, louder: "Let's go get wasted!"

"Why don't you guys go ahead? I'll get my USB and put my stuff back in the hotel."

Olive made her way through the now-empty room to the podium, feeling like a huge weight had been lifted off her shoulders. She was relaxed and relieved. Professionally, things were starting to look up: as it turned out, with adequate preparation she could actually string together several coherent sentences in front of other scientists. She also had the means to carry out her research next year, and two big names in her field had just complimented her work. She smiled, letting her mind wander to whether she should text Adam to tell him that he was right, she did make it out alive; she should probably ask how his keynote address had gone, too. If his PowerPoint had acted up and he'd mispronounced words like "microarrays" or "karyotyping," whether he planned to go to the department social. He was probably meeting up with friends, but maybe she could buy him a thank-you drink for all his help. She would even pay, for once.

"It went well," someone said.

Olive turned to find Tom standing behind her, arms folded across his chest as he leaned against the table. He looked as though he'd been staring at her for a while. "Thank you. Yours, too." His talk had been a more condensed repeat of the one he'd given at Stanford, and Olive had to admit that she'd spaced out a bit.

"Where's Adam?" he asked.

"Still giving his keynote, I think."

"Right." Tom rolled his eyes. Probably with fondness, though Olive didn't quite catch it in his expression. "He does that, doesn't he?"

"Does what?"

"Outdoes you." He pushed away from the table, ambling closer. "Well, outdoes everyone. It's not personal." She frowned, confused, wanting to ask Tom what he meant by that, but he continued, "I think you and I will get along great next year."

The reminder that Tom believed in her work enough to take her in his lab quashed her discomfort. "We will." She smiled. "Thank you so much for giving me and my project a chance. I can't wait to start working with you."

"You're welcome." He was smiling, too. "I think there are a lot of things we can gain from each other. Wouldn't you agree?"

It seemed to Olive like she had much more to gain from it than he did, but she nodded anyway. "I hope so. I think imaging and blood biomarkers complement each other perfectly, and only by combining them can we—"

"And I have what you need, don't I? The research funds. The lab space. The time and ability to mentor you properly."

"Yes. You do. I . . ."

All of a sudden, she could pick out the gray rim of his cornea. Had he gotten closer? He was tall, but not that much taller than her. He didn't usually feel *this* imposing.

"I'm grateful. So grateful. I'm sure that—"

She felt his unfamiliar smell in her nostrils, and his breath, hot and unpleasant against the corner of her mouth, and—fingers, a vise-tight grip around her upper arm, and why was he—what was he—

"What—" Heart in her throat, Olive freed her arm and took several steps back. "What are you *doing*?" Her hand came up to her biceps and—it *hurt*, where he'd clasped her.

God—had he really done that? Tried to kiss her? No, she must have imagined it. She must be going crazy, because Tom would never—

"A preview, I think."

She just stared at him, too stunned and numb to react, until he moved closer and bent once more toward her. Then it was happening all over again.

She pushed him away. As forcefully as she could, she pushed him away with both her hands on his chest, until he stumbled back with a cruel, condescending laugh. Abruptly, her lungs seized and she couldn't breathe.

"A preview of—what? Are you out of your mind?"

"Come on."

Why was he smiling? Why was that oily, hateful expression on his face? Why was he looking at her like—

"A pretty girl like you should know the score by now." He looked at her from head to toe, and the lewd gleam in his eyes made her feel disgusting. "Don't lie to me and say you didn't pick out a dress that short for my benefit. Nice legs, by the way. I can see why Adam's wasting his time with you."

"The— What are you—"

"Olive." He sighed, putting his hands in his pockets. He should have looked nonthreatening, lounging like that. But he felt like anything but. "You don't think I accepted you into my lab because you are good, do you?"

Slack-jawed, she took one more step back. One of her heels almost caught in the carpet, and she had to hold on to the table to avoid falling.

"A girl like you. Who figured out so early in her academic career that fucking well-known, successful scholars is how to get ahead." He was still smiling. The same smile Olive had once thought kind. Reassuring. "You fucked Adam, didn't you? We both know you're going to fuck me for the same reason."

She was going to vomit. She *was* going to vomit in this room, after all, and it had nothing to do with her talk. "You are disgusting."

"Am I?" He shrugged, unperturbed. "That makes two of us. You used Adam to get to me and to my lab. To this conference, too."

"I didn't. I didn't even *know* Adam when I submitted—"

"Oh, please. You're telling me you thought your pitiful abstract was selected for a talk because of its quality and scientific importance?" He made a disbelieving face. "Someone here has a very high opinion of herself, considering that her research is useless and derivative and that she can barely put together two words without stuttering like an idiot."

She froze. Her stomach sank and twisted, her feet cemented to the ground. "It's not true," she whispered.

"No? You think it's not true that scientists in the field want to impress the great Adam Carlsen enough to kiss the ass of whoever he's fucking at the moment? I certainly did when I told his very mediocre girlfriend that she could come work for me. But maybe you're right," he said, all mocking affability. "Maybe you know STEM academia better than I do."

"I'm going to tell Adam about this. I'm going to—"

"By all means." Tom widened his arms. "Go ahead. Be my guest. Do you need to borrow my phone?"

"No." Her nostrils flared. A wave of icy anger swept over her. "No." She turned around and marched to the entrance, fighting the nausea and bile climbing up her throat. She was going to find Adam. She was going to find the conference organizers and report Tom. She was never going to see his face again.

"Quick question. Who do you think Adam will believe, Olive?"

She halted abruptly, just a few feet from the door.

"Some bitch he's been fucking for about two weeks, or someone who's been a close friend for years? Someone who helped him get the most important grant of his career? Someone who's had his back since he was younger than you are? Someone who's actually a *good* scientist?"

She spun around, shaking with rage. "Why are you doing this?"

"Because I can." Tom shrugged again. "Because as advantageous as my collaboration with Adam has been, sometimes it's a bit annoying how he needs to be best at everything, and I like the idea of taking something away from him for once. Because you are very pretty, and I look forward to spending more time with you next year. Who would have guessed that Adam had such good taste?"

"You are crazy. If you think that I'll work in your lab, you are—"

"Oh, Olive. But you will. Because you see—while your work is not particularly brilliant, it does complement nicely the ongoing projects in my lab."

She let out a single, bitter laugh. "Are you really so deluded that you think I would ever collaborate with you after this?"

"Mmm. It's more that you don't have a choice. Because if you want to finish your project, my lab is your only opportunity. And if you don't . . . well. You sent me information on all your protocols, which means that I can easily replicate them. But don't worry. Maybe I'll mention you in the acknowledgment section."

She felt the ground flip under her feet. "You wouldn't," she whispered. "It's research misconduct."

"Listen, Olive. My friendly advice is: suck it up. Keep Adam happy and interested as long as possible, and then come to my lab to finally do some decent work. If you keep *me* happy, I'll make sure you can save the world from pancreatic cancer. Your nice little sob story about your mom or your aunt or your stupid kindergarten teacher dying from it is only going to get you so far. You're mediocre."

Olive turned around and ran from the room.

~~~~~~

WHEN SHE HEARD the beep of the key card, she immediately wiped her face with the sleeves of her dress. It didn't quite do the trick: she'd been crying for a solid twenty minutes, and even an entire paper towel roll wouldn't have been enough to hide what she'd been up to. Really, though, it wasn't Olive's fault. She'd been sure Adam had to attend the opening ceremony, or at least the department social after his talk. Wasn't he on the social-and-networking committee? He should have been elsewhere. Socializing. Networking. Committeeing.

But here he was. Olive heard steps as he walked inside, then him stopping at the entrance of the bedroom, and . . .

She couldn't convince her eyes to meet his. She was a mess after all, a miserable, disastrous mess. But she should at least attempt to divert Adam's attention. Maybe by saying something. Anything.

"Hey." She tried a smile, but continued to stare down at her own hands. "How did your address go?"

"What happened?" His voice was calm, pitched low.

"Did you only just finish?" Her smile was holding. Good. Good, that was good. "How was the Q and A—"

"What happened?"

"Nothing. I . . ."

She didn't manage to finish the sentence. And the smile— which, if she was honest with herself, hadn't been much of a smile to begin with—was crumbling. Olive heard Adam come closer but didn't look at him. Her closed eyelids were all that was keeping the floodgates shut, and they weren't doing a good job of it, either.

She startled when she found him kneeling in front of her. Right by her chair, his head level with hers, studying her with a worried frown. She made to hide her face in her palms, but his hand came up to her chin and lifted it up, until she had no choice but to meet his eyes. Then his fingers slid up to her cheek, cupping it as he asked, yet again, "Olive. What happened?"

"Nothing." Her voice shook. It kept disappearing somewhere, melting in the tears.

"Olive."

"Really. Nothing."

Adam stared at her, questioning, and didn't let go. "Did someone buy the last bag of chips?"

A laugh bubbled out of her, wet and not wholly under her control. "Yes. Was it you?"

"Of course." His thumb swiped across her cheekbone, stopping a falling tear. "I bought all of them."

This smile felt better than the one she'd cobbled together earlier. "I hope you have good health insurance, because you're so getting type 2 diabetes."

"Worth it."

"You monster." She must have been leaning into his hand, because his thumb was stroking her again. Ever so gently.

"Is that how you talk to your fake boyfriend?" He looked so worried. His eyes, the line of his mouth. And yet—so patient. "What happened, Olive?"

She shook her head. "I just . . ."

She couldn't tell him. And she couldn't *not* tell him. But above all, she couldn't tell him.

Who do you think Adam will believe, Olive?

She had to take a deep breath. Push Tom's voice out of her head and calm herself before continuing. Come up with something to say, something that wouldn't make the sky fall in this hotel room.

"My talk. I thought it went okay. My friends said it did. But then I heard people talking about it, and they said . . ." Adam really should stop touching her. She must be getting his whole hand wet. The sleeve of his blazer, too.

"What did they say?"

"Nothing. That it was derivative. Boring. That I stammered. They knew that I'm your girlfriend and said that was the only reason I was chosen to give a talk." She shook her head. She needed to let it go. To put it out of her head. To think carefully about what to do.

"Who? Who were they?"

Oh, Adam. "Someone. I'm not sure."

"Did you see their badges?"

"I . . . didn't pay attention."

"Were they on your panel?" There was something underneath his tone. Something pressing that hinted at violence and rage and broken bones. Adam's hand was still gentle on her cheek, but his eyes narrowed. There was a new tension in his jaw, and Olive felt a shiver run down her spine.

"No," she lied. "It doesn't matter. It's okay."

His lips pressed into a straight line, his nostrils flared, so she added, "I don't care what people think of me, anyway."

"Right," he scoffed.

This Adam, right here, was the moody, irascible Adam who grads in her program complained about. Olive shouldn't have been surprised to see him this angry, but he'd never been like this with her before.

"No, really, I don't care what people say—"

"I know you don't. But that's the problem, isn't it?" He stared at her, and he was so close. She could see how the yellows and greens mixed into the clear brown of his eyes. "It's not what *they* say. It's what *you* think. It's that you think they're right. Don't you?"

Her mouth was full of cotton. "I . . ."

"Olive. You are a great scientist. And you will become an even better one." The way he was looking at her, so earnest and serious—it was going to break her. "Whatever this asshole said, it speaks nothing of you and a whole lot of them." His fingers shifted on her skin to weave through the hair behind her ear. "Your work is brilliant."

She didn't even think it through. And even if she had, she probably couldn't have stopped herself. She just leaned forward and hid her face in his neck, hugging him tight. A terrible idea, stupid and inappropriate, and Adam was surely going to push her away, any minute now, except that . . .

His palm slid to her nape, almost as if to press her into him, and Olive just stayed there for long minutes, crying warm tears into the flesh of his throat, feeling how grounding, how warm, how solid he was—under her fingers and in her life.

You just had to go and make me fall for you, she thought, blinking against his skin. *You absolute ass.*

He didn't let her go. Not until she pulled back and wiped her cheeks again, feeling like maybe this time around she'd be able to hold it together. She sniffled, and he leaned over to grab a box of tissues from the TV table. "I really am fine."

He sighed.

"Okay, maybe . . . maybe I'm not fine right now, but I will be." She accepted the tissue that he plucked for her and blew her nose. "I just need a while to . . ."

He studied her and nodded, his eyes unreadable again.

"Thank you. For what you said. For letting me snot all over your hotel room."

He smiled. "Anytime."

"And your jacket, too. Are you . . . Are you going to the department social?" she asked, dreading the moment she would have to get out of this chair. Of this room. *Be honest*, that sensible, ever-knowing voice inside her whispered. *It's his presence that you don't want to be out of.*

"Are you?"

She shrugged. "I said I would. But I don't feel like talking to anyone right now." She dried her cheeks once more, but miraculously the flow had stopped. Adam Carlsen, responsible for 90 percent of the department's tears, had actually managed to make someone stop crying. Who would've thought? "Though I feel like the free alcohol could really help."

He stared at her pensively for a moment, biting the inside of his cheek. Then he nodded, seeming to reach some sort of decision, and stood with his hand held out to her. "Come on."

"Oh." She had to crane her neck to look up at him. "I think I'm going to wait a bit before I—"

"We're not going to the social."

We? "What?"

"Come on," he repeated, and this time Olive took his hand and didn't let go. She couldn't, with the way his fingers were closing around hers. Adam looked pointedly at her shoes, until she got the hint and slipped them on, using his arm to keep her balance.

"Where are we going?"

"To get some free alcohol. Well"—he amended—"free for you."

She almost gasped when she realized what he meant. "No,

I—Adam, no. You have to go to the department social. And to the opening ceremony. You're the keynote speaker!"

"And I keynote-spoke." He grabbed her red duffle coat from the bed and pulled her toward the entrance. "Can you walk in those shoes?"

"I—yes, but—"

"I have my key card; we don't need yours."

"Adam." She grabbed his wrist, and he immediately turned to look at her. "Adam, you can't skip those events. People will say that you—"

His smile was lopsided. "That I want to spend time with my girlfriend?"

Olive's brain stopped. Just like that. And then it started again, and—

The world was a little different.

When he tugged her hand again, she smiled and simply followed him out of the room.

Chapter Fifteen

♥ **HYPOTHESIS:** *There is no moment in life that cannot be improved by food delivered by conveyor belt.*

Everyone saw them.

People whom Olive had never met before, people whom she recognized from blog posts and science Twitter, people from her department who'd been her teachers in previous years. People who smiled at Adam, who addressed him by his first name or as Dr. Carlsen, who told him "Great talk" or "See you around." People who completely ignored Olive, and people who studied her curiously—her, and Adam, and the place where their hands were joined.

Adam mostly nodded back, only stopping to chat with Holden.

"You guys skipping the boring shit?" he asked with a knowing smile.

"Yep."

"I'll make sure to drink your booze, then. And to extend your apologies."

"No need."

"I'll just say you had a family emergency." Holden winked. "Perhaps *future-family* emergency, how does that sound?"

Adam rolled his eyes and pulled Olive outside. She had to hurry to keep up with him, not because he was walking particularly fast, but because his legs were so long, one of his strides was worth about three of hers.

"Um . . . I'm wearing heels, here."

He turned to her, his eyes traveling down her legs and then rapidly moving away. "I know. You're less vertically challenged than usual."

Her eyes narrowed. "Hey, I'm five-eight. That's actually pretty tall."

"Hm." Adam's expression was noncommittal.

"What's that face?"

"What face?"

"Your face."

"Just my regular face?"

"No, that's your 'you're not tall' face."

He smiled, just a smidge. "Are the shoes okay for walking? Should we go back?"

"They're fine, but can we slow down?"

He feigned a sigh, but he did. His hand let go of hers and pushed against her lower back to steer her to the right. She had to hide a small shiver.

"So . . ." She stuffed her fists in the pockets of her coat, trying to ignore how the tips of her fingers were still tingling. "Those free drinks you mentioned? Do they come with food?"

"I'll get you dinner." Adam's lips curved a little more. "You're not a cheap date, though."

She leaned into his side and bumped her shoulder against his biceps. It was hard not to notice that there was no give. "I really am not. I fully plan to eat and drink my feelings."

His smile was more uneven than ever. "Where do you want to go, smart-ass?"

"Let's see . . . What do you like? Aside from tap water and hard-boiled spinach?"

He gave her a dirty side-look. "How about burgers?"

"Meh." She shrugged. "I guess. If there's nothing else."

"What's wrong with burgers?"

"I don't know. They taste like foot."

"They what?"

"What about Mexican? Do you like Mexican?"

"Burgers don't taste like—"

"Or Italian? Pizza would be great. And maybe there's something celery-based that you could order."

"Burgers it is."

Olive laughed. "What about Chinese?"

"Had it for lunch."

"Well, people in China have Chinese food multiple times a day, so you shouldn't let that stop you from— *Oh*."

It took Adam two whole steps to realize that Olive had stopped in the middle of the sidewalk. He whirled around to look at her. "What?"

"There." She pointed to the red-and-white sign across the road.

Adam's gaze followed, and for a long moment he simply stared, blinking several times. And then: "No."

"There," she repeated, feeling her cheeks widen into a grin.

"Olive." There was a deep vertical line between his eyebrows. "No. There are way better restaurants we can—"

"But I want to go to that one."

"Why? There's—"

She moved closer to him and grasped the sleeve of his blazer. "Please. Please?"

Adam pinched his nose, sighed, and pursed his lips. But not

five seconds later he put his hand between her shoulder blades to guide her across the street.

~~~~~~

THE PROBLEM, HE explained in hushed tones as they waited to be seated, was not the sushi train, but the all-you-can-eat for twenty dollars.

"It's never a good sign," he told her, but his voice sounded more resigned than combative, and when the server ushered them inside, he followed her meekly to the booth. Olive marveled at the plates traveling on the conveyor belt weaving across the restaurant, unable to stop her openmouthed grin. When she remembered Adam's presence and turned her attention back to him, he was staring at her with an expression halfway between exasperated and indulgent.

"You know," he told her, eyeing a seaweed salad passing by his shoulder, "we could go to a real Japanese restaurant. I am very happy to pay for however much sushi you want to eat."

"But will it *move* around me?"

He shook his head. "I take it back: you are a *disturbingly* cheap date."

She ignored him and lifted the glass door, grabbing a roll and a chocolate doughnut. Adam muttered something that sounded a lot like "very authentic," and when the waitress stopped by he ordered them both a beer.

"What do you think this is?" Olive dipped a piece of sushi in her soy sauce. "Tuna or salmon?"

"Probably spider meat."

She popped it into her mouth. "Delicious."

"Really." He looked skeptical.

It wasn't, in all truth. But it was okay. And this, well, this was so much fun. Exactly what she needed to empty her mind of . . . everything. Everything but here and now. With Adam.

"Yep." She pushed the remaining piece toward him, silently daring him to try it.

He broke apart his chopsticks with a long-suffering expression and picked it up, chewing for a long time.

"It tastes like foot."

"No way. Here." She grabbed a bowl of edamame from the belt. "You can have this. It's basically broccoli."

He brought one to his mouth, managing to look like he didn't hate it. "We don't have to talk, by the way."

Olive tilted her head.

"You said you didn't want to talk to anyone back at the hotel. So we don't have to, if you'd rather eat this"—he glanced at the plates she had accumulated with obvious distrust—"food in silence."

You're not just anyone, seemed like a dangerous thing to say, so she smiled. "I bet you're great at silences."

"Is that a dare?"

She shook her head. "I want to talk. Just, can we not talk about the conference? Or science? Or the fact that the world is full of assholes?" *And that some of them are your close friends and collaborators?*

His hand closed into a fist on the table, jaw clenched tight as he nodded.

"Awesome. We could chat about how nice this place is—"

"It's appalling."

"—or the taste of the sushi—"

"Foot."

"—or the best movie in the Fast and Furious franchise—"

"*Fast Five*. Though I have a feeling you're going to say—"

"*Tokyo Drift*."

"Right." He sighed, and they exchanged a small smile. And then, then the smile faded and they just stared at each other, something thick and sweet coloring the air between them, magnetic and just the right side of bearable. Olive had to rip her gaze from his, because—no. No.

She turned away, and her eyes fell on a couple at a table a few feet to their right. They were the mirror image of Adam and Olive, sitting on each side of their booth, all warm glances and tentative smiles. "Do you think they're on a fake date?" she asked, leaning back against her seat.

Adam followed her gaze to the couple. "I thought those mostly involved coffee shops and sunscreen applications?"

"Nah. Only the best ones."

He laughed silently. "Well." He focused on the table, and on angling his chopsticks so that they were parallel to each other. "I can definitely recommend it."

Olive dipped her chin to hide a smile and then leaned forward to steal one edamame.

~~~~~~

IN THE ELEVATOR she held on to his biceps and took off her heels, failing disastrously at being graceful as he studied her and shook his head. "I thought you said they didn't hurt?" He sounded curious. Amused? Fond?

"That was ages ago." Olive picked them up and let them dangle from her fingers. When she straightened, Adam was again impossibly tall. "Now I am very ready to chop off my feet."

The elevator pinged, and the doors opened. "That seems counterproductive."

"Oh, you have no idea— Hey, what are you—?"

Her heart skipped what felt like a dozen beats when Adam swept her up into a full bridal carry. She yelped, and he carried her to their room, all because she had a blister on her pinkie toe. Without much of a choice, she closed her arms around his neck and sank against him, trying to make sure she'd survive if he decided to drop her. His hands were warm around her back and knee, forearms tight and strong.

He smelled amazing. He felt even better.

"You know, the room's only twenty meters away—"

"I have no idea what that means."

"Adam."

"We Americans think in feet, Canada."

"I'm too heavy."

"You really are." The ease with which he shifted her in his arms to slide the key card belied his words. "You should cut pumpkin-flavored drinks from your diet."

She pulled his hair and smiled into his shoulder. "Never."

Their name tags were still on the TV table, exactly where they'd left them, and there was a conference program half-open on Adam's bed, not to mention tote bags and a mountain of useless flyers. Olive noticed them immediately, and it was like having a thousand little splinters pressed deep into a fresh wound. It brought back every single word Tom had said to her, all his lies and his truths and his mocking insults, and . . .

Adam must have known. As soon as he put her down, he gathered everything that was conference related and stuck it on a chair facing the windows, where it was hidden from their sight, and Olive . . . She could have hugged him. She wasn't going to—she already had, twice today—but she really could have. Instead she resolutely pushed all those little splinters out of her mind, plopped herself down on her bed belly up, and stared at the ceiling.

She'd thought it would be awkward, being with him in such a small space for a whole night. And it was a little bit, or at least it had been when she'd first arrived earlier today, but now she felt calm and safe. Like her world, constantly hectic and messy and demanding, was slowing down. Easing up, just a bit.

The bedcover rustled under her head when she turned to look at Adam. He seemed relaxed, too, as he draped his jacket against the back of a chair, then took off his watch and set it neatly on the desk. The casual domesticity of it—the thought that his day and hers would end in the same place, at the same time—soothed her like a slow caress down her spine.

"Thank you. For buying me food."

He glanced at her, crinkling his nose. "I don't know that there was any food involved."

She smiled, rolling to her side. "You're not going out again?"

"Out?"

"Yeah. To meet other very important science people? Eat another seven pounds of edamame?"

"I think I've had enough networking and edamame for this decade." He took off his shoes and socks, and set them neatly by the bed.

"You're staying in, then?"

He paused and looked at her. "Unless you'd rather be alone?"

No, I would not. She propped herself up on her elbow. "Let's watch a movie."

Adam blinked at her. "Sure." He sounded surprised but not displeased. "But if your taste in movies is anything like your taste in restaurants, it'll probably—"

He didn't see the pillow coming at him. It bounced off his face and then fell to the floor, making Olive giggle and spring off the bed. "You mind if I shower, before?"

"You smart-ass."

She started rummaging through her suitcase. "You can pick the movie! I don't care which one, as long as there are no scenes in which horses are killed, because it— Crap."

"What?"

"I forgot my pajamas." She looked for her phone in the pockets of her coat. It wasn't there, and she realized that she hadn't brought it with her to the restaurant. "Have you seen my— Oh, there it is."

The battery was almost dead, probably because she had forgotten to turn off the recording after her talk. She hadn't checked her messages in a few hours, and found several unread texts—mostly from Anh and Malcolm, asking her where she was and if she still planned to come to the social, telling her to get her ass there ASAP because "the booze is flowing like a river," and then, finally, just informing her that they were all going downtown to a bar. Anh must have been well on her way to wasted by that point, because her last message read: Clallif u want tp join ♥ us, Olvie

"I forgot my pajamas and wanted to see if I could borrow something from my friends, but I don't think they'll be back for hours. Though maybe Jess didn't go with them, let me text and see if—"

"Here." Adam set something black and neatly folded on her bed. "You can use this if you want."

She studied it skeptically. "What is it?"

"A T-shirt. I slept in it yesterday, but it's probably better than the dress you're wearing. To sleep in, I mean," he added, a faint flush on his cheeks.

"Oh." She picked it up, and the T-shirt unfolded. She immediately noticed three things: it was large, so large that it would hit her mid-thigh or even lower; it smelled heavenly, a mix of Adam's skin and laundry detergent that had her wanting to bury her face in it and inhale for weeks; and on the front, it said in big, white letters . . .

"'Biology Ninja'?"

Adam scratched the back of his neck. "I didn't buy it."

"Did you . . . steal it?"

"It was a present."

"Well." She grinned. "This is one hell of a present. Doctor ninja."

He stared at her flatly. "If you tell anyone, I'll deny it."

She chuckled. "Are you sure it's okay? What will you wear?"

"Nothing."

She must have been gaping at him a little too much, because he gave her an amused look and shook his head.

"I'm kidding. I have a tee under my shirt."

She nodded and hurried into the bathroom, making a point not to meet his eyes.

Alone under the hot jet of the shower it was much harder to concentrate on stale sushi and Adam's uneven smile, and to forget why he'd ended up allowing her to cling to him for three whole hours. What Tom had done to her today was despicable, and she was going to have to report him. She was going to have to tell Adam. She was going to have to *do* something. But every time she tried to think about it rationally, she could hear his voice in her head—*mediocre* and *nice legs* and *useless and derivative* and *little sob story*—so loud that she was afraid her skull would shatter into pieces.

So she kept her shower as quick as possible, distracting herself by reading the labels of Adam's shampoo and body wash (something hypoallergenic and pH-balanced that had her rolling her eyes) and drying herself as fast as humanly possible. She took out her contacts, then stole a bit of his toothpaste. Her gaze fell on his toothbrush; it was charcoal black, down to the bristles, and she couldn't help but giggle.

When she stepped out of the bathroom, he was sitting on the edge of the bed, wearing plaid pajama pants and a white T-shirt. He was holding the TV remote in one hand and his phone in the other, looking between the two screens with a frown.

"You would."

"Would what?" he asked absentmindedly.

"Have a black toothbrush."

His mouth twitched. "You will be shocked to hear that there is no Netflix category for movies in which horses don't die."

"An obscenity, isn't it? It's much needed." She crumpled her too-short dress into a ball and stuffed it inside her bag, fantasizing that she was stuffing Tom's throat. "If I were American, I'd totally run for Congress on that platform."

"Should we fake-marry, so you can get citizenship?"

Her heart stumbled. "Oh, yes. I think it's time we fake-move-to-the-next-level."

"So"—he tapped at his phone—"I'm just googling 'dead horse,' plus the title of whatever movie sounds good."

"That's what I usually do." She padded across the room until she was standing next to him. "What do you have?"

"This one's about a linguistics professor who's asked to help decipher an alien—"

He glanced up from his phone, and immediately fell silent. His mouth opened and then shut, and his eyes skittered to her thighs, her feet, her unicorn knee socks, and quickly back to her face. No, not her face: some point above her shoulder. He cleared his throat before saying, "Glad it . . . fits." He was looking at his phone again. His grip on the remote had tightened.

It was a long beat before she realized that he was referring to his T-shirt. "Oh, yeah." She grinned. "Exactly my size, right?" It was so large that it covered pretty much the same amount of skin her dress had, but was soft and comfortable like an old shoe. "Maybe I won't give it back."

"It's all yours."

She rocked on her heels, and wondered if it would be okay if she sat next to him now. It was only convenient, since they had to choose a movie together. "Can I really sleep in it this week?"

"Of course. I'll be gone tomorrow, anyway."

"Oh." She knew that, of course. She'd known the first time he'd told her, a couple of weeks ago; she'd known this morning when she'd boarded the plane in San Francisco, and she'd known mere hours ago, when she'd used that precise piece of information to comfort herself that no matter how awkward and stressful, her stay with Adam would at least be short-lived. Except that it wasn't awkward now. And it wasn't stressful. Not nearly as much as the idea of being apart from him for several days. Of being here, of all places, without him. "How big is your suitcase?"

"Hm?"

"Can I come with you?"

He looked up at her, still smiling, but he must've noticed something in her eyes, behind the joke and the attempt at humor. Something vulnerable and imploring that she'd failed to adequately bury within herself.

"Olive." He dropped his phone and the remote on the bed. "Don't let them."

She just tilted her head. She was not going to cry again. There was no point in it. And she was not like this—this fragile, defenseless creature who second-guessed herself at every turn. At least, she didn't use to be. God, she hated Tom Benton.

"Let them?"

"Don't let them ruin this conference for you. Or science. Or make you feel any less proud of your accomplishments."

She looked down, studying the yellow of her socks as she buried her toes in the soft carpet. And then up to him again.

"You know what's really sad about this?"

He shook his head, and Olive continued.

"For a moment there, during the talk . . . I really enjoyed myself. I was panicky. Close to puking, for sure. But while I was talking to this huge group of people about my work and my hypotheses and my ideas, and explaining my reasoning and the trials and errors and why what I research is so important, I . . . I felt confident. I felt good at it. It all felt *right* and *fun*. Like science is supposed to be when you share it." She wrapped her arms around herself. "Like maybe I could be an academic, down the road. A real one. And maybe make a difference."

He nodded as though he knew exactly what she meant. "I wish I had been there, Olive."

She could tell he really did. That he regretted not being with her. But even Adam—indomitable, decisive, ever-competent Adam—couldn't be in two places at once, and the fact remained that he had *not* seen her talk.

I have no idea if you're good enough, but that's not what you should be asking yourself. What matters is whether your reason *to be in academia is good enough.* That's what he'd told her years ago in the bathroom. What she'd been repeating to herself for years whenever she'd hit a wall. But what if he'd been wrong all along? What if there *was* such a thing as good enough? What if that was what mattered the most?

"What if it's true? What if I really am mediocre?"

He didn't reply for a long moment. He just stared, a hint of frustration in his expression, a thoughtful line to his lips. And then, low and even, he said, "When I was in my second year of grad school, my adviser told me that I was a failure who would never amount to anything."

"What?" Whatever she'd expected, that wasn't it. "Why?"

"Because of an incorrect primer design. But it wasn't the first time, nor the last. And it wasn't the most trivial reason he used to berate me. Sometimes he'd publicly humiliate his grads for no reason. But that specific time stuck with me, because I remember thinking . . ." He swallowed, and his throat worked. "I remember being sure that he was right. That I would never amount to anything."

"But you . . ." *Have published articles in the* Lancet. *Have tenure and millions of dollars in research grants. Were keynote speaker at a major conference.* Olive wasn't even sure what to bring up, so she settled for, "You were a MacArthur Fellow."

"I was." He exhaled a laugh. "And five years before the Mac-Arthur grant, in the second year of my Ph.D., I spent an entire week preparing law school applications because I was sure that I'd never become a scientist."

"Wait—so what Holden said was true?" She couldn't quite believe it. "Why law school?"

He shrugged. "My parents would have loved it. And if I couldn't be a scientist, I didn't care what I'd become."

"What stopped you, then?"

He sighed. "Holden. And Tom."

"Tom," she repeated. Her stomach twisted, leaden.

"I would have dropped out of my Ph.D. program if it hadn't been for them. Our adviser was well-known in the field for being a sadist. Like I am, I suppose." His mouth curled into a bitter smile. "I was aware of his reputation before starting my Ph.D. Thing is, he was also brilliant. The very best. And I thought . . . I thought that I could take it, whatever he'd dish out at me, and that it would be worth it. I thought it would be a matter of sacrifice and discipline and hard work." There was a strain to Adam's voice, as though the topic was not one he was used to discussing.

Olive tried to be gentle when she asked, "And it wasn't?"

He shook his head. "The opposite, in a way."

"The opposite of discipline and hard work?"

"We worked hard, all right. But discipline . . . discipline would presume specifically laid-out expectations. Ideal codes of behavior are defined, and a failure to adhere to them is addressed in a productive way. That's what I thought, at least. What I still think. You said that I'm brutal with my grads, and maybe you're right—"

"Adam, I—"

"But what I try to do is set goals for them and help them achieve them. If I realize that they're not doing what we have mutually agreed needs to be done, I tell them what's wrong and what they must change. I don't baby them, I don't hide criticism in praises, I don't believe in that Oreo cookie feedback crap, and if they find me terrifying or antagonizing because of it, so be it." He took a deep breath. "But I also don't *ever* make it about them. It's always about the work. Sometimes it's well done, other times it's not, and if it's not . . . work can be redone. It can improve. I don't want them to tie their self-worth to what they produce." He paused, and he looked—no, he *felt* faraway. Like these were things he gave a great deal of thought to, like he wanted this for his students. "I hate how self-important this all sounds, but science *is* serious business, and . . . it's my duty as a scientist, I believe."

"I . . ." All of a sudden, the air in the hotel room was cold. *I'm the one who told him*, she thought, feeling her stomach flip. *I'm the one who told him repeatedly that he's terrifying and antagonizing, and that all his students hate him.* "And your adviser didn't?"

"I never quite understood what he thought. What I do know now, years later, is that he was abusive. A lot of terrible things happened under his watch—scientists were not given credit for their ideas or authorship of papers they deserved. People were publicly belittled for making mistakes that would be normal for experienced researchers—let alone trainees. Expectations were stellar, but never fully defined. Impossible deadlines were set arbitrarily, out of the blue, and grads were punished for not meeting them. Ph.D. students were constantly assigned to the same tasks, then pitted against each other and asked to compete, for my adviser's amusement. Once he put Holden and me on the same research project and told us that whoever obtained publishable results first would receive funding for the following semester."

She tried to imagine how it would feel, if Dr. Aslan openly promoted a competitive environment between Olive and her cohorts. But no—Adam and Holden had been close friends their whole lives, so the situation wasn't comparable. It would have been like being told that to receive a salary next semester, Olive would need to outscience Anh. "What did you do?"

He ran a hand through his hair, and a strand fell on his forehead. "We paired up. We figured that we had complementary skills—a pharmacology expert can achieve more with the help of a computational biologist, and vice versa. And we were right. We ran a really good study. It was exhausting, but also elating, staying up all hours to figure out how to fix our protocols. Knowing that we were the first to discover something." For a moment, he seemed to enjoy the memory. But then he pressed his lips together, rolling his jaw. "And at the end of the semester, when we presented our findings to our adviser, he told us that we'd both be without funding, because by collaborating we hadn't followed his guidelines. We spent the following spring teaching six sections of Introduction to Biology per week—on top of lab work. Holden and I were living together. I swear that I once heard him mumble 'mitochondria are the powerhouse of the cell' in his sleep."

"But . . . you gave your adviser what he wanted."

Adam shook his head. "He wanted a power play. And in the

end he got it: he punished us for not dancing to his tune and published the findings we brought to him without acknowledging our role in obtaining them."

"I . . ." Her fingers fisted in the loose fabric of her borrowed T-shirt. "Adam, I'm so sorry I ever compared you to him. I didn't mean to—"

"It's okay." He smiled at her, tight but reassuring.

It was *not* okay. Yes, Adam could be direct, painfully so. Stubborn and blunt and uncompromising. Not always kind, but never devious, or malicious. Quite the opposite: he was honest to a fault, and required from others the same discipline he clearly imposed on himself. As much as his grads complained about his harsh feedback or the long hours of work they were asked to put in the lab, they all recognized that he was a hands-on mentor without being a micromanager. Most of them graduated with several publications and moved on to excellent academic jobs.

"You didn't know."

"Still, I . . ." She bit her lip, feeling guilty. Feeling defeated. Feeling angry at Adam's adviser and at Tom for treating academia like their own personal playground. At herself, for not knowing what to do about it. "Why did no one report him?"

He closed his eyes briefly. "Because he was short-listed for a Nobel Prize. Twice. Because he had powerful friends in high places, and we thought no one would believe us. Because he could make or break careers. Because we felt that there was no real system in place to ask for help." There was a sour set to his jaw, and he was not looking at her anymore. It was so surreal, the idea of Adam Carlsen feeling powerless. And yet, his eyes told another story. "We were terrified, and probably somewhere deep down we were convinced that we'd signed up for it and we deserved it. That we were failures who would never amount to anything."

Her heart hurt for him. For herself. "I'm so, *so* sorry."

He shook his head again, and his expression somewhat cleared. "When he told me that I was a failure, I thought he was right. I was ready to give up on the one thing I cared about because of it. And Tom and Holden—they had their own issues with our adviser, of course. Everyone did. But they helped me. For some reason my adviser always seemed to know when something wrong was happening with my studies, but Tom mediated a lot between us. He took lots of crap so I wouldn't have to. He was a favorite of my adviser's and interceded to make the lab less like a battle zone."

Adam talking about Tom as though he were a hero made her nauseous, but she remained silent. This wasn't about her.

"And Holden . . . Holden stole my law school applications and made paper planes out of them. He was removed enough from what was happening to me that he could help me see things objectively. Just like I am removed from what happened to you today." His eyes were on her, now. There was a light in them that she didn't understand. "You are not mediocre, Olive. You were not invited to speak because people think that you are my girlfriend—there is no such thing, since SBD's abstracts go through a blind review process. I would know, because I've been roped into reviewing them in the past. And the work you presented is important, rigorous, and brilliant." He took a deep breath. His shoulders rose and fell in time with the thudding of her heart. "I wish you could see yourself the way I see you."

Maybe it was the words, or maybe the tone. Maybe it was the way he'd just told her something about himself, or how he'd taken her hand earlier and saved her from her misery. Her knight in black armor. Maybe it was none of it, maybe it was all of it, maybe it was always going to happen. Still—it didn't matter. Suddenly, it just didn't matter, the *why* of it, the *how*. The *after*.

All Olive cared about was that she wanted to, right now, and that seemed enough to make it all right.

It was all so slow: the step forward she took to come to stand between his knees, the rise of her hand to his face, the way her fingers cupped his jaw. Slow enough that he could have stopped her, he could have pulled out of reach, he could have said something—and he did not. He simply looked up at her, his eyes a clear, liquid brown, and Olive's heart at once jumped and quieted when he tilted his head and leaned into her palm.

It didn't surprise her, how soft his skin was beneath the night stubble, how much warmer than hers. And when she bent, for once taller than him, the shape of his lips under hers was like an old song, familiar and easy. It wasn't their first kiss, after all. Though, it was different. Calm and tentative and precious, Adam's hand light on her waist as he tilted his chin up to her, eager and pressing, like this was something he'd thought of—like he'd been wanting it, too. It wasn't their first kiss, but it was the first kiss that was *theirs*, and Olive savored it for long moments. The texture, the smell, the closeness. The slight hitch in Adam's breath, the odd pauses, the way their lips had to work a little before finding the right angles and some form of coordination.

See? She wanted to say, triumphant. To whom, she wasn't sure. *See? It was always going to be like this.* Olive grinned into his lips. And Adam—

Adam was already shaking his head when she pulled back, like a *no* had been waiting in his mouth all along, even as he returned her kiss. His fingers closed tight around her wrist, drawing her hand away from his face. "This is not a good idea."

Her smile faded. He was right. He was completely right. He was also wrong. "Why?"

"Olive." He shook his head again. Then his hand left her

waist and came up to his lips, as if to touch the kiss they'd just shared, make sure it had really happened. "This is . . . no."

He really was right. But . . . "Why?" she repeated.

Adam's fingers pressed into his eyes. His left hand was still holding her wrist, and she wondered distractedly if he was even aware of it. If he knew that his thumb was swiping back and forth across her pulse. "This is not what we're here for."

She could feel her nostrils flare. "That doesn't mean that—"

"You're not thinking clearly." He swallowed visibly. "You're upset and drunk, and—"

"I had two beers. Hours ago."

"You're a grad student, currently depending on me for a place to stay, and even if not, the power I have over you could easily turn this into a coercive dynamic that—"

"I'm—" Olive laughed. "I'm not feeling coerced, I—"

"You're in love with *someone else*!"

She almost recoiled. The way he spit out the words was that heated. It should have put her off, driven her away, once and for all drilled into her head how ridiculous this was, how disastrous an idea. It didn't, though. By now the moody, ill-tempered ass Adam meshed so well with *her* Adam, the one who bought her cookies and checked her slides and let her cry into his neck. There might have been a time when she couldn't quite reconcile the two, but they were all so clear now, the many faces of him. She wouldn't want to leave behind any of them. Not one.

"Olive." He sighed heavily, closing his eyes. The idea that he might be thinking of the woman who Holden mentioned flashed into her mind and slipped away, too painful to entertain.

She should just tell him. She should be honest with him, admit that she didn't care about Jeremy, that there was no one else. Never had been. But she was terrified, paralyzed with fear, and after the day she'd had, her heart felt so easy to break. So fragile. Adam could shatter it in a thousand pieces, and still be none the wiser.

"Olive, this is how you're feeling *now*. A month from now, a week, tomorrow, I don't want you to regret—"

"What about what *I* want?" She leaned forward, letting her words soak the silence for drawn-out seconds. "What about the fact that *I* want this? Though maybe you don't care." She squared her shoulders, blinking quickly against the prickling sensation in her eyes. "Because you don't want it, right? Maybe I'm just not attractive to you and *you* don't want this—"

It nearly made her lose her balance, the way he tugged at her wrist and pulled her hand to himself, pressing her palm flush to his groin to show her that . . . Oh.

Oh.

Yeah.

His jaw rolled as he held her gaze. "You have no fucking idea what I want."

It took her breath away, all of it. The low, guttural tone of his voice, the thick ridge under her fingers, the enraged, hungry note in his eyes. He pushed her hand away almost immediately, but it already felt too late.

It wasn't that Olive hadn't . . . the kisses they'd exchanged, they were always physical, but now it was as if something had been switched on. For a long time she'd thought Adam handsome and attractive. She'd touched him, sat on his lap, considered the vague possibility of being intimate with him. She'd thought about him, about sex, about him *and* sex, but it had always been abstract. Hazy and undefined. Like line art in black and white: just the base for a drawing that was suddenly coloring on the inside.

It was clear now, in the damp ache pooling between her

thighs, in his eyes that were all pupil, how it would be between them. Heady and sweaty and slick. Challenging. They would do things for each other, demand things of each other. They would be incredibly close. And Olive—now that she could see it, she really, *really* wanted it.

She stepped close, even closer. "Well, then." Her voice was low, but she knew he could hear her.

He shut his eyes tight. "This is not why I asked you to room with me."

"I know." Olive pushed a black strand of hair away from his forehead. "It's also not why I accepted."

His lips were parted, and he was staring down at her hand, the one that was almost wrapped around his erection a moment ago. "You said no sex."

She had said that. She remembered thinking about her rules, listing them in his office, and she remembered being certain that she would never, ever be interested in seeing Adam Carlsen for longer than ten minutes a week. "I also said it was going to be an on-campus thing. And we just went out for dinner. So." He might know what was best, but what he wanted was different. She could almost see the debris of his control, feel it slowly erode.

"I don't . . ." He straightened, infinitesimally. The line of his shoulders, his jaw—he was so tense, still avoiding her eyes. "I don't have anything."

It was a little embarrassing, the amount of time it took for her to parse the meaning of it. "Oh. It doesn't matter. I'm on birth control. And clean." She bit into her lip. "But we could also do . . . other things."

Adam swallowed, twice, and then nodded. He wasn't breathing normally. And Olive doubted he could say no at this point. That he would even want to. He did put up a good effort, though.

"What if you hate me for this, after? What if we go back and you change your mind—"

"I won't. I . . ." She stepped—God, even *closer*. She wouldn't think about after. Couldn't, didn't want to. "I've never been surer of anything. Except maybe cell theory." She smiled, hoping he'd smile back.

Adam's mouth remained straight and serious, but it scarcely mattered: the next time Olive felt his touch it was on the slope of her hip bone, under the cotton of the T-shirt he'd given her.

Chapter Sixteen

♥ **HYPOTHESIS:** *Despite what everyone says, sex is never going to be anything more than a mildly enjoyable activi— Oh.*
Oh.

It was like a layer peeled away.

Adam yanked off the shirt he was wearing in one fluid movement, and it was as though the white cotton was only one of many things tossed in a corner of the room. Olive didn't have a name for what the other things were; all she knew was that a few seconds earlier he'd seemed reluctant, almost unwilling to touch her, and now he was . . . not.

He was running the show now. Wrapping his large hands around her waist, sliding his fingertips under the elastic of her green polka-dot panties, and kissing her.

He kisses, Olive thought, *like a man starved*. Like he'd been waiting all this time. Holding back. Like the possibility of the two of them doing this had occurred to him in the past, but he'd set it aside, stored it away in a deep, dark place where it had grown into something fearsome and out of control. Olive thought she knew how it would be—they'd kissed before, after all. Except, she realized now, that *she* had always been the one to kiss him.

Maybe she was being fanciful. What did she know about different types of kisses, anyway? Still, something in her belly thrummed and liquefied when his tongue licked against hers, when he bit a tender spot on her neck, when he made a guttural noise in the back of his throat as his fingers cupped her ass through her panties. Under her shirt, his hand traveled up to her rib cage. Olive gasped and smiled into his mouth.

"You did that before."

He blinked at her, confused, pupils blown large and dark. "What?"

"The night I kissed you in the hallway. You did it that night, too."

"I did what?"

"You touched me. Here." Her hand slid to her ribs to cover his through the cotton.

He looked up at her through dark lashes, and began to lift a corner of her shirt, up her thighs and past her hip until it caught right under her breast. He leaned into her, pressing his lips against the lowest part of her ribs. Olive gasped. And gasped again when he bit her softly, and then licked across the same spot.

"Here?" he asked. She was growing light-headed. It could be how close he was, or the heat in the room. Or the fact that she was almost naked, standing in front of him in nothing but panties and socks. "Olive." His mouth traveled upward, less than an inch, teeth grazing against skin and bone. "Here?" She hadn't thought she could get this wet this quickly. Or at all. Then again, she hadn't really thought much about sex in the past few years.

"Pay attention, sweetheart." He sucked the underside of her breast. She had to hold on to his shoulders, or her knees would give out on her. "Here?"

"I . . ." It took a moment to focus, but she nodded. "Maybe.

Yes, there. It was . . . it was a good kiss." Her eyes fluttered closed, and she didn't even fight it when he took the shirt completely off her. It was his, after all. And the way he was studying her, it brooked no self-consciousness on her part. "Do you remember it?"

He was the distracted one now. Staring at her breasts like they were something spectacular, his lips parted and breath quick and shallow. "Remember what?"

"Our first kiss."

He didn't answer. Instead he looked up and down at her, eyes glazed, and said, "I want to keep you in this hotel room for a week." His hand came up to cup her breast, not exactly gentle. Just this side of too forceful, and Olive felt herself clench around nothing. "For a year."

He pushed his hand against her shoulder blades to make her arch toward him, and then closed his mouth against her breast, all teeth and tongue and wonderful, delicious suction. Olive whimpered against the back of her hand, because she hadn't known, hadn't thought that she'd be so sensitive, but her nipples were tight and raw and almost sore, and if he didn't do something, she'd—

"You're edible, Olive."

His palm pressed against her spine, and Olive arched a little more. An offering of sorts. "That's probably an insult," she breathed out with a smile, "considering that you only like wheatgrass and broccoli— *Oh*."

He could fit her entire breast in his mouth. All of it. He groaned in the back of his throat, and it was clear that he'd love to swallow her whole. Olive should touch him, too—she was the one who'd asked for this, and it followed that she should make sure that being with her was not a chore for him. Maybe put her hand back where he'd dragged it earlier and stroke? He could instruct her on how he liked it. Maybe this was a one-time thing and they were never going to talk about it again, but Olive couldn't help herself—she just wanted him to like this. To like *her*.

"This okay?" She must have lingered too long inside her head, because he was looking up at her with a frown, his thumb swiping back and forth on her hip bone. "You're tense." His voice was strained. He was cupping his cock almost absentmindedly, stroking and gripping every once in a while—when his eyes fell on the hard points of her nipples, when she shivered, when she squirmed on her feet to rub her thighs together. "We don't have to—"

"I want to. I said I did."

His throat bobbed. "It doesn't matter, what you said. You can always change your mind."

"I won't." The way he was looking at her, Olive was sure he'd protest again. But he just rested his forehead on her sternum, his breath warm against the skin he'd just licked, and let his fingertips coast the elastic of her panties, dip under the thin cotton.

"I think *I*'ve changed my mind," he murmured.

She stiffened. "I know I'm not doing anything, but if you tell me what you like, I can—"

"My favorite color must be green, after all."

She exhaled when his thumb pressed between her legs, brushing against fabric that was already dark and wet. She exhaled in a rush until there was no air left, embarrassment washing over her at the thought that now he must know exactly how much she wanted this—and at the pleasure of his finger, large and blunt, running against her seam.

He definitely knew. Because he looked back up at her, glassy-eyed and breathing fast. "Damn," he said, quiet. "Olive."

"Do you . . ." Her mouth was as dry as the desert. "Do you want me to take them off?"

"No." He shook his head. "Not yet."

"But if we—"

He hooked his finger on the elastic and pushed the cotton to the side. She was glistening, swollen and plump to her own eyes, way too far ahead, considering that they'd barely done anything. Too eager. This was embarrassing. "I'm sorry." There were two kinds of heat, the one curling tight at the bottom of her stomach, and the one rising to her cheeks. Olive could barely tell them apart. "I am . . ."

"Perfect." He wasn't really talking to her. More to himself, marveling at the way his fingertip sank so easily between her folds, parting them and gliding back and forth until Olive threw back her head and closed her eyes because the pleasure was streaming, stretching, thrumming through her and she couldn't, couldn't, *couldn't*—

"You are so beautiful." The words sounded hushed, ripped out of him. Like he wasn't going to say them. "May I?"

It took her several heartbeats to realize that he was referring to his middle finger, to the way it was circling around her entrance and tapping at it. Applying a light pressure right against the rim. So wet already.

Olive moaned. "Yes. Anything," she breathed out.

He licked her nipple, a silent thank-you, and pushed in. Or at least, he tried. Olive hissed and so did Adam, with a muted, hoarse "Fuck."

He had big fingers—that must be why they didn't fit. The first knuckle was just shy of too much, a pinching ache and the sensation of damp, uncomfortable fullness. She shifted on her heels, trying to adjust and make room, and then shifted some more, until he had to grip her hip with his other hand to keep her still. Olive held on to his shoulders, his skin sweat slicked and scorching hot under her palms. "Shh."

His thumb grazed her, and she whimpered. "It's okay. Relax."

Impossible. Though, if Olive had to be honest, the way his finger was curving inside her—it was already getting better. Not so painful now, and maybe even wetter, and if he touched her *there . . .* Her head lolled back. She clutched his muscles with her nails.

"There? Is that a good spot?"

Olive wanted to tell him that no, it was too much, but before she could open her mouth, he did it again, until she couldn't keep quiet anymore, all groans and whimpers and wet, obscene noises. Until he tried to get a little further inside, and she couldn't help wincing.

"What is it?" His voice was his regular voice, but a million times raspier. "Does it hurt?"

"No— *Oh.*"

He looked up, all flushed pale skin against dark waves. "Why are you so tense, Olive? You've done this before, right?"

"I—yes." She was not sure what compelled her to continue. Any idiot could see from a mile away that it was a terrible idea, but there was no room left for lies now that they were standing so close. So she confessed, "A couple of times. In college."

Adam went immobile. Completely motionless. His muscles flexed, coiled strong under her palms, and then they just stayed like that, tense and still as he stared up at her. "Olive."

"But it doesn't matter," she hastened to add, because he was already shaking his head, pulling away from her. It really didn't matter. Not to Olive, and therefore, it shouldn't to Adam, either. "I can figure it out—I've learned whole-cell patch clamp in a couple of hours; sex can't be much harder. And I bet you do this all the time, so you can tell me how to—"

"You'd lose."

The room was chilly. His finger was not inside her anymore, and his hand had left her hip.

"What?"

"You'd lose your bet." He sighed, wiping a hand down his face. The other one, the one that had been inside her, moved down to adjust his cock. It looked enormous by now, and he winced as he touched it. "Olive, I can't."

"Of course you can."

He shook his head. "I'm sorry."

"What? No. No, I—"

"You're basically a vir—"

"I'm not!"

"Olive."

"I am not."

"But so close to it that—"

"No, that's not the way it works. Virginity is not a continuous variable, it's categorical. Binary. Nominal. Dichotomous. Ordinal, potentially. I'm talking about chi-square, maybe Spearman's correlation, logistic regression, the logit model and that stupid sigmoid function, and . . ."

It had been weeks and it still took her breath away, the uneven tilt of his smile. How unanticipated it always was, the dimples it formed. Olive was left without air as his large palm cupped the side of her face and brought it down for a slow, warm, laughing kiss.

"You are such a smart-ass," he said against her mouth.

"Maybe." She was smiling, too. And kissing him back. Hugging him, arms draped around his neck, and she felt a shiver of pleasure when he pulled her deeper into himself.

"Olive," he said inching back, "if for any reason sex is something that you . . . that you're not comfortable with, or that you'd rather not have outside of a relationship, then—"

"No. No, it's nothing like that. I—" She took a deep breath, looking for a way to explain herself. "It's not that I want to *not* have sex. I just . . . don't particularly *want* to have it. There is something weird about my brain, and my body, and—I don't know what's wrong with me, but I don't seem to be able to experience attraction like other people. Like *normal* people. I tried to just . . . to just do it, to get it over with, and the guy I did it with was nice, but the truth is that I just don't feel any . . ." She closed her eyes. This was difficult to admit. "I don't feel any sexual attraction unless I actually get to trust and like a person, which for some reason never happens. Or, almost never. It hadn't, not in a long time, but now—I really like you, and I really trust you, and for the first time in a million years I want to—"

She couldn't ramble anymore, because he was kissing her again, this time hard and bruising, as though he wanted to absorb her into himself. "I want to do this," she said, as soon as she was able to. "With you. I really do."

"Me too, Olive." He sighed. "You have no idea."

"Then, please. Please, don't say no." She bit her lip, and then his. And then nipped at his jaw. "Please?"

He took a deep breath and nodded. She smiled and kissed the curve of his neck, and his hand splayed against her lower back.

"But," he said, "we should probably go about this a little differently."

~~~~~~

IT TOOK HER the longest time to realize his intentions. Not because she was stupid, or oblivious, or that naive about sex, but because . . .

Maybe she *was* a little naive about sex. But she truly hadn't thought about it for ages before Adam, and even then, it was never quite in these terms—him above her, pushing her legs wide open with his palms on her inner thighs and then kneeling between them. Sliding down, low.

"What are you—"

The way he parted her with his tongue, it was as though she

was butter and he meant to slice through her like a hot knife. He was slow but sure, and didn't pause when Olive's thigh stiffened against his palm, or when she tried to squirm away. He just grunted, rich and low; then ran his nose in the skin at the juncture of her abdomen, inhaling deeply; and then he licked her once more.

"Adam—stop," she pleaded, and for a moment he just nuzzled his face against her folds like he had no intention of doing any such thing. Then he lifted his head, eyes foggy, as if aware that he should be listening to her.

"Mmm?" His lips vibrated against her.

"Maybe . . . maybe you should stop?"

He went still, his hand tightening around her thigh. "Have you changed your mind?"

"No. But we should do . . . other things."

He frowned. "You don't like this?"

"No. Yes. Well, I've never . . ." The line between his eyebrows deepened. "But I'm the one who put you up to this, so we should do things that *you* are into, and not stuff for me . . ."

This time it was the flat of his tongue against her clit, pressing just enough to make her clench and exhale in a rush. The tip was circling around it, which—such a small movement, and yet it sent her hand straight to her mouth, had her biting the fleshy part of her palm.

"Adam!" Her voice sounded like someone else's. "Did you hear what I . . . ?"

"You said to do something I'm into." His breath was hot against her. "I am."

"You can't possibly want to—"

He squeezed her leg. "I can't remember a moment I didn't."

It just didn't feel like standard hookup fare, something this intimate. But it was hard to protest when he looked spellbound, staring at her, at her face and her legs and the rest of her body.

His hand was large, open over her abdomen and holding her down, inching higher and closer to her breasts, but never close enough. Lying like this, Olive was a little embarrassed of how concave her stomach was. Of the way her ribs stuck out. Adam, though, didn't seem to mind.

"Wouldn't you rather—"

A nip. "No."

"I didn't even say—"

He glanced up. "There isn't anything I'd rather do."

"But—"

He sucked on one of her lips with a loud, wet noise, and she gasped. And then his tongue was inside her, and she moaned, half in surprise, half at the feeling of— Yes.

Yes.

"Fuck," someone said. It wasn't Olive, so it must have been Adam. "Fuck." It felt incredible. Otherworldly. His tongue, dipping in and out, circling and lapping, and his nose against her skin, and the quiet sounds he made from deep in his chest whenever she contracted, and Olive was going to—she . . .

She wasn't sure she was going to come. Not with another person in the room touching her. "This might take a while," she said apologetically, hating how thin her voice sounded.

"Fuck, yes." His tongue swiped the entirety of her, a long, broad stroke. "Please." She didn't think she'd ever heard him quite this enthusiastic about anything, not even grant writing or computational biology. It kicked the whole thing a few notches higher for her, and it got worse when she noticed his arm. The one that wasn't cupping the cheek of her ass and holding her open.

He hadn't taken himself out of his pants yet, that Olive could see, and wasn't that unfair, since she was all splayed open for him. But the way his arm was shifting, how his hand was moving up and down slowly, that was just unbearable. She arched further, her spine shaping a perfect curve as the back of her head hit the pillow.

"Olive." He leaned back a few centimeters and kissed the inside of her shaking thigh. Took a deep breath with his nose, as if to hold the smell of her within himself. "You can't come yet." His lips brushed against her folds as his tongue dipped in again, and she squeezed her eyes shut. There was a liquid, burning heat blossoming in her tummy, spilling all over her. Her fingers clawed at the sheets, grasping for an anchor. This was impossible. Unmanageable.

"*Adam.*"

"Don't. Two more minutes." He sucked on— *God*, yes. *There.*

"I'm—sorry."

"One more."

"I *can't—*"

"Focus, Olive."

In the end, it was his voice that ruined everything. That quiet, possessive tone, the hint of an order in the low rasp of his words, and the pleasure broke over her like an ocean wave. Her mind snapped, and she was not wholly herself for seconds, and then minutes, and when she had a sense of the world again, he was still licking her, except more slowly, as if with no purpose but to savor her. "I want to go down on you until you pass out." His lips were so soft against her skin.

"No." Olive fisted the pillow. "I—you can't."

"Why?"

"I have to . . ." She couldn't think straight, not quite yet. Her mind was addled, stuttering.

She almost screamed when he pushed one finger inside. This time it sank like a rock into water, smooth and without obstacle, and her walls clamped on it as if to welcome Adam and hold him inside.

"Jesus." He licked her clit again, and she was too sensitive for this. Maybe. "You are"—he hooked his finger inside her, pressing against the roof of her channel, and the pleasure welled in her, washing against her edges—"so small and tight and warm."

The heat flooded within her once more, knocked the air out of her lungs, leaving her openmouthed, bright colors bursting behind her eyelids. He groaned something that was not quite coherent, and slid in another finger on the tail end of her orgasm, and the taut stretch of it, it was ruinous. Her body bloomed into something that didn't belong to her anymore, something made of bright, high peaks and lush valleys. It left her heavy and boneless, and she was not sure how long went by before she could bear to raise her palm to his forehead and gently push him away to get him to stop. He shot her a sullen glance but complied, and Olive tugged him up—because he looked like he might start again any moment, and because it would be nice, to have him next to her. Maybe he was thinking the same: he lifted himself above her, leaning his weight on his forearm; his chest pushed against her breast, one large thigh lodged firmly between her legs.

She was still wearing her stupid knee socks, and *God*, Adam was probably thinking that she was the lamest lay he'd ever—

"Can I fuck you?"

He said it, and then he kissed her, unconcerned with where his mouth had been just seconds earlier. She wondered if she should be put off by that, but she was still twitching with pleasure, contracting with aftershocks at the memory of what he'd just done. She couldn't make herself care, and it was nice to kiss him like this. So nice.

"Mmm." Her palms came up to cup his face, and she began to trace his cheekbones with her thumbs. They were red, and hot. "What?"

"Can I fuck you?" He sucked the base of her throat. "Please?" He breathed it against the shell of her ear, and—it wasn't as though she could say no. Or wanted to. She nodded her permission and reached for his cock, but he beat her to it and pulled down his pants, closing his fist around it. He was big. Larger than she'd thought he'd be, than she'd thought anyone could be. She could still feel his heart pounding rapidly against her chest as he aligned himself to her and nudged the head against her opening and—

Olive was lax now. And pliant. And still not loose enough. "*Ah.*" It didn't quite hurt, but it was nearly too much. Definitely not easy. And yet, that sensation, the push of him against every part of her, it held a promise. "You're so big."

He groaned into her neck. His entire body was vibrating with tension. "You can take it."

"I can," she told him, voice reedy, and her breath caught halfway through the second word. Women gave birth, after all. Except that he was not in, not really. Not even half. And there was just no more room.

Olive looked up at him. His eyes were closed, dark half-moons against his skin, and his jaw was tense. "What if it's too much?"

Adam lowered his lips to her ear. "Then . . ." He attempted a thrust, and maybe it was too much, but the friction was lovely. "Then I'll fuck you like this." She squeezed her eyes shut when he hit a place that made her whimper. "God, Olive."

Her entire body was pulsating. "Is there something I should be . . ."

"Just . . ." He kissed her collarbone. Their breathing was erratic by now, loud in the silence of the room. "Be quiet for a moment. So I don't come already."

Olive canted her hips, and he was rubbing that spot again. It made her thighs tremble, and she tried to open them wider. To invite him inside. "Maybe you should."

"I should?"

She nodded. They were too dazed to kiss with any kind of coordination by this point, but his lips were hot and soft when they brushed against hers. "Yes."

"Inside you?"

"If you—"

Adam's hand came up behind Olive's knee and angled it just so, spreading her legs in a way she simply hadn't thought of. Firmly holding her open.

"If you want to."

"You're so perfect, you're driving me insane."

Her insides opened to him without warning. They welcomed and pulled at him until he bottomed out, until he was wedged deep and stretching her to a point that should be breaking, but just made her feel filled, sealed, perfect.

They both exhaled. Olive lifted a hand, closed it shakily around Adam's sweaty nape.

"Hey." She smiled up at him.

He smiled back, just a little. "Hey."

His eyes were opaque, like stained glass. He moved inside her, just a hint of a thrust, and it made her entire body clench around him, until she could feel his cock twitch and pulsate inside her, like a drum. Her head fell to the pillow, and someone was groaning, something guttural and out of control.

Then Adam pulled out, pushed back in, and they annihilated the no-sex rule. In the span of a few seconds his thrusts went from tentative, exploratory, to fast and all-eclipsing. His hand slid to the small of her back, lifting her into him as he piled in, and in, and in again, rubbing inside her, against her, forcing pleasure to vibrate up her spine.

"Is this okay?" he asked against her ear, not quite managing to stop.

Olive couldn't answer. Not past the sharp hitch of her breath, the way her fingers dug desperately into the sheets. Pressure built again inside her, swelled large and consuming.

"You have to tell me, if you don't like it," he rasped. "What I'm doing." He was eager, a little clumsy, losing control and slipping out of her, having to nudge his cock back inside; he was out of focus, but so was she, too flooded by how good he felt, how stupefying the pleasure, how smoothly he slid in and out. How right this felt.

"I—"

"Olive, you have to—" He stopped with a grunt, because she canted her hips and clenched around him. Gripping him harder, sucking him deeper.

"I like it." She reached up to fist her fingers in his hair. To catch his eyes, make sure he was paying attention as she said, "I *love* it, Adam."

His control poured out. He made a crude noise and shuddered, pumping hard and muttering nonsense into her skin— how perfect she was, how beautiful, how long he'd wanted this, how he would never, *could* never let go of her. Olive felt his orgasm soar, the blinding, scalding pleasure as he trembled on top of her.

She smiled. And when new shivers began to roll down her spine, she bit Adam's shoulder and let herself go under.

Chapter Seventeen

♥ **HYPOTHESIS:** *When I think I've hit rock bottom, someone will hand me a shovel. That someone is probably Tom Benton.*

Olive drifted off after the first time, and dreamed of many strange, nonsensical things. Sushi rolls shaped like spiders. The first snowfall in Toronto, during her last year with her mother. Adam's dimples. Tom Benton's sneer as he spat the words "little sob story." Adam, again, this time serious, saying her name in his unique way.

Then she felt the mattress dip, and the sound of something being placed on the nightstand. She slowly blinked awake, disoriented in the dim light of the room. Adam was sitting on the side of the bed, pushing a lock of hair behind her ear.

"Hi." She smiled.

"Hey."

Her hand reached out to touch his thigh through the pants he'd never managed to take all the way off. He was still warm, still solid. Still there.

"How long did I sleep?"

"Not long. Maybe thirty minutes."

"Hmm." She stretched a bit against the mattress, arms above her head, and noticed the fresh glass of water on the nightstand. "Is that for me?"

He nodded, handed it to her, and she propped up on her elbow to drink it, smiling in thanks. She noticed his gaze linger on her breasts, still tender and sore from his mouth, and then drift away to his own palms.

Oh. Maybe, now that they had sex—*good sex*, Olive thought, *amazing sex*, though who knew about Adam?—he needed his own space. Maybe he wanted his own damn pillow.

She returned the empty glass and sat up. "I should move to my bed."

He shook his head with an intensity that suggested that he didn't want her to go, not anywhere, not ever. His free hand closed tight around her waist, as if to tether her to him.

Olive didn't mind.

"You sure? I suspect I might be a cover hog."

"It's fine. I run warm." He brushed a strand of hair from her forehead. "And according to someone, I look like I might snore."

She gasped in mock outrage. "How *dare* they? Tell me who said that and I will personally avenge you—" She yelped when he held the icy-cool glass against her neck, and then dissolved into laughter, drawing up her knees and trying to twist away from him. "I'm sorry—you don't snore! You sleep like a prince!"

"Damn right." He set the glass on the nightstand, appeased, but Olive remained curled up, cheeks flushed and breathing hard from fending him off. He was smiling. With dimples, too. The same smile he'd smiled into her neck earlier, against her skin, the one that had tickled her and made her laugh.

"I'm sorry about the socks, by the way." She winced. "I know it's a controversial topic."

Adam looked down at the rainbow-colored material stretched around her calves. "Socks are controversial?"

"Not socks per se. Just, keeping them on during sex?"

"Really?"

"Totally. At least according to the issue of *Cosmopolitan* we keep at home to swat cockroaches."

He shrugged, like a man who'd only ever read the *New England Journal of Medicine* and maybe *Truck-Pushing Digest*. "Why would anyone care one way or the other?"

"Maybe they don't want to unknowingly have sex with people with horrible, disfigured toes?"

"Do you have disfigured toes?"

"Truly grotesque. Circus-worthy. Antithetical to sex. Basically a built-in contraceptive."

He sighed, clearly amused. He was struggling to hold on to his moody, broody, intense act, and Olive *loved* it.

"I've seen you in flip-flops multiple times. Which, by the way, are not lab compliant."

"You must be mistaken."

"Really."

"I don't like what you're insinuating, Dr. Carlsen. I take the Stanford environmental health and safety guidelines very seriously and— What are *you*—"

He was so much larger than her, he could hold her down with one hand on her belly as he wrestled her out of her socks, and for some reason she loved every moment of it. She put up a good fight, and maybe he'd have a couple of bruises tomorrow, but when he finally managed to take them off, Olive was out of breath from laughing. Adam caressed her feet reverently, as though they were delicate and perfectly shaped instead of belonging to someone who ran two marathons a year.

"You were right," he said. Chest heaving, she looked at him curiously. "Your feet are pretty hideous."

"What?" She gasped and freed herself, pushing at his shoulder until he ended up on his back under her. He surely could have unseated her, giant that he was. And yet. "Take it back."

"You said it first."

"Take it back. My feet are cute."

"In a hideous way, maybe."

"That's *not* a thing."

His laugh blew warm against her cheek. "There's probably a German word for that. Cute, but exceptionally ugly."

She bit his lip just enough to make him feel it, and Adam—he seemed to lose that grip he always had on himself. He seemed to suddenly want more, and he flipped them until she was underneath him, turning the bite into a kiss. Or maybe it was Olive herself, since her tongue was licking his lip, exactly where she'd made it sting.

She should probably tell him to stop. She was sweaty and sticky, and should excuse herself and go take a shower. Yes, that sounded like good sex etiquette. But he felt warm and strong, positively glowing. He smelled delicious, even after all they'd done, and she couldn't help getting sidetracked and letting her arms loop around his neck. Pulling him down.

"You weigh a ton," she told him. He made to move up and away, but she wrapped her legs around his waist, holding him close. She felt so safe with him. Invincible. A true slayer. He turned her into a powerful, ferocious person, one that could destroy Tom Benton and pancreatic cancer before breakfast.

"No, I love it. Stay, please." She grinned up at him, and saw his breathing speed up.

"You *are* a cover hog." There was a spot at the base of her neck that he'd found earlier, a spot that made her sigh and arch up and melt into the pillow. He attacked it like it was his new true north. He had a way of kissing her, half cautious and half unrestrained, that had her wondering why she used to think of kissing as such a boring, aimless activity.

"I should go clean up," she said, but didn't make a move. He slid down, just a couple of inches, just enough to get distracted by her collarbone, and then by the curve of her breast. "Adam."

He ignored her and traced her jutting hip bones, and her ribs, the taut skin of her belly. He kissed every last freckle, as though to store them up in his memory, and there were so many. "I'm all sticky, Adam." She squirmed a little.

In response, his palm moved to her ass. To keep her still. "Ssh. I'll clean you up myself."

He put his finger inside her and she gasped, because— Oh God. Oh. Oh *God*. She could hear the wet noises down there, from herself and his own come, and he should be disgusted by this, and she should, too, and yet—

She wasn't. And he was groaning, as if the satisfaction of having made a mess of her, inside her, of knowing that she'd let him, was a heady thing for him. Olive closed her eyes and let herself go under, feeling him lick the skin between her thigh and abdomen, hearing low moans and gasps coming out of her own mouth, sliding her fingers in his hair to grip him more tightly against her. She was definitely clean by the time she came, slow contractions that swelled in large waves and had her thighs shaking around his head, and that was when he asked, "Can I fuck you again?"

She looked up at him, flushed and hazy with her orgasm, and bit her lip. She wanted to. She really wanted to have him on top of her, inside her, chest pushing her into the mattress and arms snaked around her body. That feeling of security, of finally belonging that seemed to get more intense the closer he got to her.

"I want to." Her hand came up to touch his arm, the one he was holding himself up on. "It's just—I'm just sore, and I—"

He immediately regretted asking. She could tell by how his body stilled before he got off her, as if to not crowd her, as if to give her space she didn't want.

"No," she panicked. "It's not that—"

"Hey." He noticed how flustered she was and bent down to kiss her.

"I do want to—"

"Olive." He curled around her. His cock rubbed against her lower back, but he instantly angled his hips away. "You're right. Let's go to sleep."

"What? No." She sat up, frowning. "I don't want to go to sleep."

He was struggling, she could tell. Trying to hide his erection. Trying not to glance at her naked body. "Your flight was early this morning. You're probably jet-lagged—"

"But we only have one night." One single night. One night for Olive to suspend the outside world. To avoid thinking about Tom, and what had happened earlier today, and the mysterious woman Adam was in love with. One night to forget that whatever feelings she had for him, they were not mutual.

"Hey." He reached up, pushing her hair behind her shoulder. "You don't owe me anything. Let's get some sleep and—"

"We have one night." Determined, she pressed her palm on his chest, straddling him. The cotton of his pants was soft against her folds. "I want the whole night." She smiled down at him, forehead against his, her hair a curtain between them and the outside world. A sanctuary of sorts. He gripped her waist like he couldn't help himself, pulling her against him, and oh, they fit so well together. "Come on, Adam. I know you're old, but you can't go to sleep just yet."

"I—" He seemed to forget what he was about to say the moment her hand slid inside his pants. His eyes closed, and he exhaled sharply, and—yes. Good. "Olive."

"Yes?"

She kept on sliding down his body. And tugging at his pants. And he made some half-hearted efforts to stop her, but he didn't seem to be fully in control, and in the end he let her take his remaining clothes off. She pulled her hair back and sat on her heels between his thighs.

Adam tried to look away and failed. "You are so beautiful." The words were low and hushed, as though they'd slipped out of his mouth. Loose and unbidden, just like everything else about this.

"I've never done this," she confessed. She didn't feel shy, probably because this was Adam.

"No. Come here."

"So it probably won't be any good."

"You—Olive. You don't have to. You shouldn't."

"Noted." She pressed a kiss against his hip, and he groaned as though she'd done something special. As though this was beyond anything. "But if you have any wishes."

"Olive. I'm going to—" Grunt. He was going to grunt, a rumbling noise coming from deep in his chest. She ran her nose on the skin of his abdomen, seeing his cock twitch with the corner of her eye.

"I love the way you smell."

"Olive."

Slowly, precisely, she wrapped her hand around the base of his erection and studied it from underneath her eyelashes. The head was shiny already, and—she didn't know much, but he seemed close. He seemed very hard, and above her his chest heaved and his lips parted and his skin flushed. He seemed like it wouldn't take much, which . . . good. But also, Olive wanted her time with him. She wanted so much time with Adam. "Someone has done this to you, before? Right?"

He nodded, like she'd expected he would. His hand fisted the sheets, trembling slightly.

"Good. So you can tell me, if I mess it up."

She said the last word against the shaft, and it felt like they were oscillating, vibrating at some short-wave frequency that burst and shattered when she touched him for real. Before parting her lips on the head of his cock she looked up at him, gave him a small smile, and that seemed to do him in. His back arched. He groaned, and ordered her in hushed tones to please, give him a moment, go slow, not let him come, and Olive wondered if his spine was melting into the same liquid, scalding pleasure she'd felt earlier.

It probably couldn't have been more obvious, that she'd never done this. And yet it seemed to turn him on beyond belief. He clearly couldn't help himself—he thrust forward, threaded his fingers in her hair, pressed her head down until her throat was tight around him. He groaned, and talked, and caught her eyes, as if constantly fascinated by the way she was looking up at him. He slurred raspy words, mumbling, "Olive, yes." "Lick the . . ." "Take it just—deeper. Make me come." She heard praises and endearments come out of his mouth—how good she was, how lovely, how perfect; obscenities about her lips and body and eyes, and maybe she would have been embarrassed, if it hadn't been for the pleasure spilling rich from both of them, overflowing their brains. It felt natural, to have Adam ask for what he wanted. To give it to him.

"Can I—?" Her teeth grazed the underside of the head, and he grunted abruptly. "In your mouth."

She only had to smile at him, and his pleasure looked nuclear, pounding through him and washing over his entire body. What Olive had felt earlier, white-hot and just shy of painful. She was still sucking gently when he regained control of his limbs and cupped her cheek.

"The things I want to do to you. You have no idea."

"I think maybe I do." She licked her lips. "Some, at least." His eyes were glazed as he stroked the corner of her mouth, and Olive wondered how she could possibly be done with this, with *him*, in just a few hours.

"I doubt it."

She leaned forward, hiding a smile into the crease of his thigh. "You can, you know." She nibbled on the hard plane of his abdomen and then looked up at him. "Do them."

She was still smiling when he pulled her up to his chest, and for a few minutes they managed to sleep.

~~~~~~

IT REALLY WAS a nice hotel room, she supposed. The large windows, mostly. And the view of Boston after dark, the traffic and the clouds and the feeling that something was happening out there, something she didn't need to be part of because she was here. With Adam.

"What language is that?" it occurred to her to ask. He couldn't quite look at her face, not with her head nestled under his chin, so he continued to draw patterns on her hip with his fingertips.

"What?"

"The book you're reading. With the tiger on the cover. German?"

"Dutch." She felt his voice vibrate, from his chest and through her flesh.

"Is it a manual on taxidermy?"

He pinched her hip, lightly, and she giggled. "Was it hard to learn? Dutch, I mean."

He inhaled the scent of her hair, thinking for a moment. "I'm not sure. I always knew it."

"Was it weird? Growing up with two languages?"

"Not really. I mostly thought in Dutch until we moved back here."

"How old was that?"

"Mmm. Nine?"

It made her smile, the idea of child Adam. "Did you speak Dutch with your parents?"

"No." He paused. "There were au pairs, mostly. Lots of them."

Olive pushed herself up to look at him, resting her chin on her hands and her hands on his chest. She watched him watch her, enjoying the play of the streetlights on his strong face. He was always handsome, but now, in the witching hours, he took her breath away.

"Were your parents busy?"

He sighed. "They were very committed to their jobs. Not very good at making time for anything else."

She hummed softly, conjuring a mental image: five-year-old Adam showing a stick-figure drawing to tall, distracted parents in dark suits surrounded by secret agents speaking into their headsets. She knew nothing about diplomats. "Were you a happy child?"

"It's . . . complicated. It was a bit of a textbook upbringing. Only child of financially rich but emotionally poor parents. I could do whatever I wanted but had no one to do it with." It sounded sad. Olive and her mom had always had very little, but she'd never felt alone. Until the cancer.

"Except Holden?"

He smiled. "Except Holden, but that was later. I think I was already set in my ways by then. I'd learned to entertain myself with . . . things. Hobbies. Activities. School. And when I was supposed to be with people, I was . . . antagonistic and unapproachable." She rolled her eyes and bit softly into his skin, making him chuckle. "I've become like my parents," he mused. "Exclusively committed to my job."

"That's not true at all. You're very good at making time for others. For me." She smiled, but he looked away as if embarrassed, and she decided to change the topic. "The only thing I can say in Dutch is *'ik hou van jou.'*" Her pronunciation must have been poor, because for a long moment Adam couldn't parse it. Then he did, and his eyes widened.

"My college roommate had a poster with 'I love you' written in every language," Olive explained. "Right across from my bed. First thing I'd see every morning after waking up."

"And at the end of year four you knew every language?"

"End of year one. She joined a sorority as a sophomore, which was for the best." She lowered her gaze, nuzzled her face in his chest, and then looked back up at him. "It's pretty stupid, if you think about it."

"Stupid?"

"Who needs to know how to say 'I love you' in every language? People barely need it in one. Sometimes not even in one." She smoothed his hair back with her fingers. "'Where's the restroom?' on the other hand . . ."

He leaned into her touch, as if soothed by it. "*Waar is de WC?*"

Olive blinked.

"That would be 'Where's the restroom?'" he explained.

"Yeah, I figured. Just . . . your voice . . ." She cleared her throat. She'd been better off without knowing how attractive he sounded when speaking another language. "Anyway. That would be a useful poster." She brushed her finger against his forehead. "What's this from?"

"My face?"

"The little scar. The one above your eyebrow."

"Ah. Just a stupid fight."

"A fight?" She chuckled. "Did one of your grads try to kill you?"

"Nah, I was a kid. Though I could see my grads pouring acetonitrile in my coffee."

"Oh, totally." She nodded in agreement. "I have one, too." She pulled her hair behind her shoulder and showed him the small, half-moon-shaped line right next to her temple.

"I know."

"You know? About my scar?"

He nodded.

"When did you notice? It's really faint."

He shrugged and began tracing it with his thumb. "What's it from?"

"I don't remember. But my mom said that when I was four there was this *huge* snowstorm in Toronto. Inches upon inches of snow piling up, the most intense in five decades, you know the drill. And everyone knew it was coming, and she'd been preparing me for days, telling me that we might end up stuck at home for a few days. I was so excited about it that I ran outside and dove headfirst into the snow—except that I did it about half an hour after the storm had started, and ended up hitting my head on a stone." She laughed softly, and so did Adam. It had been one of her mother's favorite stories. And now Olive was the only person who could tell it. It lived in her, and no one else. "I miss the snow. California is beautiful, and I hate the cold. But I really miss the snow."

He continued stroking her scar, a faint smile on his lips. And then, when the silence had settled around them, he said, "Boston will have snow. Next year."

Her heart thudded. "Yeah." Except that she wouldn't be going to Boston, not anymore. She'd have to find another lab. Or not work in a lab at all.

Adam's hand traveled up her neck, closing gently around her nape. "There are good trails for hiking, where Holden and I used to go in grad school." He hesitated before adding, "I'd love to take you."

She closed her eyes, and for a second she let herself imagine it. The black of Adam's hair against the white snow and the deep greens of the trees. Her boots sinking into the soft ground. Cold air flowing inside her lungs, and a warm hand wrapping around her own. She could almost see the flakes, fluttering behind her eyelids. Bliss.

"You'll be in California, though," she said distractedly.

A pause. Too long.

Olive opened her eyes. "Adam?"

He rolled his tongue inside his cheek, as if thinking carefully about his words. "There is a chance that I'll be moving to Boston."

She blinked at him, confused. Moving? He'd be moving? "What?" No. What was he saying? Adam was not going to leave Stanford, right? He'd never been—the flight risk had never been *real*. Right?

Except he'd never said that. Olive thought back to their conversations, and—he'd complained about the department withholding his research funds, about them suspecting that he was going to leave, about the assumptions people had made because of his collaboration with Tom, but . . . he'd never said that they were wrong. He'd said that the frozen funds had been earmarked for research—for the current year. That's why he'd wanted them released as soon as possible.

"Harvard," she whispered, feeling incredibly stupid. "You're moving to Harvard."

"It's not decided yet." His hand was still wrapped around her neck, thumb swiping back and forth across the pulse at the base of her throat. "I've been asked to interview, but there's no official offer."

"When? When will you interview?" she asked, but didn't really need his answer. It was all starting to make sense in her head. "Tomorrow. You're not going home." He'd never said he would. He'd only told her he'd be leaving the conference early. Oh God. *Stupid, Olive. Stupid.* "You're going to Harvard. To interview for the rest of the week."

"It was the only way to avoid making the department even more suspicious," he explained. "The conference was a good cover."

She nodded. It wasn't good—it was perfect. And God, she felt nauseous. And weak-kneed, even lying down. "They'll offer you the position," she murmured, even though he must already know. He was Adam Carlsen, after all. And he'd been asked to interview. They were *courting* him.

"It's not certain yet."

It was. Of course it was. "Why Harvard?" she blurted. "Why—why do you want to leave Stanford?" Her voice shook a little, even though she did her best to sound calm.

"My parents live on the East Coast, and while I have my issues with them, they're going to need me close sooner or later." He paused, but Olive could tell that he wasn't done. She braced herself. "The main reason is Tom. And the grant. I want to transition to doing more similar work, but that will only be possible if we show good results. Being in the same department as Tom would make us infinitely more productive. Professionally, moving's a no-brainer."

She'd braced herself, but it still felt like a punch in the sternum that left her void of air, caused her stomach to twist and her heart to drop. Tom. This was about *Tom*.

"Of course," she whispered. It helped her voice sound firmer. "It makes sense."

"And I could help you acclimatize, too," he offered, significantly more bashful. "If you want to. To Boston. To Tom's lab. Show you around, if you . . . if you're feeling lonely. Buy you that pumpkin stuff."

She couldn't answer that. She really—she could *not* answer that. So she hung her head for a few moments, ordered herself to buck the hell up, and lifted it again to smile at him.

She could do this. She *would* do this. "What time are you leaving tomorrow?" He was probably just moving to another hotel, closer to the Harvard campus.

"Early."

"Okay." She leaned forward and buried her face in his throat. They were not going to sleep, not one second. It would be such a waste. "You don't have to wake me up, when you leave."

"You're not going to carry my bags downstairs?"

She laughed into his neck and burrowed deeper into him. This, she thought, this was going to be their perfect night. And their last.

Chapter Eighteen

💛 **HYPOTHESIS:** *A heart will break even more easily than the weakest of hydrogen bonds.*

It wasn't the sun high in the sky that woke her up, nor housekeeping—thanks to Adam, likely, and a Do Not Disturb sign on the door. What got Olive out of bed, even though she really, *really* didn't want to face the day, was the frantic buzzing on the nightstand.

She buried her face in the pillow, extended her arm to grope her way to her phone, and then brought it to her ear.

"Yeah?" she bleated, only to find that it wasn't a call but a very long string of notifications. It included one email from Dr. Aslan congratulating her on her talk and asking for the recording, two texts from Greg (Have u seen the multichannel pipette? Nvm found it.), one from Malcolm (call me when you see this), and . . .

One hundred and forty-three from Anh.

"What the . . . ?" She blinked at the screen, unlocked her

phone, and started scrolling up. Could it be one hundred and forty-three reminders to wear sunscreen?

Anh: O

Anh: M

Anh: G

Anh: OMG

Anh: Omg omg OMFG

Anh: Where the hell are you

Anh: OLIVE

Anh: OLIVE LOUISE SMITH

Anh: (JK I know you don't have a middle name)

Anh: (But if you did it would be Louise FIGHT ME you know im right)

Anh: Where ARE U?!?!?

Anh: Your missing so much YOU ARE MISSING SO

Anh: WHERE THE HELL IS YOUR ROOM I'M COMING TO YOU

Anh: OL we need to talk about this IN PERSON!!!!!1!!!!!!!!

Anh: Are you DEAD?

Anh: You better be IT'S THE ONLY WAY I'LL FORGIVE YOU FOR MISSING THIS OL

Anh: Ol is this real life is iT jUST FANTASY SJFGAJHSGFASF

Anh: OOOOOOOOOOOOOOOOOOOOOOOOOOOOOOOOL

Olive groaned, rubbed her face, and decided to skip the other 125 messages and text Anh her room number. She went into the bathroom and reached for her toothbrush, trying not to notice that the spot where Adam's had been was now empty. Whatever Anh was freaking out about, Olive was likely going to be underwhelmed. Jeremy had Irish step-danced at the department social, or Chase had tied a cherry stem with his tongue. Great entertainment value, for sure, but Olive would survive missing either.

She dried her face, thinking that she was doing a great job of not thinking of how sore she was; of how her body was buzzing, vibrating like it had no intention of stopping, not two, not three, not five hours from now; of the faint, comforting scent of Adam on her skin.

Yeah. A great job.

When she stepped out of the bathroom, someone was about to tear down the door. She opened it to find Anh and Malcolm, who hugged her and started talking so loudly and rapidly, she could barely make out the words—though she did catch the terms "paradigm-shifting," "life-altering," and "watershed moment in history."

They chattered their way to Olive's unused bed and sat down. After a few more moments of overlapping babbling, Olive decided to intervene and lifted her hands.

"Hold on." She was already coming down with a headache. Today was going to be a nightmare, for so many reasons. "What happened?"

"The weirdest thing," Anh said.

"Coolest," Malcolm interrupted. "She means coolest."

"Where *were* you, Ol? You said you were going to join us."

"Here. I just, um, was tired after my talk, and fell asleep and—"

"Lame, Ol, *very* lame, but I have no time to berate you for your lameness because I need to catch you up with what happened last night—"

"*I* should tell her," Malcolm gave Anh a scathing look. "Since it's about me."

"Fair enough," she conceded with a flourishing gesture.

Malcolm smiled, pleased, and cleared his throat. "Ol, who have I been wanting to have sex with for the past several years?"

"Uh . . ." She scratched her temple. Off the top of her head, she could name about thirty people. "Victoria Beckham?"

"No. Well, yes. But no."

"David Beckham?"

"Also yes. But no."

"The other Spice Girl? The one in the Adidas tracksuit—"

"No. Okay, yes, but don't focus on celebrities, focus on *real life* people—"

"Holden Rodrigues," Anh blurted out impatiently. "He hooked up with Rodrigues at the department social. Ol, it is with utmost regret that I must inform you that you have been dethroned and are no longer the president of the Hot for Teacher club. Will you retire in shame or accept the treasurer position?"

Olive blinked. Several times. An inordinate amount of times. And then heard herself say, "Wow."

"Isn't it the weirdest—"

"Coolest, Anh," Malcolm interjected. "*Coolest.*"

"Things can be weird in a cool way."

"Right, but this is pure, one hundred percent cool, zero percent weird—"

"Hold up," Olive interrupted. Her headache was growing a size or two. "Holden is not even in the department. Why was he at the social?"

"No idea, but you bring up an excellent point, which is that since he's in pharmacology, we can do whatever we want without having to tell anyone."

Anh tilted her head. "Is that so?"

"Yep. We checked Stanford's socialization regulations on our way to CVS to get condoms. Basically foreplay." He closed his eyes in bliss. "Will I ever step inside a pharmacy again without getting a boner?"

Olive cleared her throat. "I'm so happy for you." She really was. Though this did feel a bit weird. "How did it happen?"

"I hit on him. It was glorious."

"He was shameless, Ol. *And* glorious. I took some pictures."

Malcolm gasped in outrage. "Okay, that's illegal and I could sue you. But if I look good in them, do send them my way."

"Will do, babe. Now tell us about the sex."

The fact that Malcolm, usually very forward with the details of his sex life, just closed his eyes and smiled, spoke volumes. Anh and Olive exchanged a long, impressed glance.

"And that's not even the best part. He wants to see me again. Today. A *date*. He used the word 'date' unprompted." He fell back on the mattress. "He's so hot. And funny. And nice. A sweet, filthy beast."

Malcolm looked so happy, Olive couldn't resist: she swallowed the lump that had taken residence in her throat sometime last night and jumped on the bed next to him, hugging him as tight as she could. Anh followed and did the same.

"I'm so happy for you, Malcolm."

"Same." Anh's voice was muffled against his hair.

"I am happy for me, too. I hope he's serious. You know when I said I was training for gold? Well, Holden's *platinum*."

"You should ask Carlsen, Ol," Anh suggested. "If he knows what Holden's intentions are."

She probably wasn't going to have the opportunity anytime soon. "I will."

Malcolm shifted a bit and turned to Olive. "Did you really fall asleep last night? Or were you and Carlsen celebrating in unmentionable ways?"

"Celebrating?"

"I told Holden that I was worried about you, and he said that you guys were probably celebrating. Something about Carlsen's funds being released? By the way, you never told me Carlsen and

Holden were best friends—it seems like a piece of information you'd want to share with your Holden-Rodrigues-fan-club-founder-and-most-vocal-member roommate—"

"Wait." Olive sat up, wide-eyed. "The funds that were released, are they . . . the frozen ones? The ones Stanford was withholding?"

"Maybe? Holden said something about the department chair finally easing up. I tried to pay attention, but talking about Carlsen is a bit of a buzzkill—no offense. Plus, I kept getting lost in Holden's eyes."

"And his butt," Anh added.

"And his butt." Malcolm sighed happily. "Such a nice butt. He has little dimples on his lower back."

"Oh my God, so does Jeremy! I want to bite them."

"Aren't they the cutest?"

Olive stopped listening and stood from the bed, grabbing her phone to read the date.

September twenty-ninth.

It was September twenty-ninth.

She had known, of course. She had known for over a month that today was coming, but in the past week she'd been too busy fretting about her talk to focus on anything else, and Adam hadn't reminded her. With everything that had happened in the past twenty-four hours, it was no surprise that he'd forgotten to mention that his funds had been released. But still. The implications of it were . . .

She closed her eyes, shut tight, while Anh and Malcolm's excited chattering kept rising in volume in the background. When she opened them, her phone lit up with a new notification. From Adam.

Adam: I have interview meetings until 4:30, but I'm free for the night. Would you like to get dinner? There are several good restaurants near campus (though a shameful lack of conveyor belts). If you're not busy, I could show you around campus, maybe even Tom's lab.

Adam: No pressure, of course.

It was almost two in the afternoon. Olive felt as though her bones weighed twice as much as the day before. She took a deep breath, straightened her shoulders, and began typing her reply to Adam.

She knew what she had to do.

SHE KNOCKED ON his door at five sharp, and he answered just a few seconds later, still dressed in slacks and a button-down that must have been his interview attire and . . .

Smiling at her. Not one of those half-baked things she'd gotten used to, but a real, true smile. With dimples, and crinkles around his eyes, and genuine happiness to see her. It shattered her heart in a million pieces before he even spoke.

"Olive."

She still hadn't figured it out, why the way he said her name was so unique. There was something packed behind it, something that didn't quite make it to the surface. A sense of possibilities. Of depth. Olive wondered if it was real, if she was hallucinating it, if he was aware. Olive wondered a lot of things, and then told herself to stop. It couldn't matter less, now.

"Come in."

It was an even fancier hotel, and Olive rolled her eyes, wondering why people felt the need to waste thousands of dollars in lodgings for Adam Carlsen when he barely paid attention to his surroundings. They should just give him a cot and donate the money to worthy causes. Endangered whales. Psoriasis. Olive.

"I brought this—I'm assuming it's yours." She took a couple of steps toward him and held out a phone charger, letting the cable end dangle, making sure that Adam wouldn't need to touch her.

"It is. Thank you."

"It was behind the bedside lamp, probably why you forgot it." She pressed her lips together. "Or maybe it's old age. Maybe dementia has already set in. All those amyloid plaques."

He glared at her, and she tried not to smile, but she already was, and he was rolling his eyes and calling her a smart-ass, and—

Here they were. Doing this, again. Dammit.

She let her eyes wander away, because—no. Not anymore. "How was the interview?"

"Good. Just day one, though."

"Of how many?"

"Too many." He sighed. "I have grant meetings with Tom scheduled, too."

Tom. Right. Of course. Of course—this was why she was here. To explain to him that—

"Thank you for coming out," he said, voice quiet and earnest. As though by hopping on a train and agreeing to see him, Olive had given him a great deal of pleasure. "I figured you might be busy with your friends."

She shook her head. "No. Anh's out with Jeremy."

"I'm sorry," he said, looking genuinely regretful for her, and it took Olive several moments to recall her lie, and his assumption that she was in love with Jeremy. Only a few weeks earlier, but it already seemed so long ago, when she hadn't been able to imagine anything worse than Adam discovering her feelings for him. It sounded so foolish after everything that had happened in the past few days. She should really come clean, but what was the point now? Let Adam think what he liked. It would serve him better than the truth, after all.

"And Malcolm is with . . . Holden."

"Ah, yes." He nodded, looking exhausted.

Olive briefly fantasized about Holden texting Adam the equivalent of what Olive and Anh had been subjected to for the past two hours, and smiled. "How bad is it?"

"Bad?"

"This thing between Malcolm and Holden?"

"Ah." Adam leaned his shoulder against the wall, folding his arms across his chest. "I think it can be very good. For Holden, at least. He really likes Malcolm."

"Did he tell you?"

"He hasn't shut up about it." He rolled his eyes. "Did you know that Holden is secretly twelve?"

She laughed. "So is Malcolm. He dates a lot, and he's usually good at managing expectations, but this thing with Holden—I had a sandwich for lunch and he randomly volunteered that Holden is allergic to peanuts. It wasn't even PB and J!"

"He's not allergic, he fakes it because he doesn't like nuts." He massaged his temple. "This morning I woke up to a haiku about Malcolm's elbows. Holden had texted it at three a.m."

"Was it good?"

He lifted one eyebrow, and she laughed again.

"They are . . ."

"The worst." Adam shook his head. "But I think Holden might need it. Someone to care about, who also cares about him."

"Malcolm, too. I'm just . . . concerned that he might want more than Holden is willing to offer?"

"Believe me, Holden is very ready to file taxes jointly."

"Good. I'm glad." She smiled. And then felt her smile fade, just as quickly. "One-sided relationships are really . . . not good." *I would know. And maybe you would, too.*

He studied his own palm, undoubtedly thinking about the woman Holden had mentioned. "No. No, they're not."

It was a weird kind of ache, the jealousy. Confusing, unfamil-iar, not something she was used to. Half cutting, half disorient-ing and aimless, so different from the loneliness she'd felt since she was fifteen. Olive missed her mother every day, but with time she'd been able to harness her pain and turn it into motivation for her work. Into purpose. Jealousy, though . . . the misery of it didn't come with any gain. Only restless thoughts, and some-thing squeezing at her chest whenever her mind turned to Adam.

"I need to ask you something," he said. The seriousness of his tone made her look up.

"Sure."

"The people you overheard at the conference yesterday . . ."

She stiffened. "I'd rather not—"

"I won't force you to do anything. But whoever they were, I want . . . I think you should consider filing a complaint."

Oh God. *God.* Was this some cruel joke? "You really like com-plaints, don't you?" She laughed once, a weak attempt at humor.

"I'm serious, Olive. And if you decide you want to do it, I'll help you however I can. I could come with you and talk with SBD's organizers, or we could go through Stanford's Title IX office—"

"No. I . . . Adam, no. I'm not going to file a complaint." She rubbed her eyes with the tips of her fingers, feeling as though this was one giant, painful prank. Except that Adam had no idea. He actually wanted to protect her, when all Olive wanted was . . . to protect him. "I've already decided. It would do more harm than good."

"I know why you think that. I felt the same during grad school, with my mentor. We all did. But there *are* ways to do it. Whoever this person is, they—"

"Adam, I—" She ran one hand down her face. "I need you to drop this. Please."

He studied her, silent for several minutes, and then nodded. "Okay. Of course." He pushed away from the wall and straightened, clearly unhappy to let the subject go but making an effort to do so. "Would you like to go to dinner? There's a Mexican restaurant nearby. Or sushi—*real* sushi. And a movie theater. Maybe there are one or two movies playing in which horses don't die."

"I'm not . . . I'm not hungry, actually."

"Oh." His expression was teasing. Gentle. "I didn't know that was possible."

"Me neither." She chuckled weakly, and then forced herself to continue. "Today is September twenty-ninth."

A beat. Adam studied her, patient and curious. "It is."

She bit into her lower lip. "Do you know what the chair has decided about your funds?"

"Oh, right. The funds will be unfrozen." He seemed happy, his eyes brilliant in an almost boyish way. It broke her heart a little. "I meant to tell you tonight at dinner."

"That's great." She managed a smile, small and pitiful in her mounting anxiety. "That's really great, Adam. I'm happy for you."

"Must have been your sunscreen skills."

"Yeah." Her laugh sounded fake. "I'll have to put them on my CV. Fake girlfriend with extensive experience. Microsoft Office and excellent sunscreen skills. Available immediately, only serious callers."

"Not immediately." He looked at her curiously. Tenderly. "Not for a while, I'd say."

The weight, the one that had been pressing into her stomach since she'd realized what needed to be done, sank heavier. Now—this was it. The coda. The moment it all ended. Olive could do this, and she would, and things would be all the better for it.

"I think I should be." She swallowed, and it was like acid down her throat. "Available." She scanned his face, noticed his confusion, and clenched her fist in the hem of her sweater. "We gave ourselves a deadline, Adam. And we accomplished everything we wanted. Jeremy and Anh are solid—I doubt they even remember that Jeremy and I used to date. And your funds have been released, which is amazing. The truth is . . ."

Her eyes stung. She closed them tight, managing to push the tears back. Barely.

The truth, Adam, is that your friend, your collaborator, a person you clearly love and are close to, is horrid and despicable. He told me things that might be truths, or maybe lies—I don't know. I'm not sure. I'm not sure of anything anymore, and I would love to ask you, so badly. But I'm terrified that he might be right, and that you won't believe me. And I'm even more terrified that you will believe me, and that what I tell you will force you to give up something that is very important to you: your friendship and your work with him. I'm terrified of everything, as you can see. So, instead of telling you that truth, I will tell you another truth. A truth that, I think, will be best for you. A truth that will take me out of the equation, but will make its result better. Because I'm starting to wonder if this is what being in love is. Being okay with ripping yourself to shreds, so the other person can stay whole.

She inhaled deeply. "The truth is, we did great. And it's time we call it quits."

She could tell from how his lips parted, from his disoriented eyes searching hers, that he wasn't yet parsing what she'd said. "I don't think we'll need to explicitly tell anyone," she continued. "People won't see us together, and after a while they'll think that . . . that it didn't work out. That we broke up. And maybe you . . ." This was the hardest part. But he deserved to hear it.

He'd told her the same, after all, when he'd believed her in love with Jeremy. "I wish you all the best, Adam. At Harvard, and . . . with your real girlfriend. Whoever you may choose. I cannot imagine anyone not reciprocating your feelings."

She could pinpoint the exact moment it dawned on him. She could tease apart the feelings struggling in his face—the surprise, the confusion, a hint of stubbornness, a split second of vulnerability that all melted in a blank, empty expression. Then she could see his throat work.

"Right," he said. "Right." He was staring at his shoes, absolutely motionless. Slowly accepting her words.

Olive took a step back and rocked on her heels. Outside, an iPhone rang, and a few seconds later someone burst into laughter. Normal noises, on a normal day. Normal, all of this.

"It's for the best," she said, because the silence between them—that, she just couldn't stand. "It's what we agreed on."

"Whatever you want." His voice was hoarse, and he seemed . . . absent. Retreated to some place inside himself. "Whatever you need."

"I can't thank you enough for everything you've done for me. Not just about Anh. When we met, I felt so alone, and . . ." For a moment she couldn't continue. "Thank you for all the pumpkin spice, and for that Western blot, and for hiding your taxidermied squirrels when I visited, and . . ."

She couldn't bring herself to go on anymore, not without choking on her words. The stinging in her eyes was burning now, threatening to spill over, so she nodded once, decisively, a period to this dangling sentence with no end in sight.

And that would have been it. It would have surely been the end. They would have left it at that, if Olive hadn't passed him on her way to the door. If he hadn't reached out and stopped her with a hand on her wrist. If he hadn't immediately pulled that hand back and stared at it with an appalled expression, as if shocked that he'd dared to touch her without asking for permission first.

If he hadn't said, "Olive. If you ever need anything, anything at all. *Anything.* Whenever. You can come to me." His jaw worked, like there were other words, words he was keeping inside. "I *want* you to come to me."

She almost didn't register wiping wetness off her cheek with the back of her hand, or moving closer to him. It was his scent that jolted her alert—soap and something dark, subtle but oh so familiar. Her brain had him mapped out, stored away across all senses. Eyes to his almost smile, hands to his skin, the smell of him in her nostrils. She didn't even need to think about what to do, just push up on her toes, press her fingers against his biceps, and kiss him gently on the cheek. His skin was soft and warm and a little prickly; unexpected, but not unwelcome.

An apt goodbye, she thought. Appropriate. Acceptable.

And so was his hand coming up to her lower back, pulling her into his body and stopping her from sliding back on her heels, or the way his head turned, until her lips were not brushing the skin of his cheek anymore. Her breath hitched, a chuff against the corner of his mouth, and for a few precious seconds she just savored it, the deep pleasure that ran through them both as they closed their eyes and let themselves just *be*, here, with each other.

Quiet. Still. One last moment.

Then Olive opened her mouth and turned her head, breathing against his lips, "Please."

Adam groaned deep in his chest. But she was the one who closed the space between them, who deepened the kiss, who combed her hands into his hair, short nails scraping against his scalp. She was the one who pulled him even closer, and he was the one who pushed her back against the wall and moaned into her mouth.

It was frightening. Frightening, how good this felt. How easy it would be to never stop. To let time stretch and unbend, forget about everything else, and simply stay in this moment forever.

But Adam pulled back first, holding her eyes as he tried to collect himself.

"It was good, wasn't it?" Olive asked, with a small, wistful smile.

She wasn't herself sure what she was referring to. Maybe his arms around her. Maybe this last kiss. Maybe everything else. The sunscreen, his ridiculous answers on his favorite color, the quiet conversations late at night . . . all of it had been so very good.

"It was." Adam's voice sounded too deep to be his own. When he pressed his lips against her forehead one last time, she felt her love for him swell fuller than a river in flood.

"I think I should leave," she told him gently, without looking at him. He let her go wordlessly, so she did.

When she heard the click of the door closing behind her, it was like falling from a great height.

Chapter Nineteen

~~~~~~

💙 **HYPOTHESIS:** *When in doubt, asking a friend will save my ass.*

Olive spent the following day in the hotel, sleeping, crying, and doing the very thing that had gotten her into this mess to begin with: lying. She told Malcolm and Anh that she'd be busy with friends from college for the entire day, pulled the blackout curtains together, and then buried herself in her bed. Which, technically, was Adam's bed.

She didn't let herself think about the situation too much. Something inside her—her heart, very possibly—was broken in several large pieces, not shattered as much as neatly snapped in half, and then in half again. All she could do was sit down amid the debris of her feelings and wallow. Sleeping through most of the day helped dull the pain a great deal. Numb, she was rapidly starting to realize, was good.

She lied the day after, too. Feigned a last-minute request from Dr. Aslan when asked to join her friends at the conference or on excursions around Boston, and then took a deep, fortifying breath.

She drew the curtains open, forced her blood to start flowing again (with fifty crunches, fifty jumping jacks, and fifty push-ups, though she cheated on the last by going on her knees), then showered and brushed her teeth for the first time in thirty-six hours.

It wasn't easy. Seeing Adam's Biology Ninja T-shirt in the mirror made her tear up, but she reminded herself that she'd made her choice. She'd decided to put Adam's well-being first, and she didn't regret it. But she'd be damned if she let Tom Fucking Benton take credit for a project she had worked on for *years*. A project that meant the world to her. Maybe her life was nothing but a little sob story, but it was *her* little sob story.

Her heart may be broken, but her brain was doing just fine.

Adam had said that the reason most professors hadn't bothered to reply, perhaps even read her email, was that she was a student. So she followed his advice: she emailed Dr. Aslan and asked her to introduce Olive to all the researchers she'd previously contacted, plus the two people who'd been on her panel and had shown interest in her work. Dr. Aslan was close to retirement, and had more or less given up on producing science, but she was still a full professor at Stanford. It had to mean something.

Then Olive googled extensively about research ethics, plagiarism, and theft of ideas. The issue was a little murky, given that Olive had—quite recklessly, she now realized—described all her protocols in detail in her report for Tom. But once she began examining the situation with a clearer head, she decided that it wasn't as dire as she'd initially thought. The report she'd written, after all, was well-structured and thorough. With a few tweaks she could turn it into a scholarly publication. It would hopefully go quickly through peer review, and the findings would be credited under her name.

What she decided to focus on was that despite all his insults and rude comments, Tom, one of the top cancer researchers in the United States, had expressed interest in stealing her research ideas. She took it as a very, *very* backhanded compliment.

She spent the next several hours carefully avoiding thoughts of Adam and instead researching other potential scientists who might be able to support her the following year. It was a long shot, but she had to try. When someone knocked on her door, it was already the middle of the afternoon, and she'd added three new names to her list. She quickly put on clothes to answer, expecting housekeeping. When Anh and Malcolm stormed inside, she cursed herself for never checking the peephole. She truly deserved to be axed by a serial killer.

"Okay," Anh said, throwing herself onto Olive's still-made bed, "you have two sentences to convince me that I shouldn't be mad at you for forgetting to ask how my outreach event went."

"Shit!" Olive covered her mouth with her hand. "I am so sorry. How did it go?"

"Perfect." Anh's eyes were shiny with happiness. "We had such great attendance and everyone loved it. We're thinking of making this a yearly thing, and formally establishing an organization. Peer-to-peer mentoring! Hear this: every grad is assigned *two* undergrads. Once they get into grad school, they mentor *two* more undergrads each. And in ten years we take over the entire damn world."

Olive looked at her, speechless. "This is . . . you're amazing."

"I am, aren't I? Okay, now's your turn to grovel. Aaand, go."

Olive opened her mouth, but for a long time nothing really came out. "I don't really have an excuse. I was just busy with . . . something Dr. Aslan asked me to finish."

"This is ridiculous. You are in Boston. You should be out there in an Irish pub pretending you love the Red Sox and eating Dunkies, not doing *work*. For your *boss*."

"We're technically here for a work conference," Olive pointed out.

"Conference shmonference." Malcolm joined Anh on the bed.

"Can we please go out, the three of us?" Anh begged. "Let's do the Freedom Trail. With ice cream. And beer."

"Where's Jeremy?"

"Presenting his poster. And I'm bored." Anh's grin was impish.

Olive was not in the mood for socializing, or beer, or freedom trails, but at some point she was going to have to learn to productively navigate society with a broken heart.

She smiled and said, "Let me check my email, and then we can go." She had, inexplicably, accumulated about fifteen messages in the thirty minutes since she'd last checked, only one of which wasn't spam.

Today, 3:11 p.m.

FROM: Aysegul-Aslan@stanford.edu

TO: Olive-Smith@stanford.edu

SUBJECT: Reaching out to researchers for pancreatic cancer project

Olive,

I'd be happy to introduce you and ask scholars about opportunities for you in their labs. I agree that they might be more welcoming if the email comes from me. Send me your list, please.

BTW, you still haven't sent the recording of your talk. I cannot wait to listen to it!

Warmly,

Aysegul Aslan, Ph.D.

Olive did some mental calculations to determine whether it was polite to send the list and not the recording (probably not), sighed, and started AirDropping the file to her laptop. When she realized that it was several hours long, because she'd forgotten to stop her phone after her talk, her sigh morphed into a groan. "This'll take a while, guys. I have to send Dr. Aslan an audio file, and I'll need to edit it beforehand."

"Fine," Anh huffed. "Malcolm, would you like to entertain us with tales of your date with Holden?"

"Okay, first, he wore the cutest baby-blue button-down."

"Baby-blue?"

"Shut your mouth with that skeptical tone. Then he got me one flower."

"Where did he get the flower?"

"Not sure."

Olive poked around the MP3, trying to figure out where to cut the file. The ending was just minute after minute of silence, from when she'd left her phone in the hotel room. "Maybe he stole it from the buffet?" she said absentmindedly. "I think I saw pink carnations downstairs."

"Was it a pink carnation?"

"Maybe."

Anh cackled. "And they say romance is dead."

"Shut up. Then, toward the beginning of the date, something happened. Something catastrophic that could only ever happen to *me*, given that my entire damn family is obsessed with science and, therefore, attends *all* the conferences. *All of them*."

"No. Tell me you didn't—"

"Yes. When we got to the restaurant, we found my mother, father, uncle, and grandfather. Who insisted on us joining them. Which means that my first date with Holden was a freaking *Thanksgiving dinner*."

Olive looked up from her laptop and shared an appalled look with Anh. "How bad was it?"

"Funny that you ask, because it is with the utmost disconcert that I must say: it was fucking *spectacular*. They loved him—because he's a badass scientist and because he is smoother than an organic smoothie—and in the span of two hours he somehow managed to help me convince my parents that my plan of being an industry scientist is bomb. I'm not kidding—this morning my mother called and was all about how I have grown as a person and am finally in control of my future and how my dating choices reflect that. She said that Dad agrees. Can you believe it? Anyway. After dinner we got ice cream and then we went back to Holden's hotel room and sixty-nined like the world was about to end—"

"A girl like you. Who figured out so early in her academic career that fucking well-known, successful scholars is how to get ahead. You fucked Adam, didn't you? We both know you're going to fuck me for the same reas—"

Olive slammed the spacebar, immediately stopping the replay of the recording. Her heart was pounding in her chest—first from confusion, then from the realization of what she'd inadvertently recorded, and finally from anger at hearing the words again. She brought a trembling hand to her lips, trying to purge Tom's voice from her head. She had spent two days trying to recover, and now—

"The hell was that?" Malcolm asked.

"Ol?" Anh's tentative voice reminded her that she was not alone in the room. She looked up and found that her friends had sat up. They were staring at her, wide-eyed with concern and shock.

Olive shook her head. She didn't want to—no, she didn't have the strength to explain. "Nothing. Just . . ."

"I recognize it," Anh said, coming to sit next to her. "I recognize the voice. From that talk we went to." She paused, searching Olive's eyes. "That was Tom Benton, wasn't it?"

"What the—" Malcolm stood. There was real alarm blooming in his voice. Anger, too. "Ol, why do you have a recording of Tom Benton saying shit like that? What happened?"

Olive looked up at him, then at Anh, then at him again. They were studying her with worried, incredulous expressions. Anh must have taken Olive's hand at some point. She told herself that she needed to be strong, to be pragmatic, to be numb, but . . .

"I just . . ."

She tried. She really did try. But her face crumpled, and the last few days crashed and burned into her. Olive leaned forward, buried her head in Anh's lap, and let herself burst into tears.

~~~~~~

OLIVE HAD NO intention of hearing Tom spout his poison again, so she gave her friends her headphones, went to the bathroom, and let the faucet run until they'd finished listening. It took less than ten minutes, but she sobbed throughout. When Malcolm and Anh came in, they sat next to her on the floor. Anh was crying, too, fat, angry drops sliding down her cheeks.

At least there's a bathtub we can flood, Olive thought while handing her the toilet paper roll she'd been hoarding.

"He's the most disgusting, detestable, shameful, disgraceful human being," Malcolm said. "I hope he has explosive diarrhea as we speak. I hope he gets genital warts. I hope he has to live saddled by the largest, most painful hemorrhoid in the universe. I hope he—"

Anh interrupted him. "Does Adam know?"

Olive shook her head.

"You need to tell him. And then the two of you need to report Benton's ass and get him kicked out of academia."

"No, I . . . I can't."

"Ol, listen to me. What Tom said is sexual harassment. There is no way Adam wouldn't believe you—not to mention that you have a *recording*."

"It doesn't matter."

"Of course it does!"

Olive wiped her cheeks with her palms. "If I tell Adam, he's not going to want to collaborate with Tom anymore, and the project they're working on is too important to him. Not to mention that he wants to move to Harvard next year, and—"

Anh snorted. "No, he doesn't."

"Yes. He told me that—"

"Ol, I've seen the way he looks at you. He's head over feet. There is no way he'll want to move to Boston if you're not going—and I'm sure as hell not letting you go work for this dipshit . . . What?" Her eyes darted from Olive to Malcolm, who were exchanging a long glance. "Why are you guys looking at each other like that? And why are you making your inside-joke faces?"

Malcolm sighed, pinching the bridge of his nose. "Okay Anh, listen carefully. And before you ask—no, I'm not making this up. This is real life." He took a deep breath before starting. "Carlsen and Olive never dated. They pretended so you'd believe that Olive wasn't into Jeremy anymore—which she never was in the first place. Not sure what Carlsen was getting out of the arrangement, I forgot to ask. But halfway through the fake-dating Olive caught feelings for Carlsen, proceeded to lie to him about it, and pretended to be in love with someone else. But then . . ." He gave Olive a side glance. "Well. I didn't want to be nosy, but judging from the fact that the other day only one bed in this hotel room was unmade, I'm pretty sure there have been some . . . recent developments."

It was so painfully accurate, Olive had to bury her face in her knees. Just in time to hear Anh say, "This is not real life."

"It is."

"Nuh-uh. This is a Hallmark movie. Or a poorly written young adult novel. That will *not* sell well. Olive, tell Malcolm to keep his day job, he'll never make it as a writer."

Olive made herself look up, and Anh's frown was the deepest she'd ever seen. "It's true, Anh. I am so sorry I lied to you. I didn't want to, but—"

"You fake-dated Adam Carlsen?"

Olive nodded.

"God, I *knew* that kiss was weird."

She lifted her hands defensively. "Anh, I'm sorry—"

"You fake-dated *Adam. Fucking. Carlsen?*"

"It seemed like a good idea, and—"

"But I saw you kiss him! In the biology building parking lot!"

"Only because you forced me to—"

"But you sat on his lap!"

"Once again, *you* forced me to—not the coolest moment in our friendship, by the way—"

"But you put sunscreen on him! In front of at least one hundred people!"

"Only because *someone* put me up to it. Do you sense a pattern?"

Anh shook her head, as if suddenly appalled at her own actions. "I just—you guys looked so good·together! It was so obvious from the way Adam stared at you that he was *wild* about you. And the opposite—you looked at him like he was the only guy on earth and then—it always seemed like you were forcing yourself to hold back on him, and I wanted you to know that you could express your feelings if you wanted to—I really thought I was helping you, and—*you fake-dated Adam Carlsen?*"

Olive sighed. "Listen, I'm sorry I lied. Please, don't hate me, I—"

"I don't *hate* you."

Oh? "You . . . don't?"

"Of course not." Anh was indignant. "I low-key hate *myself* for forcing you to do all that stuff. Well, maybe not 'hate,' but I'd write myself a strongly worded email. And I'm incredibly flattered that you'd do something like that for me. I mean, it was misguided, and ridiculous, and needlessly convoluted, and you're a living, breathing, rom-com trope machine, and . . . God, Ol, you're such an idiot. But a very lovable idiot, and *my* idiot." She shook her head, incredulous, but squeezed her hand on Olive's knee and glanced at Malcolm. "Wait. Is your thing with Rodrigues real? Or are you two pretending to bone so a judge will give him custody of his recently orphaned godchildren?"

"Very real." Malcolm's smile was smug. "We fuck like bunnies."

"Fantastic. Well, Ol, we'll talk about this more. *A lot* more. We'll probably only talk about the greatest fake-dating event of the twenty-first century for millennia to come, but for now we should focus on Tom, and . . . it changes nothing, whether you and Adam are together. I still think he'd want to know. *I'd* want to know. Ol, if the situation were inverted, if you were the one who stood to lose something and Adam had been sexually harassed—"

"I haven't."

"Yes, Ol, you *have*." Anh's eyes were earnest, burning into hers, and it occurred to Olive then, the enormity of what had happened. Of what Tom had done.

She took a shuddering breath. "If the situation were inverted, I would want to know. But it's different."

"Why is it different?"

Because I'm in love with Adam. And he's not in love with me. Olive massaged her temples, trying to think against the mounting headache. "I don't want to take something he loves away from him. Adam respects and admires Tom, and I know Tom's had Adam's back in the past. Maybe he's better off not knowing."

"If only there were a way to find out what Adam would prefer," Malcolm said.

Olive sniffled in response. "Yeah."

"If only there were someone who knows Adam *very* well that we might ask," Malcolm said, louder this time.

"Yeah," Anh repeated, "that would be great. But there isn't, so—"

"*If only* there were someone in this room who recently started dating Adam's closest friend of nearly three decades," Malcolm near-yelled, full of passive-aggressive indignity, and Anh and Olive exchanged a wide-eyed look.

"Holden!"

"You could ask Holden for advice!"

Malcolm huffed. "You two can be so smart and yet so slow."

Olive suddenly recalled something. "Holden hates Tom."

"Uh? Why does he hate him?"

"I don't know." She shrugged. "Adam wrote it off as some odd personality quirk of Holden's, but—"

"Hey. My man's personality is perfect."

"Maybe there is something else?"

Anh nodded energetically. "Malcolm, where can Olive find Holden right this minute?"

"I don't know. But"—he tapped his phone with a smug smile—"I happen to have his number right here."

~~~~~~

HOLDEN (OR HOLDEN BubbleButt, as Malcolm had saved him in his contacts) was just finishing up his talk. Olive caught the last five minutes of it—something about crystallography she neither understood nor wanted to—and was totally unsurprised by how smooth and charismatic a speaker he was. She approached him on the podium once he was done answering questions, and he smiled when he noticed her walk up the stairs, seeming genuinely happy to see her.

"Olive. My new roommate-in-law!"

"Right. Yes. Um, great talk." She ordered herself to stop wringing her hands. "I wanted to ask you a question . . ."

"Is it about the nucleic acids in the fourth slide? Because I totally BS'd my way through them. My Ph.D. student made the figure, and she's way smarter than me."

"No. The question is about Adam—"

Holden's expression brightened.

"Well, actually, it's about Tom Benton."

It darkened just as quickly. "What about Tom?"

Right. What about Tom, precisely? Olive wasn't quite sure how to approach the topic. She wasn't even sure what she meant to ask. Sure, she could have barfed up her entire life story for Holden and begged him to fix this mess for her, but somehow it didn't seem like a good idea. She racked her brain for a moment, and then landed on: "Did you know that Adam is thinking about moving to Boston?"

"Yeah." Holden rolled his eyes and pointed at the tall windows. There were large, ominous clouds threatening to explode with torrential rain. The wind, already chilly in September, was shaking a lonely hickory tree. "Who *wouldn't* want to move here from California?" he scoffed.

Olive liked the idea of seasons, but she kept the thought to herself. "Do you think . . . Do you think he'd be happy here?"

Holden studied her intensely for a minute. "You know, you were already my favorite girlfriend of Adam's—not that there were many; you're the only woman who could compete with computational modeling in about a decade—but that question wins you a lifelong number-one plaque." He pondered the matter for a minute. "I think Adam could be happy here—in his own way, of course. Broodingly, unenthusiastically happy. But yes, happy. Provided that you are here, too."

Olive had to stop herself from snorting.

"Provided that Tom behaves."

"Why do you say that? About Tom? I . . . I don't mean to pry, but you told me to watch my back with him in Stanford. You . . . don't like him?"

He sighed. "It's not that I don't like him—even though I don't. It's more that I don't trust him."

"Why, though? Adam told me about the things Tom did for him when your adviser was abusive."

"See, this is where a big part of my mistrust comes in." Holden worried at his lower lip, as if deciding whether and how to continue. "Did Tom intercede to save Adam's ass on numerous occasions? Sure. It's undeniable. But how did those occasions come about to begin with? Our adviser was a piece of work, but he was not a micromanager. By the time we joined his lab, he was too busy being a famous asshole to know what was going on in day-to-day lab business. Which is why he had postdocs like Tom mentor grad students like Adam and me and de facto run the lab. And yet, he knew about every single minor screwup of Adam's. Every few weeks he'd come in, tell Adam that he was a failure of a human being for minor stuff like switching reagents or dropping a beaker, and then Tom, our adviser's most-trusted postdoc, would publicly intervene on behalf of Adam and save the day. The pattern was eerily specific, and only for Adam—who was by far the most promising student in our program. Destined for greatness and all that. Initially, it made me a bit suspicious that Tom was purposefully sabotaging Adam. But in recent years I've been wondering if what he wanted was something else altogether. . . ."

"Did you tell Adam?"

"Yes. But I had no proof, and Adam . . . well, you know him. He is stubbornly, unwaveringly loyal, and he was more than a little grateful to Tom." He shrugged. "They ended up becoming bros, and they've been close friends ever since."

"Did it bother you?"

"Not per se, no. I realize I might sound jealous of their friendship, but the truth is that Adam has always been too focused and single-minded to have many friends. I'd have been happy for him, truly. But Tom . . ."

Olive nodded. Yeah. *Tom.* "Why would he do this? This . . . weird vendetta against Adam?"

Holden sighed. "This is why Adam dismissed my concerns. There really isn't an obvious reason. The truth is, I don't think Tom hates Adam. Or at least, I don't think it's that simple. But I do believe that Tom is smart, and very, very cunning. That there probably is some jealousy involved, some desire to take advantage of Adam, to maybe control or have power over him. Adam tends to downplay his accomplishments, but he's one of the best scientists of our generation. Having influence over him . . . that's a privilege, and no small feat."

"Yeah." She nodded again. The question, the one she'd come here to ask, was starting to take shape in her mind. "Knowing all of this. Knowing how important Tom is to Adam, if you had proof of . . . of how Tom really is, would you show Adam?"

To his credit, Holden didn't ask what the proof was, or proof of what. He scanned Olive's face with an intent, thoughtful expression, and when he spoke, his words were careful.

"I can't answer that for you. I don't think I should." He drummed his fingers on the podium, as if deep in thought. "But I do want to tell you three things. The first you probably already know: Adam is first and foremost a scientist. So am I, and so are you. And good science only happens when we draw conclusions based on all available evidence—not just the ones that are easy, or that confirm our hypotheses. Wouldn't you agree?"

Olive nodded, and he continued.

"The second is something you may or may not be aware of, because it has to do with politics and academia, which are not easy to fully grasp until you find yourself sitting through five-hour-long faculty meetings every other week. But here's the deal: the collaboration between Adam and Tom benefits Tom more than it does Adam. Which is why Adam is the main investigator of the grant they were awarded. Tom is . . . well, replaceable. Don't get me wrong, he's a very good scientist, but most of his fame is due to him having been our former adviser's best and brightest. He inherited a lab that was an already well-oiled machine and kept it going. Adam created his own research line from the ground up, and . . . I think he tends to forget how good he is. Which is probably for the best, because he's already pretty insufferable." He huffed. "Can you imagine if he had a big ego, too?"

Olive laughed at that, and the sound came out oddly wet. When she raised her hands to her cheeks, she was not surprised to find them glistening. Apparently, weeping silently was her new baseline state.

"The last thing," Holden continued, unbothered by the waterworks, "is something you probably do not know." He paused. "Adam has been recruited by a lot of institutions in the past. *A lot.* He's been offered money, prestigious positions, unlimited access to facilities and equipment. That includes Harvard—this year was not their first attempt at bringing him in. But it's the first time he's *agreed* to interview. And he only agreed after you decided to go work in Tom's lab." He gave her a gentle smile, and then looked away, beginning to collect his things and slide them inside his backpack. "Make of that what you will, Olive."

Chapter Twenty

♥ **HYPOTHESIS:** *People who cross me will come to regret it.*

She had to lie.

Again.

It was becoming a bit of a habit, and while she spun an elaborate tale for the secretary of Harvard's biology department, one in which she was a grad student of Dr. Carlsen's who needed to track him down immediately to relay a crucial message in person, she swore to herself that this would be the last time. It was too stressful. Too difficult. Not worth the strain on her cardiovascular and psychophysical health.

Plus, she sucked at it. The department secretary didn't look like she believed a word of what Olive said, but she must have decided that there was no harm in telling her where the biology faculty had taken Adam out for dinner—according to Yelp, a fancy restaurant that was less than a ten-minute Uber ride away. Olive looked down at her ripped jeans and lilac Converse and wondered if they'd let her in. Then she wondered if Adam would be mad. Then she wondered if she was making a mistake and screwing up her own life,

Adam's life, her Uber driver's life. She was very tempted to change her destination to the conference hotel when the car pulled up to the curb, and the driver—Sarah Helen, according to the app—turned around with a smile. "Here we are."

"Thank you." Olive started getting out of the passenger seat and found that she couldn't move her legs.

"Are you okay?" Sarah Helen asked.

"Yeah. Just, un . . ."

"Are you gonna puke in my car?"

Olive shook her head. No. Yes. "Maybe?"

"Don't, or I'll destroy your rating."

Olive nodded and tried to slide out of the seat. Her limbs were still nonresponsive.

Sarah Helen frowned. "Hey, what's wrong?"

"I just . . ." There was a lump in her throat. "I need to do a thing. That I don't want to do."

Sarah Helen hummed. "Is it a work thing, or a love thing?"

"Uh . . . both."

"Yikes." Sarah Helen scrunched up her nose. "Double threat. Can you put it off?"

"No, not really."

"Can you ask someone else to do it for you?"

"No."

"Can you change your name, cauterize your fingertips, enter the witness protection program, and disappear?"

"Um, not sure. I'm not an American citizen, though."

"Probably no, then. Can you say 'fuck it' and deal with the consequences?"

Olive closed her eyes and thought about it. What, exactly, would the consequences be if she didn't do what she was planning to? Tom would be free to keep on being an absolute piece of shit, for one. And Adam would never know that he was being taken advantage of. He would move to Boston. And Olive would never have a chance to talk to him again, and all that he'd meant to her would end . . .

In a lie.

A lie, after a lot of lies. So many lies she'd told, so many true things she could have said but never did, all because she'd been too scared of the truth, of driving the people she loved away from her. All because she'd been afraid to lose them. All because she hadn't wanted to be alone again.

Well, the lying hadn't worked out too well. In fact, it had downright sucked lately. Time for plan B, then.

Time for some truth.

"No. I don't want to deal with the consequences."

Sarah Helen smiled. "Then, my friend, you better go do your thing." She pressed a button, and the passenger door unlocked with a clunk. "And you better give me a perfect rating. For the free psychotherapy."

This time, Olive managed to get out of the car. She tipped Sarah Helen 150 percent, took a deep breath, and made her way into the restaurant.

~~~~~

SHE FOUND ADAM immediately. He was big, after all, and the restaurant was not, which made for a pretty quick search. Not to mention that he was sitting with about ten people who looked a lot like very serious Harvard professors. And, of course, Tom.

Fuck my life, she thought, slipping past the busy hostess and walking toward Adam. She figured that her bright red duffle coat would attract his attention, then she'd gesticulate for him to check his phone, and text him to please, please, *please* give her five minutes of his time when dinner was over. She figured that telling him tonight was the best option—his interview would be over tomorrow, and he'd be able to make his decision with the truth at his disposal. She figured her plan might work.

She had *not* figured that Adam would notice her while in conversation with a young, beautiful faculty member. She had *not* figured that he'd suddenly stop speaking, eyes widening and lips parting; that he'd mutter "Excuse me" while staring at Olive and stand from the table, ignoring the curious looks in his direction; that he'd march to the entrance, where Olive was, with quick, long strides and a concerned expression.

"Olive, are you okay?" he asked her, and—

Oh. His voice. And his eyes. And the way his hands came up, as if to touch her, to make sure that she was intact and really there—though right before his fingers could close around her biceps he hesitated and let them fall back to his sides.

It broke her heart a little.

"I'm fine." She attempted a smile. "I . . . I'm sorry to interrupt this. I know it's important, that you want to move to Boston, and—this is inappropriate. But it's now or never, and I wasn't sure if I'd have the courage to . . ." She was rambling. So she took a deep breath and started again. "I need to tell you something. Something that happened. With—"

"Hey, Olive."

Tom. But of course. "Hi, Tom." Olive held Adam's gaze and didn't look at him. He did not deserve to be looked at. "Can you give us a minute of privacy?"

She could see his oily, fake smile with the corner of her eye. "Olive, I know you're young and don't know how these things work, but Adam's here to interview for a very important position, and he can't just—"

"Leave," Adam ordered, voice low and cold.

Olive closed her eyes and nodded, taking a step back. Fine. It was fine. It was Adam's right not to talk to her. "Okay. I'm sorry, I—"

"Not you. Tom, leave us."

Oh. Oh. Well, then.

"Dude," Tom said, sounding amused, "you can't just get up from the table in the middle of an interview dinner and—"

"Leave," Adam repeated.

Tom laughed, brazen. "No. Not unless you're coming with me. We're collaborators, and if you act like an asshole during a dinner with my department because of some student you're screwing, it will reflect poorly on me. You need to come back to the table and—"

"A pretty girl like you should know the score by now. Don't lie to me and say you didn't pick out a dress that short for my benefit. Nice legs, by the way. I can see why Adam's wasting his time with you."

Neither Adam nor Tom had seen Olive take out her phone, or press Play. They both struggled for a second, confused— they'd clearly heard the words but were unsure where they came from. Until the recording restarted.

"Olive. You don't think I accepted you into my lab because you are good, do you? A girl like you. Who figured out so early in her academic career that fucking well-known, successful scholars is how to get ahead. You fucked Adam, didn't you? We both know you're going to fuck me for the same reason."

"What the—" Tom took a step forward, hand extended to grab the phone from Olive. He didn't get far, because Adam pushed him away with a palm on his chest, making him stumble several steps back.

He still wasn't looking at Tom. And not at Olive, either. He was staring down at her phone, something dark and dangerous and frighteningly still in his expression. She should have probably been scared. Maybe she was, a little.

"—you're telling me you thought your pitiful abstract was selected for a talk because of its quality and scientific importance? Someone here has a very high opinion of herself, considering that

her research is useless and derivative and that she can barely put
together two words without stuttering like an idiot—"

"It was him," Adam whispered. His voice was low, barely a
whisper, deceptively calm. His eyes, unreadable. "It was Tom.
The reason you were crying."

Olive could only nod. In the background, Tom's recorded
voice droned on and on. Talking about how mediocre she was.
How Adam would never believe her. Calling her names.

"This is ridiculous." Tom was coming closer again, re-
attempting to take the phone away. "I'm not sure what this
bitch's problem is, but she's clearly—"

Adam exploded so fast, she didn't even see him move. One
moment he stood in front of her, and the next he was pinning
Tom against the wall.

"I'm going to kill you," he gritted out, little more than a
growl. "If you say another word about the woman I love, if you
look at her, if you even *think* about her—I'm going to *fucking*
kill you."

"Adam—" Tom choked out.

"Actually, I will kill you anyway."

People were running toward them. The hostess, a waiter, a
few faculty members from Adam's table. They were forming a
crowd, yelling in confusion and trying to pull Adam off Tom—
with no success. Olive's mind went to Adam pushing Cherie's
truck, and she almost laughed in a moment of hysteria. Almost.

"Adam," she called. Her voice was barely audible in the chaos
going on around them, but it was what got through to him. He
turned to look at her, and there were entire worlds in his eyes.
"Adam, don't," she whispered. "He's not worth it."

Just like that, Adam took a step back and let Tom go. An
elderly gentleman—probably a Harvard dean—began laying
into him, asking for explanations, telling him how unacceptable

his behavior was. Adam ignored him, and everyone else. He headed straight for Olive, and—

He cradled her head with both hands, fingers sliding through her hair and holding her tight as he lowered his forehead to hers. He was warm, and smelled like himself, like *safe* and *home*. His thumbs swept through the mess of tears on her cheeks. "I'm sorry. I'm so sorry. I didn't know, and I'm sorry, I'm sorry, I'm sorry—"

"It's not your fault," she managed to mumble, but he didn't seem to hear her.

"I'm sorry. I'm—"

"Dr. Carlsen," a male voice boomed loudly from behind them, and she felt Adam's body stiffen against hers. "I demand an explanation."

Adam paid no heed to the man, and kept holding Olive.

"*Dr. Carlsen*," he repeated, "this is *unacceptable*—"

"Adam," Olive whispered. "You have to answer him."

Adam exhaled. Then he pressed a long, lingering kiss to Olive's forehead before reluctantly disentangling himself. When she was finally able to get a good look at him, he seemed more like his usual self.

Calm. Angry at the entire world. In charge.

"Send me that recording immediately," he murmured at her. She nodded, and he turned to the elderly man who'd just approached them. "We need to talk. Privately. Your office?" The other man looked shocked and offended, but he nodded stiffly. Behind him, Tom was making a fuss, and Adam clenched his jaw. "Keep him away from me." He turned to Olive before leaving, bending closer to her and lowering his voice. His palm was warm against her elbow.

"I am going to take care of this," he told her. There was something determined, earnest in his eyes. Olive had never felt safer, or more loved. "And then I'll come find you, and I'll take care of you."

Chapter Twenty-One

♥ **HYPOTHESIS:** *Wearing expired contact lenses will cause bacterial and/or fungal infections that will have repercussions for years to come.*

"Holden sent a message for you."

Olive looked away from the window and to Malcolm, who'd turned off airplane mode the second they'd landed in Charlotte for their layover. "Holden?"

"Yeah. Well, it's technically from Carlsen."

Her heart skipped a beat.

"He lost his phone charger and can't text you, but he and Holden are on their way back to SFO."

"Ah." She nodded, feeling a small rush of relief. That explained Adam's silence. He hadn't been in touch since last night. She'd worried that he'd been arrested and was pondering emptying her savings account to help cover his bail. All twelve dollars and sixteen cents. "Where's their layover?"

"No layover." Malcolm rolled his eyes. "Direct flight. They'll be at SFO ten minutes after us, even though they're only now leaving Boston. Eat the rich."

"Did Holden say anything about . . ."

Malcolm shook his head. "Their plane is about to leave, but we can wait for them at SFO. I'm sure Adam will have some updates for you."

"You just want to make out with Holden, don't you?"

Malcolm smiled and leaned his head against her shoulder. "My kalamata knows me well."

It seemed impossible that she'd been gone for less than a week. That all the chaos had unfolded in the span of a few days. Olive felt dazed, shell-shocked, as though her brain was winded from running a marathon. She was tired and wanted to sleep. She was hungry and wanted to eat. She was angry and wanted to see Tom get what he deserved. She was anxious, as twitchy as a damaged nerve, and she wanted a hug. Preferably from Adam.

In San Francisco, she folded her now-useless coat inside her suitcase and then sat on it. She checked her phone for new messages while Malcolm went to buy a bottle of Diet Coke. There were several from Anh, just checking in from Boston, and one from her landlord about the elevator being out of commission. She rolled her eyes, switched to her academic email, and found several unread messages flagged as important.

She tapped on the red exclamation point and opened one.

Today, 5:15 p.m.
FROM: Anna-Wiley@berkeley.edu
TO: Aysegul-Aslan@stanford.edu
· CC: Olive-Smith@stanford.edu
SUBJECT: Re: Pancreatic Cancer Project

Aysegul,
Thank you for reaching out to me. I had the privilege of seeing Olive Smith's talk at SBD—we were on the same

panel—and I was very impressed with her work on early detection tools for pancreatic cancer. I'd love to have her in my lab next year! Maybe the three of us can chat more on the phone soon?

Best,
Anna

Olive gasped. She covered her mouth with her hand, and immediately opened another email.

Today, 3:19 p.m.
FROM: Robert-Gordon@umn.edu
TO: Aysegul-Aslan@stanford.edu, Olive-Smith@stanford.edu
SUBJECT: Pancreatic Cancer Project

Dr. Aslan, Ms. Smith,
Your work on pancreatic cancer is fascinating, and I would welcome the opportunity for a collaboration. We should set up a Zoom meeting.
-R

There were two more emails. *Four total* from cancer researchers, all following up on Dr. Aslan's introductory message and saying they'd love having Olive in their labs. She felt a surge of happiness so violent, it almost made her dizzy.

"Ol, look who I ran into."

Olive shot up to her feet. Malcolm was there, holding Holden's hand, and barely a step behind them—

Adam. Looking tired, and handsome, and as large in real life as he'd been in her mind for the past twenty-four hours. Looking straight at her. Olive recalled the words he'd said last night in the restaurant and felt her cheeks heat, her chest constrict, her heart beat out of her skin.

"Hear me out," Holden started without even saying hi, "the four of us: double date. Tonight."

Adam ignored him and came to stand next Olive. "How are you?" he asked in a low tone.

"Good." For the first time in days, it wasn't even a lie. Adam was here. And all those emails were in her inbox. "You?"

"Good," he replied with a half smile, and she had a weird feeling that much like her, he wasn't lying. Her heart picked up even more.

"What about Chinese?" Holden interjected. "Everyone like Chinese here?"

"I'm cool with Chinese," Malcolm muttered, though he didn't seem enthusiastic at the idea of a double date. Likely because he didn't want to sit across from Adam for an entire meal and relive the trauma of his graduate advisory committee meetings.

"Olive?"

"Um . . . I like Chinese."

"Perfect. So does Adam, so—"

"I'm not having dinner out," Adam said.

Holden frowned. "Why?"

"I have better things to do."

"Like what? Olive's coming, too."

"Leave Olive alone. She's tired, and we're busy."

"I have access to your Google Calendar, asshole. You're not busy. If you don't want to hang out with me, you can just be honest."

"I don't want to hang out with you."

"You little shit. After the week we just had. And on my *birthday*."

Adam recoiled slightly. "What? It's not your birthday."

"Yes, it is."

"Your birthday is April tenth."

"Is it, though?"

Adam closed his eyes, scratching his forehead. "Holden, we've talked daily for the past twenty-five years, and I have been to at least five Power Rangers–themed birthday parties of yours. The last one was when you turned seventeen."

Malcolm attempted to cover his laugh with a cough.

"I know when your birthday is."

"You always had it wrong, I was just too nice to tell you." He clasped Adam's shoulder. "So, Chinese to celebrate the blessing of my birth?"

"Why not Thai?" Malcolm interjected, addressing Holden and ignoring Adam.

Holden made a whiny noise and started saying something about the lack of good larb in Stanford, something Olive would have normally been interested in hearing, except that—

Adam was looking at her again. From several inches above Holden's and Malcolm's heads, Adam was looking at her with an expression that was half apologetic, half annoyed, and . . . all intimate, really. Something familiar they'd shared before. Olive felt something inside her melt and suppressed a smile.

Suddenly, dinner seemed like a great idea.

It will be fun, she mouthed at him while Holden and Malcolm were busy arguing about whether they should just try that new burger place.

It will be excruciating, he mouthed back barely parting his lips, looking resigned and put-upon and just so amazingly *Adam* that Olive couldn't help but burst into laughter.

Holden and Malcolm stopped arguing and turned to her. "What?"

"Nothing," Olive said. The corner of Adam's mouth was curling up, too.

"Why are you laughing, Ol?"

She opened her mouth to deflect, but Adam beat her to it.

"Fine. We'll go." He said "we" like he and Olive were a "we," like it had never been fake after all, and her breath caught in her throat. "But I'm excused from any birthday-related outings for the next year. Actually, make it the next two. And veto on the new burger place."

Holden fist-pumped, and then frowned. "Why veto on burgers?"

"Because," he said, holding Olive's eyes, "burgers taste like foot."

~~~~~~~

"WE SHOULD START by addressing the obvious," Holden said, chewing on the complimentary appetizers, and Olive tensed in her seat. She wasn't sure she wanted to discuss the Tom situation with Malcolm and Holden before talking about it with Adam alone.

As it turned out, she shouldn't have worried.

"Which is that Malcolm and Adam hate each other."

Next to her in the booth, Adam frowned in confusion. Malcolm, who was sitting across from Olive, covered his face with his palms and groaned.

"I am reliably informed," Holden continued, undeterred, "that Adam called Malcolm's experiments 'sloppy' and 'a misuse of research funds' during a committee meeting, and that Malcolm took offense to that. Now, Adam, I've been telling Malcolm that you were probably just having a bad day—maybe one of your grads had split an infinitive in an email, or your arugula salad wasn't organic enough. Do you have anything to say for yourself?"

"Uh . . ." Adam's frown deepened, and so did Malcolm's facepalm. Holden waited pointedly for an answer, and Olive watched it all unfold, wondering if she should take out her phone and film this car crash. "I have no recollection of that committee meeting. Though it does sound like something I would say."

"Great. Now tell Malcolm it wasn't personal, so we can move on and have fried rice."

"Oh my God," Malcolm muttered. "Holden, please."

"I'm not having fried rice," Adam said.

"You can have raw bamboo while the normal people have fried rice. But as of right now, my boyfriend thinks that his BFF's boyfriend and my own BFF has it out for him, and it's cramping my double-dating style, so please."

Adam blinked slowly. "BFF?"

"Adam." Holden pointed at a grimacing Malcolm with his thumb. "Now, please."

Adam sighed heavily, but he turned to Malcolm. "Whatever I said or did, it was not personal. I've been told that I can be needlessly antagonistic. And unapproachable."

Olive didn't get to see Malcolm's reaction. Because she was busy studying Adam and the slight curl on his lips, the one that became an almost smile when he looked at Olive and met her eyes. For a second, the brief second she held his gaze before he looked away, it was just the two of them. And this sort-of-past they shared, their stupid inside jokes, the way they'd teased each other in the late-summer sunlight.

"Perfect." Holden clapped his hands, intrusively loud. "Egg rolls for appetizer, yes?"

It was a good idea, this dinner. This night, this table, this moment. Sitting next to Adam, smelling the petrichor, watching the dark splotches on the gray cotton of his Henley from the storm that had started just as they'd slipped inside the restaurant. They would have to talk, later, have a serious conversation about Tom and many other things. But for now it was the way it had always been between Adam and her: like slipping into a favorite dress, one she'd thought lost inside her closet, and finding that it fit as comfortably as it used to.

"I want egg rolls." She glanced at Adam. His hair was starting to get long again, so she did what felt natural: reached out and flattened his cowlick. "I'm going to take a wild guess and assume that you hate egg rolls, just like everything else that's good in the world."

He mouthed *smart-ass* right as the waiter brought their waters and set the menus on the table. Three menus, to be precise. Holden and Malcolm each took one, and Olive and Adam exchanged a loaded, amused look and grabbed the remaining one to share. It worked perfectly: he angled it so that the veggie section was on his side and all manner of fried entrées were on hers. It was serendipitous enough that she let out a laugh.

Adam tapped his index finger on the drink section. "Look at this abomination," he murmured. His lips were close to her ear—a chuff of hot air, intimate and pleasant in the blasting AC.

She grinned. "No way."

"Appalling."

"Amazing, you mean."

"I do not."

"This is my new favorite restaurant."

"You haven't even tried it yet."

"It will be spectacular."

"It will be horrific—"

A throat cleared, reminding them that they were not alone. Malcolm and Holden were both staring—Malcolm with a shrewd, suspicious expression, and Holden with a knowing smile. "What's all that about?"

"Oh." Olive's cheeks warmed a little. "Nothing. They just have pumpkin spice bubble tea."

Malcolm pretended to gag. "Ugh, Ol. *Gross.*"

"Shut up."

"It sounds great." Holden smiled and leaned into Malcolm. "We should get one to split."

"Excuse me?"

Olive tried not to laugh at Malcolm's horrified expression. "Don't get Malcolm started on pumpkin spice," she told Holden in an exaggerated whisper.

"Oh, shit." Holden clutched his chest in mock terror.

"This is a serious matter." Malcolm let his menu fall on the table. "Pumpkin spice is Satan's dandruff, harbinger of the apocalypse, and it tastes like ass—not in the good way." Next to Olive Adam nodded slowly, highly impressed with Malcolm's rant. "One pumpkin spice latte contains the same amount of sugar you'd find in fifty Skittles—and *no pumpkin whatsoever.* Look it up."

Adam stared at Malcolm with something very similar to admiration. Holden met Olive's eyes and told her conspiratorially, "Our boyfriends have so much in common."

"They do. They think hating entire harmless families of food is a personality trait."

"Pumpkin spice is not harmless. It's a radioactive, overpowering sugar bomb that worms its way into every sort of product and is single-handedly responsible for the extinction of the Caribbean monk seal. And you"—he pointed his finger at Holden—"are on thin ice."

"What—why?"

"I can't date someone who doesn't respect my stance on pumpkin spice."

"To be fair it's not a very respectable stance—" Holden noticed Malcolm's glare and lifted his hands defensively. "I had no idea, babe."

"You should have."

Adam clucked his tongue, amused. "Yes, Holden. Do better." He leaned back in his seat, and his shoulder brushed against Olive's. Holden gave him the finger.

"Adam knows and respects Olive's stance on hamburgers, and they're not even—" Whatever Malcolm had been about to say, he had the sense to stop himself. "Well, if Adam knows, you should know about the pumpkin spice."

"Wasn't Adam a dick until, like, twelve seconds ago?"

"How the turntables," Adam murmured. Olive reached out to pinch him on the side, but he stopped her with a hand around her wrist.

Evil, she mouthed at him. He just smiled, evilly, studying Malcolm and Holden a little too gleefully.

"Come on. It's not even comparable," Holden was saying. "Olive and Adam have been together for years. We met less than a week ago."

"They have not," Malcolm corrected him, wagging a finger. Adam's hand was still curled around her wrist. "They started dating, like, a month before we did."

"No," Holden insisted. "Adam was into her for ages. He probably secretly studied her eating habits and compiled seventeen databases and built machine-learning algorithms to predict her culinary preferences—"

Olive burst into laughter. "He did not." She took a sip of water, still smiling. "We only just started hanging out. At the beginning of the fall semester."

"Yes, but you knew each other from earlier." Holden was

frowning. "You two met the year before you started your Ph.D. here, when you came for your interview, and he's been pining after you ever since."

Olive shook her head and laughed, turning to Adam to share her amusement. Except that Adam was staring at her already, and he did not look amused. He looked . . . something else. Worried maybe, or apologetic, or resigned. Panicky? And just like that, the restaurant was silent. The pitter-patter of rain on the windows, people's chatter, the clinking of silverware—it all receded; the floor tilted, shook a little, and the AC was just this side of too cold. At some point, Adam's fingers had let go of her wrist.

Olive thought back to the bathroom incident. To burning eyes and wet cheeks, the smell of reagent and clean, male skin. The blur of a large, dark figure standing in front of her with his deep, reassuring, amused voice. The panic of being twenty-three and alone and having no idea what she should be doing, where she should be going, what the right choice was.

Is mine a good enough reason to go to grad school?

It's the best one.

All of a sudden, things had seemed simple enough.

It had been Adam, after all. Olive had been right.

What she hadn't been right about was whether *he* remembered her.

"Yes," she said. She wasn't smiling anymore. Adam was still holding her gaze. "I guess he has."

Chapter Twenty-Two

♥ **HYPOTHESIS:** *When given a choice between A (telling a lie) and B (telling the truth), I will inevitably end up selecting . . .*
No. Not this time.

Olive had no doubt that Holden's tales were highly embellished and the result of years of comedy workshopping, but she still couldn't help laughing harder than ever before.

"And I'm awakened by this waterfall pouring down on me—"

Adam rolled his eyes. "It was a drop."

"And I'm asking myself why it's raining inside the cabin, when I realize that it's coming from the top bunk and that Adam, who was, like, thirteen at the time—"

"Six. I was six, and you were seven."

"Had pissed the bed, and the piss was seeping through the mattress and onto me."

Olive's hands flew up to cover her mouth, not quite succeeding at hiding her amusement—just like she'd failed when Holden had recounted that a dalmatian puppy had once bitten Adam's ass through his jeans, or that he'd been voted "Most likely to make people cry" in his senior yearbook.

At least Adam didn't act embarrassed, and not nearly as up-set as he'd seemed after Holden had talked about him pining after her. Which explained . . . so many things.

Everything, maybe.

"Man. Six years old." Malcolm shook his head and wiped his eyes.

"I was sick."

"Still. Seems kind of old to have an accident?"

Adam simply stared at Malcolm until he lowered his gaze. "Uh, maybe not that old after all," he muttered.

There was a large bowl of fortune cookies by the register. Olive noticed it on her way out of the restaurant, let out a de-lighted squeal, and dipped her hand in to fish out four plastic pack-ages. She handed one each to Malcolm and Holden, and held out another for Adam with a mischievous smile. "You hate these, don't you?"

"I don't." He accepted the cookie. "I just think they taste like Styrofoam."

"Probably have similar nutritional values, too," Malcolm muttered as they slipped out into the chilly humidity of the early night. Surprisingly, he and Adam were finding lots of common ground.

It wasn't raining anymore, but the street was shiny in the light under a lamppost; a soft breeze made the leaves rustle and stray drops of water scatter to the ground. The air was fresh in Olive's lungs, pleasantly so after the hours spent in the restau-rant. She unrolled her sleeves, accidentally brushing her hand against Adam's abs. She smiled up at him, playfully apologetic; he flushed and averted his eyes.

"'He who laughs at himself never runs out of things to laugh at.'" Holden popped a bit of fortune cookie in his mouth, blinking at the message inside. "Is that shade?" He looked around, indignant. "Did this fortune cookie just throw shade at me?"

"Sounds like it," Malcolm answered. "Mine says 'Why not treat yourself to a good time instead of waiting for somebody else to do it?' I think my cookie just shaded you, too, babe."

"What's wrong with this batch?" Holden pointed at Adam and Olive. "What do yours say?"

Olive was already opening hers, nibbling on a corner as she pulled the paper out. It was very banal, and yet her heart skipped beat. "Mine's normal," she informed Holden.

"You're lying."

"Nope."

"What does it say?"

"'It's never too late to tell the truth.'" She shrugged, and turned to throw away the plastic wrapper. At the last moment, she decided to keep the strip of paper and slip it inside her jeans' back pocket.

"Adam, open yours."

"Nah."

"Come on."

"I'm not going to eat a piece of cardboard because it hurt your feelings."

"You're a shit friend."

"According to the fortune cookie industry, you're a shit boyfriend, so—"

"Give it here," Olive interjected, plucking the cookie out of Adam's hand. "I'll eat it. And read it."

The parking lot was completely empty, save for Adam's and Malcolm's cars. Holden had ridden from the airport with Adam, but he and Malcolm were planning to spend the night at Holden's apartment to walk Fleming, his dog.

"Adam's giving you a ride, right, Ol?"

"No need. It's less than a ten-minute walk home."

"But what about your suitcase?"

"It's not heavy, and I—" She stopped abruptly, worried her lip for a second while she contemplated the possibilities, and then felt herself smile, at once tentative and purposeful. "Actually, Adam will walk me home. Right?"

He was silent and inscrutable for a moment. Then he calmly said, "Of course," slipped his keys in the pocket of his jeans, and slid the strap of Olive's duffel bag over his shoulder.

"Where do you live?" he asked when Holden was not within earshot anymore.

She pointed silently. "You sure you want to carry my bag? I heard it's easy to throw out your back, once you reach a certain age."

He glared at her, and Olive laughed, falling into step with him as they headed out of the parking lot. The street was silent, except for the soles of her Converse catching on the wet concrete and Malcolm's car passing them by a few seconds later.

"Hey," Holden asked from the passenger window. "What did Adam's fortune cookie say?"

"Mmm." Olive made a show to look at the strip. "Not much. Just 'Holden Rodrigues, Ph.D., is a loser.'" Malcolm sped up just as Holden flipped her off, making her burst into laughter.

"What does it really say?" Adam asked when they were finally alone.

Olive handed him the crumpled paper and remained silent as he angled it to read it in the lamplight. She wasn't surprised when she saw a muscle jump in his jaw, or when he slid the fortune into the pocket of his jeans. She knew what it said, after all.

You can fall in love: someone will catch you.

"Can we talk about Tom?" she asked, sidestepping a puddle. "We don't have to, but if we can . . ."

"We can. We should." She saw his throat work. "Harvard's going to fire him, of course. Other disciplinary measures are still being decided—there were meetings until very late last night." He gave her a quick glance. "That's why I didn't call you earlier. Harvard's Title IX coordinator should be in touch with you soon."

Good. "What about your grant?"

His jaw clenched. "I'm not sure. I'll figure something out—or not. I don't particularly care at the moment."

It surprised her. And then it didn't, not when she considered that the professional implications of Tom's betrayal couldn't have cut as deeply as the personal ones. "I'm sorry, Adam. I know he was your friend—"

"He wasn't." Adam abruptly stopped in the middle of the street. He turned to her, his eyes a clear, deep brown. "I had no idea, Olive. I thought I knew him, but . . ." His Adam's apple bobbed. "I should never have trusted him with you. I'm sorry."

He said it—"with you"—like Olive was something special, uniquely precious to him. His most beloved treasure. It made her want to shiver, and laugh, and weep at the same time. It made her happy and confused.

"I was . . . I was afraid you might be mad at me. For ruining things. Your relationship with Tom, and maybe . . . maybe you won't be able to move to Boston anymore."

He shook his head. "I don't care. I couldn't care less about any of it." He held her eyes for a long moment, his mouth working as though he was swallowing the rest of his words. But he never continued, so Olive nodded and turned around, starting to walk again.

"I think I've found another lab. To finish my study. Closer, so I won't have to move next year." She pushed her hair behind her ear and smiled at him. There was something intrinsically enjoyable in having him next to her, so physical and undeniable. She felt it on some primal, visceral level, the giddy happiness that always came with his presence. Suddenly, Tom was the last thing she wanted to discuss with Adam. "Dinner was nice. And you were right, by the way."

"About the pumpkin sludge?"

"No, that was *amazing*. About Holden. He really is insufferable."

"He grows on you, after a decade or so."

"Does he?"

"Nah. Not really."

"Poor Holden." She huffed out a small laugh. "You weren't the only one who remembered, by the way."

He glanced at her. "Remembered what?"

"Our meeting. The one in the bathroom, when I came to interview."

Olive thought that maybe his step faltered for a split second. Or maybe it didn't. Still, there was a tinge of uncertainty in the deep breath he took.

"Did you really?"

"Yup. It just took me a while to realize that it was you. Why didn't you say anything?" She was so curious about what had been going on in Adam's head in the past few days, weeks, years. She was starting to imagine quite a bit, but some things . . . some things he'd have to clear up for her.

"Because you introduced yourself like we'd never met before." She thought maybe he was flushing a little. Maybe not. Maybe it was impossible to tell, in the starless sky and the faint yellow lights. "And I'd been . . . I'd been thinking about you. For years. And I didn't want to . . ."

She could only imagine. They'd passed each other in the hallways, been at countless department research symposiums and
seminars together. She hadn't thought anything of it, but
now . . . now she wondered what *he* had thought.

He'd been going on and on about this amazing girl *for
years, but he was concerned about being in the same department*, Holden had said.

And Olive had assumed so much. She had been so wrong.

"You didn't need to lie, you know," she said, not accusing.

He adjusted the strap of her suitcase on his shoulder. "I
didn't."

"You sort of did. By omission."

"True. Are you . . ." He pressed his lips together. "Are you
upset?"

"No, not really. It's really not that bad a lie."

"It's not?"

She nibbled on her thumbnail for a moment. "I've said much
worse, myself. And I didn't bring up our meeting, either, even
after I made the connection."

"Still, if you feel—"

"I'm not upset," she said, gentle but final. She looked up at
him, willing him to understand. Trying to figure out how to tell
him. How to *show* him. "I am . . . other things." She smiled.
"Glad, for instance. That you remembered me, from that day."

"You . . ." A pause. "You are very memorable."

"Ha. I'm not, really. I was no one—part of a huge incoming
cohort." She snorted and looked down to her feet. Her steps had
to be much quicker than his to keep up with his longer legs. "I
hated my first year. It was so stressful."

He glanced at her, surprised. "Do you remember your first
seminar talk?"

"I do. Why?"

"Your elevator pitch—you called it a turbolift pitch. You put a picture from *The Next Generation* on your slides."

"Oh, yes. I did." She let out a low laugh. "I didn't know you were a Trekkie."

"I had a phase. And that year's picnic, when we got rained on. You were playing freeze tag with someone's kids for hours. They loved you—they had to physically peel the youngest off you to get him inside the car."

"Dr. Moss's kids." She looked at him curiously. A light breeze rose and ruffled his hair, but he didn't seem to mind. "I didn't think you liked kids. The opposite, actually."

He lifted one eyebrow. "I don't like twenty-five-year-olds who act like toddlers. I don't mind them if they're actually three."

Olive smiled. "Adam, the fact that you knew who I was . . . Did it have anything to do with your decision to pretend to date me?"

About a dozen expressions crossed his face as he looked for an answer, and she couldn't pick apart a single one. "I wanted to help you, Olive."

"I know. I believe that." She rubbed her fingers against her mouth. "But was that all?"

He pressed his lips together. Exhaled. Closed his eyes, and for a split second looked like he was having his teeth and his soul pulled out. Then he said, resigned, "No."

"No," she repeated, pensive. "This is my place, by the way." She pointed at the tall brick building on the corner.

"Right." Adam looked around, studying her street. "Should I carry your bag upstairs?"

"I . . . Maybe later. There is something I need to tell you. Before."

"Of course."

He stopped in front of her, and she looked up at him, at the lines of his handsome, familiar face. There was only fresh breeze between them, and whatever distance Adam had seen fit to keep. Her stubborn, mercurial fake boyfriend. Wonderfully, perfectly unique. Delightfully one of a kind. Olive felt her heart overflow.

She took a deep breath. "The thing is, Adam . . . I was stupid. And wrong." She played nervously with a lock of her hair, then let her hand drift down to her stomach, and—okay. Okay. She was going to tell him. She would do this. Now. "It's like—it's like statistical hypothesis testing. Type I error. It's scary, isn't it?"

He frowned. She could tell he had no idea where she was going with this. "Type I error?"

"A false positive. Thinking that something is happening when it's not."

"I know what type I error is—"

"Yes, of course. It's just . . . in the past few weeks, what terrified me was the idea that I could misread a situation. That I could convince myself of something that wasn't true. See something that wasn't there just because I wanted to see it. A scientist's worst nightmare, right?"

"Right." His brows furrowed. "That is why in your analyses you set a level of significance that is—"

"But the thing is, type II error is bad, too."

Her eyes bore into his, hesitant and urgent all at once. She was frightened—so frightened by what she was about to say. But also exhilarated for him to finally know. Determined to get it out.

"Yes," he agreed slowly, confused. "False negatives are bad, too."

"That's the thing with science. We're drilled to believe that false positives are bad, but false negatives are just as terrifying."

She swallowed. "Not being able to see something, even if it's in front of your eyes. Purposefully making yourself blind, just because you're afraid of seeing too much."

"Are you saying that statistics graduate education is inadequate?"

She exhaled a laugh, suddenly flushed, even in the dark cool of the night. Her eyes were starting to sting. "Maybe. But also . . . I think that *I* have been inadequate. And I don't want to be, not anymore."

"Olive." He took one step closer, just a few inches. Not enough to crowd, but plenty for her to feel his warmth. "Are you okay?"

"There have been . . . so many things that have happened, before I even met you, and I think they messed me up a little. I've mostly lived in fear of being alone, and . . . I'll tell you about them, if you want. First, I have to figure it out on my own, why shielding myself with a bunch of lies seemed like a better idea than admitting even one ounce of truth. But I think . . ."

She took a deep, shuddering breath. There was a tear, one single tear that she could feel sliding down her cheek. Adam saw it and mouthed her name.

"I think that somewhere along the way I forgot that I was something. I forgot myself."

She was the one who stepped closer. The one who put her hand on the hem of his shirt, who tugged gently and held on to it, who started touching him and crying and smiling at the same time. "There are two things I want to tell you, Adam."

"What can I—"

"Please. Just let me tell you."

He wasn't very good at it. At standing there and doing nothing while her eyes welled fuller and fuller. She could tell that he felt useless, his hands dangling in fists at his sides, and she . . .

she loved him even more for it. For looking at her like she was the beginning and end of his every thought.

"The first thing is that I lied to you. And my lie was not just by omission."

"Olive—"

"It was a real lie. A bad one. A stupid one. I let you—no, I *made* you think that I had feelings for someone else, when in truth . . . I didn't. I never did."

His hand came up to cup the side of her face. "What do you—"

"But that's not very important."

"Olive." He pulled her closer, pressing his lips against her forehead. "It doesn't matter. Whatever it is that you're crying about, I will fix it. I will make it right. I—"

"Adam," she interrupted him with a wet smile. "It's not important, because the second thing, that's what really matters."

They were so close, now. She could smell his scent and his warmth, and his hands were cradling her face, thumbs swiping back and forth to dry her cheeks.

"Sweetheart," he murmured. "What is the second thing?"

She was still crying, but she'd never been happier. So she said it, probably in the worst accent he'd ever heard.

"*Ik hou van jou*, Adam."

Epilogue

〰〰〰〰〰〰〰〰〰〰〰〰〰〰〰〰〰〰〰〰

♥ **RESULTS:** *Careful analyses of the data collected, accounting for potential confounds, statistical error, and experimenter's bias, show that when I fall in love . . . things don't actually turn out to be that bad.*

Ten months later

"Stand there. You were standing right there."

"Was I?"

He was humoring her. A little. That deliciously put-upon expression had become Olive's favorite over the past year. "A bit closer to the water fountain. Perfect." She took a step back to admire her handiwork and then winked at him as she took out her phone to snap a quick picture. She briefly considered swapping it for her current screensaver—a selfie of the two of them in Joshua Tree a few weeks earlier, Adam squinting in the sun and Olive pressing her lips to his cheek—but then thought better of it.

Their summer had been full of hiking trips, and delicious ice cream, and late-night kisses on Adam's balcony, laughing and sharing untold stories and looking up at the stars, so much brighter than the ones Olive had once climbed on a ladder to stick to the ceiling of her bedroom. She was going to start working at a cancer lab at Berkeley in less than a week, which would mean a busier, more stressful schedule and a bit of a commute. And yet, she couldn't wait.

"Just stand there," she ordered. "Look antagonistic and unapproachable. And say 'pumpkin spice.'"

He rolled his eyes. "What's your plan if someone comes in?"

Olive glanced around the biology building. The hallway was silent and deserted, and the dim after-hours lights made Adam's hair look almost blue. It was late, and summer, and the weekend to boot: no one was going to come in. Even if they did, Olive Smith and Adam Carlsen were old news by now. "Like who?"

"Anh might show up. To help you re-create the magic."

"Pretty sure she's out with Jeremy."

"Jeremy? The guy you're in love with?"

Olive stuck her tongue out at him and glanced down at her phone. Happy. She was so happy, and she didn't even know why. Except that she did know.

"Okay. In one minute."

"You can't know the exact time." Adam's tone was patient and indulgent. "Not to the minute."

"Wrong. I ran a Western blot that night. I looked at my lab logs, and I reconstructed both the when and the where down to the error bars. I am a thorough scientist."

"Hm." Adam folded his arms across his chest. "How did that blotting turn out?"

"Not the point." She grinned. "What were you doing here, by the way?"

"What do you mean?"

"A year ago. Why were you walking around the department at night?"

"I can't remember. Maybe I had a deadline. Or maybe I was going home." He shrugged, and scanned the hallway until his eyes fell on the water fountain. "Maybe I was thirsty."

"Maybe." She took a step closer. "Maybe you were secretly hoping for a kiss."

He gave her a long, amused look. "Maybe."

She took another step, and another, and another. And then her alarm beeped, once, right as she came to stand in front of him. Another intrusion of his personal space. But this time, when she pushed up on her toes, when she wrapped her arms around his neck, Adam's hands pulled her deeper into himself.

It had been one year. Exactly one year. And by now his body was so familiar to her, she knew the breadth of his shoulders, the scratch of his stubble, the scent of his skin, all by heart; she could feel the smile in his eyes.

Olive sank into him, let him support her weight, and then moved until her mouth was almost level with his ear. She pressed her lips against its shell, and whispered softly into his skin.

"May I kiss you, Dr. Carlsen?"

Author's Note

~~~~~~~~~~~~~~~~~~~~~~~~~~~~~~~~~~~~~

I write stories set in academia because academia is all I know. It can be a very insular, all-consuming, isolating environment. In the past decade, I've had excellent (women) mentors who constantly supported me, but I could name dozens of instances in which I felt as though I was a massive failure blundering her way through science. But that, as everyone who's been there knows, is grad school: a stressful, high-pressure, competitive endeavor. Academia has its own special way of tearing apart work-life balance, wearing people down, and making them forget that they are worth more than the number of papers they publish or the grant money they are able to rake in.

Taking the thing I love the most (writing love stories) and giving it a STEM academia backdrop has been surprisingly therapeutic. My experiences have not been the same as Olive's (no academic fake dating for me, boo), but I still managed to pour many of my frustrations, joys, and disappointments into her adventures. Just like Olive, in the past few years I have felt lonely, determined, helpless, scared, happy, cornered, inadequate, misunderstood, enthusiastic. Writing *The Love Hypothesis* gave me the opportunity to turn these experiences around with a humorous, sometimes self-indulgent spin, and to realize that I could put my own misadventures into perspective—sometimes even laugh at them! For this reason—and I know I probably shouldn't say it—this book means as much to me as my Ph.D. dissertation did.

Okay—that's a lie. It means waaay more.

If you're not familiar with it, a few words about a topic that comes up quite a bit in the book: Title IX is a US federal law that prohibits any kind of discrimination on the basis of gender in all institutions that receive federal funding (i.e., most universities). It legally compels schools to respond to and remedy situations of misconduct ranging from hostile work environments to harassment and assault. Covered schools have Title IX coordinators, whose job is to handle complaints and violations and to educate an institution's community about their rights. Title IX has been and currently is critical to guarantee equal access to education and to protect students and employees against gender-based discrimination.

Lastly: the women in STEM organizations Anh mentions in the book are fictionalized, but most universities host chapters of similar organizations. For real-life resources on supporting women academics in STEM, visit awis.org. For resources that specifically support BIPOC women academics in STEM, visit sswoc.org.

Acknowledgments

First, just allow me to say: asgfgsfasdgfadg. I cannot believe this book exists. Truly, afgjsdfafksjfadg.

Second, allow me to further say: this book would *not* exist if approximately two hundred people hadn't held my hand for the past two years. *Cue end credits song.* In a very disorganized order, I must acknowledge:

Thao Le, my marvelous agent (your DM changed my life, for the very best); Sarah Blumenstock, my fantastic editor (who is *not* that kind of editor); Rebecca and Alannah, my very first betas (and shout-out to Alannah for the title!); my gremlins, for being gremalicious and for always defending the c.p.; Daddy Lucy and Jen (thank you for all the reads and the SM and the infinite hand-holding), Claire, Court, Julie, Katie, Kat, Kelly, Margaret, and my wife, Sabine (ALIMONE!) (as well as Jess, Shep, and Trix, my honorary grems). My Words Are Hard buds, for the whining support: Celia, Kate, Sarah, and Victoria. My TMers, who believed in me from the start: Court, Dani, Christy, Kate, Mar, Marie, and Rachelle; Caitie, for being the first IRL person who made me feel like I could talk about all of this; Margo Lipschultz and Jennie Conway, for the precious feedback on early drafts; Frankie, for the timeliest of prompts; Psi, for inspiring me with her beautiful writing; the Berkletes, for the pooping and the knotting; Sharon Ibbotson, for the invaluable editorial input and encouragement; Stephanie, Jordan, Lindsey Merril, and Kat, for beta reading my manuscript and helping me fix it; Lilith, for the stunning art and the amazing cover, as well as the peeps at Penguin Creative; Bridget O'Toole and Jessica Brock for helping me make people think that they might want to read this book; everyone at Berkley who has helped getting this manuscript in shape behind the scenes; Rian Johnson, for doing The Thing that inspired me to do All The Things.

The truth is, I never saw myself as someone who'd ever write anything but science articles. And I probably never would have if it hadn't been for all the fanfiction authors who posted amazing pieces online and encouraged me to start writing myself. And I certainly wouldn't have had the guts to start writing original fiction if it hadn't been for the support, the cheering, the encouragement, the con-crit I got from the Star Trek and Star Wars/Reylo fandoms. To everyone who has left a comment or kudos on my fics, who has given me shout-outs on social media, who has reached out in DMs, who has drawn art for me or made a mood board, who has cheered me on, who has taken the time to read something I've written: thank you. Really, thank you so much. I owe you a lot.

Last, and let's be real, also definitely least: some half-hearted thanks to Stefan, for all the love and the patience. You better not be reading this, you pretentious hipster.

~~~~~~~~~~~~~~~~~~~~~~~~~~~~~~~~

Don't miss

Love on the Brain

coming soon from Berkley Jove!

~~~~~~~~~~~~~~~~~~~~~~~~~~~~~~~~

"By the way, you can get leprosy from armadillos."

I peel my nose away from the airplane window and glance at Rocío, my research assistant. "Really?"

"Yep. They got it from humans millennia ago, and now they're giving it back to us." She shrugs. "Revenge and cold dishes and all that."

I scrutinize her beautiful face for hints that she's lying. Her large dark eyes, heavily rimmed with eyeliner, are inscrutable. Her hair is so Vantablack, it absorbs 99 percent of visible light. Her mouth is full, curved downward in its typical pout.

Nope. I got nothing. "Is this for real?"

"Would I ever lie to you?"

"Last week you swore to me that Stephen King was writing a Winnie-the-Pooh spin-off." And I believed her. Like I believed that Lady Gaga is a known satanist, or that badminton racquets are made from human bones and intestines. Chaotic goth misanthropy and creepy deadpan sarcasm are her brand, and I should know better than to take her seriously. Problem is, every once in a while she'll throw in a crazy-sounding story that upon further inspection (i.e., a Google search) is revealed to be true. For instance, did you know that the *Texas Chainsaw Massacre* was inspired by a true story? Before Rocío, I didn't. And I slept significantly better.

"Don't believe me, then." She shrugs, going back to her grad school admission prep book. "Go pet the leper armadillos and die."

She's such a weirdo. I adore her.

"Hey, you sure you're going to be fine, away from Alex for the next few months?" I feel a little guilty for taking her away from her boyfriend. When I was twenty-two, if someone had asked me to be apart from Tim for months, I'd have walked into the sea. Then again, hindsight has proven beyond doubt that I was a complete idiot, and Rocío seems pretty enthused for the opportunity. She plans to apply to Johns Hopkins's neuro program in the fall, and the NASA line on her CV won't hurt. She even hugged me when I invited her to come along—a moment of weakness I'm sure she deeply regrets.

"Fine? Are you kidding?" She looks at me like I'm insane. "Three months in Texas, do you know how many times I'll get to see La Llorona?"

"La . . . what?"

She rolls her eyes and pops in her AirPods. "You really know *nothing* about famed feminist ghosts."

I bite back a smile and turn back to the window. In 1905, Dr. Curie decided to invest her Nobel Prize money into hiring her first research assistant. I wonder if she, too, ended up working with a mildly terrifying, Cthulhu-worshipping emo girl. I stare at the clouds until I'm bored, and then I take my phone out of my pocket and connect to the complimentary in-flight Wi-Fi. I glance at Rocío, making sure that she's not paying attention to me, and angle my screen away.

I'm not a very secretive person, mostly out of laziness: I refuse to take on the cognitive labor of tracking lies and omissions. I do, however, have one secret. One single piece of information that I've never shared with anyone—not even my sister. Don't get me wrong, I trust Reike with my life, but I also know her well enough to picture the scene: she is wearing a flowy sundress and flirting with a Scottish shepherd she met in a trattoria on the Amalfi Coast. They decide to do the shrooms they just purchased from a Belarusian farmer, and mid-trip she accidentally blurts out the one thing she's been expressly forbidden to repeat: her twin sister, Bee, runs one of the most popular and controversial accounts on Academic Twitter. The Scottish shepherd's cousin is a closeted men's rights activist who sends me a dead possum in the mail and rats me out to his insane friends, and I get fired.

No, thank you. I love my job (and possums) too much for this.

I created @WhatWouldMarieDo during my first semester of grad school. I was teaching a neuroanatomy class and decided to give my students an anonymous mid-semester survey to ask for honest feedback on how to improve the course. What I got was . . . not that. I was told that my lectures would be more interesting if I delivered them naked. That I should gain some weight, get a boob job, stop dying my hair "unnatural colors," get rid of my piercings. I was even given a phone number to call if I was "ever in the mood for a ten-inch dick." (Yeah, right.)

The messages were pretty appalling, but what sent me sobbing in a bathroom stall was the reactions of the other students in my cohort—Tim included. They laughed the comments off as harmless pranks and dissuaded me from reporting them to the department chair, telling me that I'd be making a stink about nothing.

They were, of course, all men.

(Seriously: Why *are* men?)

That night I fell asleep crying. The following day, I got up, wondered how many other women in STEM felt as alone as I did, and impulsively downloaded Twitter and made @WhatWouldMarieDo. I slapped on a poorly photoshopped pic of Dr. Curie wearing sunglasses and a one-line bio: *Making the periodic table girlier since 1889 (she/her)*. I just wanted to scream into the void. I honestly didn't think that anyone would even see my first Tweet. But I was wrong.

> @WhatWouldMarieDo What would Dr. Curie, first female professor at La Sorbonne, do if one of her students asked her to deliver her lectures naked?

> @198888 She would shorten his half-life.

> @annahhhh RAT HIM OUT TO PIERRE!!!

> @emily89 Put some polonium in his pants and watch his dick shrivel.

> @bioworm55 Nuke him NUKE HIM

> @lucyinthesea Has this happened to you? God I'm so sorry. Once a student said something about my ass and it was so gross and no one believed me.

Over half a decade later, after a handful of *Chronicle of Higher Education* nods, a *New York Times* article, and about a million followers, WWMD is my happy place. What's best is, I think the same is true for many others. The account has evolved into a therapeutic community of sorts, used by women in STEM to tell their stories, exchange advice, and . . . bitch.

Oh, we bitch. We bitch a lot, and it's glorious.

> @BiologySarah Hey, @WhatWouldMarieDo if she weren't given authorship on a project that was originally her idea and that she worked on for over one year? All other authors are men, because *of course* they are.

"Yikes." I scrunch my face and quote-tweet Sarah.

> Marie would slip some radium in their coffee. Also, she would consider reporting this to her institution's Office of Research Integrity, making sure to document every step of the process ♥

I hit send, drum my fingers on the armrest, and wait. My answers are not the main attraction of the account, not in the least. The real reason people reach out to WWMD is . . .

Yep. This. I feel my grin widen as the replies start coming in.

> @DrAllixx This happened to me, too. I was the only woman and only POC in the author lineup and my name suddenly disappeared during revisions. DM if u want to chat, Sarah.

> @AmyBernard I am a member of the Women in Science Association, and we have advice for situations like this on our website (they're sadly common)!

@TheGeologician Going through the same situation
rn @BiologySarah. I did report it to ORI and it's still
unfolding but I'm happy to talk if you need to vent.

@SteveHarrison Dude, breaking news: you're lying
to yourself. Your contributions aren't VALUABLE
enough to warrant authorship. Your team did you a
favor letting you tag along for a while but if you're
not smart enough, you're OUT. Not everything is
about being a woman, sometimes you're just A
LOSER 🧑🏻

It is a truth universally acknowledged that a community of
women trying to mind their own business must be in want of a
random man's opinion.

I've long learned that engaging with basement-dwelling STEM-
lords who come online looking for a fight is never a good idea—the
last thing I want is to provide free entertainment for their fragile
egos. If they want to blow off some steam, they can buy a gym
membership or play third-person-shooter video games. Like normal people.

I make to hide @SteveHarrison's delightful contribution but
notice that someone has replied to him.

@Shmacademics Yeah, Marie, sometimes you're just
a loser. Steve would know.

I chuckle.

@WhatWouldMarieDo Aw, Steve. Don't be too hard
on yourself.

@Shmacademics He is just a boy, standing in front of a girl, asking her to do twice as much work as he ever did in order to prove that she's worthy of becoming a scientist.

@WhatWouldMarieDo Steve, you old romantic.

@SteveHarrison Fuck you. This ridiculous push for women in STEM is ruining STEM. People should get jobs because they're good NOT BECAUSE THEY HAVE VAGINAS. But now people feel like they have to hire women and they get jobs over men who are MORE QUALIFIED. This is the end of STEM AND IT'S WRONG.

@WhatWouldMarieDo I can see you're upset about this, Steve.

@Shmacademics There, there.

Steve blocks both of us, and I chuckle again, drawing a curious glance from Rocío. @Shmacademics is another hugely popular account on Academic Twitter, and by far my favorite. He mostly tweets about how he should be writing, makes fun of elitism and ivory-tower academics, and points out bad or biased science. I was initially a bit distrustful of him—his bio says "he/him," and we all know how cis men on the internet can be. But he and I ended up forming an alliance of sorts. When the STEM-lords take offense at the sheer idea of women in STEM and start pitchforking in my mentions, he helps me ridicule them a little. I'm not sure when we started direct messaging, when I stopped being afraid that he was secretly a retired Gamergater out to doxx me, or when I began considering him a friend. But a handful of years later, here we are, chatting about half a dozen different things a couple of times a week, without having even exchanged real names. Is it weird, knowing that Shmac had lice three times in second grade but not which time zone he lives in? A bit. But it's also liberating. Plus, having opinions online can be very dangerous. The internet is a sea full of creepy, cybercriminal fish, and if Mark Zuckerberg can cover his laptop webcam with a piece of tape, I reserve the right to keep things painfully anonymous.

The flight attendant offers me a glass of water from a tray. I shake my head, smile, and DM Shmac.

Marie: I think Steve doesn't want to play with us anymore.
Shmac: I think Steve wasn't held enough as a tadpole.
Marie: Lol!
Shmac: How's life?
Marie: Good! Cool new project starting next week. My ticket away from my gross boss
Shmac: I hope so. Can't believe dude's still around.
Marie: The power of connections. And inertia. What about you?
Shmac: Work's interesting.
Marie: Good interesting?
Shmac: Politicky interesting. So, no.
Marie: I'm afraid to ask. How's the rest?
Shmac: Weird.
Marie: Did your cat poop in your shoe again?
Shmac: No, but I did find a tomato in my boot the other day.
Marie: Send pics next time! What's going on?
Shmac: Nothing, really.
Marie: Oh, come on!

Shmac: How do you even know something's going on?

Marie: Your lack of exclamation points!

Shmac: !!!!!!!11!!1!!1!!!!

Marie: Shmac.

Shmac: FYI, I'm sighing deeply.

Marie: I bet. Tell me!

Shmac: It's a girl.

Marie: Ooooh! Tell me EVERYTHING!!!!!!!11!!1!!!!!

Shmac: There isn't much to tell.

Marie: Did you just meet her?

Shmac: No. She's someone I've known for a long time, and now she's back.

Shmac: And she is married.

Marie: To you?

Shmac: Depressingly, no.

Shmac: Sorry—we're restructuring the lab. Gotta go before someone destroys a 5 mil piece of equipment. Talk later.

Marie: Sure, but I'll want to know everything about your affair with a married woman

Shmac: I wish.

It's nice to know that Shmac is always a click away, especially now that I'm flying into the Wardass's frosty, unwelcoming lap.

I switch to my email app to check if Levi has finally answered the email I sent three days ago. It was just a couple of lines— *Hey, long time no see, I look forward to working together again, would you like to meet to discuss BLINK this weekend?*—but he must have been too busy to reply. Or too full of contempt. Or both.

Ugh.

I lean back against the headrest and close my eyes, wondering how Dr. Curie would deal with Levi Ward. She'd probably hide some radioactive isotopes in his pockets, grab popcorn, and watch nuclear decay work its magic.

Yep, sounds about right.

After a few minutes, I fall asleep. I dream that Levi is part armadillo: his skin glows a faint, sallow green, and he's digging a tomato out of his boot with an expensive piece of equipment. Even with all of that, the weirdest thing about him is that he's finally being nice to me.

~~~~~~

WE'RE PUT UP in small furnished apartments in a lodging facility just outside the Johnson Space Center, only a couple of minutes from the Sullivan Discovery Building, where we'll be working. I can't believe how short my commute is going to be.

"Bet you'll still manage to be late all the time," Rocío tells me, and I glare at her while unlocking my door. It's not my fault if I've spent a sizable chunk of my formative years in Italy, where time is but a polite suggestion.

The place is considerably nicer than the apartment I rent—maybe because of the raccoon incident, probably because I buy 90 percent of my furniture from the as-is bargain corner at Ikea. It has a balcony, a dishwasher, and—huge improvement on my quality of life—a toilet that flushes 100 percent of the times I push the lever. Truly paradigm shifting. I excitedly open and close every single cupboard (they're all empty; I'm not sure what I expected), take pictures to send Reike and my coworkers, stick my favorite Marie Curie magnet to the fridge (a picture of her holding a beaker that says "I'm pretty rad"), hang my hummingbird feeder on the balcony, and then . . .

It's still only two-thirty p.m. Ugh.

Not that I'm one of those people who hates having free time. I could easily spend five solid hours napping, rewatching an entire season of *The Office* while eating Twizzlers, or moving to step 2 of the couch-to-5K plan I'm still very . . . okay, *sort of* committed to. But I am here! In Houston! Near the Space Center! About to start the coolest project of my life!

It's Friday, and I'm not due to check in until Monday, but I'm brimming with nervous energy. So I text Rocío to ask whether she wants to check out the Space Center with me (*No.*) or to grab dinner together (*I only eat animal carcasses.*).

She's so mean. I love her.

My first impression of Houston is: big. Closely followed by: humid, and then by: humidly big. In Maryland, remnants of snow still cling to the ground, but the Space Center is already lush and green, a mix of open spaces and large buildings and old NASA aircraft on display. There are families visiting, which reminds me a little of an amusement park. I can't believe I'm going to be seeing rockets on my way to work for the next three months. It sure beats the perv crossing guard who works on the NIH campus.

The Discovery Building is on the outskirts of the center. It's wide, futuristic, and three-storied, with glass walls and a complicated-looking stair system I can't quite figure out. I step inside the marble hall, wondering if my new office will have a window. I'm not used to natural light; the sudden intake of vitamin D might kill me.

"I'm Bee Königswasser." I smile at the receptionist. "I'm starting work here on Monday, and I was wondering if I could take a look around?"

He gives me an apologetic smile. "I can't let you in if you don't have an ID badge. The engineering labs are upstairs—high-security areas."

Right. Yes. The engineering labs. Levi's labs. He's probably up there, hard at work. Engineering. Labbing. Not answering my emails.

"No problem, that's understandable. I'll just—"

"Dr. Königswasser? Bee?"

I turn around. There is a blond young man behind me. He's nonthreateningly handsome, medium height, smiling at me like we're old friends even though he doesn't look familiar. " . . . Hi?"

"I didn't mean to eavesdrop, but I caught your name, and . . . I'm Guy. Guy Kowalsky?"

The name clicks immediately. I break into a grin. "Guy! It's so nice to meet you in person." When I was first notified of BLINK, Guy was my point of contact for logistics questions, and he and I emailed back and forth a few times. He's an astronaut— *an actual astronaut!*—working on BLINK while he's grounded. He seemed so familiar with the project, I initially assumed he'd be my co-lead.

He shakes my hand warmly. "I love your work! I've read all your articles—you'll be such an asset to the project."

"Likewise. I can't wait to collaborate."

If I weren't dehydrated from the flight, I'd probably tear up. I cannot believe that this man, this nice, pleasant man who has given me more positive interactions in one minute than Dr. Wardass did in one year, could have been my co-lead. I must have pissed off some god. Zeus? Eros? Must be Poseidon. Shouldn't have peed in the Baltic Sea during my misspent youth.

"Why don't I show you around? You can come in as my guest." He nods to the receptionist and gestures at me to follow him.

"I wouldn't want to take you away from . . . astronauting?"

"I'm between missions. Giving you a tour beats debugging any day." He shrugs, something boyishly charming about him. We'll get along great, I already know it.

"Have you lived in Houston long?" I ask as we step into the elevator.

"About eight years. Came to NASA right out of grad school. Applied for the Astronaut Corps, did the training, then a mission." I do some math in my head. It would put him in his mid-thirties, older than I initially thought. "The past two or so, I worked on BLINK's precursor. Engineering the structure of the helmet, figuring out the wireless system. But we got to a point where we needed a neurostimulation expert on board." He gives me a warm smile.

"I cannot wait to see what we cook up together." I also cannot wait to find out why Levi was given the lead of this project over someone who has been on it for five years. It just seems unfair. To Guy *and* to me.

The elevator doors open, and he points to a quaint-looking café in the corner. "That place over there—amazing sandwiches, worst coffee in the world. You hungry?"

"No, thanks."

"You sure? It's on me. The egg sandwiches are almost as good as the coffee is bad."

"I don't really eat eggs."

"Let me guess, a vegan?"

I nod. I try hard to break the stereotypes that plague my people and not use the word "vegan" in my first three meetings with a new acquaintance, but if they're the ones to mention it, all bets are off.

"I should introduce you to my daughter. She recently announced that she won't eat animal products anymore." He sighs. "Last weekend I poured regular milk in her cereal figuring she wouldn't know the difference. She told me that her legal team will be in touch."

"How old is she?"

"Just turned six."

I laugh. "Good luck with that."

I stopped having meat at seven, when I realized that the delicious *pollo* nuggets my Sicilian grandmother served nearly every day and the cute *galline* grazing about the farm were more . . . connected than I originally suspected. Stunning plot twist, I know. Reike wasn't nearly as distraught: when I frantically explained that "Pigs have families, too. A mom and a dad and siblings that will miss them," she just nodded thoughtfully and said, "What you're saying is, we should eat the whole family?" I went fully vegan a couple of years later. Meanwhile, my sister has made it her life's goal to eat enough animal products for two. Together we emit one normal person's carbon footprint.

"The engineering labs are down this hallway," Guy says. The space is an interesting mix of glass and wood, and I can see inside some of the rooms. "A bit cluttered, and most people are off today—we're shuffling around equipment and reorganizing the space. We've got lots of ongoing projects, but BLINK's everyone's favorite child. The other astronauts pop by every once in a while just to ask how much longer it will be until their fancy swag is ready."

I grin. "For real?"

"Yep."

Making fancy swag for astronauts is my literal job description. I can add it to my LinkedIn profile. Not that anyone uses LinkedIn.

"The neuroscience labs—your labs—will be on the right. This way there are—" His phone rings. "Sorry—mind if I take it?"

"Not at all." I smile at his beaver phone case ("Nature's Engineer") and look away.

I wonder whether Guy would think I'm lame if I snapped a few pictures of the building for my friends. I decide that I can live with that, but when I take out my phone, I hear a noise from down the hallway. It's soft and chirpy, and sounds a lot like a . . .

"Meow."

I glance back at Guy. He's busy explaining how to put on *Moana* to someone very young, so I decide to investigate. Most of the rooms are deserted, labs full of large, abstruse equipment that looks like it belongs to . . . well. NASA. I hear male voices somewhere in the building, but no sign of the—

"Meow."

I turn around. A few feet away, staring at me with a curious expression, is a beautiful young calico.

"And who might you be?" I slowly hold out my hand. The kitten comes closer, delicately sniffs my fingers, and gives me a welcoming headbutt.

I laugh. "You're such a sweet girl." I squat down to scratch her under her chin. She nips my finger, a playful love bite. "Aren't you the most *purr*-fect little baby? I feel so *fur*-tunate to have met you."

She gives me a disdainful look and turns away. I think she understands puns.

"Come on, I was just *kitten*." Another outraged glare. Then she jumps on a nearby cart, piled ceiling-high with boxes and heavy, precarious-looking equipment. "Where are you going?"

I squint, trying to figure out where she disappeared, and that's when I realize it. The piece of equipment? The precarious-looking one? It actually *is* precarious. And the cat poked it just enough to dislodge it. And it's falling on my head.

Right.

About.

Now.

I have less than three seconds to move away. Which is too bad, because my entire body is suddenly made of stone, unresponsive to my brain's commands. I stand there, terrified, paralyzed, and close my eyes as a jumbled chaos of thoughts twists through my head. *Is the cat okay? Am I going to die? Oh God, I am going to die. Squashed by a tungsten anvil like Wile E. Coyote. I am a twenty-first century Pierre Curie, about to get my skull crushed by a horse-drawn cart. Except that I have no chair in the physics department of the University of Paris to leave to my lovely spouse, Marie. Except that I have barely done a tenth of all the science I meant to do. Except that I wanted so many things and I never oh my God any second now—*

Something slams into my body, shoving me aside and into the wall.

Everything is pain.

For a couple of seconds. Then the pain is over, and everything is *noise*: metal clanking as it plunges to the floor, horrified screaming, a shrill "meow" somewhere in the distance, and, closer to my ear . . . someone is panting. Less than an inch from me.

I open my eyes, gasping for breath, and . . .

Green.

All I can see is green. Not dark, like the grass outside; not dull, like the pistachios I had on the plane. This green is light, piercing, intense. Familiar, but hard to place, not unlike—

Eyes. I'm looking up into the greenest eyes I've ever seen. Eyes that I've seen before. Eyes surrounded by wavy black hair and a face that's angles and sharp edges and full lips, a face that's offensively, imperfectly handsome. A face attached to a large, solid body—a body that is pinning me to the wall, a body made of a broad chest and two thighs that could moonlight as redwoods. Easily. One is slotted between my legs and it's holding me up. Unyielding. This man even smells like a forest—and *that mouth*. That mouth is still breathing heavily on top of me, probably from the effort of whisking me off from under seven hundred pounds of mechanical engineering tools, and—

I *know* that mouth.

Levi.

Levi.

I haven't seen Levi Ward in six years. Six blessed, blissful years. And now here he is, pushing me into a wall in the middle of NASA's Space Center, and he looks . . . he looks . . .

"Levi!" someone yells. The clanking goes silent. What was meant to fall has settled on the floor. "Are you okay?"

Levi doesn't move, nor does he look away. His mouth works, and so does his throat. His lips part to say something, but no sound comes out. Instead a hand, at once rushed and gentle, reaches up to cup my face. It's so large, I feel perfectly cradled. Engulfed in green, cozy warmth. I whimper when it leaves my skin, a plaintive, involuntary sound from deep in my throat, but I stop when I realize that it's only shifting to the back of my skull. To the hollow of my collarbone. To my brow, pushing back my hair.

It's a cautious touch. Pressing but delicate. Lingering but urgent. As though he is studying me. Trying to make sure that I'm all in one piece. Memorizing me.

I lift my eyes, and for the first time I notice the deep, unmasked concern in Levi's eyes.

His lips move, and I think that, maybe—is he mouthing my name? Once, and then again? Like it's some kind of prayer?

"Levi? Levi, is she—"

My eyelids fall closed, and everything goes dark.

See Adam pine for Olive in this special bonus chapter!

There is a brief moment, just a handful of seconds after Olive's mouth first presses against his own, in which Adam considers coming clean to her.

It's a shit idea. One of his worst to date, even after truly out-doing himself in the last month. He was the one to propose this farce to Olive, as though anything good could ever come of pre-tending to be in a relationship with the only woman he's looked at twice in the past decade. And he was the one to offer that she room with him, even though there are about thirty people in Boston who could put him up for the night.

He should have reached out to grad school friends. Jack's in Pasadena now, but George still lives here. So do Annika and Riley. Tom, of course, though he'd probably ask why Adam's not staying with Olive and make a few more jabs about how "whipped" he is. He'd have to make excuses, come up with a few lies, which . . . annoying. Tom can be annoying. People are annoying.

But at least Adam wouldn't be right here, with Olive's hand soft on his face, her lips moving clumsily against his own, hesitant, delicate, a little fumbling in a way that tells him she hasn't done this in a while, and . . .

Adam's cock is as hard as a rock. He's thirty-four years old. He's fully clothed, barely touching a woman who's fully clothed herself, and yet this kiss is without a doubt the most profoundly erotic experience of his life.

This must be it, the thing that's fucking with his head. The reason he's considering telling her everything. But Olive's lips are cool, her damp hair tickles his face, and her skin smells sweet, edible, glowing. Like the shower she took a handful of feet from him, the one he sternly ordered himself not to think about. He managed not to, at least until he realized that she hadn't locked herself inside the bathroom. That's when he forgot to breathe; only cheap plywood and opportunity between them, and Olive trusted him to stay put.

Not that he would ever do anything else. But Adam has it even worse than he thought, if the idea of this girl trusting him with basic human decency has more of an effect on him than full-blown pornography.

"You're in love with her, aren't you?" Holden had asked last week, noticing that Adam's eyes kept straying to his phone rather than watching the game on TV. And Adam rolled his eyes, looked back to the screen, and answered, *"I just want her to be safe. And happy. And to have what she needs."* Holden didn't say anything, just nodded and smiled knowingly, and that was the closest Adam had come to punching him since grad school.

So, what if Adam went ahead and did it? What if he told Olive the truth?

Pretty fucking tragic twist of fate, but you don't seem to remember that we first met years ago. An issue, since I remember a little too well. I like no one, absolutely no one, but I liked you from the start. I liked you when I didn't know you, and now that I do know you it's only gotten worse. Sometimes, often, always, I think about you before falling asleep. Then I dream of you, and when I wake up my head's still there, stuck on something funny, beautiful, filthy, intelligent that's all about you. It's been going on for a while, longer than you think, longer than you can imagine, and I should have told you, but I have this impression, this certainty that you're half a second from running away, that I should give you enough reasons to stay. Is there anything I can do for you? I'll take you grocery shopping and fill your fridge when we're back home. Buy you a new bike and a case of decent reagent and that sludge you drink. Kill the people who made you cry. Is there something you need? Name it. It's yours. If I have it, it's yours.

There is no scenario in which any of this won't send her screaming. And after the last few days, weeks, years, all Olive needs is to have a little quiet. A safe space. A place to run *to*, not *from*. So Adam makes his decision: he tucks the truth away one more time, and when she pulls back, a faint smile on her lips and a hopeful look in her eyes, he shakes his head.

"Olive, this is . . . no."

"Why?" There is a frown between her brows. That Adam put there himself, because he is fucking *bad* for her.

"This is not what we're here for."

Her nostrils flare. "That doesn't mean that—"

"You're not thinking clearly. You're upset and drunk, and—"

She rolls her eyes, impatient, and his hands itch to pull her closer. Kiss her again. Kiss her in every fucking place. She's a brat. An incessant, outrageous smart-ass, and he has to clench his fist to avoid reaching for her.

"I had two beers. *Hours* ago," she says irritably, and Adam feels himself grow just as irritated. He's in no condition to fight her on this. Not when he's already busy fighting himself.

"You're a grad student, currently depending on me for a place to stay, and even if you weren't, the power I have over you could easily turn this into a coercive dynamic that—"

She laughs. Like the one thing that scares the shit out of him and keeps him awake at night—that she'll get hurt from this thing they're doing, that there are signals he's not picking up on, that he is harming her or taking advantage—is little more than a funny joke. "I'm not feeling coerced." She scoffs, like the possibility is ridiculous to her. Maybe it's her tone, maybe her scent in his nostrils, but Adam's control snaps.

"You're in love with *someone else*," he tells her, angry, cruel, sparing nothing.

And Olive stops laughing. Instead she flinches, nearly recoils away from him, and Adam instantly wants to punch himself and take it back.

Great job, asshole. Throw it in her face. Remind her that the guy she does care about is off somewhere with her closest friend. It's not like you know exactly *how it feels, wanting someone who'd rather be with someone else. It's not like you can relate every fucking minute you spend with her.*

"Olive." He pinches the bridge of his nose, trying to calm down. Being brusque and short-tempered should be nothing new to him, but Olive does something to the chemistry of his brain, something that makes him mellow, patient, as content as someone like him can hope to be. A snarly, feral beast, tamed at last. Problem is, neither of them seems to be doing great tonight. Olive is tired and confused. Adam is tired, too, but also horny, and tempted, and ground down to the bones after weeks and weeks of wanting and not having. More than a little pathetic about this girl.

He needs to be better, because this is not about him. He promised himself at the very start that his time with Olive would always be about *her*, and that's why he needs to attempt something radical to his nature: diplomacy.

He closes his eyes, and takes a deep breath, and thinks of a sensitive way of saying, *You think you want me to fuck you, but you don't. The problem is, I really, really do, which makes this a risky conversation for us to have. You should go to sleep. Get some rest while, three feet away from you, I try to forget that black dress of yours. Or the time you brought up the idea of us fucking in my office. Or when you wiggled in my lap for one hour, and all I could think was that in a just world, an ideal world, this thing we're doing would be real, and those intrusive, half-formulated, lurid fantasies I have about you wouldn't send you screaming, and—*

"Adam, I . . ."

He needs to wrap up this conversation and then go for a ten-mile run. He's exhausted and not fit to be around.

"Olive, this is how you're feeling *now*," he says, trying to sound reasonable even though he feels anything but. Olive presses her lips together; her nostrils flare, and Adam powers through. "A month from now, a week, tomorrow, I don't want you to regret . . ." He trails off the second he notices something: maybe she isn't *angry*? Because what she looks like is . . . *hurt*? Betrayed? Blinking quickly, like she's about to cry again.

He snaps his mouth shut. No. She's not going to feel like that. Not because of *him*. "Olive—"

"What about what *I* want?" She leans forward, eyes blazing. Okay, she's angry all right. Fiercely, beautifully so. "What about the fact that *I* want this? Though maybe you don't care, because you don't want it, right? Maybe I'm just not attractive to you, and *you* don't want this—"

He really *is* fucking exhausted. Or his control would be better than this: closing his fingers around her wrist and pulling her
hand down to his cock. It's hard, he's hard, he's hard all the
time, and if she wants to lie to herself, then so be it, but not on
his damn watch.

"You have no fucking idea what I want," he hisses.

Except that now she must. His jaw rolls. He holds her wide,
shocked eyes; presses her even closer; and shows her *exactly*
what he wants, what she does, what he deals with, what it's been
like for the past three years, and—

Shit. Adam immediately lets go of her and looks away, but
the damage is done, and this—*this* is why he shouldn't be allowed *anywhere* near her. If he cannot be trusted not to spill
the extent to which he's gone for her, he needs to get the hell
out of here. He even makes to stand, but stops the second she
whispers, "Well, then."

He glances up. Olive's expression has cleared. She looks
calmer all of a sudden. Relieved. Determined. Like—and this
makes absolutely no sense—the one thing she's afraid of is not
Adam himself but the idea of him *rejecting* her.

She steps close. Closer still. Her smell is in his nostrils, her
thighs press against the insides of his own, and this was heady
and harrowing twenty seconds ago, but it's rapidly becoming
unbearable. How beautiful she is—it confuses him. It's a constant pressure that doesn't let go, and Adam has to shut his eyes
tight just to pretend that she's not within reach. "This is not why
I asked you to room with me."

"I know." She's touching him now. Of her own free will.
Pushing hair away from his forehead. Her fingers are cool and
soft and capable, the same fingers she does science with, and he
wants to lean into her. "It's also not why I accepted." *You don't
like being touched, dickhead*, he reminds himself. *You hate it,*

in fact. Remember who you were, back when your life wasn't a montage of the times this girl touched you because she had to?

"When we started this, you said no sex," he points out, in a half-hearted, last-ditch attempt at stopping this. Like he'd ever tell her no. The things he would do for her. The things he would do *to* her.

"I also said it was going to be an on-campus thing. And we just went out for dinner. So." She shrugs her shoulders. The fabric of his shirt ripples against her breasts, and, okay.

Okay.

He's considering this. He cannot stop himself.

"I don't . . ." He rubs his forehead. *Don't say it. It'll mess you up. Basic self-preservation. Don't do it.* But he knows that if she asks, he'll fuck her. Even just to take her mind away from what's bothering her. He'll hopefully make it good enough, and tomorrow she'll act like nothing happened.

Adam's life won't ever be the same.

"I don't have anything," he says.

She stares at him for a long moment, uncomprehending. Then her cheeks redden. "Oh, it doesn't matter. I'm on birth control. And clean." She bites into her lip, and he feels it like a hand on his own body. "But we could also do . . . other things."

Other things.

Other *things.*

Ah, yes. Other things.

He lets his eyes roam her for a moment. As stupefied as he was by her waves and her makeup and that nearly-too-short dress, she'll never be more lovely to him than with her face scrubbed pink, her hair messy and wild. Her body is lithe, graceful, strong, and he takes in the shapeless T-shirt, the slight swell of her breasts, the curves of her hips. All things he hasn't allowed himself to look at for weeks—for *years*. It never mattered:

they were always there, stuck in his brain. The curve of her lower back while she opened the seminar door with her shoulder. The line of her throat as she drank from a water bottle. A graceful stretch and a sliver of stomach skin.

He can think of *other things* to do with her. With every single part of her. So many indecent, beautiful, obscene things. *What's too much, Olive? What can I ask you to do, how many times? You should be careful. Set boundaries. Tell me what you want.*

"After." Adam swallows. Takes a deep breath. Tells himself to wind down. *Nothing might happen. Maybe she wants to make out a little. Fool around. Be held. It's fine.* "What if you hate me for this, after? What if we go back and you change your mind—"

"I won't. I . . ." She comes even closer. "I've never been surer of anything. Except maybe cell theory." She smiles. First tentative, then hopeful, then bright, and then she leans over to kiss him again, and . . .

He never stood a chance. Never, and certainly not this time, when it's so different from all the others. They've kissed before, sure, and . . . it's been nice. Too nice, sometimes, but also interrupted. Frustrating. Unfinished. Performative. Always the start of something, never the end. This time, though . . . This time there's no one around, and after a moment of reluctance, Adam lets himself do what he wants.

He deepens the kiss. Brings Olive closer. Inhales the scent of her, familiar by now, soft skin and sugar and fake-dating Wednesdays. He's wanted her for so long, this feels like something imagined, right out of a dream. He could start by devouring her. By going on his knees and burying his face in her sweet pussy. By taking off her top, memorizing every inch of her for *after.* He won't rush her, though, so he makes himself get rid of his own shirt to feel more of her skin and then stays put, sitting on the side of the bed like a big, hulking animal trying to play nice. It doesn't feel like this'll be enough, not with the way she gasps every time his tongue brushes against hers, not when his palm is cupping her ass, but he *can* go slow. He *can* feel her nipples, pointy and hard against his chest, but he'll be okay just sucking at a spot on her throat. He *can* let his hand slide up to rest on the soft underside of her breast, but he doesn't need to see it. And he *can* . . .

Olive is saying something. And Adam's brain is too dazed to parse language. "What?"

"You did it that night, too." She's smiling. All he wants to think about is making her come. Can he do it? It's been a while. He wishes he had more practice. For her.

"I did what?"

"You touched me. Here." Her hand covers his through the cotton, and he takes it as permission. He lifts her shirt slowly, giving her time to object, stopping the instant her breath catches, at the first sign of hesitation. Right under her tits, which almost have him groaning in desperation, but—no. Patient. He can be fucking patient till she's comfortable.

He waits, and meanwhile he presses his lips against her ribs. Bites softly. Licks. She tastes sweet, and he wonders if she'd let him go down on her. Seems like asking for too much, but maybe.

"Here?" he says. "Olive. Here?" The underside of her breast is right there, and she's not answering him, just clutching him like she'll fall if she doesn't, and okay. Okay, yes: he wants to fuck her into the mattress. No point in pretending he doesn't. "Pay attention, sweetheart." The underside of her breast is right there, so he runs his tongue across it, he sucks on it, and she whimpers. "Here?"

He doesn't hear her answer. He's a little distracted, because her shirt is finally coming off, and . . .

There is a split second of insecurity, he thinks. A short moment of hesitation when he can tell that Olive is thinking of covering herself. Her back nearly hunches; Adam can almost smell the panic between them, and he's ready to put a stop to this, right now. But then her shoulders square, like she's decided that she doesn't mind showing him her body after all, and . . .

Okay.

Yeah.

So it's been a long time for him. Years, he'd guess. Not since grad school, and even then he never quite . . . There was about a decade or so in which Adam thought he'd had just enough sex in his life to know with the utmost certainty that he wasn't interested in having any more. No real reason for it, just . . . no. And then—Olive. He'd almost laughed in his office at being asked to be secretive about dating other women. At the reptilian, greedy part of his brain, thinking: *Are there any? I thought it was just you.*

"Do you remember it?" she's saying, and her breasts. Her small, beautiful tits. The long dip in the center of her stomach. Her toned, smooth legs. He wants to tuck her underneath him for safekeeping. For months.

"Remember what?" he asks, absent, transfixed. His own voice sounds distant.

"Our first kiss."

"I want to keep you in this hotel room for a week," he murmurs, because it's the truth. Can he touch her? He'll stop if she tells him to. But. "For a year."

He's losing track of time. Missing beats. Not out of control but getting bolder. He splays his hand against her back, brings her closer to his mouth, arches her up like an offering, and he misses a bit of what comes after because it feels *that* good. He doesn't want to be rough, but the noises Olive is making are spellbinding: breathless moans and sharp inhales.

Then her muscles tense. It's sudden, and he feels it the second it happens, like a bucket of ice over his head. He immediately pulls back. "This okay?"

She's in her head about something. Her expression is faraway, and as much as his cock hurts, something switches in his brain. He wants to lick her tits, yes, but he wants to reassure her more.

He sets his hand on her hip, thumb swiping back and forth on her hip bone, trying to look at her face. "You're tense. We don't have to—"

"I want to." She sounds scared. A little defensive. Definitely in her head. "I said I did."

"It doesn't matter what you said. You can always change your mind."

"I won't."

She's stubborn. She's stubborn, and he likes that about her, just like every other damn thing, but this . . . He's just not willing to risk moving this along if she's having any doubt. So he squeezes his cock till he's near pain and stops. Slows down. Brings her into himself, rests his forehead on her sternum, matches his breathing with hers, feels her arms form a loose loop around his neck, lets himself smell the sweetness between them. It takes several moments, but she slowly softens, relaxing into him. First pliant, her nose rubbing softly against his hair, then restless. Eager all over again.

Holden and his stupid, supremely idiotic questions. Of course Adam is in love with Olive, of fucking course. And that's why this is nice, too. Just being with her. Near her. A little painful, maybe, but a whole lot nice.

"I think *I've* changed my mind," he says against her skin. His fingers are tracing the elastic of her panties—cotton, green polka dots. He's going to steal them once they're done. He's going to build a shrine for them. Do unspeakable things with them.

"I know I'm not doing anything," Olive says, something reedy in her voice, "but if you tell me what you like, I can—"

"My favorite color must be green, after all."

She's wet already. Adam cannot quite believe it, so he presses his thumb to her panties, just to make sure. But once his finger is there, he cannot help himself. He moves the tip up and down between her legs, over and over. He wants to remember this moment. Store it for later. Archive it in his DNA.

"Do you . . . Do you want me to take them off?"

Yes. But no. This underwear is probably all that's between her and Adam begging her to let him fuck her. Better on for now. "No. Not yet."

She squirms, impatient. "But if we—"

He pushes the cotton to the side because he cannot stop himself, and that's a mistake. She looks ready. Ripe. A perfect piece of fruit. He wonders if it means that he could fuck her now. That it could be fast, a little messy, and she'd still be okay. She'd take it. She'd enjoy it. He'd make it good, hopefully. Maybe. If he remembers how. If he doesn't blow it in twenty seconds. If he doesn't blow it right now just looking at his fingers trace her glistening pussy, circle around her clit, disappear between her plump folds—and she's wet, she's really fucking *wet*, wet in a way that makes it easy to lie to himself and pretend that it's *him* she wants, not just anyone who'll take her mind off a shitty day. He watches her arch up, close her eyes, let out a low moan, exhale something that is so obviously pleasure. Adam strokes himself and *knows* it, that he's going to come just from looking at her.

"You are so beautiful." He can't remember ever saying it to a woman before—why state obvious facts—but with Olive the words burst out of him. "May I?" he rasps against her nipples when he finds her entrance, not quite sounding like himself, and the second his finger is inside her, he—

"Fuck." It's a tight fit, which makes his cock twitch even harder. His vision darkens to black spots. For a few seconds he can feel his heartbeat drumming in his ears, pleasure stabbing in his loins. He forgets about everything that's not Olive, everything that's not the places where he's touching her. She feels like the best thing that's ever happened to him, but better. And then . . . then she's moving. Squirming while impaled on his finger, in a way that broadcasts very little enjoyment, and the wave of pleasure that was about to crash right into him, it abruptly recedes.

Adam freezes.

"Hey. Shh." This is not really working—him in her. So he tries to still her hips, and when that doesn't do the trick he grazes her clit again with his thumb, hoping it will help her soften. She whimpers, closes a hand around his arm with trembling fingers. Her nipples are hard little pebbles, and she seems to like it, seems to breathe faster and break into a sweat and maybe want more— but she stays just as tight. "It's okay. Relax." He tries to stretch her. Work his finger in a little deeper. See where he can go. She's wet inside, really wet, and it shouldn't be this difficult, he doesn't think.

Problem is, he cannot read her. Not consistently. Granted, he has very little recent experience, and even less clarity of mind with Olive grinding against his hand. She lets out soft groans, deep breaths, but then she'll wince, claw her nails into his biceps, and that's putting the brakes on pretty quickly for him, the idea that she might be in any kind of pain. "Does it hurt?" he tries to ask. She shakes her head, but a second later he sees her flinch. "Why are you so tense, Olive?" he asks, distracted, staring at his finger inside her. "You've done this before, right?"

It's a stupid question, and he instantly wants to punch himself for asking it. Of course she's done this before—look at her. She's not like Adam. She probably does this—

"I—yes, a couple of times. In college."

Adam goes still. His mind empties, then blanks. Then the enormity of what is happening hits him like a freight train, and he gently pulls away, shaking his head.

This is . . . no. No. It's a mistake. She clearly doesn't take sex lightly, which means that she deserves to have it with someone . . . better. Someone else. Someone who's not this much older than her, who never failed her friend's dissertation proposal, who doesn't need to set an alarm for one a.m. to remember to stop working and go to sleep. Someone who didn't spend the last several years pining across lecture rooms, someone who doesn't picture her when he—

"But it doesn't matter. I can figure it out. I've learned whole-cell patch clamp in a couple of hours; sex can't be much harder," she says quickly. Like she's under the impression that he's put off by her inexperience. "And I bet you do this all the time, so you can tell me how to—"

"You'd lose."

"What?"

"You'd lose your bet." He sighs. His stupid, moronic cock has never been this hard. Because part of him likes this. The lie he could spin to himself: that this means something to her. That *he* means something to her. "I can't."

"Of course you can."

He shakes his head. "I'm sorry."

"What? No. No, I—"

"You're basically a vir—"

"I'm not!"

"Olive."

"I am not."

"But so close to it that—"

"No, that's not the way it works. Virginity is not a continuous variable, it's categorical. Binary. Nominal. Dichotomous. Ordinal, potentially. I'm talking about chi-square, maybe Spearman's correlation, logistic regression, the logit model and that stupid sigmoid function, and . . ."

She does *this* every single time. Makes him want to laugh, like he's somehow not really the sulky, humorless person he knows himself to be. Every Wednesday she makes him forget that he's supposed to be antagonistic and unapproachable, to hate the entire world, and even though it's a terrible idea, he's touching her again, smiling against her mouth while she laughs into his, telling her between kisses to stop being a smart-ass, and then, once they're too close again: "Olive, if for any reason sex is something that you're not comfortable with, or that you'd rather not have outside of a relationship, then—"

"No. No, it's nothing like that. I—" He pulls back and watches her, patient. Wanting to understand. "It's not that I want to *not* have sex. I just . . . don't particularly *want* to have it. There is something weird about my brain, and my body, and— I don't know what's wrong with me, but I don't seem to be able to experience attraction like other people. Like *normal* people. I tried to just . . . to just do it, to get it over with, and the guy I did it with was nice, but the truth is that I just don't feel any . . . sexual attraction unless I actually get to trust and like a person, which for some reason never happens. Or, almost never. It hadn't, not in a long time, but now—I really like you, and I really trust you, and for the first time in a million years I want to . . ."

Adam wants to tell her that there's nothing weird with her brain. That he'd forgotten sex was something he was *supposed* to want for years before meeting her. That he knows exactly what she's saying. But it's a risky truth to admit amid the lies, and so he just looks at her, takes in her words, and for the first time in weeks wonders if maybe there is hope.

He hasn't let himself before. He's not one to lie, not even to himself, and the delusion that this will end in anything but a clean cut on September twenty-ninth is a dangerous one to entertain. But if Olive trusts him. If she *trusts* him.

Maybe not now. Nor soon. She's in love with someone else, and these things take time. But next year they'll be both here in Boston, and maybe, if she already *trusts* him, Adam could convince her to let him take care of her. He doesn't want anything in return. She doesn't need to fall for him, because he loves her enough for the both of them. But if she *trusts* him—

"I want to do this," she's telling him. "With you. I really do."

Adam can feel his heart expand, grow full of something fragile and unfamiliar. "Me too, Olive. You have no idea."

"Then, please. Please, don't say no. Please?" She nibbles on his lip, his jaw, the skin under his ear, until he takes a deep breath and nods and realizes that if this is going to happen—and it is, it absolutely fucking is—he needs to be better at it. Make her comfortable. So he picks her up and deposits her on his bed, smiling at the surprised, laughing yelp she lets out.

"Okay?" he asks when she's on her back. He shifts on top of her, taking in her small nod and the new view—her fanning hair, pale skin, jutting hip bones. He wants to lick them. Then he wants to feed her sugary foods, keep her warm and safe till her ribs don't stick out so much anymore. The skin of her belly—he will think about it years from now, get himself off to the memories of each soft freckle. He takes her panties off, finally, *finally*, and she's wearing knee-high socks, bright and happy, and . . . just like everything else she's ever done, he's apparently into that. He's into that *a lot*.

"Adam?"

Her voice is airy, and he takes it as an ask to hurry up. To push her legs wide open with his palms on her inner thighs and smell her lovely honey scent. She's wet and sticky under his lips, smooth and soft, and he thinks he blacks out from it a little. From the pleasure of doing this to her, of exploring her with his tongue. He's almost sure he's done this before, and even though he doesn't remember when, or with whom, he's positive she was nothing like Olive. Her ass fits perfectly in his palms, he can span her hips with his fingers, and it's a bit of a power trip, the way he can easily angle her for him to lick, and . . . she's lithe. Especially compared to the oafish, lumbering mountain Adam is. He's tried very hard to pretend it doesn't turn him on to the extent that it does, but . . . no. Not possible to lie to himself, not when he's sucking on the lips of her pussy and she's moaning into the palm of her hand. It makes him want to get closer, learn her even more, and—

And then she's telling him to stop.

It takes a moment to penetrate the trance he's been put into, but when it does, he goes still. "Have you changed your mind?"

"No. But we should do . . . other things."

"You don't like this?"

"No. Yes. Well, I've never . . ."

Adam tries to imagine having sex with Olive and not begging her to let him do this. Seems absurd. Beyond belief.

"But I'm the one who put you up to this," she adds, "so we should do things that *you* are into, and not stuff for me . . ."

He finally catches her meaning and growls deep in his throat. He closes his eyes, lays his forehead against her thighs, and contemplates trashing the entire damn hotel room. But it would scare Olive, and do absolutely nothing to convince her that she is beautiful and fuckable, that he wants to absorb her into himself and lick her dry, that this is for *him* more than for her. So he opts for something else: pressing his tongue against her clit, gripping her squirming waist to still her, to make her take his fingers and his tongue inside her. He holds her wide open, watches her arch on the mattress in a beautiful, perfect bow. He hears her soft noises and feels her tense, clutch at his hair and shoulders with a frustrated, impatient sort of desperation, like she wants to come but she's afraid she won't, and he loves the feeling of it, the illusion that this precipice they're hovering on together is unending, hidden in space and time. An arc of pleasure, suspended. But then she comes with sweet whimpers and slow, strong contractions, and Adam's gut tightens, and his vision whitens. He'd love to fuck her, but he might come from just this, and that's okay. He wants to watch her again. She's sensitive, writhing, laughing, small and tight and warm, beautiful, so beautiful, so powerful and perfect and beautiful. When it's too much, when she pulls him up to her, he presses her into bed with his legs and his arms and his hands, watches her twitch with the last aftershocks of pleasure, feels her little heart beat, a drum against his own. In this moment, he has everything. Every last thing he needs.

"Can I fuck you?" he asks against her mouth.

She kisses him back. Pulls him closer. Traces his hot, sweaty skin. He's not worthy, but he wants her anyway. "Mmm?"

"Can I fuck you? Please?"

She nods and reaches down for him, but he's not sure there's time for it. He's hard in a way that's painful and urgent, different from ever before, and Olive's flawless, soft, tight pussy is right there, ready for him, and when he begins to slide inside, his existence narrows to bare details: the pressure around his cock, strained, world defining; Olive's eyes, shocked wide, holding his own; the air between them, warm, heavy.

"You're so big," she gasps.

He groans into her neck. Maybe he is big. Still. "You can take it." Nothing, nothing exists except for the pleasure tingling at the base of his spine.

"I can," she agrees. Adam has to close his eyes, or it will be over right now. He rocks inside her, and it's torture. Delicious, drowning torture. "What if it's too much?"

It seems like a distinct possibility. He can't imagine thrusting into her the way he needs to because she's small, and he's not. "Then I'll fuck you like this." It's already getting better. She's still sealed tight around him, but he's making progress, getting a little farther, and the way she pulsates around him is splendidly, obscenely good. They're both breathing fast, loud. She's not positioned right for him to push deeper, that's the problem. He lets his hand slide to her thigh and shifts it to open her more. Just a little more.

"Is there something I should be—"

"Shhh. Be quiet for a moment. So I don't come already."

She's starting to move underneath him. Like she's impatient for this to progress, even though he's about to snap from the tension of keeping it slow. He wants to sink his teeth into her. Tether her to him. Keep her in check. He withdraws a bit, which his body hates and which seems pretty fucking stupid, but pushing back in is beyond anything.

"Maybe you should."

He should what? Ah, yeah. They're talking about him coming. "I should?"

She nods, and he wants to kiss her; she wants to kiss him, too, but they're not quite able to do it, too distracted, too dazed, and he lets out a silent laugh, thinking about the two of them attempting this. Both of them barely knowing what they're doing and yet somehow making this spectacular, magnificent chaos. "Inside you?"

She nods, like whatever he'd ask of her, she'd give him. "If you want to."

He does. He thinks of it a lot—base, filthy fantasies of making a mess on her, making a mess *in* her, leaving his mark. He has lots of those. A few more than he should. "You're driving me insane," he says into her clavicle, and that's when something gives. A second of slick friction. Then he finds himself as deep as he can go, and everything stops.

The universe rearranges into something better.

They're both still for a moment. Then they exhale sharp sounds in the silent room. Olive lifts a hand, just to run her fingers through his hair, and Adam is speechless. Mindless.

This is— Jesus. Oh, God.

She smiles at him, happy, hopeful, beautiful, and says, "Hey."

Adam smiles, too, and thinks, *This is it.* He thinks, *I love you.* He thinks, *Maybe, one day, you'll even let me tell you.*

And he says, "Hey."

Photo courtesy of the author

Ali Hazelwood is the *New York Times* bestselling author of *The Love Hypothesis*, as well as the writer of peer-reviewed articles about brain science, in which no one makes out and the ever after is not always happy. Originally from Italy, she lived in Germany and Japan before moving to the United States to pursue a Ph.D. in neuroscience. She recently became a professor, which absolutely terrifies her. When Ali is not at work, she can be found running, eating cake pops, or watching sci-fi movies with her two feline overlords (and her slightly-less-feline husband).

CONNECT ONLINE

AliHazelwood.com
🐦 EverSoAli
📷 AliHazelwood